BOOKS BY MARIO VARGAS LLOSA

THE REAL LIFE OF
ALEJANDRO MAYTA

THE REAL LIFE OF ALEJANDRO MAYTA

MARIO VARGAS LLOSA

Translated by Alfred Mac Adam

AVENTURA
The Vintage Library of Contemporary World Literature

*Vintage Books
A Division of Random House
New York*

First Aventura edition, December 1986

English translation copyright © 1986 by
Farrar, Straus and Giroux, Inc.
All rights reserved under International and
Pan-American Copyright Conventions.
Published in the United States by Random House, Inc.,
New York, and simultaneously in Canada by
Random House of Canada Limited, Toronto.
Originally published in Spain as
La Historia de Mayta *by*
Editorial Seix Barral, S.A., Barcelona, in 1984.
Copyright © 1984 by Mario Vargas Llosa.
This translation originally published by
Farrar, Straus and Giroux, Inc., in 1986.

Library of Congress Cataloging in Publication Data
Vargas Llosa, Mario, 1936–
The real life of Alejandro Mayta
(Aventura)
Translation of: La historia de Mayta.
1. Mayta, Alejandro—Fiction. I. Title.
PQ8498.32.A65H513   1986b   863   86-40169
ISBN 0-394-74776-3 (pbk.)
Manufactured in the United States of America
10 9 8 7 6 5 4 3 2 1

THE REAL LIFE OF
ALEJANDRO MAYTA

One

A morning jog along the Malecón de Barranco, when the dew
still hangs heavy in the air and makes the sidewalks slippery and
shiny, is just the way to start off the day. Even in summer, the
sky is gray, because the sun never shines on this neighborhood
before ten. The fog blurs the edges of things—the profiles of
sea gulls, the pelican that flies over the broken line of cliffs that
run along the sea. The water looks like lead, dark green, smoking,
rough, with patches of foam. The waves form parallel rows as
they roll in, and sometimes a fishing boat bounces over them.
Sometimes a gust of wind parts the clouds, and out in the distance
La Punta and the ocher islands of San Lorenzo and El Frontón
materialize. It's beautiful, as long as you concentrate on the landscape and the birds, because everything man-made there is ugly.

The houses are ugly, imitations of imitations. Fear, in the shape
of gates, walls, sirens, and spotlights, suffocates them. Television
antennas form a ghostly forest. Ugly, too, is the garbage that
piles up on the outer edge of the Malecón and spills down its
face. Why is it that this part of the city—which has the best

3

view—is a garbage dump? Laziness. Why don't the property owners tell their servants to stop dumping garbage right under their noses? Because they know that if theirs didn't, the neighbors' servants or the workers from the Parque de Barranco would. Even the regular garbagemen do: I see them while I'm running, throwing garbage down there they should be carrying to the dump. That's why people have resigned themselves to the vultures, roaches, mice, and the stinking garbage dump whose birth and growth I've witnessed on my morning runs: a daily vision of stray dogs scratching in the dump under clouds of flies. Over the past few years, I've also gotten used to seeing stray kids, stray men, and stray women along with the stray dogs, all painstakingly digging through the trash looking for something to eat, something to sell, something to wear. The spectacle of misery was once limited exclusively to the slums, then it spread downtown, and now it is the common property of the whole city, even the exclusive residential neighborhoods—Miraflores, Barranco, San Isidro. If you live in Lima, you can get used to misery and grime, you can go crazy, or you can blow your brains out.

But I'm sure Mayta never got used to any of it. At the Salesian School, we'd be about to take the bus to Magdalena, where we both lived, when he'd suddenly run to give don Medaro, a ragged blind man with an out-of-tune violin who was always standing at the door of the María Auxiliadora Church, the bread-and-cheese snack the priests gave us at our last recess. And on Monday he would give don Medaro a *real*, which he must have saved from his own allowance. Once, during one of our Communion classes, he made Father Luis jump by asking him point-blank, "Why are there rich and poor people, Father? Aren't we all God's children?" He was always talking about the poor, the blind, the lame, the orphaned, the mad people wandering the streets. The last time I saw him, years after we had left the Salesian School, he brought up his old theme while we were having coffee in the Plaza San Martín: "Have you seen how many beggars there are in Lima? Thousands upon thousands."

4

Even before his famous hunger strike, lots of us in the class thought he would become a priest. In those days, to care about the poor was something we thought only a future priest would do, not something a revolutionary would do. Back then, we knew a lot about religion, very little about politics, and absolutely nothing about revolution. Mayta was a curly-haired, pudgy kid with flat feet and wide spaces between his teeth. He waddled: his feet looked like clock hands permanently set at ten minutes to two. He always wore short pants, a sweater with green stripes, and a scarf to keep warm. He would even keep that scarf on during class. We would tease him a lot for worrying about the poor, for serving at Mass, for praying and crossing himself so devoutly, for being so bad at soccer, and, most of all, for being named Mayta. All he'd say was, "Go pick your noses."

Even though his family was of modest means, he wasn't the poorest student in the school. The Salesian students could pass for public-school kids because our school wasn't just for the lily-whites, as Santa María or La Inmaculada were, but for poorer kids from the lower middle class—the children of bureaucrats, petty officials, soldiers, unsuccessful professional men, artisans, and even the children of skilled laborers. Pure whites were a minority at our school: there were lots of mulattoes, black-and-Indian combinations, Chinese, Japs, "almost whites," and tons of Indians. But even though many of us had copper-colored skin, high cheekbones, flat noses, and coarse hair, the only one I can remember with an Indian name was Mayta. Otherwise, he was no more Indian than the rest of us. His pale skin was greenish, his hair curly, and his features typically Peruvian—a mestizo.

He lived around the corner from La Magdalena Church, in a narrow house with its paint peeling off and no back yard. I got to know the place very well because over the course of a month I went there every afternoon. We read *The Count of Monte Cristo* aloud to each other. I got the book for my birthday, and we both loved it. Mayta's mother worked as a nurse in the maternity ward and gave people shots at home. We would see her from the bus when she opened the door for Mayta. She was a robust woman with gray hair, and she would always give her son a quick kiss as if he were late. We never saw his father, and I was sure he didn't exist. Mayta swore he was always on the road doing some job or other: he was an engineer (the most respected profession at the time).

I've finished running. Twenty minutes out and back between Parque Salazar and my house seems appropriate. Besides, as I ran I managed to forget I was running, and I dredged up memories of the classes at the Salesian School, Mayta's superserious face, his waddle, and his high-pitched voice. There he is, I see him, I hear him, and I will go on seeing and hearing him as I catch my breath, leaf through the paper, eat breakfast, shower, and begin work.

His mother died when we were in our third year and Mayta went to live with an aunt who was also his godmother. He always spoke tenderly of her and told us how she gave him Christmas presents, birthday presents, and took him to the movies. She really must have been a good person, because Mayta kept up his relationship with doña Josefa after he was out on his own. Despite his irregular life, he went on visiting her over the years, and it was in her house that he had that encounter with Vallejos. I wonder how doña Josefa Arrisueño is doing now, twenty-five years after that party. I've been wondering ever since I called her, overcame her misgivings, and persuaded her to let me visit her. I'm still wondering as I get off the bus that leaves me on the corner of Paseo de la República and Avenida Angamos, where the Surquillo district begins. It's a neighborhood I know well. When I was a kid, I'd come here with my friends on party nights to drink beer in El Triunfo, or I'd bring shoes to be fixed or clothes to be altered, or I'd come to see cowboy films in the neighborhood's uncomfortable, smelly theaters—the Primavera, the Leoncio Prado, and the Maximil. It's one of the few neighborhoods in Lima that has barely changed at all. It's still full of shoemakers, tailors, alleys, printing shops with compositors setting type by hand, city garages, cavernous stores,

6

cheap bars, storage depots, dumpy shops, gangs of punks on the corners, and kids playing soccer right in the street, with cars, trucks, and ice-cream carts going by. The crowds on the sidewalks, the badly painted one- or two-story houses, the oily puddles, the hungry dogs: they all seem the same as they did then.

But now these streets that once housed only thugs and prostitutes are also marijuana and cocaine centers. The drug traffic is worse here than in La Victoria, Rímac, Porvenir, or the slums. At night, these leprous corners, these sordid tenements, these pathetic saloons all turn into drug drops where marijuana and cocaine are bought and sold. Every day, they find another crude laboratory that processes cocaine. When the party that changed Mayta's life took place, none of these things existed. There were few people in Lima who knew how to smoke marijuana, and cocaine was something for bohemian types and high-class nightclubs, something only a few night people would use to get rid of their hangovers so they could go on partying. Cocaine was far from being the most prosperous business in the country, and it wasn't spreading all over the city. But none of this drug business is visible now as I walk along Jirón Dante toward the intersection with Jirón González Prada, just as Mayta must have walked that night to get to his aunt-godmother's house—that is, if he came by bus or streetcar. In 1958, the streetcars still rattled along where cars from Zanjón now whiz by.

He was tired, foggy, with a slight buzzing in his head and a tremendous desire to soak his feet. There was no better remedy for physical or mental fatigue: that fresh, liquid sensation on his soles, arches, and toes relieved fatigue, dejection, and bad moods, and raised his morale. He had been walking since dawn, trying to sell *Workers Voice* in the Plaza Unión to the workers who were getting off the buses and streetcars and going into the factories on Avenida Argentina. Later, he had made two trips from the room on Jirón Zepita to Plaza Buenos Aires, in Cocharcas, first carrying some stencils and later an article by Daniel Guérin, translated from a French magazine, about colonialism in Indochina.

He had been on his feet for hours in the tiny print shop in Cocharcas, which, despite everything, still went on publishing the paper (with a bogus masthead, and payment in advance). He helped the compositor set the type and he corrected the proofs. Later, taking only one bus instead of the two that were really needed, he went to Rímac, where, every Wednesday in a tiny room on Avenida Francisco Pizarro, he would lead a study group of students from the University of San Marcos and the Engineering School. Afterward, without taking a break, with his stomach growling because all day he'd eaten only a dish of rice and greens in the university restaurant on Jirón Moquegua (he got in with an ID card from God knows when, which he updated from time to time), he attended the meeting of the Central Committee of the Revolutionary Workers' Party (Trotskyist), in the garage over on Jirón Zorritas, which lasted two long, smoky, polemical hours.

Who would have wanted to go to a party after a day like that? Plus, he always hated parties. His knees were shaking, and he felt as though he were walking on hot coals. But how could he not go? Except when he was away or in jail, he had never missed one of his aunt's parties. And in the future, tired or not, with his feet a wreck or not, he would not miss one, even if it meant just dropping in for a minute, just long enough to tell his aunt he loved her. The house was filled with noise. The door opened straightaway: "Hello, godson."

"Hello, godmother," Mayta said. "Happy birthday."

"Mrs. Josefa Arrisueño?"

"Yes. Come in, come in."

She's well preserved. She has to be over seventy, but she sure doesn't show it: no wrinkles, and very little gray in her dark hair. She's plump, but she has a nice figure. Wide hips. She's wearing a lilac-colored dress with a red sash. The room is big, dark, with unmatched chairs, a big mirror, a sewing machine, a television set, a table, a Lord of Miracles, a San Martín de Porres,

8

photos on the wall, and a vase filled with wax roses. Did the party where Mayta met Vallejos take place here?

"Right here." Mrs. Arrisueño nods, looking around the room. She points to a rocker loaded with magazines. "I can just see them there, yakking away."

There weren't many people, but lots of smoke, the clinking of glasses, and the waltz "Idolo" at full blast. One couple was dancing and several were keeping time to the music, clapping hands or humming. Mayta, as always, felt out of place and sensed he might make a fool of himself at any moment. He would never be at ease in company. The table and chairs had been pushed into a corner so there would be space for dancing. Someone had a guitar under his arm. The people one might expect to see were there, and some others as well: her cousins, lovers, neighbors, relatives, and friends one would remember from other birthdays. But the skinny chatterbox—this was the first time he'd ever been seen there.

"He wasn't a friend of the family's," says Mrs. Arrisueño, "but a lover or relative or something of a friend of Zoilita's, my eldest daughter. She brought him, and no one knew anything about him."

But they soon found out he was a nice guy, a good dancer, a good drinker, a smooth talker, and knew lots of jokes. Mayta said hello to his cousins, took a ham sandwich in one hand and a glass of beer in the other, and looked for a chair where he could collapse. The only free one was next to the skinny guy, who was standing there gesturing, holding forth to a chorus of three: the cousins Zoilita and Alicia and an old man in slippers. Trying to pass unnoticed, Mayta sat down next to them so he could let a respectable amount of time pass and then go home to sleep.

"He'd never stay long," says Mrs. Arrisueño, rummaging through her pockets for a handkerchief. "He didn't like parties. He wasn't like other people. Never, not even when he was a kid. Always serious, always a little gentleman. His mother would say, 'He was born old.' She was my sister, see? Mayta's birth was the tragedy of her life, because the moment she figured out

9

she was pregnant, her boyfriend disappeared. Never saw him again. Do you think Mayta was that way because he had no father? He only came to my birthday parties to be polite. I brought him here when my sister died. He was the boy God never gave me. I only had girls. Zoilita and Alicia. They're both in Venezuela, married, with children. Doing fine. I might have been able to remarry, but my daughters were so against it that I stayed a widow. A big mistake, let me tell you. Because now look at my life: I'm all alone, like a mushroom, a target for the thieves who'll break in here any time now. My daughters send me a little something every month. If it weren't for them, I'd be in a bad way, see?"

As she speaks, she looks me over, just barely dissimulating her curiosity. Her voice cracks once in a while, just like Mayta's; her hands are big; and even though she smiles from time to time, her eyes are sad and watery. She complains about the rising cost of living, about the muggings—"There's not a single woman in this neighborhood who hasn't been attacked at least once"— about the robbery at the branch of the Banco de Crédito where so many poor people got shot, and about not being able to go to Venezuela too, where the streets are paved with gold.

"At the Salesian, we all thought Mayta would become a priest," I say to her.

"That's what my sister thought, too." She nods, blowing her nose. "Me, too. He would make the sign of the cross whenever he passed a church; he went to Communion every Sunday. A little saint. Who'd ever have said it—I mean, that he would turn out to be a communist. In those days, it didn't seem possible that a kid as religious as that would become a communist. But that's all changed; now there are lots of communist priests, right? I can remember perfectly the day he walked through that door."

He came up to her with his schoolbooks under his arm, and then, with his fist clenched as if he were going to punch himself, he recited in one breath what he had come to announce to her, the decision that had kept him awake all night: "Godmother, we eat

10

a lot, we don't think about the poor. Do you know what they eat? I'm telling you that, from now on, I'm only going to have some soup at lunch and some bread at night. Just like don Medaro, the blind man."

"That little trick landed him in the hospital," doña Josefa remembers.

The little trick went on for several months and he got thinner and thinner, without any of us in the class being able to figure out why, until Father Giovanni, full of admiration, told us when they took Mayta to Loayza Hospital. "All this time he's been fasting so he could be one with the poor, out of human and Christian solidarity," he said softly, shocked at what Mayta's godmother had come to report to the school authorities. The news left us confused, so much so that we didn't dare make fun of him when he came back, cured by injections and tonics. "This boy will cause a stir," Father Giovanni would say. He sure did, but not in the way you thought, Father.

"It was bad luck that he got it in his head to come that night." Mrs. Arrisueño sighs. "If he hadn't come, he wouldn't have met Vallejos and nothing of what happened would have happened. Because Vallejos was the instigator, everybody knows it. Mayta would come, give me a hug, and leave after a little while. But that night he was the very last to go, yakking away with Vallejos over in that corner. It must be twenty-five years ago and I remember as if it were yesterday. Revolution this, revolution that. The whole blessed night."

Revolution? Mayta turned to look at him. Had the young fellow spoken, or was it the old man in slippers?

"Yessir, tomorrow," repeated the skinny guy, raising the glass he held in his right hand. "The socialist revolution could begin tomorrow if we wanted. I'm telling you, mister."

Mayta yawned again and then stretched, his body tickling all over. The skinny guy went on talking about the socialist revolution with the same sauciness with which he'd told traveling-salesman jokes a moment before, the same tone he'd used to

11

describe the last bout of "our national honor, Frontado." Despite his weariness, Mayta began to listen. What was going on in Cuba was nothing compared to what could happen in Peru if we wanted it to. The day the Andes start shaking, the whole country will tremble. Could he be a member of APRA? A party man? A real communist at Godmother's get-together? Impossible. Mayta never remembered anyone talking politics in this house.

"And just what is going on in Cuba?" asked cousin Zoilita.

"Well, Fidel Castro swore he wouldn't cut his beard off until he brought Batista down." The skinny guy laughed. "Haven't you seen what those guys from the 26 of July Movement are doing everywhere? They put a flag on the Statue of Liberty in New York. Batista's sinking fast, he's done for."

"Who is Batista?" asked cousin Alicia.

"A despot," Skinny adamantly explained. "The dictator of Cuba. What's going on there is nothing compared to what can happen here. Thanks to our geography, I mean. A real gift from God to the revolution. When the Indians rise up, Peru will be a volcano."

"Okay, but now go and dance," said cousin Zoilita. "People came here to dance. I'm going to put something fast on."

"Revolutions are serious business; I, for one, don't support them," Mayta heard the old man in slippers say in a gravelly voice. "When APRA rose up in Trujillo in 1930, there was a real bloodbath. The APRA people got into the barracks and liquidated I don't know how many officers. Sánchez Cerro sent planes and tanks and crushed them, and they shot a thousand APRAs in the Chan Chan ruins."

"Were you there?" asked Skinny excitedly. Mayta thought: Revolutions and soccer matches are all the same for this guy.

"I was in Huánuco, in my barbershop," said the old man in slippers. "Rumors about the killing reached all the way there. The few APRAs in Huánuco were picked up and jailed. The prefect, a little army man with a bad temper who liked women a lot, did it. Colonel Badulaque."

After a bit, cousin Alicia also went off to dance and Skinny seemed depressed that his whole audience was the old man. Then he saw Mayta and raised his glass to him: "Hello there, buddy."

"How do you do," said Mayta, raising his glass in turn.

"My name is Vallejos," Skinny said, shaking hands.

"Mine's Mayta."

"From talking so much, I lost my partner." Vallejos laughed, pointing to a girl with bangs. She was dancing with Pepote (who was trying his best to get cheek-to-cheek while "Contigo a la distancia" was on)—a distant cousin of Alicia and Zoilita's. "If he squeezes her any tighter, Alci's gonna haul off and sock him."

He looked eighteen or nineteen because of his elegant figure, his smooth face, and his practically crew-cut hair, but, thought Mayta, he can't be so young. His gestures, his tone of voice, and his self-assurance would suggest someone who's been around. He had big white teeth that made his dark face cheerful. He was one of the few who wore a jacket and tie, and also a handkerchief in his jacket pocket. He was always smiling, and there was something direct and effusive about him. He took out a pack of Incas and offered Mayta one. Then he lit it.

"If the APRA revolution of 1930 had been a success, things would sure be different," he said vehemently, exhaling smoke from his nose and mouth. "There wouldn't be so much injustice and inequality. The heads that have to roll would already be gone, and Peru would be a different place. Don't think I'm in APRA, but let's give Caesar his due. I'm a socialist, buddy, no matter what they say about soldiers and socialism not mixing."

"A soldier?" Mayta winced.

"Second lieutenant." Vallejos nodded. "I graduated last year in Chorrillos."

Jesus. Now he understood Vallejos's haircut and his impulsive manner. Was this what they called a natural leader? Incredible that an army man would talk like that.

"It was a historic party," Mrs. Josefa affirms. "Because Mayta and Vallejos met, and so did my nephew Pepote and Alci. He fell in love with her and stopped being the lazy playboy he'd been. He got a job, married Alci, and they went to Venezuela,

13

too—who wouldn't? But it seems they've parted now. I hope it's only gossip. Ah, you recognize him, right? Yes, it's Mayta. Years and years ago."

In the picture, faded and yellowed around the edges, he looks forty or over. It's a snapshot taken by some public photographer in an unrecognizable plaza in bad light. He's standing, with a shawl over his shoulders and an expression of discomfort, as if the glare of the sun made his eyes itch or as if posing in public in front of passersby embarrassed him. In his right hand he has a satchel or a package or a briefcase, and though the picture is blurred, you can see how badly dressed he is: baggy pants, a jacket that hangs, his shirt collar too wide, and a tie with a badly tied, ridiculous little knot. Revolutionaries wore ties in those days. He's got messy long hair; his face is rather different from the way I remember it, fuller, frowning, a taut seriousness. That's what you see in the photo: a tired man. Tired from not having slept enough, from having walked a lot, or, maybe, tired from something that's much older, the fatigue of a life that has reached a boundary, not old age yet, but something that might well be old age if behind it there is, as in Mayta's case, nothing but lost illusions, frustrations, mistakes, enemies, political deceptions, want, bad food, jail, police stations, an underground life, failures of all kinds and nothing even remotely resembling a victory. And nevertheless, in that exhausted and tense countenance, there glows as well, somehow, that secret, intact integrity in the face of setbacks which it always thrilled me to find in him over the years, that juvenile purity, capable of reacting with the same indignation to any injustice, in Peru or at the ends of the earth, and that honest belief that the most urgent task, the one that could not be shirked, was to change the world. An extraordinary snapshot, indeed, that caught Mayta full-length, the Mayta that Vallejos met that night.

"I asked him to have it taken," says doña Josefa, putting it back on the mantel. "So I could have a remembrance of him. See these photos? They're all relatives, some really distant ones. Most are dead now. Were you two very friendly?"

14

"We didn't see each other for many years," I tell her. "Later we ran into each other a few times, but only rarely."

Doña Josefa Arrisueño looks at me, and I know what she's thinking. I would like to ease her doubts, to calm her, but it's impossible because at this point I know as little about my plans for Mayta as she herself does.

"What will you write about him?" she whispers, running her tongue over her thick lips. "His life?"

"No, not his life," I answer, trying to say something that won't confuse her even more. "Something inspired by his life. Not a biography, but a novel. A very free history of the period, Mayta's world, the things that happened in those years."

"Why him?" she asks, working herself up. "There are others who are more famous. The poet Javier Heraud, for example. Or the people in the Radical Left Movement, de la Puente, Lobatón, the ones people always talk about. Why Mayta? No one remembers him."

She's right. Why? Because his case was the first in a series that would typify the period? Because he was the most absurd? Because he was the most tragic? Because his person and his story hold something ineffably moving, something that, over and beyond its political and moral implications, is like an X-ray of Peruvian misfortune?

"In other words, you don't believe in the revolution." Vallejos pretended to be shocked. "In other words, you are one of those who believe that Peru will always be the same until the end of the world."

Mayta smiled and shook his head. "Peru will change. The revolution will come," he explained, with infinite patience. "But it will come in its own time. It's not as easy as you say."

"In fact, it *is* easy—I say so because I know so." Vallejos's face glistened with sweat, and his eyes were as fiery as his words. "It's easy if you know the topography of the mountains, if you know how to fire a Mauser, and if the Indians rise up."

"If the Indians rise up." Mayta sighed. "As easy as winning the lottery."

He'd never dreamed that his godmother's birthday party could be such fun. He had thought at the outset: This guy's a provocateur, an informer. He knows who I am and wants to loosen my tongue. But after talking with him awhile, he was sure he wasn't any of those things; he was a stray angel with wings who had no idea where he'd landed. Yet he felt no desire to tease him. He liked to listen to him talk about the revolution as if it were a kind of game or a set in a match, something you could bring off with a little effort and ingenuity. There was so much confidence and innocence in the boy that it made him want to go on listening to his crazy ideas all night. He wasn't tired anymore and he was on his third glass of beer. Pepote kept dancing with Alci—the *chotis* "Madrid," by Agustín Lara, sung by all the guests—but the lieutenant didn't seem to care a bit. He had dragged a chair next to Mayta's, and straddling it, he explained that fifty determined, well-armed men using Cáceres's hit-and-run tactics could light the fuse of the Andes powder keg. He's so young he could be my son, Mayta thought. And so cute he must have all the girls he wants.

"And what do you do for a living?" Vallejos asked.

It was a question that always made him uncomfortable, although he was ready for it. His answer—half truth, half lie—sounded falser to him than it had at other times. "I'm a journalist," he said, wondering how Vallejos would react if he heard him say, "I do what you talk about. Revolution. What do you think of that?"

"For which paper?"

"For France-Presse. I do translations."

"So you speak frog." Vallejos made a face. "Where'd you learn it?"

"By himself, with a dictionary, and a grammar someone won in a raffle," doña Josefa tells me. "You may not believe me, but I saw him with my own eyes. He would lock himself up in his room and repeat words for hours and hours. The parish priest in Surquillo would lend him magazines. He would say to me, 'I already understand a little, godmother. I'm picking it up.' Finally, he did understand it, because he would spend days reading books in French, believe me."

"Of course I believe you," I tell her. "I'm not surprised he learned by himself. When he got some idea in his head, he saw it through. I've known few people as tenacious as Mayta."

"He could have been a lawyer, a professional man," laments doña Josefa. "Did you know he got into San Marcos on the first try? And high up on the list. He was still a boy, sixteen or seventeen at the most. He could have had a degree when he was twenty-four or twenty-five. What a waste, my God! And for what? For politics, that's what. Pure waste!"

"He didn't stay at the university long, isn't that right?"

"Within a few months, or a year at the most, he was thrown in jail," doña Josefa says. "That's when the calamities began. He didn't come back here, he lived by himself. From then on, it went from bad to worse. Where's your godson? Hiding out. Where's Mayta these days? In jail. Have they let him out? Yes, but they're looking for him again. If I were to tell you the number of times the police came here to turn the place upside down, to treat me disrespectfully, to scare me out of my wits, you'd think I was exaggerating. If I tell you fifty times, I'm shortening the list. Instead of winning cases with the mind God gave him. Is that any kind of life?"

"Yes, it is," I gently contradict her. "A hard life, if you like, but also intense and coherent. Preferable to many others, ma'am. I can't imagine Mayta growing old in some office, doing the same thing day after day."

"Well, you may be right," doña Josefa agrees—more from good manners than out of conviction. "From the time he was a child, you could see he wouldn't have a life like everyone else's. Has anyone ever seen a snotnose kid stop eating one day because there are people in the world going hungry? I didn't believe it, right? He had his soup and left the rest. And at night he had his bread. Zoilita, Alicia, and I would tease him: 'You gorge yourself when no one can see you, you trickster.' But it turned out that wasn't so. That's all he ate. And if he was like that as a kid, why wouldn't he be the way he was when he grew up?"

"Did you see *And God Created Woman*, with Brigitte Bardot?" asked Vallejos, changing the subject. "I saw it yesterday. Long legs, so long they come right out of the screen. I'd like to go to Paris someday and see Brigitte Bardot in the flesh."

"Shut up and dance." Alci had just gotten loose from Pepote and was tugging Vallejos out of his chair. "I'm not going to spend the whole night dancing with this lug. It's like dancing with a leech. Come on, a mambo."

"A mambo!" the lieutenant intoned. "Terrific! A mambo!"

A minute later, he was spinning like a top. He was a good dancer: he moved his hands, he knew trick steps, he sang. He inspired the others, who began to form wheels, conga lines, change partners. Soon the room was a whirl that left you dizzy. Mayta got up and pushed his chair against the wall to give the dancers more space. Would he ever dance like Vallejos? Never. Compared with Mayta, even Pepote was an ace. Smiling, Mayta remembered how he always felt like a Neanderthal whenever he had to dance with Adelaida, even the easiest dances. It wasn't his body that was awkward; it was that timidity, modesty, visceral inhibition that came from being so close to a woman that turned him into a bear. That's why he had decided not to dance unless forced into it, as when cousin Alicia or cousin Zoila made him, which could happen any moment. Did Leon Davidovitch know how to dance? Sure he did. Didn't Natalia Sedova say that, revolution aside, he was the most normal of men? An affectionate father, a loving husband, a good gardener; he loved to feed rabbits. The most normal thing in normal men is that they like to dance. To them, dancing did not seem, as it did to him, something ridiculous, a frivolity, a waste of time, a forgetting of important things. You are not a normal man, remember that, he thought. When the mambo was over, there was applause. They had opened the windows facing the street to let fresh air into

18

the room, and Mayta could see the couples with their faces pressed against the window frames, the lieutenant with his masculine eyes bulging, gazing hungrily at the women. His godmother made an announcement: there was chicken soup, and she needed help to serve it. Alci ran to the kitchen. Vallejos came and sat down next to Mayta again, sweating. He offered him a cigarette.

"In reality, I am here and not here." He winked jokingly. "Because I should be in Jauja. I live there. I'm in charge of the jail. I shouldn't leave, but I get out whenever I can. Ever been to Jauja?"

"I've been to other places in the mountains," said Mayta, "but never to Jauja."

"The first capital of Peru!" Vallejos played the fool. "Jauja! Jauja! What a shame you've never been there. All Peruvians should visit Jauja!"

Mayta then heard him launch, with no preamble, into a discourse about Indian life. The real Peru was in the mountains and not along the coast, among the Indians and condors and the peaks of the Andes, not here in Lima, a foreign, lazy, anti-Peruvian city, because from the time the Spaniards had founded it, it had looked toward Europe and the United States and turned its back on Peru. These were things Mayta had heard and read often, but they sounded different coming from the lieutenant's mouth. The novelty was in the clean and smiling way he said them, blowing out gray smoke rings at the same time. There was something spontaneous and lively in his manner of speaking that made whatever he was saying sound even better. Why did this boy arouse in him that nostalgia, that sensation of something altogether extinct. Because he's sound, thought Mayta. He's not perverted. Politics hasn't killed his joy in living. He's probably never taken part in politics of any kind. That's why he's irresponsible, that's why he says whatever comes into his head. There seemed to be no guile, no hidden intentions, no prefabricated rhetoric in the lieutenant. He was still in that adolescence in which politics consists exclusively of feelings, moral indignation, rebellion, idealism, dreams, generosity, disinterestedness, mysticism. Yes, those things do still exist, Mayta. There they were, incarnate—who the fuck would have thought it—in a little army officer. Listen to what he says. The injustice of it all was monstrous, any millionaire had more money than a million poor people, the dogs of the rich ate better than the Indians in the mountains, that iniquity had to be stopped, the people had to be mobilized, the haciendas had to be taken over, the barracks seized, the troops, who came from the people, made to revolt, unleash strikes, remake society from top to bottom, do justice. What envy. There he was, young, slim, handsome, smiling, talkative, with his invisible wings, believing that the revolution was a question of honesty, bravery, disinterestedness, daring. He didn't suspect and would perhaps never know that the revolution was a long act of patience, an infinite routine, a terribly sordid thing, a thousand and one wants, a thousand and one vile deeds, a thousand and one . . . But here comes the chicken soup, and Mayta's mouth watered when he smelled the aroma of the steaming bowl Alci put into his hands.

"How much work, and also what an expense every birthday," doña Josefa remembers. "I was in debt for a long time after. People broke glasses, vases. The house the next morning looked like a battleground or as if there had been an earthquake. But I took the trouble every year because it was a tradition in the neighborhood. Many relatives and friends saw each other only that one day a year: I did it for them as well, so as not to deprive them. Here, in Surquillo, my birthday parties were like national holidays or Christmas. Everything's changed, now there's no room in life for parties. The last time was the year that Alicita and her husband went to Venezuela. Now on my birthday I watch TV and then go to bed."

She looks sadly around the room devoid of people, as if putting back into those chairs, corners, and windows all the relatives and friends who would come to sing "Happy Birthday" to her, to applaud her good cooking, and she sighs. Now she looks seventy years old. Did she know if any relative had Mayta's notebooks and his articles? Her distrust rekindles.

"What relatives?" she murmurs, making a face. "The only relative Mayta ever had was me, and he never even brought a box of matches here, because whenever the police were looking for him this was the first place they came to. Besides, I never knew he was a writer or anything like that."

Yes, he wrote, and once in a while I read the articles that would come out in those little newspapers—handbills, really—in which he collaborated, and which he printed himself, and which are not to be found anywhere, not even in the National Library, or in any private library. But it's natural that doña Josefa never knew about *Workers Voice*, or any of the other little papers. Neither did the vast majority of the people in this country, especially those for whom they were written and printed. By the same token, doña Josefa was right: he wasn't a writer, or anything like that. Even though it would have pained him, he was a real intellectual. I still remember the hard tone in which he referred to intellectuals, in that last conversation we had in Plaza San Martín. They weren't good for much, according to him.

"At least the ones from this country." He was specific. "They get too sensualized too soon, they have no solid convictions. Their morality is worth approximately the price of a plane ticket to a youth congress, a peace congress, etc. That's why the ones who don't sell themselves for a Yankee scholarship, or to the Congress for the Freedom of Culture, let themselves be bribed by Stalinism and become party members."

He pointed out that Vallejos, surprised at what he had said and at the tone in which he had said it, looked him up and down, with his spoon suspended midway between his mouth and the bowl. He had upset him and, in a way, put him on his guard. A bad job, Mayta, a very bad job. Why did he let his temper and impatience get the better of him when the subject was intellectuals? What was Leon Davidovich, after all? He was an intellectual, and a genial one, and Vladimir Ilyich as well. But both of them had been, above and beyond everything else, revolutionaries. Didn't

21

you blow off steam against the intellectuals out of spite, because in Peru they were all reactionaries or Stalinists, and not a single one a Trotskyist?

"All I mean is, you can't count much on intellectuals for the revolution." Mayta tried to smooth things over, raising his voice so he could be heard over the *huaracha* "La Negra Tomasa." "Not at first, in any case. First come the workers, then the peasants. The intellectuals bring up the rear."

"What about Fidel Castro and the 26 of July people in the mountains of Cuba, aren't they intellectuals?" countered Vallejos.

"Maybe they are," admitted Mayta. "But that revolution is still green. And it isn't a socialist revolution but a petit-bourgeois revolution. Two very different things."

The lieutenant stared at him, intrigued. "At least you think about those things," he said, recovering his aplomb and his smile between spoonfuls of soup. "At least you don't get bored talking about the revolution."

"No, it doesn't bore me." Mayta smiled at him. "On the contrary."

My fellow student Mayta—he never became "sensualized." Of all the impressions I have of him from those fleeting encounters we had over the course of the years, the strongest is of the frugality that emanated from his person, from his appearance, from his gestures. Even in his way of sitting in a café, of looking over the menu, of telling the waiter his choice, even in his way of accepting a cigarette, there was something ascetic. That was what gave authority, a respectable aura, to his political theories, no matter how wild they may have seemed to me, no matter how lacking in disciples he was. The last time I saw him, weeks before the party where he met Vallejos, he was over forty and had spent at least twenty years in the struggle. No matter how much anyone might dig into his life, not even his worst enemies could accuse him of profiting, even once, from politics. On the contrary, the most consistent aspect of his career was always to have taken, with a kind of infallible intuition, all the necessary steps so that things would turn out for the worst, so that he would be entangled in problems and complications. "What he is is an amateur suicide," a friend we had in common once said to me. "An amateur, not a real suicide," he repeated. "Someone who likes to kill himself bit by bit." The idea set off sparks in my head, because it was so unexpected, so picturesque, like that phrase I'm sure I heard him use that time, in his diatribe against intellectuals.

"What are you laughing at?"

"At the phrase 'to get sensualized.' Where did you get it?"

"I've probably just invented it." Mayta smiled. "Okay. There are probably better ones. To go soft, to slip. But you understand what I mean. Small concessions that mine your morals. A little trip, a scholarship, anything that panders to your vanity. Imperialism is adept at those traps. And Stalinism, too. Workers or peasants fall easily. Intellectuals grab on to the bottle as soon as they have it in front of their mouths. Later they invent theories to justify their betrayal."

I told him he was more or less quoting Arthur Koestler, who had said those "skillful imbeciles" were capable of preaching neutrality in the face of bubonic plague because they had acquired the diabolical art of being able to prove everything they believed and of believing everything they could prove. I was sure he would reply that quoting a known agent of the CIA like Koestler was the absolute limit, but, to my surprise, I heard him say: "Koestler? Oh, right. No one has described the psychological terrorism of Stalinism better."

"Watch it, now. That's the road that leads to Washington and free enterprise," I said, to provoke him.

"You're wrong," he said. "That's the road to permanent revolution and Leon Davidovich. Trotsky, to his friends."

"And who is Trotsky?" said Vallejos.

"A revolutionary," Mayta clarified. "He's dead. A great thinker."

"From Peru?" insinuated the lieutenant timidly.

"Russian," said Mayta. "He died in Mexico."

23

"Enough politics, or I'll throw you both out," Zoilita insisted. "Come on, cousin, you haven't danced even once. Come on, let's dance this waltz."

"Dance, dance," Alci begged for help, from Pepote's arms.

"With whom?" said Vallejos. "I've lost my partner."

"With me," said Alicia, dragging him to the floor.

Mayta found himself in the middle of the floor, trying to follow the beat of "Lucy Smith," the lyrics of which Zoilita hummed in a cute way. He tried to sing too, to smile, while he felt his cramped muscles and an enormous shame at having the lieutenant see how poorly he danced. The room can't have changed much since then; except for wear and tear, this must be the same furniture as that night. It isn't difficult to imagine the room overflowing with people, smoke, the smell of beer, the sweat on people's faces, the music blaring, and, even, to discover them, in that corner next to the vase with wax roses, sitting one out, immersed in chatter about the only subject that mattered to Mayta—the revolution—a chat that lasted until dawn. The external scene—faces, gestures, clothing, objects—is there, quite visible. But not what happened within Mayta and the young lieutenant over the course of those hours. Did a current of sympathy flow from the first moment between the two, an affinity, the reciprocal intuition of a common denominator? There are friendships at first sight, more often perhaps than loves. Or was the relation between them from the outset exclusively political, an alliance of two men pledged to a common cause? In any case, they met here, and here began for both of them—although in the disorder of the party neither could suspect it—the most important event of their lives.

"If you do write something, don't mention me at all," doña Josefa Arrisueño begs me. "Or at least change my name and, above all, the address of the house. Many years have gone by, but in this country you never know. See you soon."

"I hope we do see each other soon," said Vallejos. "Let's continue our talk another time. I have to thank you because, you know, I've learned a great deal."

24

"See you, ma'am." We shake hands, and I thank her for her patience.

I go back to Barranco on foot. As I cross Miraflores, the party fades little by little and I find myself evoking an image of that hunger strike that Mayta went on when he was fourteen or fifteen years old, so he could be on a par with the poor. Out of all that talk with his aunt-godmother, the image that remains clearest in my mind is that midday bowl of soup and that slice of bread at night: all he ate for three months.

"See you soon." Mayta nodded. "Yes, of course, we'll go on talking."

Two

The Action for Development Center is located on Avenida Pardo in Miraflores. It's in one of the last of the old low-rise buildings to resist the advance of "urban development," the skyscrapers that have replaced these brick-and-wood houses and the gardens that surround them. Once the old houses were graced with shade, the rustle of leaves, and the chatter of sparrows—the effect of the ficus trees, once the lords of the street and now mere pygmies, reduced by the scale of the giant buildings. The good taste of Moisés—of *Doctor* Moisés Barbi Leyva, as the receptionist reminds me—has filled the house with colonial furniture that fits in perfectly with the building itself, which is one of those forties copies of the architecture of our colonial era: balconies with awnings, Sevilian patios, Moorish-style arches, tiled fountains. It has a certain charm. The whole house glows, and you can see people working in the rooms that face the garden, itself well trimmed and neat. Two armed guards who frisk me to see if I'm carrying a gun patrol the entranceway. While I wait to see Moisés, I look over the center's most recent publications, all on view in a display case illuminated by fluorescent light: studies on economy, statistics, sociology, politics, and history, all nicely printed, with a kind of prehistoric seabird colophon on the title pages.

Moisés Barbi Leyva is the backbone of the Action for Development Center. Thanks to his ability to wheel and deal, to his magnetic personality, and his prodigious appetite for work, the center is one of the most active cultural entities in the country. What is extraordinary about Moisés, beyond his cyclonic will and his bulletproof optimism, is his ability to negotiate, an anti-Hegelian science that consists in reconciling opposites, like San Martín de Porres—also from Lima—getting a dog, a mouse, and a cat all to eat from the same plate. Thanks to Moisés's eclectic genius, the center gets subventions, grants, and loans from capitalists and communists, from the most conservative governments and foundations as well as the most revolutionary, Washington and Moscow, Bonn and Havana, Paris and Beijing. They all think the center is *their* institution. Naturally, they are all wrong. The Action for Development Center belongs to Moisés Barbi Leyva and will belong to no one else until he dies. And doubtless it will die with him, because there is no one in this country capable of replacing him.

In Mayta's time, Moisés was a radical revolutionary. Now he is a progressive intellectual. His genius lies in having maintained intact his image as a man of the left, of having actually strengthened it as the center prospered—and he along with it. In the same way, he has been able to maintain excellent relations with the most violently opposed ideological adversaries; he has been able to get along with all the governments this country has had in the last twenty years, without selling out to any of them. He has a masterly sense of proportion and distance and knows how to counteract any concession that might seem excessive toward any one side with a compensatory rhetorical outburst toward the other. When I hear him at a cocktail party speak out all too forcefully against the rape of our natural resources by multinational corporations or against imperialist perversions of our

Third World culture, I know that this year the U.S. contributions to the center's programs have been larger than those of the opposition. And if, at an exhibition or concert, I hear him alarmed about Soviet intervention in Afganistan or pained at the repression of Solidarity in Poland, it's that this time he's received some help from the Eastern Bloc. With feints and shifts like these, he can always prove his ideological independence and that of the institution he heads.

Every Peruvian politician capable of reading a book—there aren't that many—considers him his intellectual mentor and is sure the center works directly for him. In a vague sort of way, they're all right. Moisés has been wise enough to make all of them feel that getting along well with his institution is necessary for them, and that feeling is in fact no illusion, because the right-wingers linked with the center feel like reformers, social democrats, almost socialists by virtue of that connection; the same connection makes the left-wingers socially acceptable, moderates them, tricks them out with a certain scientific gloss, an intellectual varnish. Moisés makes the military men feel like civilians, the priests like laymen, and the bourgeois like proletarians, true native sons of the nation.

Because he is successful, Moisés arouses venomous envy. Many people say the very worst about him and make fun of the wine-colored Cadillac in which he is driven around. The most virulent bad-mouthing comes, of course, from the progressive intellectuals who, thanks to the center—to Moisés—eat, wear clothes, write, publish, travel to congresses, and increase their status as progressives. He knows what people say about him, but he doesn't let it bother him. And if it does bother him, he covers it up. His success in life and the preservation of his image are based on a philosophy from which he never deviates: people may hate Moisés Barbi Leyva, but Moisés Barbi Leyva hates no one. His only enemies are abstract monsters—imperialism, latifundism, militarism, the oligarchy, the CIA, etc.—which are as useful for his purposes as are his friends (the rest of humanity). The intractable fanatic that Mayta was thirty years ago would doubtless

28

have said that Moisés was the typical example of the revolutionary intellectual who "got sensualized," which is probably the case. But would he have recognized that, despite all the deals he has to make and the acts he has to put on in this bedeviling country he lives in, Moisés Barbi Leyva has managed things so that several dozen intellectuals have earned a living, have worked instead of wasting their time in university cliques corrupted by frustration and intrigues, and at least the same number have traveled, taken special courses, and kept up a fertile association with their colleagues in the rest of the world? Would he recognize that, even if he is "sensualized," Moisés Barbi Leyva has done, all by himself, what the Ministry of Education, the Institute of Culture, or any of the universities in Peru should have done? No, he wouldn't recognize any of it. Because those things for Mayta were distractions from the primordial task, the only obligation for anyone with eyes to see and enough decency to take action: the revolutionary struggle.

"How are you?" Moisés shakes hands with me.

"And how are you, comrade?" replies Mayta.

He was the second to arrive, a rare event, because for as long as the committee had been meeting he had been there to open the garage on Jirón Zorritos, the local headquarters of RWP(T). The seven members of the committee all had keys and all of them had at one time or another slept in the garage if they had no other place or if they had some work to do. The two university students on the committee, Comrade Anatolio and Comrade Medardo, studied for their examinations there.

"Today I beat you." Comrade Medardo was shocked. "A miracle."

"Last night I went to a party and didn't get to bed until late."

"You, at a party?" Comrade Medardo laughed. "Another miracle."

"Something interesting," Mayta explained. "But not what you're thinking. I'm going to report to the committee right now."

The outside of the garage had nothing that would even suggest the kind of activities that went on there. Inside, you saw first a

29

poster with the bearded faces of Marx, Lenin, and Trotsky that Comrade Jacinto had brought back from a congress of Trotskyist organizations in Montevideo. Stacked against the walls were piles of *Workers Voice* and handbills, manifestos and statements favoring strikes or denouncing them, which they had never got around to handing out. There were a couple of chairs with their bottoms hanging out, and a few three-legged stools that looked as though they might belong either to a milkmaid or to a medium. Some mattresses were piled on top of each other and covered with a blanket. They were also used as seats when necessary. On a bookshelf made of boards and bricks, a few books covered with plaster dust languished, and in a corner there was the skeleton of a tricycle without wheels. The local office of the RWP(T) was so tiny that, with only a third of the committee present, it looked as though there was a quorum.

"Mayta?" Moisés leans back in his desk chair and gives me an incredulous look.

"Mayta," I say. "You remember him, don't you?"

He recovers his aplomb and his smile. "Of course, how could I ever forget him. But it's just strange. Is there anyone anywhere in Peru who remembers Mayta?"

"Barely any. That's why I have to squeeze out the memories of the few who do remember."

I know he'll help me, because Moisés is an obliging type, always willing to help anyone. But I realize at the same time he'll have to break through his own psychological reservations, do himself a kind of violence, since he had worked closely with Mayta and they had certainly been friends. Is he made uncomfortable by the memory of Comrade Mayta in this office full of leather-bound books, a parchment map of old Peru, and some fornicating pre-Colombian deities from Huacas in a glass case? Does having to speak again about the activities and illusions he and Mayta shared make him feel he is in a slightly false situation? Probably. Remembering Mayta makes even me—and I was never one of Mayta's political buddies—ill at ease, so the important director of the Action for Development Center must . . .

30

"He was a good guy," he says prudently. At the same time, he looks at me as if to discover in my deepest, most secret innermost self my own opinion of Mayta. "An idealist, well-intentioned. But naïve, deluded. At least, as far as that rotten business in Jauja is concerned, I have a clean conscience. I told him he was getting into a mess and I tried to get him to reconsider. A waste of time, of course, because he was stubborn as a mule."

"I'm trying to reconstruct the beginning of his political life," I explain. "I don't know much, except that when he was still a kid, before the university, or in the first year, he joined APRA. And later . . ."

"And later he became everything, that's the truth," says Moisés. "APRA, communist, revisionist, Trotskyist. Every sect, every group. The only reason he wasn't in more is that in those days there weren't more. Nowadays he'd have more options. Here in the center we are charting all the parties, groups, alliances, factions, and leftist fronts there are in Peru. How many would you think? More than thirty." He drums his fingers on the desk and assumes a pensive attitude.

"But there's one thing you have to recognize," he quickly adds in a very serious voice. "There wasn't a drop of opportunism in any of those changes. He may have been unstable, wild, whatever you like, but he was also the fairest person in the world. And another thing. He had a self-destructive streak. He was always heterodox, a rebel by nature. As soon as he got involved in something, he began to dissent and he ended up in the dissenting faction. Disagreeing was his strongest instinct. Poor Comrade Mayta! What a fucked-up life, don't you think?"

"The meeting is called to order," said Comrade Jacinto. He was secretary general of the RWP(T) and the oldest of the five present. Two committee members were missing: Comrade Pallardi and Comrade Carlos. After waiting half an hour for them, they had decided to begin without them. Comrade Jacinto, in a gravelly voice, "read" the minutes of the last meeting, three weeks ago. As a precaution, they took no written minutes, but the secretary general jotted down the principal theme of each dis-

31

cussion in a notebook and now he was looking at it—he squinted as he spoke. How old was Comrade Jacinto? Sixty, maybe older. A solid, upright *cholo*, he had a crest of hair over his forehead and an athletic air that made him seem younger. He was a relic in the organization and had lived its history since back in the forties, when they held those meetings at the poet Rafael Méndez Dorich's house. Trotsky's ideas were brought to Peru by a handful of surrealists who had come back from Paris—Pablo de Westphalen, Abril de Viveo, and César Moro. Comrade Jacinto was one of the founders of the first Trotskyist organizations, the Marxist Workers' Group (in 1946), the forerunner of the Revolutionary Workers' Party. In Fertilizantes, S.A. (Fertisa), where he had worked for twenty years, he had always been a member (a minority member, of course) of the union directorate —this despite the hostility of APRAs and Communist Party men. Why had he remained a Trotskyist instead of joining one of the other groups? Mayta was happy about it, but never understood it. The whole Trotskyist old guard, all of Comrade Jacinto's contemporaries, had stayed in RWP. Why, then, was he in the Revolutionary Workers' Party (T[rotskyist])? So he wouldn't lose touch with the young people? That must have been the reason, because Mayta doubted that the international Trotskyist polemic that raged over the revisionism of Michel Pablo, secretary of the Fourth International, mattered much to Comrade Jacinto.

"*Workers Voice*," said the secretary general. "That's the most urgent matter."

"Left-wing childishness, being in love with contradiction, I don't know what to call it," says Moisés. "The affliction of the ultra-left. To be the most revolutionary, to be further to the left than So-and-so, to be more radical than the other guy. That was Mayta's attitude all his life. When we were in APRA Youth, snotnose punks still wet behind the ears, APRA still underground, Manuel Seoane gave us a talk about Haya de la Torre's theory of historical space and time, how he had refuted and gone beyond Marxist dialectic. Mayta, of course, declared that we had to study Marxism so we would know just what we had refuted and gone beyond. He formed a circle, and within a few months the APRA Youth had to discipline us. And that's how, without our knowing it, we ended up collaborating with the Communist Party. The concrete result was the Panóptico prison. Our baptism of fire."

He laughs and I laugh. But we're not laughing at the same thing. Moisés is laughing at the games played by the precociously politicized children he and Mayta were then, and by laughing he tries to convince me that it was all unimportant, a case of political measles, anecdotes gone with the wind. I'm laughing at two photographs I have just discovered in the office. They face each other and balance each other out in their silver frames: Moisés shaking hands with Senator Robert Kennedy when Kennedy was in Peru promoting the Alliance for Progress, and Moisés next to Premier Mao Ze-dong in Beijing, with a delegation of Latin Americans. In both, he flashes a smile of neutrality.

"The person in charge may report," says Comrade Jacinto.

The person in charge of *Workers Voice* was Mayta. He shook his head to dispel both the image of Lieutenant Vallejos and the drowsiness that had been bothering him since he had awakened that morning after only three hours of sleep. He stood up and took out the three-by-five card with the outline of what he intended to say.

"That's the truth, comrades. *Workers Voice* is our most urgent problem, and we have to resolve it today, right now," he said, stifling a yawn. "In fact, there are two problems and we should take them up separately. The first, the problem of the name, has come up because the divisionists have withdrawn. The second is the usual problem, money."

All of them knew what was going on, but Mayta spelled it out for them in great detail. Experience had shown him that being prolix in presenting an idea saved time later on in the discussion. Item one: Should they go on calling the party newspaper *Workers Voice*, with the T added! After all, the divisionists had brought out their own paper, which they called *Workers Voice*,

33

even using the same logo, to make the working class believe that they represented the continuation of the Revolutionary Workers' Party and that the RWP(T) was the splinter group. A sleazy move, of course. But facts have to be faced. How could there be two Revolutionary Workers' Parties without the workers getting confused? And two *Workers Voice*, even if one of them had the letter T for Trotskyist all over it, would confuse them even more. By the same token, the articles for the next issue were already set, over in the Cocharcas print shop, so a decision had to be made right away. Would it be *Workers Voice (T)*, or should the name be changed? Mayta paused to light up a cigarette, and to see if Comrades Jacinto, Medardo, Anatolio, or Joaquín would say anything. Since they remained silent, Mayta went on, exhaling smoke. "The other matter is that we need five hundred *soles* to pay the printer. The business manager told me that beginning with the next issue they'll have to charge us more, to meet the rising cost of paper. Twenty percent."

The Cocharcas shop charged them two thousand *soles* to print a thousand copies, two pages each, and they sold the paper for three *soles*. Theoretically, if they sold out the issue, they would have had a profit of a thousand *soles*. In practice, the stands and paperboys charged a fifty percent commission for each copy, so that—naturally, they had no advertising—they lost fifty cents per copy. They only made a profit on the copies they sold themselves outside factories, universities, and unions. But, except for rare occasions—and those stacks of yellowed papers that demoralizingly surrounded the central committee of the RWP(T) in the garage on Jirón Zorritos were testimony to how rare they were—they had never sold out the thousand copies. Besides, many of the copies that made it to the street weren't sold but were given away. The *Workers Voice* always ran at a loss, and now with the split, things had got worse.

Mayta attempted an encouraging smile. "Comrades, it isn't the end of the world. Don't be so downcast. Let's try to find a solution."

"They threw him out of the Communist Party when he was in

prison, if I'm remembering right," Moisés recalls. "Probably I'm wrong. I get confused with all those schisms and reconciliations."

"Was he in the Communist Party for long?" I ask him. "Were you both in it?"

"We were in and not in, depending on how you look at it. We never officially joined and we didn't have cards. But no one had a card in those days. The party was proscribed and was tiny. We collaborated as sympathizers more than as militants. In jail, Mayta, with his spirit of contradiction, began to feel heretical sympathies. We began to read Trotsky, I dragged along by him. In Frontón, he was already lecturing the prisoners about double power, permanent revolution, the stagnation of Stalinism. One day he got word that the party had expelled him, accusing him of being ultra-left, of being a divisionist, a provocateur, a Trotskyite, etc. A little later, I was exiled to Argentina. When I got back, Mayta was carrying on the fight in the RWP. But aren't you hungry? Let's have some lunch."

It's a splendid summer afternoon, with a white sun overhead that cheers up houses, people, and trees. In Moisés's sparkling, wine-colored Cadillac, we go out into the streets of Miraflores. There are many more police patrols out than on other days, and many more army jeeps filled with helmeted soldiers. A sandbag-protected machine-gun nest manned by Marines has been set up at the entrance to the Diagonal. As we pass, I see that the officer in charge is speaking over a walkie-talkie. On a day like this, the only place to eat is at the seaside, Moisés says. The Costa Verde or the Suizo de La Herradura? The Costa Verde is closer and better defended against possible attack. On the way, we talk about the RWP in the last years of Odría's dictatorship, 1955 and 1956, when the political prisoners were let out of jail and the exiles came home.

"Just between us, all that business with the RWP was a joke," Moisés says. "A serious joke, of course, for the men who dedicated their lives to it and got screwed. A tragic joke for the ones who got killed. And a joke in bad taste for the ones who dried out their brains writing jerk-off pamphlets and getting caught up in sterile polemics. But, no matter how you look at it, a joke with no sense to it at all."

Just as we feared, the Costa Verde is crowded. At the door, the restaurant's security people frisk us, and Moisés leaves his revolver with the guards. They hand him a yellow check slip. While we wait for a table to come free, we sit under a straw awning next to the breakwater. We drink a cold beer, watch the waves break, and feel the spray on our faces.

"How many members did the RWP have in Mayta's time?" I ask.

Moisés stares into space and takes a long drink that leaves a beer mustache on his face. He removes it with his napkin. He turns his head, and a mocking little smile floats over his face. "Never more than twenty," he murmurs. He speaks in such a low voice that I have to lean over to hear him. "That was the most. We celebrated in a Chinese restaurant. We had twenty members. A little later, the divisions began. Pabloists and Anti-Pabloists. Do you remember Comrade Michel Pablo? The RWP and the RWP(T). Were we Pabloists or Antis? I swear I can't even remember. It was Mayta who got us involved in those ideological subtleties. Now I remember. We were Pabloists and they were Antis. Seven of us, and thirteen of them. They got the name and we had to add a capital T to our RWP. Neither group grew after the split; that I know for sure. That's how it went, until the Jauja business. Then the two RWPs disappeared, and another story began. Which was good for me. I was exiled in Paris, where I could write my thesis and devote myself to serious things."

"The points of view are clear, and the arguing is hot," said Comrade Anatolio.

"You're right," grunted the secretary general. "We'll vote with a show of hands. How many in favor?"

Mayta's suggestion—to change the name of *Workers Voice (T)* to *Proletarian Voice*—was rejected, three to two. Comrade Jacinto's vote broke the tie. The answer Medardo and Anatolio gave to Mayta's and Joaquín's argument about the confusion caused by the existence of two papers with the same name attacking each other was that changing the name would seem to be giving in to the divisionists, admitting that they were the real RWP, not the RWP(T). And wasn't it the RWP(T) that was holding to the party line? Besides, to give them the name of the paper as well as the name of the organization—wasn't that like rewarding betrayal? According to Medardo and Anatolio, the similarity of the titles, a transitory problem, would no longer confuse the workers as soon as the workers saw how the content of the articles, editorials, the news itself—the doctrinal coherence —defined the situation, revealing which was the genuinely Marxist, anti-bureaucratic newspaper, and which the fraud. The discussion was harsh, extremely long, and Mayta thought how much more fun he had had talking the night before with that silly, idealistic boy. I've lost this vote because I'm befuddled by lack of sleep, he thought. Oh, well, what difference did it make? If keeping the title meant they'd have more problems distributing *Workers Voice (T)*, he would request a review of the decision when all seven members of the committee were present.

"You mean there were really only seven of you when Mayta met Second Lieutenant Vallejos?"

"So you remember Vallejos, too." Moisés smiles. He studies the menu and orders a shrimp *ceviche* and scallops with rice. I've left the choice to him, having told him that a sensualized economist like himself could do a better job than I ever could. "Yes, seven. I don't remember all their names—their real names —but I do remember their party names. Comrade Jacinto, Comrade Anatolio, Comrade Joaquín. I was Comrade Medardo. Have you noticed how the Costa Verde's menu has declined since rationing went into effect? If we go on like this, every restaurant in Lima will close down."

They've given us a table in back, and we can just barely see the ocean. It's blocked by the heads of the other customers— tourists, couples, employees celebrating some company birthday. There must be an important politician or a member of the board of directors among them, because I see four bodyguards dressed in business suits, and carrying automatic rifles, sitting at a nearby table. They are silently drinking beer, keeping an eye on everything that goes on in the restaurant. The talk, the laughter, the clatter of dishes and glasses drowns out the surf.

"With Vallejos, then, you were eight," I say to him. "Your memory's tricked you."

"Vallejos was never in the party," he replies instantly. "The idea of a party with only seven members sounds like a joke, doesn't it? Vallejos was never a member. As a matter of fact, I never met the man. The first time I saw him was in the papers."

He speaks with absolute certainty, and I have to believe him. Why would he lie? In any case, what he says surprises me, even more than the number of militants in the RWP(T). I imagined it was small, but not as tiny as that. I had imagined a scenario that I now have to discard—Mayta bringing Vallejos to the garage on Jirón Zorritos, introducing him to his comrades, incorporating him into the party structure as secretary of defense . . . Another idea down the drain.

"Now, when I say seven, I mean seven full-time professionals," Moisés clarifies after a moment. "There were also the fellow travelers, students and workers with whom we set up study groups. And we had some influence in some unions—Fertisa, for example, and Civil Construction."

The waiter brings the *ceviche*, and the shrimp look fresh and moist. You can sense the *picante* in the very aroma. We drink and eat, and as soon as we finish, we get back down to business. "Are you sure you never saw Vallejos?"

"Mayta was the only one who saw him. For a long time, anyhow. Later on, we named a special commission. The Action Group. Anatolio, Mayta, and Jacinto, I think. They all saw him for sure, a few times at least. The rest of us, never. Don't you understand? He was in the army. What were we? Underground revolutionaries. And him? A second lieutenant!"

"He's been ordered to infiltrate our group," said Comrade Joaquín. "At least that much is clear, I hope."

"That's what I thought at first, of course," Mayta agrees.

"Let's review the facts, comrades. Are they that dumb? Would they send a lieutenant to infiltrate the party who spouts off about the socialist revolution at a birthday gathering? I got him to spill his guts, and he doesn't know what he's talking about. His heart's in the right place, but he's naïve, emotional. He talks about revolution without knowing what it is. He's an ideological virgin. The revolution for him is Fidel Castro and his happy band of bearded heroes taking potshots out in the Sierra Maestra. It sounds like a good thing to him, but he just doesn't understand how it works. Mind you, I've only had a little time to sound him out, that's as far as it goes."

He sat down and was talking rather impatiently because over the course of the three-hour session he had finished off all his cigarettes and he was dying for a smoke. Why didn't he believe Vallejos could be an intelligence officer ordered to gather information about the RWP(T)? And if he were? Was it so strange the army would resort to such a crude plan? Weren't the cops, the military men, and the whole Peruvian bourgeoisie all crude? But the jovial and exuberant image of the young chatterbox again dispelled his suspicion.

He listened to Comrade Jacinto agree with him: "Maybe they have ordered him to infiltrate us. At least we have the advantage over him of knowing who he is. We can take the necessary precautions. If they're giving us the chance to infiltrate them, it's our revolutionary obligation to take advantage of it, comrades."

That's how a subject that had provoked innumerable arguments in the RWP(T) suddenly resurfaced. Should the party have as one of its goals infiltrating the Army, the Navy, and the Air Force, in order to form cells made up of soldiers, sailors, and airmen? Or to indoctrinate the troops about their common cause with the proletariat and the peasants? Or was it a mistake to present the idea of a class struggle to the military, because over and beyond their social differences, there was an institutional link, an esprit de corps that united enlisted men and officers in an unbreachable unity? Mayta was sorry he had reported on the lieutenant. This was going to go on for hours. He dreamed about soaking his swollen feet in a washbasin. He had done it that morning when he came home from the party over in Surquillo, happy that he had gone over to give his aunt-godmother a hug. He had fallen asleep with wet feet, dreaming that he and Vallejos were running a race on a beach that could have been Agua Dulce, empty of swimmers, at dawn. He was falling behind, and the boy kept turning back to cheer him on, laughing. "Get a move on, come on, or are you getting so old you've run out of breath, Mayta?"

"Those meetings would drag on for hours. By the end, we'd all lose our voices," says Moisés, digging into the rice. "For example: Should Mayta go on seeing Vallejos or be on the safe side and drop him? Things like that, you just didn't decide in a minute. Oh, no. You had to analyze the circumstances, the causes, and the effects. We had to wring out a slew of hypotheses. The October Revolution, the relationship among socialist, capitalist, and bureaucratic-imperialist forces in the world, the development of the class struggle on all five continents, the pauperization of the neocolonial nations, monopolistic concentration . . ."

He started out smiling, but now his expression is sour. He puts the fork he was just raising to his mouth back down on his plate. Just a second ago, he was eating heartily, praising the Costa Verde's cook: "How much longer do you think we'll be able to eat like this with what's going on?" Suddenly he's lost his appetite. Have the memories he's dredged up as a favor to me depressed him?

"Mayta and Vallejos did me a huge favor," he murmurs, for the third time that morning. "If it hadn't been for them, I would still be in some dinky group trying to sell fifty copies of a bi-weekly newsletter, knowing all the time the workers would never read it, or that, if they did read it, they would never understand it." He wipes his mouth and gestures to the waiter to remove his plate.

"When the Vallejos business began, I no longer believed in what we were doing," he adds, with a funerary air. "I realized full well that it wouldn't lead anywhere, except back to jail once in a while, into exile once in a while, and to political and personal frustration. Nevertheless . . . Inertia, something like that, or something I can't define. A panic about feeling disloyal, a traitor. To the comrades, to the party, to your own self. A terror about wiping out in one shot something that, for better or for worse, represented years of struggle and sacrifice. Priests who leave the Church must feel the same thing." He looks at me at that moment as if he had just noticed I was still there.

"Did Mayta ever feel discouraged?"

"I don't know, maybe not, he was like granite." He is thoughtful for a moment and then shrugs. "Maybe he did, but secretly. I suppose we all have those flashes of lucidity in which we see we are at the bottom of a well, without a ladder. But we would never admit it, not for a second. Yes, Mayta and Vallejos did me a big favor."

"You repeat it so often it seems as though you don't believe it. Or that the favor hasn't really been of any use to you."

"It really hasn't been much use to me," he affirms with a sad gesture.

And when I laugh and make fun of him, telling him that he's one of the few Peruvian intellectuals who have achieved independence, and that, in addition, he is one of the few about whom one can say that he does things and helps to do things for his colleagues, he disarms me with an ironic look. Am I talking about Action for Development? Yes, I am: it's helped Peru and certainly contributed more to the nation than twenty years of party militancy. Yes, it also helped the people whose books it published; it got them grants and liberated them from that whorehouse of a university. But it had frustrated Moisés. Not in the same way the RWP(T) had, of course. He had always wanted—he looks at me as if wondering whether I'm worth the revelation—to be one of them. To do research, to publish. An old, very ambitious project that he knew full well he would never carry out: an economic history of Peru. General and detailed, from the pre-Inca cultures to our own times. Forgotten, like all his other academic projects! To keep the center alive

41

meant being an administrator, a diplomat, a publicity agent, and, most of all, a bureaucrat twenty-four hours a day. No—twenty-eight, thirty. For him, the day was thirty hours long.

"Don't you think it's wonderful that an ex-Trotskyist who spent his youth fulminating against the bureaucracy should end up a bureaucrat?" he asks, trying to recover his good humor.

"There's nothing more to be said," protested Comrade Joaquín. "There's nothing more to be said about the subject and that's it."

How right you are, thought Mayta, nothing more to be said, and besides, what was it they were discussing? A while ago—it was Comrade Medardo's fault, because he had brought up the question of the participation of soldiers' soviets in the Russian Revolution—they were arguing about the sailors' rebellion in Kronstadt and how it was crushed. According to Medardo, that anti-socialist rebellion, in March of 1921, was solid evidence of the doubtful class consciousness of the troops and of the risks of relying on the revolutionary potential of soldiers. On a talking spree, Comrade Jacinto explained that, instead of speaking about their behavior in 1921, Medardo should remember what the Kronstadt sailors had done in 1905. Weren't they the first to rise up against the tsar? And in 1917, weren't they ahead of the majority of factories in forming a soviet? The discussion then drifted to Trotsky's attitude toward Kronstadt. Medardo and Anatolio remembered that in his *History of the Revolution* he had approved, as a lesser evil, the repression of the uprising because it was objectively counterrevolutionary and aided both the White Russians and the imperialist powers. But Mayta was sure that Trotsky had rectified that thesis later and clarified it: he didn't participate in the repression of the sailors, which had been, exclusively, the work of the Petrograd committee, headed by Zinoviev. He even went so far as to write that it was at the time of the liquidation of the rebel sailors during the Lenin government that the first manifestations of the anti-proletarian crimes of Stalinist bureaucratization had emerged. Finally, because of an unforeseen twist, the discussion ground to a halt on the question of whether the translations of Trotsky into Spanish were any good. "There's no way we can vote on this," Mayta stated. "Let's see if there's a consensus. Even though it hardly seems probable to me, I recognize that Vallejos may be under orders to infiltrate us or provoke us in some way. On the other hand, as Comrade Jacinto has said, we should not pass up the opportunity to win over a young officer. Here's my proposal. I'll make contact with him, I'll sound him out, I'll see if there is any way to attract him. Without, of course, giving him any information about the party. If I smell something suspicious, that's it. If I don't, well, we'll cross that bridge when we come to it."

Either because they were tired or because he was persuasive, they accepted. When he saw those four heads nod in agreement, he was overjoyed: now he could go out and buy cigarettes, have a smoke.

"In any case, if he had any crises, he certainly concealed them," Moisés says. "That's one thing I always envied him: how sure he was about what he was doing. Not only in the RWP(T), but before, too, when he was a Moscow man and in APRA."

"How do you explain all those changes? Did he just change ideologies, or were there psychological reasons?"

"I'd say moral reasons," Moisés corrects me. "Although to talk about morality in Mayta's case may seem incongruous to you."

In his eyes, there burns a malicious light. Is he expecting a little insinuation from me so he can start gossiping?

"It doesn't seem incongruous to me at all," I assure him. "I always suspected that Mayta's political shifts were more emotional and ethical than ideological."

"The search for perfection, for the pure." Moisés smiles. "He was a very good Catholic when he was a boy. He even went on a hunger strike so he could know how the poor lived. Did you know that? That's maybe why he was that way. When you start looking for purity in politics, you eventually get to unreality."

He observes me for a moment in silence while the waiter pours our coffee. Many of the Costa Verde's customers have left, including the important man and his bodyguards with their automatic rifles. In addition to being able to hear the sound of the sea again, we can just make out, over on the left, among the Barranquito jetties, a few surfers waiting for their wave, sitting astride their boards like horsemen. "An attack from the sea would be really easy," someone says. "There's no beach patrol. We've got to tell the boss."

"What is it about Mayta that interests you so much?" Moisés asks me, as he uses the tip of his tongue to check the temperature of the coffee. "Of all the revolutionaries of those years, he is the most obscure."

I don't know how to go on. If I could, I would tell him, but at this moment I only know that I want to know, even invent, Mayta's story, and as lifelike as possible. I could give him moral, social, and ideological reasons, and show him that Mayta's story is the most important, the one that most urgently needs to be told. But it would all be a lie. I truthfully do not know why Mayta's story intrigues and disturbs me.

"Perhaps I know why," Moisés says. "Because his story was the first, before the triumph of the Cuban Revolution. Before that event which split the left in two."

He may be right, it may well be because of the precursory character of the adventure. It's also true that it inaugurated a new era in Peru, something neither Mayta nor Vallejos could guess at the time. But it's also possible that the whole historical context has no more importance than as decor and that the obscurely suggestive element I see in it consists of the truculence, marginality, rebelliousness, delirium, and excess which all came together in that episode of which my fellow Salesian School chum was the leading character.

"A progressive military man? Are you sure there is such a thing?" mocks Comrade Medardo. "The APRA people have spent their lives looking for one, so he could make their revolution for them and open the doors of the Palace to them. They've grown old without finding him. Do you want the same thing to happen to us?"

"It's not going to happen." Mayta smiles. "Because we aren't going to stage a barracks coup but bring about *the* revolution. Don't worry, comrade."

"Well, I for one am worrying," said Comrade Jacinto. "But about something more terrestrial. Did Comrade Carlos pay the rent? I don't want the old lady down here again."

The meeting was over, and since they never left all at once, Anatolio and Joaquín had gone first. Mayta and Jacinto waited a few minutes before leaving. Mayta smiled as he remembered that night. The old lady had walked in unexpectedly right in the middle of a hot discussion of the agrarian reform that Paz Estenssoro's Revolutionary Nationalist Movement had instituted in Bolivia. Her entrance had left all of them stupefied, as if the person who opened the door were an informer and not that fragile little figure with white hair and a bent back, leaning on a metal cane.

"Good evening, Mrs. Blomberg," Comrade Carlos reacted. "What a surprise."

"Why didn't you knock?" protested Comrade Jacinto.

"I don't have to knock on the door to my own garage, do I?" retorted the offended Mrs. Blomberg. "We agreed that you would pay the rent on the first. What happened?"

"We're a bit behind because of the bank strike," said Comrade Carlos, stepping forward, trying to block Mrs. Blomberg's view of the poster with the bearded men and of the stacks of *Workers Voice*. "Here's the check, see?"

Mrs. Blomberg calmed down when she saw Comrade Carlos take an envelope out of his pocket. She looked over the check carefully, nodded, and said goodbye, muttering all the while that in the future they should pay on time because at her age she wasn't in any shape to go around collecting rents from house to house. They had a fit of laughing, forgot the discussion, and began to dream up scenarios. Could Mrs. Blomberg have seen Marx, Lenin, and Trotsky? Could she be on her way to the police station? Would the garage be raided that night? They had told her they were renting the garage as the headquarters for a chess club, and about the only thing the old lady wouldn't see in her quick visit was a chessboard or a pawn. But the police never came, so Mrs. Blomberg must have noticed nothing suspicious.

"Unless this lieutenant of yours who wants to start a revolution is an outcome of that visit," said Medardo. "Instead of raiding us, infiltrating us."

"After all these months?" Mayta demurred, afraid to reopen a discussion that would keep him from his cigarette. "We'll know soon enough. Ten minutes have gone by. Shall we go?"

"We'll have to find out why Pallardi and Carlos didn't come," said Jacinto.

"Carlos was the only one of the seven who led a normal life," Moisés says. "A contractor, he owned a brickworks. He paid the garage rent, the printer, and he paid for the handbills. We all chipped in, but our contributions were nothing. His wife wished we'd drop dead."

"And Mayta? At France-Presse he couldn't have earned much."

"And he spent half his salary or more on the party," Moisés adds. "His wife hated us, too, of course."

"Mayta had a wife?"

"Mayta was married as legally as can be." Moisés laughs. "But not for long. To a woman named Adelaida—she worked in a bank. A real cutie. Something we never understood. You didn't know Mayta was married?"

I knew nothing about it. They left together and locked the garage door. At the corner store they stopped off so Mayta could buy a pack of Incas. He offered them to Jacinto and Medardo and lit up his own so hastily he actually burned his fingers. Heading toward Avenida Alfonso Ugarte, he took several deep drags, half closing his eyes, enjoying to the fullest the pleasure of inhaling and exhaling those diminutive clouds of smoke that faded into the night.

"I know why I can't stop thinking about the lieutenant's face," he thought aloud.

"That soldier boy's made us lose a lot of time," complained Medardo. "Three hours, for a second lieutenant!"

Mayta went on as if he hadn't heard a word: "It's either because he's ignorant or because he's inexperienced, or who knows why—he was talking about the revolution the way we never talked."

"Don't use dem big words wit' me, sir, ah's jus a worker, not uh intelleftual," mocked Jacinto.

It was a joke he made so often that Mayta had begun to wonder if in fact Comrade Jacinto didn't envy the *intelleftuals* he said he respected so little. At that moment, the three of them had to hug the wall to keep from being run over by a crowded bus that came sliding over the sidewalk.

"He talked with humor, joyfully," added Mayta. "As if he were talking about something healthy and beautiful. We've lost that kind of enthusiasm."

"You mean we've gotten old," joked Jacinto. "Maybe you have, but I'm still growing."

But Mayta wasn't in the mood for jokes and went on speaking anxiously, hastily: "We're too wound up in theory, too serious, too politicizing. I don't know . . . Listening to that kid spout off about the socialist revolution made me envy him. Being involved in the struggle for so long hardens you, sure, but it's bad to lose your illusions. It's bad that the methods we use make us forget our goals, comrades."

Did they understand what he wanted to tell them? He felt he was getting upset and changed the subject. When he left them on Alfonso Ugarte to go to his room on Zepita Street, the idea kept buzzing in his head. In front of the Loyaza Hospital, as he waited for a break in the river of cars, trucks, and buses that choked the four lanes, he suddenly understood an association that had been flitting, ghostlike, through his mind since the previous night. That's what it was: the university.

That disillusioning year, those courses on history, literature, and philosophy he'd signed up for at San Marcos University. He had quickly concluded that the professors had lost their love of teaching somewhere along the line, if in fact they had ever had any love for the great works and great ideas they were supposed to teach. To judge by what they were teaching and the kind of papers they expected from their students, it would seem that some kind of inversion had taken place in their dull, mediocre wits. The Spanish literature professor seemed convinced that it was more important to read what Leo Spitzer had written about García Lorca than to read Lorca himself, or to read Amado Alonso's book on Neruda's poetry than to read Neruda. And the history professor deemed the sources of Peruvian history more important than Peruvian history. For the philosophy professor, form was more important than ideas and their impact on action . . . Culture for them had dried up, had become a vain science, sterile erudition separated from life. He had told himself then that this was what was to be expected from bourgeois culture, from bourgeois idealism—leaving life behind. He had withdrawn from the university in disgust: real culture was just the opposite of what they were teaching.

But had he, Jacinto, Medardo, the comrades of the RWP(T), and those in the other RWP become just as academic? Had they forgotten the true hierarchy of things—that there was a difference between essentials and extraneous matters? Had their revolutionary work become as esoteric and pedantic as literature, history, and philosophy had for the professors at San Marcos? Listening to Vallejos was like being awakened from a dream: "Don't forget the essentials, Mayta. Don't get tangled up in superfluous things, comrade." He knew nothing, had read nothing, was a virgin—all of that—but in one sense he had an advantage over all of them: the revolution for him was action, something tangible, heaven on earth, the reign of justice, equality, fraternity. He could guess what images the revolution took on in Vallejos's mind: peasants breaking the chains the bosses had shackled them with, workers who went from being servants to being masters of machines and shops, a society in which surplus value no longer fattens up a minority but reverts back to the workers . . . and he felt a shiver run down his spine.

Wasn't he at the corner of Cañete and Zepita? He woke from his reverie and rubbed his arms. Damn! How absentminded can you get? The corner of Cañete and Zepita was one he always avoided, because of the bad taste it left in his mouth whenever he went near it. Right there, in front of the newsstand, the gray-green car had stopped with a screech that still whined in his ears. Before he could figure out what was happening, four thugs got out and he saw four pistols pointed at him. He was frisked, pushed around, and shoved into the car. He had been in police stations and various jails before, but that was the worst and the longest time, the first in which he had been worked over. He thought he would go mad and considered suicide. Ever since, he had avoided that corner, out of a kind of superstition he would have been ashamed to admit. He turned onto Zepita and slowly walked the two blocks to his house. His weariness as usual concentrated in his feet. Damned flat feet. I'm a fakir, he thought. Walking on thousands of tiny needles . . . He thought: The revolution is a party for that brand-new lieutenant.

He had the second attic room in a house on a dead-end street lined with two-story buildings, an area about nine by fifteen feet, overflowing with books, magazines, and newspapers scattered all over the floor. There was a bed without a headboard, with a mattress and one blanket. A few shirts and some trousers hung from nails in the wall, and behind the door there was a mirror and a little shelf with his shaving things. A dangling bulb shone a dirty light on the room, which was made even smaller by its incredible disorder. As soon as he entered, he went down on all fours to drag out from under the bed—the dust made him sneeze—the chipped basin which was probably the object he treasured most in the place.

The rooms had no bath. In the patio, there were two common lavatories and a faucet, where all the neighbors got water for washing and cooking. During the day there were always lines,

49

but not at night, so Mayta went down, filled his basin, and returned to his room—carefully, so he wouldn't spill a drop—all in a few minutes. He undressed, lay down on his bed, and sank his feet in the basin. Ah, how restful. He had often fallen asleep giving himself a footbath, and would awaken sneezing and frozen to death. But he didn't fall asleep this time. While the fresh, soothing sensation spread from his feet to his ankles and legs and the fatigue diminished, he thought that even if it had no concrete effect, it was a good thing that someone reminded him: what happened to those literati, historians, and philosophers at San Marcos should not happen to a revolutionary. A revolutionary should not forget that he lives, fights, and dies to make revolution and not to . . .

"Let's get the check," says Moisés. "Enough talk. I'll pay. Rather, the center will pay. Stick that wallet where the sun won't shine on it."

But there is no more sun. The sky has clouded over, and when we leave the Costa Verde, it looks like winter. One of those typical afternoons in Lima, wet, with a low sky that threatens and blusters, promising a storm that never comes. When he picks up his pistol at the entrance—"It's a 7.65 Browning," he tells me—Moisés checks to see if the safety is on. He puts it in the glove compartment.

"At least tell me what you've got so far," he says as we roll along Quebrada Armendáriz in his wine-colored Cadillac.

"A forty-year-old man with flat feet, who's spent his life in the catacombs of theoretical revolution (or should I say revolutionary intrigue?)," I sum up for him. "In APRA, an APRA dissident; in the Communist Party, a Communist Party dissident; finally, a Trotskyist. Every variant, all the contradictions of the left during the fifties. He lived underground, was jailed, and lived in permanent indigence. But . . ."

"But what?"

"But the frustration didn't embitter him or even corrupt him. He stays honest, idealistic, despite that castrating life. Does that sound about right?"

"Basically, yes," affirms Moisés as he slows down to let me off. "But have you ever thought how difficult it is to be corrupted in this country of ours? You have to have opportunities. Most people are honest because they have no choice, don't you think? Did you ever wonder how Mayta would have reacted if he'd been given a chance to be corrupted?"

"I figure he always behaved in such a way that he never put himself in the path of corruption."

"You don't have much to go on yet," concludes Moisés.

Off in the distance, we hear shots.

Three

To get there from Barranco, you have to go to downtown Lima, cross the Rímac—a squalid creek this time of year—at the Ricardo Palma bridge, go along Piedra Liza and skirt the San Cristóbal hills. It's a long, risky, and at certain times of the day extremely slow route because of all the traffic. It also charts the gradual impoverishment of Lima: the prosperity of Miraflores and San Isidro progressively decays and grows ugly in Lince and La Victoria, then resurges illusively in the downtown area, with the tedious towers of banks, mutual-fund and insurance companies—among which nevertheless there proliferate promiscuous tenements and old houses that stay upright only by a miracle. But immediately after you cross the river, in the so-called Bajo el Puente sector, the city decomposes into vacant lots, where huts thrown together out of matting and rubble have sprung up, slums mixed in with garbage dumps that go on for miles. Once this marginal Lima was only poor, but now it's a place of blood and terror as well.

When you come to Avenida de los Chasquis, the asphalt gives

out and the potholes take over, but a car can still bounce along a few more yards, fenced-in lots on either side, and broken streetlights—the kids smash the bulbs with slingshots. Since it's my second visit, I won't be so dumb as to go beyond the store where I got stuck last time. My last trip involved some slapstick comedy. When I finally figured out that I was definitely stuck in the mud, I asked some boys talking on the corner to give me a push. They helped me, but before getting down to pushing, they held a knife to my throat and threatened to kill me if I didn't give them everything I had. They took my watch, my wallet, my shoes, and my shirt. They allowed me to keep my trousers. While they pushed the car, we talked. Were there many murders in the neighborhood? Quite a few. Political assassinations? Yeah, them too. Just yesterday, a decapitated body was found just down the way there, with a sign on it: "Stinking Squealer."

I park and walk among dumps that double as pigpens. The pigs root around in these mounds of garbage, and I have to wave both hands around to keep the flies off. On top of and in between the mounds of garbage huddle the huts, made of tin cans, bricks, cement (some), adobe, wood, and with tin roofs (some). They are all half started, never finished, always decrepit, leaning on one another, collapsing or about to collapse, swarming with people who look at me with the same indolence as the last time. Until a few months ago, political violence did not affect the slums on the outskirts of Lima as much as it affected the residential neighborhoods and the downtown area. But now most of the people assassinated or kidnapped by revolutionary commandos, the armed forces, or the counterrevolutionary death squads come from these zones.

There are more old men than young, more women than men, and from time to time I have the impression that I'm not in Lima or even on the coast but in some village in the Andes: sandals, Indian skirts, ponchos, vests with llamas embroidered on them, dialogues in Quechua. Do they really live better in this stink and scum than in the mountain villages they have abandoned to come to Lima? Sociologists, economists, and anthropologists assure us that, as amazing as it might seem, this is the case. Their expectations for bettering themselves and for simply surviving are greater, it seems, in these fetid dumps than in the plateaus of Ancash, Puno, or Cajamarca, where drought, epidemics, barren land, and unemployment decimate the Indian towns. This is probably true. How else can you explain someone's choosing to live in these dumps and this filth?

"For them, it's the lesser of two evils, a better choice," said Mayta. "But if you think that just because there is misery in these slums they must contain revolutionary potential, you're mistaken. These people aren't proletarians: they're lumpen. They have no class consciousness, because they aren't a class. They can't even imagine what the class struggle is."

"Then they're like me." Vallejos smiled. "What the fuck is the class struggle?"

"The motor of history," explained Mayta, very serious, full of his role as professor. "The struggle that results from the contrary interests of each class in society. Interests innate in the role of each class in the production of wealth. There are those who own capital, those who own property, those who own knowledge. And there are those who own nothing but their labor: the workers. And there are as well the marginal people, those people from the slums, the lumpen. Are you getting confused?"

"Just hungry." Vallejos yawned. "These talks always give me an appetite. Let's forget the class struggle for today and have a nice cold beer. I'm inviting you to have lunch at my parents' house. My sister is coming out. A big event. She's worse off than if she were in a barracks. I'll introduce you. And the next time we see each other, I'll bring the surprise I told you about."

They were in Mayta's tiny room, Mayta sitting on the floor and the second lieutenant on the bed. From outside came the sounds of voices, laughter, and automobiles. Minute dust motes floated around them like weightless little animals.

"If you go on this way, you won't learn anything about Marxism." Mayta gave up. "The fact is, you don't have much of a teacher. I always complicate the things I teach."

"You're better than many of the ones I had in military school." Vallejos encouraged him with a laugh. "You know what happens to me? I'm really interested in Marxism, but all those abstractions get me. I'm much more open to practical, concrete things. By the way, should I tell you my plan for revolution before we have the beer, or later?"

"I'll only listen to your inspired plan if you pass the test," Mayta said, following his lead. "So what the fuck is the class struggle?"

"The big fish eats the little fish," said Vallejos, cackling. "What else could it be, brother? To know that a landowner with a thousand acres and his Indians hate each other, you don't have to do much studying. Well, did I get a hundred? Now, my plan is gonna knock your socks off, Mayta. Even more when you see the surprise. Will you come to lunch? I want you to meet my sister."

"Mother? Sister? Miss?"

"Juanita," she decides. "We're better off calling each other by name. After all, we're about the same age, right? And this is María."

The two women wear leather sandals, and from the bench I'm sitting on, I can see their toes: Juanita's are still, and María's wiggle around nervously. Juanita is dark, energetic, with thick arms and legs, and dark down on her upper lip. María is small and light-skinned, with clear eyes and an absent expression.

"A Pasteurina or a glass of water?" Juanita asks me. "Better for us if you have a soda, because around here water is gold. Just to get it, you have to go all the way to Avenida de los Chasquis."

The place reminds me of a cabin out in the San Cristóbal hills where two Frenchwomen, sisters in the congregation of Father de Foucauld, lived. That was long ago. Here the walls are also whitewashed and bare, the floor covered with straw mats; the blankets make you think this could be the dwelling of a desert nomad.

"All we need is sun," says María. "Father Charles de Foucauld. I read his book *In the Heart of the Masses*. It was famous at one time."

"I read it, too," says Juanita. "I don't remember much. I never did have a good memory, even when I was young."

"What a shame." Nowhere do I see a crucifix, an image of the Virgin, a religious picture, a missal. Nothing that might allude to the fact that the inhabitants are nuns. "About that lack of memory. Because I . . ."

"Well, that's something else. Of course I remember him." Juanita chides me with a look, as she hands me the Pasteurina. Then her tone changes: "I haven't forgotten my brother, of course."

"What about Mayta?" I ask her, swigging that tepid, overly sweet stuff straight from the bottle.

"I remember him, too." Juanita nods. "I saw him only once. At my parents' house. I don't remember much, because that was the next-to-the-last time I talked to my brother. The last time was two weeks later. All he did was talk about his friend Mayta. He really liked him and admired him. His influence was . . . Perhaps I'd better say nothing."

"Ah, so that's what it's about." María uses a piece of cardboard to shoo the flies away from her face. Neither wears a habit, only flannel skirts and gray blouses. But in the way they wear their clothes, in the way their hair is held back in a net, in the way they talk and move, you can see they are nuns. "At least it's about them and not about us. We were nervous, now I can say it, because publicity is bad for the things we do."

"And just what is it we do?" mocked Mayta, with a sarcastic laugh. "We've taken over the town, the police station, the jail, we've got all the weapons in Jauja. What now? Head for the hills like mountain goats?"

"Not like mountain goats," replied the second lieutenant,

without getting angry. "We can go on horseback, burro, mule, by truck, or on foot. On foot is best, because there's no better way to get around in the mountains. It's easy to see you don't know much about the mountains, buddy."

"It's true, I really don't know much about them," admitted Mayta. "I'm really ashamed."

"Well, we can help you there. Come with me tomorrow to Jauja." Vallejos nudged him with his elbow. "You'll have a free place to stay, and free food. Just the weekend, man. I'll show you the country, we can go to the Indian towns, you'll see the real Peru. But listen, now: don't open the surprise. You promised. Or I'll take it back."

They were sitting on the sand at Agua Dulce, gazing over the deserted beach. All around them were fluttering sea gulls, and a salty, moist breeze wet their faces. What could this surprise be? The package was wrapped so carefully, as if it contained something precious. And it was really heavy.

"Of course I'd like to go to Jauja," said Mayta. "But . . ."

"But you can't pay the bus fare," Vallejos cut in. "Don't worry. I'll buy you a ticket."

"We'll see. Let's get back to business," Mayta insisted. "Serious business. Did you read the little book I gave you?"

"I liked it and I understood everything, except for a couple of Russian names. Know why I liked it, Mayta? Because it is more practical than theoretical. *What Is to Be Done? What Is to Be Done?* Lenin knew what had to be done, buddy. He was a man of action, like me. So my plan looked like kid stuff to you?"

"Well, at least you read Lenin, and at least you like him. You're making progress." Mayta avoided answering directly. "Want me to tell you something? You were right, your sister really impressed me. She didn't seem like a nun. She made me remember old times. When I was a kid, I was as devout as she is, did you know that?"

"He looked older than he was," Juanita says. "He was in his forties, wasn't he? And since my brother looked younger than he was, they looked like father and son. It was during one of my rare visits to my family. At that time, the two of us were cloistered. Not like these snots who live half the time in the convent and half the time out on the street."

María protests. She waves her piece of cardboard in front of her face very fast, driving the flies crazy. They're not only all around us, buzzing our heads: they dot the walls, like nailheads. I already know what's in this package, Mayta thought. I know what the surprise is. He felt a wave of heat in his chest and thought: He's crazy. How old can Juanita be? Undecipherable: petite, ramrod straight; her gestures and movements released waves of energy, and her slightly bucked teeth were always biting her lower lip. Could she have been a novice in Spain and lived there for a long time? Because her accent was remotely Spanish, the accent of a Spanish woman whose *j*'s and *r*'s had lost their edges, the *z*'s and *c*'s their roundness, but whose spoken Spanish hadn't yet taken on the Lima drawl. What are you doing here, Mayta? he thought, feeling uncomfortable. What are you doing here with a nun? He unobtrusively stretched out his hand and felt for the surprise. Yes, indeed—a gun.

"I thought the two of you were in the same order," I say to them.

"Then you are sadly mistaken," María replies. She smiles often, but Juanita is serious even when she makes jokes. Outside, there is a furious barking, as if a pack of dogs were fighting. "I was with the proletarian nuns, she with the aristocratic nuns. Now both of us are lumpen."

We begin talking about Mayta and Vallejos, but without knowing it, we digress into a discussion of local crime. At the beginning, the revolutionaries were quite strong here: they solicited money in broad daylight, even held meetings. They would kill people from time to time, accusing them of being traitors. Then the freedom squads appeared, cutting off heads, mutilating, and burning real or supposed accomplices of the revolutionaries with acid. Violence has increased. Juanita believes, nevertheless, that there are still more ordinary crimes than political crimes, and that common murderers disguise their crimes as political assassinations.

"A few days ago, a guy in the neighborhood killed his wife because she was jealous of him," María tells. "And his brothers-in-law saw him trying to cover up the crime by hanging one of those famous 'Squealer Bitch' signs on her."

"Let's go back to what brought me here," I suggest. "The revolution that began to take shape during those years. The one Mayta and your brother were involved in. It was the first of many. It charted the process that has ended in what we are all living through now."

"It may turn out that the great revolution of those years wasn't any of the ones you think it was, but ours," Juanita interrupts me. "Because—have all these murders and attacks produced anything positive? Violence only breeds violence. And things haven't changed, have they? There is more poverty than ever, here, out in the country, out in the mountains, everywhere."

"Did you talk about that?" I ask her. "Did Mayta talk to you about the poor, about misery?"

"We talked about religion," Juanita says. "And don't think I brought the subject up. It was him."

"Yes, very Catholic, but no more—I'm free of those illusions," Mayta murmurs, sorry he's said it here, afraid that Vallejos's sister will be offended. "Don't you ever have doubts?"

"From the moment I wake up until I go to bed," she says softly. "Whoever told you that faith and doubts don't go together?"

"I mean"—Mayta grows bolder—"isn't it a hoax to say that the mission of Catholic schools is to educate the elite? Is it really possible to infuse the children of the classes in power with the evangelical principles of charity and love for one's neighbor? Have you ever thought about that?"

"I think about that and much worse things." The nun smiled at him. "Rather, we both think. It's true. When I took orders, we all thought that, along with power and wealth, God had given those families a mission as far as their disinherited brothers were concerned. That those girls who were the head of the social body—if we could educate them well—would take charge of making the rest of the body better, the arms and the legs. But now none of us thinks that is the way to change the world."

And Mayta, surprised, listened to her tell about the scheme she and her schoolmates had worked up. They didn't stop until the free school for the poor in Sophianum was closed. The little girls from paying families all had a little girl in the school, a poor girl. The better-off girls brought in sweets, clothes, and once a year visited the poor girls' homes with presents. They would go in the family car with Mommy; or sometimes only the chauffeur dropped off the Christmas cake. Disgusting, shameful. Could you call that practicing charity? The nuns had brought the matter up so often, criticized, written, and protested so much that, finally, the free school of Sophianum was closed.

"Then we aren't so far apart, after all, Mother." Mayta was shocked. "I'm happy to hear you talk this way. May I quote you something a great man once said? That when humanity has fought all the revolutions necessary to end injustice, a new religion will be born."

"Who needs a new religion when we already have the true one?" replied the nun, passing him the cookies. "Have one."

"Trotsky," Mayta clarified. "A revolutionary, an atheist. But he respected the problem of faith."

"All that stuff about how the revolution liberates the people's energy, you can understand right here." Vallejos threw a stone at a pelican. "Did my plan seem that bad to you? Or did you say it just to bust my balls, Mayta?"

"It seemed a monstrous deformity to us." Juanita shrugs, making a discouraged gesture. "And now I wonder if, deformity and all, it wasn't better for those girls to have a place where they could learn to read and where they would get at least one Christmas cake a year. I don't know, I'm not so sure anymore that we did the right thing. What were the results? At the school there were thirty-two nuns and twenty or so sisters. That's the usual proportion in most schools. The congregations have collapsed . . .

Was our crisis of social conscience such a good thing? Was the sacrifice of my brother a good thing?"

She tries to smile, as if excusing herself for having involved me in her confusion.

"It's logical, it's a piece of cake, it's money in the bank." Vallejos was getting excited. "If the Indians work for a boss who exploits them, they work unwillingly and produce very little. When they work for themselves, they will produce more, and that will benefit all of society. Need cigarettes, brother?"

"As long as a parasitic class doesn't come into existence to expropriate and use for its own advantage the efforts of the proletariat and the peasants," Mayta explained to him. "As long as a bureaucratic class doesn't accumulate enough power to create a new unjust social structure. And to avoid that, Leon Davidovich conceived the permanent revolution. God, I even bore myself with these lectures."

"I'd like to go to a soccer match, how about you?" Vallejos sighed. "I got out of Jauja to see the classic Alianza–U match and I don't want to miss it. Come on, I'm inviting you."

"What's your answer to that question?" I say to her when I see she's stopped talking. "Did the silent revolution of those years help the Church or hurt it?"

"It helped us, the ones who lost our false illusions, but it didn't help the faith. As to the other nuns, I can't say," María says. And, turning to Juanita: "What was Mayta like?"

"He always spoke softly, courteously, and he dressed very modestly," Juanita recalls. "He tried to shock me with his anti-religious attitudes. But I rather think I shocked him. He had no idea what was going on in the convents, seminaries, the parishes. He knew nothing about our revolution . . . He opened his eyes wide and said, 'We're not so far apart, after all.' The years have proven him correct, don't you think?"

And she tells me that Father Miguel, a priest in the neighborhood who mysteriously disappeared a few years ago, is, it seems, the famous Comrade Leoncio who led the bloody attack on the Palace of Government a month ago.

"I doubt it," María protests. "Father Miguel was a loudmouth. Fiery as far as words go, but nothing but a blowhard. I'm sure the police or the freedom squads killed him."

Yes, that's what it was. Not a revolver or an automatic pistol, but a short, light sub-machine gun that looked factory-fresh: black, oily, and shiny. Mayta stared at it hypnotized. Making an effort, he took his eyes off the weapon, which trembled in his hands, and looked around, all the time with the feeling that from among the books and papers scattered around his room the informers were crawling out, pointing a finger at him, laughing their heads off: "We've got you now, Mayta." "You've had it now, Mayta," "Right in the act, Mayta." This kid's foolish, a nut, he thought. A . . . But he felt no ill will toward the lieutenant. Instead, the benevolence inspired by a prank played by a favorite child, and the desire to see him again as soon as possible. To box his ears, he thought. To tell him . . .

"When I'm with you, I feel funny somehow. I don't know whether to tell you or not. I hope you don't get mad. May I speak frankly?"

The stadium was half empty, and they had arrived very early. The preliminary match hadn't even begun.

"Of course," said Vallejos, exhaling smoke from his mouth and nose. "I can guess. Are you going to tell me my revolutionary plan is half-assed? Or are you going to get on me again about the surprise?"

"How long have we been seeing each other?" asks Mayta. "Two months?"

"We're really tight, though, right?" Vallejos says as he applauds a kick made by a small, extremely agile wing. "What were you going to say?"

"That sometimes I think we're wasting our time."

Vallejos forgot the match. "You mean, about lending me books and teaching me Marxism?"

"Not because you don't understand what I teach you," Mayta clarified. "You're smart enough to understand dialectical materialism, or anything else."

"That's good," said Vallejos, returning to the match. "I thought you were wasting your time because I'm a jerk."

"No, you're no jerk." Mayta smiled at the lieutenant's profile. "The fact is, when I'm talking to you, knowing what you're thinking, knowing you yourself, I think that theory, instead of helping you, can actually get in your way."

"Darn! Almost a goal. Nice shot." Vallejos got up to clap.

"In that sense, understand?" Mayta went on.

"I don't understand a thing," Vallejos said. "Now I am a jerk. Are you trying to tell me to forget my plan, that I was wrong to give you the sub-machine gun? What do you mean, brother? Goal! All right!"

"In theory, revolutionary spontaneity is bad," Mayta said. "If there is no doctrine, no scientific knowledge, the impulse is wasted in anarchic gestures. But you have an instinctive resistance to getting tangled up in theory. Maybe you're right. Perhaps, thanks to that instinct, what happened to us won't happen to you . . ."

"Us?" asked Vallejos, turning to look at him.

"From worrying so much about being well prepared in doctrinal terms, we forgot the practical, and . . ."

He fell silent because there was a huge uproar in the stands: firecrackers were going off, and a rain of confetti came down on the field. You'd made a mistake, Mayta.

"You haven't answered me," Vallejos insisted, without looking at him, contemplating his cigarette. Was he an informer? "You said *us*, and I asked who *us* is. You didn't answer, buddy."

"Revolutionary Peruvians, Marxist Peruvians," Mayta spelled it out, scrutinizing him. Was he an agent ordered to find out about them, to provoke them? "We know a lot about Leninism and Trotskyism, but we don't know how to reach the masses. That's what I meant."

"I asked him if he at least believed in God, if his political ideas were compatible with the Christian faith," Juanita says.

"I shouldn't have asked you that, brother," Vallejos begged pardon, contrite, the two of them immersed in the flood of

63

people emptying out of the stadium. "I'm sorry. I don't want you to tell me anything."

"What can I tell you that you don't already know?" Mayta said. "I'm happy we came, even if the match was no good. It's been ages since . . ."

"I want to tell you just one thing," Vallejos declared, taking him by the arm. "I understand that you have your doubts about me."

"You're nuts," said Mayta. "Why should I have doubts about you?"

"Because I'm a soldier, and because you don't know me all that well," said Vallejos. "I can understand that you'd hide certain things from me. I don't want to know anything about your political life, Mayta. I play fair and square with my friends, and I think of you as a friend. If I pull a fast one on you, you've got a way to even the score—the surprise . . ."

"The revolution and the Catholic religion are incompatible," asserts Mayta softly. "Don't fool yourself, Mother."

"You're the one who's fouled up. You're also way behind the times," Juanita jokes. "Do you think I'm put out when I hear religion called the opiate of the people? It may have been, probably was, in any case. But that's all finished. Everything is changing. We're going to bring about the revolution, too. Don't laugh."

Had the era of progressive priests and nuns already begun then in Peru? Juanita says yes, but I have my doubts. Anyway, it was in such an early stage of development, as yet so inarticulate, that Mayta couldn't have had any idea of it. Would he have been pleased? The ex-child who had gone on a hunger strike to be like the poor, would he have been happy that Monsignor Bambarén, bishop of the slums, wore his famous ring with the pontifical coat of arms on one side and the hammer and sickle on the other? Would he have been happy that Father Gustavo Gutiérrez conceived liberation theology by explaining that bringing about the socialist revolution was the obligation of every Catholic? That Monsignor Méndez Arceo advised the Mexican faithful to go to Cuba as they used to go to Lourdes? Yes, no doubt about it. Maybe he would have gone on being a Catholic, as have so many these days. Did he give one the feeling that he was dogmatic, a man of rigid ideas?

Juanita thinks it over for a moment. "Yes, I think so, a dogmatic man." She nods. "At least he wasn't at all flexible about religion. We only spoke for a while, perhaps I didn't understand what kind of man he was. I thought about him a lot later on. He had a huge influence on my brother. He changed his life. He made him read, which was something he almost never did before. Communist books, of course. I tried to warn him: 'You know he's catechizing you?'"

"Yes, I know, but I learn a lot of things from him, sister."

"My brother was an idealist, a rebel, with an innate sense of justice," adds Juanita. "He found a mentor in Mayta, one who manipulated him as he saw fit."

"So, as far as you're concerned, Mayta was calling the shots?" I ask her. "Do you think he planned it all, that he put the Jauja business into Vallejos's head?"

"No, because I don't know how to use it." Mayta was doubtful. "I'll make you a confession. I've never even fired a cap gun in my entire life. But, going back to what you said before about friendship, I have to warn you about one thing."

"Don't warn me about anything, I already asked you to excuse my indiscretion," said Vallejos. "I'd rather hear one of your speeches. Let's go on with double power, that idea of undercutting the bourgeoisie and the imperialists slowly but surely."

"Not even friendship comes before the revolution for a revolutionary: get that through your head and never forget it," said Mayta. "Revolution, above all things. Then comes the rest. That's what I tried to explain to your sister the other afternoon. Her ideas are good, she goes as far as a Catholic can. But that's just not enough. If you believe in heaven and hell, then what happens here on earth will always take a back seat to all that. And there will never be a revolution. I trust you and I think of you as a great friend. If I hide anything, if . . ."

"Okay, okay. I've already asked you to forgive me, can't we forget it?" Vallejos wanted to shut him up. "So you've never fired a gun? Tomorrow we'll go over by Lurín, with the surprise. I'll give you a lesson. Firing a sub-machine gun is much easier than the thesis of double power."

"Of course, that was what had to happen," Juanita said. But she does not seem all that sure, judging by the way she says it. "Mayta was an old hand at politics, a professional revolutionary. My brother was an impulsive kid Mayta could dominate just by his age and his knowledge."

"I don't know. I'm just not sure," I said to her. "Sometimes I think it was the other way around."

"That's silly," said María, joining in. "How could a kid get a savvy old guy like that involved in as crazy a deal as that?"

Exactly, Mother. Mayta was a revolutionary from the shadowy side. He had spent his life conspiring and fighting in insignificant little groups like the one he was a member of. And suddenly, just when he was reaching the age at which people usually retire from militant activism, someone turned up who opened the doors of action to him for the first time. Could there have been anything as captivating for a man like Mayta than out of the blue having someone stick a sub-machine gun in his hands?

"This is make-believe, a novel," says Juanita, with a smile that forgives me for my transgression. "This isn't at all like the real story, in any case."

"It won't be the real story, but, just as you say, a novel." I confirm her ideas. "A faint, remote, and, if you like, false version."

"Then why work so hard at it?" she insinuates with irony. "Why try to find out everything that happened, why come to confess to me like this. Why not just lie and make the whole thing up from top to bottom?"

"Because I'm a realist, in my novels I always try to lie knowing why I do it," I explain. "That's how I work. And I think the only way to write stories is to start with History—with a capital H."

"I wonder if we ever really know what you call History with a capital H," María interrupts. "Or if there's as much make-believe in history as in novels. For example, the things we were talking about. So much has been said about revolutionary priests, about Marxist infiltration in the Church . . . But no one comes up with the obvious answer."

"Which is?"

"The despair and anger you feel at having to see hunger and sickness day and night, the feeling of impotence in the face of so much injustice," said Mayta, always choosing his words carefully so as not to offend. The nun noticed that he barely moved his lips as he spoke. "Above all, realize that the people who can do something never will. Politicians, the rich, the ones in the driver's seat, the ones with power."

"But why would you lose your faith because of that?" asked Vallejos's sister, astonished. "I would think it would make it stronger, that it would . . ."

Mayta went on, his tone hardening: "No matter how strong your faith is, there comes a moment when you say, *That's it*. It just can't be possible that the remedy for so much iniquity is the promise of eternal life. That's how it was, Mother. Seeing that hell was right here in the streets of Lima. Especially over in El Montón. Ever been to El Montón?"

Another shack city, one of the first, no worse, no more miserable than this one where Juanita and María live. Things have gotten much worse since that time when Mayta confessed to the nun; the shacks have proliferated, and in addition to misery and unemployment, there is murder now. Was it really the spectacle of Montón that fifty years ago transformed the devout little boy that Mayta was into a rebel? Contact with that world has not had the same effect, in any case, on Juanita and María. Neither gives the impression of being desperate, outraged, or

67

even resigned, and at least as far as I can see, living with iniquity has not convinced them that the solution is assassination and bombs. They went on being nuns, right? Would the shots fade into echoes in the Lurín desert?

"No." Vallejos aimed, fired, and the noise wasn't as loud as Mayta thought it would be. His palms were sweaty with expectation. "No, they weren't for me, I lied to you. The books, well, in fact I bring them all to Jauja so the joeboys can read them. I have faith in you, Mayta. I'm going to tell you something I wouldn't even tell the person I love most in the world, my sister."

As he spoke, he put the sub-machine gun in Mayta's hands. He showed him how to brace it, how to take off the safety, how to aim, squeeze the trigger, load and unload.

"A big mistake. Never talk about things like that," Mayta admonished him, his voice shaken by the jolt he had felt in his body as he heard the burst of fire and realized from the vibration in his wrists that it was he who had fired. Off in the distance, the sand extended, yellowish, ocher, bluish, indifferent. "It's a simple matter of security. Nothing to do with you, but with the others, don't you understand? Anyone can do whatever he likes with his life. But no one should endanger his comrades, the revolution, just to show a friend he trusts him. And suppose I worked for the cops?"

"That's not your style. Even if you wanted, you couldn't be a squealer." Vallejos laughed. "What do you think? Easy, huh?"

"You know, it's really easy," Mayta agreed, touching the muzzle and burning his fingers. "Don't tell me any more about the joeboys. I don't need proof of your friendship, jerk-off."

A hot breeze had come up and the salt flats looked as if they were being bombarded with grains of sand. It was true that the second lieutenant had chosen the perfect place—who would hear the shots in this solitude? He shouldn't think he knew all he had to know. The main thing was not loading, unloading, aiming, and firing, but cleaning the weapon and knowing how to take it apart and put it back together.

"I told you because I had a purpose." Vallejos returned to the subject, gesturing at the same time that they should head back to the highway, because the land breeze was going to suffocate them. "I need your help, brother. They're boys from the Colegio San José, over in Jauja. Really young, fourth or fifth year. We got to be friends playing soccer on the little field near the jail. The joeboys."

They walked on the sand with their heads bent to the wind, their feet buried up to the ankles in the soft earth. Mayta quickly forgot the shooting lesson and his anger of a moment before, intrigued by what the second lieutenant was saying.

"Don't tell me anything that'll make you sorry you did," Mayta reminded him, even though he was beside himself with curiosity.

"Shut the fuck up." Vallejos had tied his handkerchief over his face to protect himself from the sand. "The joeboys and I went from soccer to having a few beers together, then to little parties, to the movies, and to meetings. Since we've been holding these meetings, I've tried to teach them the things you teach me. A teacher from the Colegio San José helps me out. He says he's a socialist, too."

"You give classes in Marxism?" Mayta asks.

"You bet, the only true science," Vallejos says, gesticulating. "The antidote to all those idealist, metaphysical ideas they get pumped into their heads. Just as you yourself would have said it in your own flowery style, brother."

A moment before, when he was showing Mayta how to shoot, he was a dextrous athlete, a commander. And now he was a timid boy, awkwardly telling him his story. Through the rain of sand, Mayta looked at him. He imagined the women who had kissed those clean-cut features, bitten those fine lips, who had writhed under the lieutenant's body.

"You know you really knock me out?" he exclaimed. "I thought my classes in Marxism bored you to death."

"Sometimes they do—to be frank—and other times I get lost," Vallejos admitted. "Permanent revolution, for example.

69

It's too many things all at the same time. So I've scrambled the joeboys' brains. That's why I'm always asking you to come to Jauja. Come on, give me a hand with them. Those boys are pure dynamite, Mayta."

"Of course we're still nuns, but without the disguise." María smiles. "We've got a surplus of jobs, not vows. They free us up from teaching and let us work here. The congregation helps us out as best they can."

Do Juanita and María have the feeling they really are helping in a positive way by living in this shack city? They must. Otherwise, the risk they run by living here under these conditions would be inexplicable. A day doesn't go by without some priest, nun, or social worker in the slums being attacked. Setting aside whether what they do is useful or not, it's impossible not to envy them the faith that gives them the strength to withstand this daily horror. I tell them that as I walked here I had the feeling I was crossing all the circles of hell.

"It must be even worse there," Juanita says, without smiling.

"You've never been in this place before, young man?" María interjects.

"No, I've never been in El Montón," Juanita replied.

"I have, often, when I was a kid, when I was such a devout Catholic," said Mayta. She noticed that he had an abstracted— nostalgic?—expression on his face. With some boys from Catholic Action. There was a Canadian mission in the dump. Two priests and a few laymen. I remember one young, red-faced, tall priest who was a doctor. 'Nothing I've learned is of any use,' he would say. He couldn't stand the fact that children were dying like flies, he couldn't bear the high incidence of tuberculosis, and that at the same time the newspapers were filled with page after page on parties, banquets, the weddings of the rich. I was fifteen. I would go back to my own home and at night I could not pray. God doesn't hear, I would think. He covers His ears so He can't hear and His eyes so He doesn't have to see what's going on in El Montón. Then one day I was convinced. To fight against all that, I had to stop believing in God, Mother."

To Juanita, it seemed like drawing an absurd conclusion from correct premises, and she told him so. But she was moved by the fervor she saw in him.

"I've had my moments of anguish about my faith, too," she said. "But, happily, I've never gotten to the point of demanding a reckoning from God."

"We don't talk only about theory, but about practical things as well," Vallejos went on. They were walking along the highway toward Lima, trying to flag down a truck or a bus, the sub-machine gun concealed in a bag.

"Practical things—you mean like how to make Molotov cocktails, set dynamite charges, manufacture bombs?" mocked Mayta. "Practical things—you mean like your revolutionary plan of the other day?"

"Everything in its proper time, brother," Vallejos said, as always in a jovial tone. "Practical things—I mean like going to the Indian communities to see the problems of the peasants on site. And to see solutions. Because those Indians have begun to move, to occupy the lands they have been demanding for themselves for centuries."

"To recover them, you mean," Mayta said softly. He fixed a curious gaze on Vallejos. He was disconcerted, as if, despite the fact that they had been seeing each other for so many weeks, he was just now discovering the real Vallejos. "Those lands belonged to them, don't forget."

"Exactly, the recovery of lands is what I mean," agreed the second lieutenant. "We go and talk with the peasants, and the boys see that those Indians, without the help of any party, are beginning to break their chains. That's how the boys are learning the way the revolution will come to this country. Professor Ubilluz helps me out with the theory, but you'd help me much more, brother. Will you come to Jauja?"

"Well, I have to say you've left me gaping," Mayta said.

"Shut your mouth before it gets filled with sand." Vallejos laughed. "Look, that bus's going to stop."

"So you've got your group and all," repeated Mayta, rubbing

71

his eyes, which were irritated from all the dust. "A Marxist studies circle. In Jauja! Plus you've made contact with peasant groups. Which means that . . ."

"Which means that, while you talk about the revolution, I do it." The lieutenant gave him a pat on the back. "Fuckin' right. I'm a man of action. You, you're a theoretician. We've got to put it all together. Theory and practice, buddy. We'll get the people moving, and no one'll be able to stop them. We'll do great things. Shake hands and swear you'll come out to Jauja. Our Peru is a great place, brother!"

He looked like an excited, happy kid, with his impeccable uniform and his crew cut. Once again, Mayta felt happy to be with him. They took a corner table and ordered two coffees from the Chinese storekeeper. Mayta imagined they were both the same age, both boys, and that they had sealed their friendship with blood.

"Nowadays, there are lots of priests and nuns in the Church just like that Canadian priest from El Montón," the Mother said, not at all upset. "The Church has always known what misery is, and, whatever you say, it has always done what it could to alleviate it. But now, it's true, it has understood that injustice is not individual but social. The Church no longer accepts the fact that the few have everything while the majority has nothing. We know that under today's conditions purely spiritual aid is nothing but a joke . . . But I'm wandering from the subject."

"No, that *is* the subject," Mayta urged her on. "Misery, the millions of hungry people in Peru. The only subject that counts. Is there a solution? What is it? Who's got it? God? No, Mother. The revolution."

The afternoon has slipped by, and when I get around to looking at my watch, I see I've been there for almost four hours. I would have liked to hear what Juanita heard, to hear from Mayta's mouth how he lost his faith. Over the course of our conversation, children have appeared at the half-open door from time to time: they poke their heads in, spy on us, get bored, and go away. How many of them have been recruited by the insurgents? Did my old schoolmate ever tell me about his trips to El Montón to lend a hand to the Canadian mission? How many of them will kill or be killed? Juanita has stepped over to the nearby clinic to see if there are any problems. Did he go every afternoon, after classes at the Salesian School let out, or did he only go on Sundays?

The clinic is open from eight to nine, run by two volunteer doctors who take turns; in the afternoons, a male and a female nurse come to give vaccinations and first aid. Did Mayta help the redheaded, desperate, angry priest bury the babies wiped out by hunger and infection, did his eyes fill with tears, did his heart pound in his breast, did his childish, believer's imagination soar to heaven to ask why: Why do you permit this to happen, Lord? Next to the clinic, in a shack made from boards, is the office of Communal Action. Along with the clinic, that office is the reason why Juanita and María are in the slum. Did the Canadian mission where Mayta did volunteer work look like this one? Did a lawyer go to that one to give free legal counsel to the neighborhood, was there also a technical adviser to advise them on establishing businesses? Mayta would go there, would plunge into all that misery, his faith would begin to falter, and at the Salesian he wouldn't say a word about it. With me, he went on talking about serials and how terrific it would be to see a picture based on *The Count of Monte Cristo*.

Juanita and María tell me they worked for a few years in the bottling plant at San Juan de Lurigancho, but that since the plant closed they have devoted themselves exclusively to Communal Action. Their respective orders send them enough to live on. Why did he confide just like that in a person he was meeting for the first time? Because she was a nun, because she inspired affection, because the nun was the sister of his new friend, or because he suddenly felt a wave of melancholy, remembering the ardent faith he'd felt as a Salesian student?

"When the terrorism started, we were really frightened," María says. "We thought they'd blow the place up and destroy everything. But so much time has passed that we don't even remember anymore. We've been lucky. Even though there's been some violence around here, they haven't touched us yet."

"Is your family very Catholic?" asked Mayta. "Didn't you have problems with . . . ?"

"They're Catholics, but more out of routine than conviction." The nun smiled. "Like most people. Sure I had problems. They were really astonished when I told them I wanted to be a nun. For my mother, it was the end of the world. For my father, it was as if I had been buried alive. But they've gotten used to it."

"One son in the army and one daughter in the convent," said Mayta. "It was the usual pattern in aristocratic families in colonial times."

"Come on out," called Vallejos from the table. "Talk with the rest of the family, too, and don't monopolize my sister—we never get to see her."

Both teach morning classes in the little school they've set up in Communal Action. On Sundays, when the priest comes to say Mass, the place turns into a chapel. He hasn't come often of late: someone blew up his church and he's had problems with his nerves ever since.

"It doesn't look as if it was the freedom squads that did it, but some neighborhood kids who wanted to play a little trick on him, knowing he's so chickenhearted," María says. "The poor man has never said a single word about politics, and his only weakness is chocolate. But after the blast, and with his nerves, he's lost more than twenty pounds."

"Does it seem to you that I speak of him with some anger and resentment?" Juanita makes a curious face, and I see she is not asking just for the sake of asking. It's something that must have been bothering her now for a long time.

"No, I didn't sense anything like that," I say to her. "What I've noticed is that you try to avoid mentioning Mayta by name. You always beat around the bush instead of saying 'Mayta.' Is it because of the Jauja thing, because you're sure he pushed Vallejos into it?"

"I'm not sure about that," Juanita denies it. "It's possible that my brother is also to blame. But even though I don't want to, I realize that I still resent him a little. Not because of Jauja. But because he made him doubt. That last time we were together, I asked him, 'Are you going to become an atheist like your friend Mayta? Are you going that way, too?' He didn't give me the answer I was looking for. He just shrugged his shoulders and said: 'I probably will, sister, because the revolution is the most important thing.' "

"Father Ernesto Cardenal also said the revolution was the most important thing," María recalls. She adds that—she doesn't know why—the redheaded priest Mayta talked about reminded her of the visits to Peru of, first, Ivan Ilyich, and then Ernesto Cardenal.

"Yes, it's true, what would Mayta have said that afternoon when we talked, if he had known that we would be hearing things like that from within the Church," Juanita says. "Even though I thought I was up on everything, I was shocked when Ivan Ilyich came. Could it be a priest saying those things? Had our revolution gotten to that point? It certainly wasn't a silent revolution any longer."

"But Ivan Ilyich wasn't anything," interposes María, her blue eyes filled with mischief. "You had to hear Ernesto Cardenal to get the good stuff. Where we were teaching, some of us asked special permission to go to the National Institute of Culture and the Teatro Pardo y Aliaga to see him."

"Now he's a government minister in his country, a real political figure, right?" asked Juanita.

"Yes, I'll go to Jauja with you," Mayta promised him in a low voice. "But, for God's sake, let's be discreet. Above all, after what you've told me. What you're doing with those boys is subversion, comrade. You're risking your career, and lots of other things."

"Look who's talking. And who fills my head with subversive propaganda every time we meet?"

75

They started laughing, and the Chinese man who was bringing them their coffee asked what the joke was. "A traveling-salesman joke," said the lieutenant.

"The next time you come to Lima, we'll fix a date for me to go to Jauja," Mayta promised him. "But give me your word you won't say a thing to your group about my visit."

"Secrets, secrets, you've got a mania for secrets," Vallejos protested. "Yeah, I know: security is vital. But you can't always be so finicky, brother. Shall I tell you about secrets? Pepote, that creep from your aunt's party, took Alci from me. I went to see her and I found her with him. Holding hands. 'Let me introduce my boyfriend,' she said. They set me up as their audience."

It didn't seem to bother him, since he laughed as he told the story. No, he wouldn't say a thing to the joeboys or to Ubilluz, it would be a surprise. Now he had to take off. They parted with a heartfelt handshake, and Mayta watched him leave the store, ramrod-straight and solid in his uniform, walking toward Avenida España. As he watched him disappear, he thought that this was the third time they were meeting in the same place. Was it smart? The police station was just down the way, and it wouldn't be odd to see informers having coffee there. So he had formed—on his own, taking his chances—a Marxist circle. Who would have guessed? He half closed his eyes and saw, at an altitude of about nine thousand feet, their adolescent, mountain-Indian faces, their rosy cheeks, their stringy hair, their wide mountaineer's chests. He saw them chasing a ball, sweating, excited. The second lieutenant running with them, as if he were one of them, but he was taller, more agile, stronger, more skillful, kicking, charging, and with every jump, kick, or charge, his muscles would harden. After the game, he saw them crowded into a whitewashed adobe room—through the windows, you could see white clouds skimming over purple peaks. They would be listening attentively to the lieutenant, who would be showing them Lenin's *What Is to Be Done*, saying, "Boys, this is pure dynamite." He didn't laugh. He felt not the slightest desire to make fun of him, to say to himself what he had been saying about Vallejos to his comrades in the RWP(T): "He's very young, but he's made of good stuff." "He's good, but he's got to grow up." He felt, at this moment, considerable admiration for Vallejos, a bit of envy for his youth and enthusiasm, and something more, something intimate and warm. At the next meeting of the Central Committee of the RWP(T), he would request a discussion because the Jauja business was now taking on a new character. He was about to get up from his corner table—Vallejos had paid the check before he left—when he discovered the bulge in his trousers. His face and body burned. He realized he was trembling with desire.

"We'll walk you," Juanita says.

We talk for a while at their door, in the dusk that will soon be night. I tell them not to bother, that I've left the car about three-quarters of a mile away, why should they walk all that way?

"It's not to be nice," María says. "We don't want you to get mugged again."

"I haven't got anything for them to steal," I tell them. "Just the car key and this notebook. The notes don't mean anything—whatever hasn't found its way into my memory doesn't get into the novel."

But there's no way to dissuade them and they go out with me into the stench and heat of the dump. I walk between them and I call them my bodyguards as we make our way through the crazy terrain consisting of shacks, caves, stands, pigsties, children tumbling down the garbage hills, unexpected dogs. The people all seem to be at their doors or walking through the heat, and you hear conversations, jokes, curses. Once in a while, I trip on a hole or on a stone, no matter how carefully I walk, but María and Juanita walk easily, as if they know every obstacle in the road by heart.

"Thefts and muggings are worse than the political crimes," Juanita repeats. "Because of unemployment and drugs. There were always thieves in the neighborhood, of course. But, before, they went out of the neighborhood, to steal from rich people.

Because there's no work, because of drugs, because of the war, there's not a drop of neighborhood solidarity left. Now the poor rob and kill the poor.

"It's become a big problem," she adds. "As soon as it gets dark, unless you have a knife—and if you do, you're one of the killers—unless you just don't know what you're doing or you're dead drunk, you just don't walk around here, because you know you'll get mugged. The thieves break into houses in broad daylight and the assaults often turn into murder. The people's despair is boundless, that's why these things happen. For instance, the poor guy the people from the next slum found trying to rape a little girl: they poured kerosene over him and burned him alive."

"Just yesterday, they found a cocaine laboratory here," María says.

What would Mayta say about all this? In those days, drugs were almost nonexistent, a toy for refined night people. Now, on the other hand . . . They can't keep medicines in the clinic, I listen to them tell me. At night, they bring all the drugs home and hide them in a safe place, under some trunk. Because every night thieves break in to steal the bottles, the pills, the ampules. Not to get better—that's what the clinic is for, and the medicines are free. They take them to get high. They think any medicine is a drug and take whatever they find. Lots of thieves turn up at the clinic the next day, suffering from diarrhea, vomiting, and worse. The neighborhood kids get high on banana skins, on floripondio leaves, on glue, on anything. What would Mayta say about all that? I can't even guess, and besides, I can't concentrate on Mayta's memory, because in the context of so much misery his story shrinks to nothing and evaporates. Any unknown face is a tempting target—is it María who's talking?

"This is also the red-light district of the zone," Juanita adds. Or is it that in this ignominious context it isn't Mayta but literature that seems useless? "Really painful, don't you think? To sell yourself to live is bad enough. But to do it here, surrounded by garbage and pigs . . ."

"The explanation is that they get business here," notes María.

That's a bad thought. If, like the Canadian priest in Mayta's anecdote, I also succumb to despair, I won't write this novel. That won't help anyone. No matter how ephemeral it is, a novel is something, while despair is nothing. Do they feel secure trotting around the neighborhood at night? Up till now, thank God, nothing's happened to them. Not even with the crazy drunks who might not be able to recognize them.

"Maybe we're so ugly we don't tempt anyone." María guffaws.

"Both doctors have been attacked," Juanita says. "But they still keep coming."

I try to go on talking, but I get distracted. I try to go back to Mayta, but I just can't, because again and again the image of the poet Ernesto Cardenal eclipses Mayta's image. Cardenal's image when he came to Lima—fifteen years ago?—and made such an impression on María. I haven't told them I also went to hear him at the National Institute of Culture and at the Teatro Pardo y Aliaga, and that he made a vivid impression on me, too. I haven't said that I'll always be sorry I heard him, because since then I haven't been able to read his poetry, which I had liked before. Isn't that wrong? Does one thing have anything to do with the other? It must, in some way I can't explain. But the relationship exists because I feel it.

He came on stage dressed like Che Guevara, and in the question-and-answer session he responded to the demagoguery of some agitators in the audience with more demagoguery than even they wanted to hear. He did and said everything necessary to earn the approbation and applause of the most recalcitrant: there was no difference between the Kingdom of God and communist society; the Church had become a whore, but thanks to the revolution it would become pure again, as it was becoming in Cuba; the Vatican, a capitalist cave which had always defended the powerful, was now the servant of the Pentagon; the fact that there was only one party in Cuba and in the U.S.S.R. meant the elite had the task of stirring up the masses, exactly as

Christ had wanted the Church to do with the people; it was immoral to speak against the forced-labor camps in the U.S.S.R. —how could anyone believe capitalist propaganda?

And the final act of pure theater: waving his hands, he announced to the world that the recent cyclone that hit Lake Nicaragua was the result of some ballistic experiments carried out by the United States . . . I still have a vivid impression of his insincerity and his histrionics. Ever since then, I've tried to avoid meeting the writers I like, so that the same thing that happened with the poet Cardenal doesn't happen with them. Every time I try to read him, something like acid flows out of the book and ruins it—the memory of the man who wrote it.

We've reached the car. The door on the driver's side has been broken open. Since there was nothing to take, the thief, to get even, has slit the seat, and the stain indicates that he's urinated on it. I tell Juanita and María that he's done me a favor, because now I'll have to change the seat covers, which were worn out, anyway. But they, sincerely sorry for me, and angry, pity me.

Four

"Sooner or later, the story will have to be written," says the senator, moving around in his seat until he finds a comfortable position for his bad leg. "The true story, not the myth. But the time isn't right just yet."

I had asked that our conversation take place somewhere quiet, but he insisted that I come to the Congress Bar. Just as I feared, someone's always interrupting us: colleagues and reporters come up to us, say hello to him, gossip, ask him questions. Ever since the attack that left him lame, he is one of the most popular members of Congress. We are talking intermittently, with long pauses. I explain once again that I'm not trying to write the "true story" of Alejandro Mayta. I only want to garner as much information, as many opinions about him as I can, so that later I can add a large dose of fancy to all that data, so I can create something that will be an unrecognizable version of what actually happened. His bulging, distrustful little eyes scrutinize me unsympathetically.

"As far as what's happening today is concerned, no one should do anything that might hinder the great process of unification that is taking place among the democratic left-wing organizations, the only thing that can save Peru in today's circumstances," he says softly. "Mayta's story, even if twenty-five years have gone by, may still make some old wounds bleed."

He's a thin man who speaks easily. He dresses elegantly and has lots of gray mixed into his thick curly hair. From time to time, his bad leg seems to give him some pain, because he rubs it hard. He writes well, for a politician. That skill opened to him the higher spheres of General Velasco's military government, to which he was an adviser. He invented a good number of the high-sounding phrases that conferred a progressive aura on the dictatorship, and he was the editor of one of the confiscated newspapers. He wrote speeches for General Velasco (you could tell which ones, because certain sociojuridical expressions got tangled in the general's teeth). He and his small group represented the regime's radical wing. Now, Senator Campos is a moderate personality, attacked by the extreme right, the Maoist and Trotskyist ultra-left. The guerrillas have condemned him to death, and so have the liberty squads. These death squads—a sign of the absurd times we live in—declare that he is the secret leader of the subversives. A few months ago, a bomb destroyed his car, wounding his chauffeur and maiming his left leg, which he can no longer bend. Who threw the bomb? No one knows.

"But, after all," he exclaims suddenly, just when I think there's no way to make him speak and I'm about to leave, "if you've learned so many things already, you'd better know the main thing: Mayta collaborated with Army Intelligence and probably with the CIA."

"That's not true," protested Mayta.

"It is," countered Anatolio. "Lenin and Trotsky always condemned terrorism."

"Direct action is not terrorism," said Mayta, "but pure and simple revolutionary insurrection. If Lenin and Trotsky condemned that, then I don't know what they did all their lives.

Figure it out, Anatolio. We're forgetting the most important thing. Our job is the revolution, the first task of any Marxist. Isn't it incredible that a second lieutenant has to remind us of it?"

"Will you accept at least that Lenin and Trotsky condemned terrorism?" Anatolio made a tactical retreat.

"So long as we take careful note of the differences, I do, too," Mayta agreed. "Blind terrorism, cut off from the masses, estranges the people from the revolutionary vanguard. We are going to be something else: the spark that lights the fuse, the snowball that turns into an avalanche."

"You're waxing poetic today." Anatolio burst out laughing, with a laugh that seemed too loud for the small room.

Not a poet, he thought. A man with a dream, a man who's been rejuvenated. And with an optimism he hadn't felt for years. It was as if the mounds of books and newspapers piled around him were burning with a mild, all-encompassing fire that, instead of burning him, kept his body and his soul in a kind of incandescence. Was this happiness? The discussion of the Central Committee of the RWP(T) had been impassioned, the most emotional that he could recall in many years. Right after the meeting, he had gone to the Plazuela del Teatro Segura, to France-Presse. He translated for around four hours, and despite all that mindless work, he felt fresh and lucid. His report on the second lieutenant had been approved, as had his proposal to take Vallejos's plan into consideration. Work program, action plan —what jargon, he thought. The agreement was, in fact, transcendent: to carry out the revolution now, once and for all. As he expounded, Mayta spoke with such conviction that he moved his comrades: he saw it in their faces and in the fact that they listened to him without interrupting even once. Yes, it could be done, as long as a revolutionary organization like the RWP(T) directed it—not a well-intentioned boy lacking ideological solidity. He half closed his eyes, and the image materialized, clear and sharp: a small, well-armed, well-equipped vanguard, with urban support and clear ideas about their strategic goals. Their accomplishments would be the focal point from which the revolution would radiate outward toward the rest of the nation—the flint and steel that would spark the revolutionary blaze. Hadn't the objective conditions existed since time immemorial in Peru, a country with such glaring class contradictions? That initial nucleus, by means of daring attacks of armed propaganda, would set about creating the subjective conditions that would induce the workers and peasants to join the action. The figure of Anatolio, standing at the corner of the bed where Mayta was sitting, brought him back to the present.

"Well, I'm going down to see if there's still a line." He'd already gone down twice, and both times he'd found someone waiting at the outhouse door. Mayta saw him come out bent over, holding his stomach. What a good thing it was that Anatolio had come over tonight, what a good thing that today, when finally something important was happening, today when something new was happening, he had someone with whom to share the torrent of ideas in his head. The party has taken a decisive step, he thought. He was stretched out on his bed, resting on his right arm as if on a pillow. The Central Committee of the RWP(T), after approving the idea of his working with Vallejos, had named an Action Group—Comrade Jacinto, Comrade Anatolio, and Mayta himself—to prepare a schedule of activities. It was decided that Mayta would go to Jauja immediately, to see on the spot what Vallejos's outfit looked like and what kind of contacts he had made with the Indian communities in Mantaro Valley. Then the other two members of the Action Group would also go up to the mountains, to coordinate the work. The RWP(T) meeting broke up with everyone in a state of euphoria, and Mayta remained exalted even as he translated releases for France-Presse. He was still euphoric when he reached his room on Jirón Zepita. Just where the dead-end street began, he saw a youthful figure waiting for him, teeth glistening in the semi-darkness.

"I was so shaken up by all that that I came by to see if we could talk awhile," said Anatolio. "Are you very tired?"

"Just the opposite. Let's go on up." Mayta patted him on the back. "I'm all excited, too—it's just what our little pal Vallejos says, pure dynamite."

There were rumors, insinuations, gossip, even a handbill that went around San Marcos University—all accusing him. Of being an infiltrator? Of being an informer? Then there appeared two articles containing disturbing facts about Mayta's activities.

"An informer?" I interrupt him. "But all of you . . ."

Senator Campos raises his hand and stops me dead. "We were Trotskyists, just as Mayta was, and those attacks came from the Stalinists, so at first we paid no attention," he explains, shrugging. "They always called those of us in the RWP half-breed squealers. Trotskyists and Stalinists always fought like cats and dogs. The basic idea was always 'Your worst enemy is the guy most like you; get rid of him even if you have to sell your soul.' "

He falls silent, because once again a reporter has come up to ask if what they've said in another newspaper is true; namely, that because he's been frightened by the threats on his life, the senator is preparing to flee the country, under the pretext that he is going to have his leg operated on again. The senator laughs. "A pack of lies. Unless I'm bumped off, the Peruvian people will have me around for quite some time." The reporter leaves, happily writing down that last remark. We ask for another coffee. "I know, I know, we over here in the Congress abuse our privileges by drinking coffee several times a day, while, for people on the outside, coffee's become a luxury item. But don't worry, it won't go on this way. The guy with the coffee concession had a reserve stock, but it's giving out." He goes on for a while, discoursing about the havoc the war has wrought: rationing, insecurity, the psychosis the people are living through these days, with the rumors about the presence of foreign troops in national territory.

"The fact is that our Soviet comrades knew everything," he suddenly adds to what he had been saying to me. "The word had to be passed to them from above. Moscow, the KGB. That's how they probably found out about Mayta's duplicity."

85

He puts a cigarette in his holder, lights it, takes a drag, and rubs his leg. His face has turned sad, as if he was wondering if he hadn't told me too much. He and my old schoolmate fought the same fight, shared the same political dreams, the same underground life, the same persecution. How can he just tell me in that indifferent way that Mayta was a lousy stool pigeon?

"You know that Mayta was in and out of jail quite often." He drops ashes in the empty coffee cup. "That must have been where they blackmailed him into working for them. Some people harden in jail; others get soft."

He looks at me, measuring the effect of his words. He seems calm, sure of himself, with that amiable expression he never loses, even in the most heated arguments. Why does he hate his old comrade?

"Those things are always difficult to prove."

There, in some moment of the past, an unrecognizable Mayta, wrapped in greasy scarves, passes notebooks written in invisible ink that contain names, plans, and places to an army officer obviously uncomfortable in civilian clothes and a distrustful foreigner who just can't get his Spanish prepositions right.

"Impossible to prove, rather," he clarifies. "And yet, on one occasion, we did find some things out for sure." He takes a deep breath and lets me have it: "During the time of General Velasco, we found out that the CIA practically ran our Intelligence service. Many names were revealed. Mayta's was one of them. And when we took a good look at things, remembering back, we saw a few events in a different light. His behavior was suspicious from the time he met Vallejos."

"That's a sizable accusation," I tell him. "A spy for the army and a CIA agent at the same time . . ."

"Spy, agent—those are big words," he modifies. "Informer, instrument, perhaps victim. Have you spoken with anyone else who knew Mayta then?"

"Moisés Barbi Leyva. How is it he knew nothing about all this? Moisés was involved in all the planning for the Jauja thing, he even saw Mayta the day before . . ."

"Moisés is a guy who knows a lot of things." Senator Campos smiles.

Is he going to tell me now that Moisés is a CIA agent? No, he could never make an accusation like that against the director of a center that has already published two of his sociopolitical tomes—one of them with an introduction by Barbi Leyva himself.

"Moisés is a prudent man, full of interests to defend," he blurts out, in a mildly acid tone. "His philosophy nowadays is what's done is done. It's the only way to live, if you want to avoid problems. Unfortunately, I'm not like him. I've never hesitated to speak up. That's why I ended up with a game leg—I always say what I think. Someday I'll get killed for it. What I can do, of course, is look my family in the eye without feeling shame."

He turns aside for a moment, as if upset at allowing himself to be drawn into such an autobiographical outpouring.

"What does Moisés think of the Mayta of those days?" he asks me, keeping his eyes fixed on the toes of his shoes.

"He thinks Mayta was a rather naïve idealist," I tell him. "A headstrong man full of conflicts, but a revolutionary through and through."

He continues to meditate, shrouded in cigarette smoke. "I told you: it's better not to take the lid off that pot. There are some stinks in there that would make lots of people choke." He pauses a moment, smiles, and unloads: "It was Moisés who read the charge that Mayta was an infiltrator the night we expelled him from the RWP(T)."

He's left me speechless. In the small garage, now turned into a courtroom, an adolescent, thundering Moisés ends his deposition by waving a handful of irrefutable evidence. Squealer! Informer! Pale, slumped over underneath the poster bearing the effigies of the ideologues, my schoolmate utters not a syllable. The door opened and Anatolio entered.

"I thought maybe you'd fallen in," Mayta greeted him.

"Whew, now I can breathe more easily." Anatolio laughed,

closing the door. He had moistened his hair, face, and chest, and his chest glistened with drops of water. He carried his shirt in his hand, and Mayta watched him carefully lay it out at the foot of the cot. What a little kid he is, he thought. The bones of his slim torso were just barely visible, and a tangle of hair glistened in the middle of his chest. His arms were long and well shaped. Mayta had noticed him for the first time four years before, while he was lecturing at the Civil Construction Union. Every minute or so, a group of boys from the Communist Youth would interrupt him, chanting the usual party line against Trotsky and Trotskyism: Hitler's allies, agents of imperialism, lackeys of Wall Street. Anatolio was the most aggressive, a young guy with big eyes and dark hair, sitting in the front row. Would he be the one to give the signal for the others to attack him? Despite everything, there was something in the boy Mayta found likable. He had felt one of those twinges he'd had before —and been wrong then. This time he was right. When Mayta left the Union, his spirits more tranquil, he went up to the boy and offered to buy him a coffee, "so we can go on airing our differences." He didn't have to make the offer twice. Later on, when he was a member of the RWP(T), Anatolio would say to him, "You brainwashed me in the best Jesuit style, comrade." It was true, he had done an affectionate and clever job on him. He'd lent him books, magazines, had convinced him to join a Marxist studies circle which he was leading, had bought him myriad coffees and persuaded him that Trotskyism was the only true Marxism, revolution without bureaucracy, despotism, or corruption. And now there he was, young and good-looking, naked from the waist up, standing under the single, dusty light in the room, flattening out his shirt. He thought: Ever since I got involved with Vallejos, I haven't seen Anatolio's face in my dreams. He was sure: not even once. A good thing Anatolio was in the Action Group. Of all the people in the party, Mayta got along best with Anatolio. It was also Anatolio over whom he had most influence. Whenever they'd agreed to go out to sell the *Workers Voice* or to pass out handbills in the Plaza Unión or at the entrances to the factories on Avenida Argentina, Anatolio never kept him waiting, even though he lived over in Callao.

"I really wish I didn't have to go across town at this time of night . . ."

"If you don't mind being uncomfortable, stay here."

All the comrades of the Central Committee of the RWP(T) had slept at one time or another in the little room. And occasionally, several at the same time, all piled on top of each other.

"I really don't want you to have a bad night because of me," said Anatolio. "You should have a bigger bed, in case of emergencies."

Mayta smiled at him. His body, inflamed, had become tense. He made an effort to think about Jauja. Did they kick him out of the party after Jauja?

"Before," he corrects me, getting satisfaction out of my discomfort. "Immediately before. If my memory doesn't fail me, they announced that Mayta had resigned from the RWP(T). A pious fiction, so that the enemy wouldn't see any cracks in our façade. But he was kicked out. Then the Jauja affair took place and there was no way to clear things up. Do you remember how they clamped down on us? Some of us were jailed, and the others went underground. Mayta was forgotten. That's how history is written, my friend. On account of the confusion and the reactionary offensive unleashed because of the Jauja thing, Mayta and Vallejos turned into heroes . . ."

He becomes meditative, weighing the extravagant elements in the story. I let him reflect without pressing him, sure he hasn't finished yet. The self-sacrificing Mayta transformed into a two-faced monster, weaving a really risky plot just to trap his comrades? It's too hard to swallow, and besides, I think it would be impossible to justify in a novel unless I were to write about the unreal world of thrillers.

"Nowadays, none of that matters," the senator adds. "Because the right failed. They wanted to liquidate the left once and for all. All they succeeded in doing was hold it up for a few years. Then came Cuba and in 1963 the Javier Heraud

89

business. In '65, the guerrillas from the Radical Left Movement and the National Liberation Front. Defeat after defeat for insurrectionist theses. Now they've got what they want. Except that . . ."

"Except that . . ." I say.

"Except that this is no longer revolution, but apocalypse. Could anyone have ever imagined that Peru would be living a permanent bloodletting like this?" He looks at me. "What's going on now has definitively turned the page on the Mayta and Vallejos story. I'm sure there's not a soul who remembers it. What else?"

"Vallejos," I say to him. "Was he a provocateur, too?"

He takes a drag on his cigarette holder and breathes out a mouthful of smoke, turning his head to one side so the smoke doesn't go into my face.

"There's no proof about Vallejos. He may have been Mayta's tool." He gestures again. "Seems probable, doesn't it? Mayta was a cunning old fox, Vallejos an unseasoned kid. But, I repeat, there's no proof."

He always speaks smoothly, greeting people who pass by.

"You know that Mayta spent his life changing parties," he adds. "Always on the left. Was he just fickle, or was he clever? Even I—and I knew him well—could never tell. He was as slippery as an eel. There was no way to know him completely. In any case, he was with all of them at one time or another, all the progressive organizations. A suspicious pattern, don't you think?"

"What about all the times he was in jail?" I ask. "The Penitentiary, the Sexto, the Frontón."

"The way I hear it is that he never spent much time in jail," the senator insinuates. "He was in lots of different jails, but never really in jail. All I know is that his name was on the Intelligence service books."

He speaks with equanimity, without the slightest sign of ill will toward the man he's accusing of lying day and night over the course of years, betraying and knifing in the back the people who believed in him, organizing an insurrection just so there'd be a pretext for a general repression of the left. He hates Mayta's guts, no doubt about it. Everything he tells me, everything he suggests against Mayta must come from way back. He must have been thinking and rethinking it, saying and resaying it for twenty-five years. Is there any foundation of truth underneath this mountain of hatred? Is it all a game to vilify Mayta's memory for all those who remember him? Where does this hatred come from? Is it political, personal, or both?

"It was really something Machiavellian." He pries the butt out of the cigarette holder with a match and puts it out in the ashtray. "In the beginning, we couldn't believe it—the refinement with which he'd set up the trap seemed impossible. A masterly operation."

"Did it seem likely that the Intelligence services and the CIA would organize a plot like that?" I interrupt him. "Just to liquidate a seven-man organization?"

"Six, six." Senator Campos laughs. "Don't forget that Mayta was one of them." But he quickly turns serious. "The target of the trap wasn't just the RWP(T) but the whole left. A preventive operation: nip any revolutionary movements in Peru in the bud. But we ruined the surprise, there was a provocation, but it didn't have the results they hoped it would. Insignificant as we were, it was the RWP(T) which saved the left from a bloodbath like the one going on now in Peru."

"How did the RWP(T) make the plot fail?" I ask him. "The Jauja thing happened, didn't it?"

"We made at least ninety percent of it fail," he points out. "They only got ten percent of what they wanted. How many of us were jailed? How many had to hide out? They had us where they wanted us for four or five years. But they didn't finish us off, which is what they wanted."

"Wasn't the price high?" I ask. "Because Mayta, Vallejos . . ."

His gesture silences me. "It's risky being a provocateur and an informer," he affirms with severity. "They failed and they paid the price, of course. Isn't that how things work in that business? Besides, there's other proof. Check the survivors. What's happened to them? What did they do afterward? What are they doing now?"

It would seem that over the years Senator Campos has lost the habit of self-criticism.

"I always thought the revolution would begin with a general strike," Anatolio said.

"A Sorelian detour, an anarchist error," said Mayta sarcastically. "Neither Marx nor Lenin nor Trotsky ever said that a general strike would be the only method. Have you forgotten China? What was Mao's method? Strikes, or revolutionary war? Slide back, or you'll fall off the bed."

Anatolio slid back from the edge.

"If the plan works, there will never be a coming together of the people and the soldiers," he said. "It will be war to the death."

"We have to break old patterns and discard empty formulas." Mayta kept his ears open, because it was usually at that time of night that he would hear the sounds. Despite his anxiety, he would have preferred not to go on talking politics with Anatolio. What should they talk about, then? Anything, but not that militance that had established an abstract solidarity, an impersonal fraternity between them. He added, "It's harder for me than for you, because I'm older."

The two of them could barely fit on the narrow cot, which creaked if one of them made the slightest movement. They had removed their shirts and their shoes, but still had their trousers on. They had put out the light, and the glow from the streetlamp could be seen through the window. Far off, from time to time, they could hear the lewd howl of a cat in heat: it was nighttime.

"I'll confess something to you, Anatolio," Mayta said. On his back, resting on his right arm, he had smoked an entire pack in a few hours. Despite those pains in his chest, he still felt like smoking. His anxiety was suffocating him. He thought: Calm down, Mayta. Don't make a fool of yourself, okay, Mayta? "This is the most important moment of my life. I'm sure it is, Anatolio."

"It is for everybody," said the boy, like an echo. "The most important in the life of the party. And I hope in the history of Peru."

"It's different for you," Mayta said. "You're a kid. And so's Pallardi. You two are just beginning your lives as revolutionaries, and you're starting out right. I'm over forty already."

"You call that old? Don't they say that life begins at forty?"

"No, it's old age that begins at forty," Mayta murmured. "I've been in this game for almost twenty-five years. Over the last few months, over this last year, most of all since we split up and there are only seven of us, all this time I've had one little idea ringing in my ear: Mayta, you're wasting your time."

There was silence, broken finally by the howls of the cat.

"I get depressed sometimes myself," he heard Anatolio say. "When things don't go right, it's only human to paint the whole picture black. But I'm really surprised to hear you say it, Mayta. Because if there's one thing I've always admired about you, it's your optimism."

It was hot, and when their forearms brushed, they were moist with sweat. Anatolio was also flat on his back, and Mayta could see in the semi-darkness his bare feet next to his own. He thought that at any moment their feet would touch.

"Get me right," he said, covering up his discomfort. "I'm not depressed about having dedicated my life to the revolution. That could never happen, Anatolio. Every time I walk down the street and I see the country I live in, I know there can be nothing more important for me. I just wonder if I've wasted my time, if I've taken the wrong road."

"If you're going to tell me you've lost your belief in Leon Davidovich and Trotskyism, I'll kill you," Anatolio joked. "I hope I haven't read all that crap just for fun."

But Mayta wasn't in the mood for jokes. He was experiencing

exaltation and at the same time anguish. His heart was beating so hard, he said to himself, that Anatolio could probably hear it. The dust piled up on the books, papers, and magazines all over the room tickled his nose. Hold in that sneeze, or you'll die, he thought, absurdly.

"We've lost too much time, Anatolio. In byzantine problems —mental masturbation totally unrelated to the real world. We're disconnected from the masses, we have no roots in the people. What kind of revolution were we going to bring about? You're very young. But I've been in this thing for a long time, and the revolution isn't an inch closer to taking place. Today, for the first time, I've felt we were advancing, that the revolution wasn't a dream, but flesh and blood."

"Calm down, brother," Anatolio said to him, stretching out his hand and patting him on the leg. Mayta recoiled, as if instead of affectionately touching him, Anatolio had punched him. "Today, in the Central Committee meeting, when you presented your proposal for going into direct action, when you asked how long we would go on wasting time, you went right to our hearts. I never heard you speak so well, Mayta. It came right from your guts. I was thinking: Let's go out to the mountains right now, what are we waiting for. I felt a knot in my throat, I swear."

Mayta turned on his side, making an effort, and saw Anatolio's profile take shape against the cloudy background of the bookshelf. Anatolio's curly hair, his smooth forehead, his white teeth, his slightly parted lips.

"We are going to begin another life," he whispered. "Out of the cave, into the air, out of garage and café intrigue to working with the masses and directly attacking the enemy. We are going to plunge right into the heart of the people, Anatolio."

His face was very close to the boy's bare shoulder. A smell, strong and elemental, of human flesh assailed his nose and made him dizzy. His bent knees grazed Anatolio's leg. In the semi-darkness, Mayta could just barely make out Anatolio's unmoving profile. Did he have his eyes open? His breathing made his chest move rhythmically. Slowly, he stretched out his moist and trembling right hand, and feeling around, he found Anatolio's trousers.

"Let me jerk you off," he whispered in an agonizing voice, feeling that his whole body was burning. "Let me, Anatolio."

"And, last but not least, there is one other matter we haven't gone into, but that, if we want to get to the bottom of things, we're going to have to bring up." Senator Campos sighs—sorry, one might say, for bringing the matter up. "You know that Mayta was a homosexual, of course."

"In our country, people always accuse their enemies of being homosexuals. It's hard to prove, though. Does it have anything to do with Jauja?"

"Yes, you see it must have been the way they got to him," he adds. "That's how they got him up against the wall and made him work for them. His Achilles' heel. All he had to do was give in once. What could he do then but go on collaborating?"

"I learned from Moisés that he got married."

"All queers get married." The senator smiles. "It's the handiest disguise there is. Aside from the fact that it was a joke, his marriage was a disaster. It only lasted a minute."

The Senate has been called to order, or maybe it's the deputies, because a growing noise and the sound of briefcases hitting tables comes from the hall. We hear amplified voices. The bar empties. Senator Campos says softly: "We are going to appeal directly to the minister. The Chamber is going to demand that he tell us once and for all if foreign troops have actually entered national territory." But he doesn't seem to be in a hurry. He goes on talking without losing that scientific objectivity he uses to cover up his hatred.

"Perhaps the explanation is in all that," he reflects, playing with his cigarette holder. "Is it possible to be sure of a homosexual? An incomplete, feminine being open to all kinds of weakness, and that includes being an informer."

Growing excited, carried away by the theme, he forgets Mayta and Jauja and explains to me that homosexuality is intimately linked to the division of classes and to bourgeois culture. Why, if this isn't so, are there virtually no homosexuals in socialist countries? It's no accident, it doesn't come about because the air of those latitudes makes people more virtuous. It's a shame the socialist countries are fomenting subversion in Peru. Because there is a lot to imitate in those countries. The culture of idleness, that dispirited emptiness, that existential insecurity typical of the bourgeoisie that even comes to have doubts about the sex it was born with. Being queer is to lack definition—a good image.

"Aren't you ashamed?" he heard him say. "To take advantage of me because we're friends, because I'm in your house. Aren't you ashamed, Mayta?"

Anatolio was sitting up, on the edge of the bed, with his elbows on his knees and his hands together, holding up his chin. A slick shine from the window fell on his back and gave his smooth skin a dark green glow in which you could see his ribs.

"Yes, I'm ashamed," Mayta whispered. He struggled to speak. "Forget what happened."

"I thought we were friends," the boy said, his voice breaking, his face turned away from Mayta. He passed from rage to disdain and back to rage. "What a lousy trick, fuck! Did you think I was a queer?"

"I know you aren't," whispered Mayta. The heat of a moment before had given way to a cold that went right through his bones: he tried to think about Vallejos, about Jauja, about the exalting and purifying days to come. "Don't make me feel worse than I already feel."

"And how the fuck do you think I feel?" whined Anatolio. He moved, the little cot groaned, and Mayta thought the boy was going to stand up, slip on his shirt, and leave, slamming the door behind him. But the cot became quiet once again, and those taut shoulders were still there. "You've fucked it all up,

Mayta. What a jerk you are. You sure picked a good moment. Today, of all days."

"Did anything really happen?" Mayta murmured. "Don't be such a kid. You're talking as if we'd both died."

"As far as I'm concerned, you died tonight."

Just then, they heard above their heads tiny sounds: light, multiple, invisible, repugnant, shapeless. For a few seconds it seemed like an earthquake. The old beams in the ceiling vibrated and it seemed as though they would fall down on the two of them. Then, in the same arbitrary way they had begun, the sounds disappeared. On other nights, they set Mayta's nerves on edge. Today he listened to them thankfully. He felt Anatolio's rigidity and saw his head pitched forward, listening to see if the rats were coming back: he had forgotten, he had forgotten. And Mayta thought about his neighbors sleeping three in a bed, four in a bed, eight in a bed, in those little rooms lined up in the shape of a horseshoe, indifferent to the garbage, the sounds of rats. At that moment, he envied them.

"Rats," he stammered. "In the attic. Dozens of them. They chase around, fight, then they calm down. They can't get in here. Don't worry."

"I'm not worried," Anatolio said. And then, after a moment: "Where I live, in Callao, there are rats, too. But under the floorboards, in the drains, in . . . But not over my head."

"At first, I had nightmares," Mayta said. He was speaking more clearly. Regaining control over his muscles, he could breathe. "I've set out traps, poison. Once we even got the city to fumigate. Useless. They go away for a few days and then they come back."

"Cats are better than poison or traps," said Anatolio. "You should get yourself one. Anything would be better than that fucking symphony over your head."

As if she thought Anatolio had been talking about her, the cat in heat began to howl obscenely down the street. Mayta's heart gave a leap: Anatolio seemed to be smiling.

"In the RWP(T), an Action Group was formed to prepare the Jauja thing with Vallejos. You were one of its members, right? What were your activities?"

"We had few activities, although some were quite funny." With an ironic gesture, the senator cheapens the whole episode and turns it into mischief. "For example, we spent an afternoon grinding up charcoal and buying saltpeter and sulfur to make gunpowder. We didn't turn out a single ounce, as far as I remember."

He moves his head, amused, and slowly lights another cigarette. He exhales upward and contemplates the spirals on the capitals of the column. Even the waiters have gone, and the Congress Bar seems larger. There, in the center of the hall, a burst of applause resounds. "I hope the Chamber will make the minister tell us the whole truth. We want to know if there are American Marines in Peru." The senator reflects, forgetting me for a few seconds. "And if the Cubans are in fact ready to invade us from Bolivia."

"We in the Action Group began to confirm our suspicions" —he quickly returns to the subject. "We had already put Mayta under surveillance, without his noticing it. Ever since he turned up without any prior notice, with that stuff about having found a revolutionary army man. A second lieutenant who was going to start the revolution in the mountains, whom we were supposed to support. Just think back, imagine it's 1958. Wasn't it suspicious? But it wasn't until later, when, despite our misgivings, he got us involved in the Jauja adventure, that he began to smell really fishy."

While his accusations against Mayta and Vallejos don't upset me, the senator's methods do: he's as slippery as a snake, like quicksilver—impossible to catch in your bare hand. He speaks in an absolutely objective way, so that, listening to him, you'd think that Mayta's duplicity was axiomatic. At the same time, despite all my efforts, I can't get a single bit of incontrovertible evidence out of him, nothing beyond that web of suppositions and hypotheses he weaves all around me. "People are saying now that the Cubans are probably already over the border and that they are the ones fighting in Cuzco and Puno," he suddenly says, loudly. "Now we'll find out for sure."

I bring him back to our subject. "Do you remember any specific things that made you suspect Mayta?"

"Any number of things," he says instantly, as he exhales a mouthful of smoke. "Things that, taken in isolation, might not mean anything but, grouped together, become damning evidence."

"Are you thinking of something concrete?"

"One day, out of the blue, he suggested we bring other political groups into the insurrection project," says the senator. "Beginning with the CP. He'd even begun to negotiate. Do you realize what that meant?"

"Frankly, no," I reply. "All the left-wing parties, Stalinists, Maoists, Trotskyists, accepted years later the idea of an alliance, joint operations, even combining in a single party. Why was something suspicious then that hasn't been thought so ever since?"

"Ever since means twenty-five years later," he says with irony. "A quarter century ago, a Trotskyist just could not propose that we invite the Stalinists to work with us. In those days, it would have been something like the Vatican suggesting that all Catholics convert to Islam. The very suggestion was a confession. The Stalinists hated Mayta with all their heart. And he hated them, at least he appeared to. Can you imagine Trotsky calling Stalin in to work with him?" He nods in regret. "His game was obvious."

"I never believed it," Anatolio said. "Some of the others in the party do believe it. I always defended you, saying it was a bunch of lies."

"If talking about it is going to make you forget it, okay, let's talk." Mayta spoke softly. "If not, let's not talk about it. It's hard for me to talk about it, Anatolio, and I've always been confused about it. I've been in the dark about it for years and years, trying to understand."

"Do you want me to take off?" Anatolio asked. "I'll leave right away."

But he didn't move a muscle. Why couldn't Mayta stop thinking about those families in the other little rooms, piled up in the darkness, parents, children, stepchildren, sharing mattresses, blankets, the stale air and the bad smells of the night? Why did he have them before his mind's eye now, when he normally never thought about them?

"I don't want you to go," he said. "I want you to forget what happened, and for us never to mention it again."

A car, making an incredible racket, impertinent, doubtless ancient and patched up from one end to the other, crossed a nearby street, shaking the windows in their frames.

"I don't know," Anatolio said. "I don't know if I'll be able to forget it and let everything go back to being what it was. What got into you, Mayta? How could you do it?"

"Well, since you really want to know, I'll tell you," he heard himself saying, with a firmness that surprised him. He closed his eyes, and fearing that once again his mouth would disobey him at any moment, he went on: "Ever since the Central Committee meeting, I've been happy. It's as if I'd got new blood, because of this idea of going into action. I was . . . you know how I was, Anatolio. That was why I did it. Excitement, enthusiasm. It's wrong, animal instincts blind our reason. I felt a desire to touch you, to caress you. I've felt the same way many times since I met you. But I was always able to control myself, and you never noticed. Tonight I just couldn't contain myself. I know that you could never want to have me touch you. The most I could ever hope to get from someone like you, Anatolio, would be to let me jerk him off."

"I'll have to inform the party and request them to expel you."

"And now I really do have to say goodbye," Senator Campos suddenly says, looking at his watch, his head turning toward the Chamber. "There's going to be a discussion of the plan to lower the draft age to fifteen. Fifteen-year-old soldier boys, can you imagine? Of course, the other side uses grade-school kids . . ."

He stands up, and I do likewise. I thank him for the time he's given me, even though, as I tell him to his face, I find myself frustrated. Those harsh charges against Mayta and his interpretation of Jauja as a mere trap do not seem well-founded to me. He goes on smiling amiably.

"I don't know if I've acted properly in speaking to you so frankly," he says to me. "It's one of my defects, I know it. But in this case, for political reasons, it would be better not to stir up the mud and spatter people with it. But, after all, you aren't a historian but a novelist. If you had said I'm going to write an essay, a sociopolitical study, I wouldn't have said a word. Fiction is different. You can believe what I've said or not, of course."

I inform him that all the testimonials I get, true or false, are useful to me. Did it seem to him I would discard his assertions? He's wrong. What I use is not the truth of the testimonies but their power to suggest, their power as inventions, their color, their dramatic strength. And I certainly do have the feeling that he knows more than he's told me.

"And I was blabbing like a parrot," he replies, without changing expression. "There are things I wouldn't tell even if they were to skin me alive. My friend, let's render unto time what is proper to time and to history what is proper to history."

We walk toward the main exit. The hallways of Congress are crowded: commissions come to meet with members of Congress, women with steno pads, and supporters of various political parties, who, under the eye of men wearing armbands, stand on line to go up to the gallery above the Chamber of Deputies, where the debate on the new draft law promises to be red-hot. There are security agents everywhere: police with rifles, detectives in street clothes carrying sub-machine guns, and the personal bodyguards of the congressmen. These last are not allowed in the Chamber, so they stroll about the halls, not even bothering to hide the pistols they carry in holsters or simply stuck into their trouser tops. The police carefully frisk everyone who crosses the vestibule, obliging them to open all packages, purses, and briefcases. They are looking for explosives. But even these precautions haven't prevented two attacks within the Congress itself over the past weeks: one of them was really serious— dynamite that exploded in the senatorial chamber, leaving two dead and three wounded. Senator Campos limps, supporting himself on a cane, and waves to all and sundry. He escorts me to the door. We pass through that space crammed with people, weapons, and political disputation that seems like a minefield. I get the feeling that all it would take would be a minor incident and the whole Congress would blow up like a powder keg.

"How wonderful, a breath of fresh air," the senator says, at the door. "I don't know how many hours I've been here, and the air is just foul with so much smoke. Okay, I've contributed my widow's mite. I smoke a lot. I'll have to give it up one of these days. I know I can do it—I've already given up smoking half a dozen times."

He takes me by the arm, but just to whisper in my ear: "As for what we've discussed here, I haven't said a word about anything. Not about Mayta, not about Jauja, nothing. No one's going to accuse me of undermining the democratic left in these times by reviving a polemic about prehistoric events. If you were to use my name, I'd have to deny everything," he goes on as if he were joking, although both of us know that just below his light tone there lies a warning. "The left decided to bury that episode, and that's the only reasonable idea just now. A time will come for a full airing of the matter."

"I understand you perfectly, Senator. Don't worry about a thing."

"If you were to have me say something, I'd have to sue you for libel," he says, winking at me and at the same time patting, as if by accident, the bulge in his jacket where his pistol is. "Now you know the truth, use it—but not my name."

He extends a cordial hand toward me and winks again in a roguish way: he's got short, thin fingers. Hard to imagine them squeezing a trigger.

"Have you ever envied the bourgeoisie?" Mayta asked.

"Why are you asking me that?" says Anatolio, surprised.

"Because I, who was always scornful of them, envy them something," Mayta said. Would he laugh?

"What's that?"

"Being able to take a bath every day." Mayta was sure the boy would at least smile, but he never saw even the slightest sign of it. He was still sitting on the edge of the cot. He'd turned a bit to the side, so that now Mayta could see his long, dark, bony, serious profile, bathed in the light coming through the window. He had wide, prominent lips, and his large teeth seemed to glow.

"Mayta."

"Yes, Anatolio?"

"Do you think our relationship can go back to what it was before tonight?"

"Yes, the same as it was before," said Mayta. "Nothing's really happened, Anatolio. Did anything really happen? Get it through your head, once and for all."

Just for a brief second, and very faintly, the pitter-pat of little feet in the attic came back, and Mayta noticed that the boy stiffened and tensed up.

"I don't know how you can sleep with that noise every night."

"I can sleep with that noise because I don't have any choice," Mayta replied. "But it isn't true that you can get used to anything, as people say. I haven't gotten used to not being able to take a bath whenever I want. Even if I can't remember when I had an apartment with a private bath. It was probably when I lived with my aunt Josefa over in Surquillo a million years ago. Even so, it's something I miss every day. When I come home tired and I can only wash myself like a cat down in the patio and I carry a pan of water up here to soak my feet, I think how

103

terrific it would be to take a shower, to get under the water and feel it wash away the filth, the problems. To sleep all refreshed . . . What a good life the bourgeoisie have, Anatolio."

"There's no public bath around here?"

"There is one five blocks from here, where I go once or twice a week," said Mayta. "But I don't always have the money. A bath costs the same as a meal at the university dining hall. I can live without bathing, but not without eating. Do you have a shower at your place?"

"Yeah," said Anatolio. "The problem is, there isn't always water."

"You lucky dog." Mayta yawned. "See, in some ways you're a little bit bourgeois yourself."

Again, Anatolio did not smile. They were silent and still, each one in his place. Although it was dark, Mayta noted the signs of dawn on the other side of the tiny window—a couple of car horns, indistinct voices, movement. Could it be five, or perhaps six? They had stayed up the whole night. He felt weak, as if he had made some great effort or had gotten over a serious illness.

"Let's sleep awhile," he said, turning over on his back. He covered his eyes with his forearm and slid over as far as he could to make room. "It must be very late. Tomorrow, I mean today, we'll have to kick ass."

Anatolio said nothing, but after a bit, Mayta felt him move, heard the bed creak, and glimpsed him stretch out, also on his back, next to him, but careful not to touch him.

"Mayta."

"Yes, Anatolio?"

The boy said nothing, even though Mayta waited quite a while. He felt him breathing anxiously. Then Mayta's unruly body began to heat up again.

"Go to sleep," he repeated. "And tomorrow all we think about is Jauja, Anatolio."

"You can give me a hand job if you want," Mayta heard him

whisper timidly. And, in an even lower, frightened voice: "But nothing more than that, Mayta."

Senator Anatolio Campos goes his way, and I remain at the head of the main staircase of the Congress, facing the river of people, mini-buses, cars, buses, the hustle and bustle of Plaza Bolívar. Until I lose sight of it along Avenida Abancay, I watch a decrepit city bus, gray and leaning over to the right, whose exhaust pipe, flush with the top of the roof, spouts a column of black smoke. Clinging to its doors, a cancerous growth of people miraculously hangs on, just grazing the cars, the light posts, and the pedestrians. Everyone's on his way home. On every corner, there's a compact mass waiting for the buses and mini-buses. When the vehicle stops, there is a melee of pushing, shouting, shoving, insults. They are all humble, sweaty people, men and women for whom this street fighting, all to clamber onto those stinking hulks—on which, when they finally get on, they travel a half hour or forty-five minutes, standing, crowded together, angry—is an everyday routine. And these Peruvians, despite their poorly made, slightly absurd clothes, their sleazy skirts, their greasy ties, are members of a minority blessed by fortune. No matter how modest and monotonous their lives may be, they have jobs as office girls or minor officials, they have their little salaries, their social security, their retirement guaranteed. Highly privileged people, compared with those barefoot *cholitos* over there: I'm watching them pull a cart filled with empty bottles, cutting through the traffic, spitting. I also see that family in rags—a woman of indeterminate age, four kids covered with scales of grime—who from the stairs of the Museum of the Inquisition stretch their hands out toward me automatically, as soon as they see I'm close: "Some spare change, boss." "Anything you can give, mister."

Suddenly, instead of continuing toward Plaza San Martín, I decide to go into the Museum of the Inquisition. I haven't been here for a long time, maybe since the last time I saw my schoolmate Mayta. As I go through the museum, I can't get his face out of my mind, as if that image of a prematurely aged, tired man that I saw in the photo in his godmother's house were evoked in some irresistible way by the place I'm visiting. What's the connection? What secret thread links this all-powerful institution, which for three centuries kept guard over Catholic orthodoxy in Peru and the rest of South America, and the obscure revolutionary militant who twenty-five years ago, for a brief moment, flashed like a bolt of lightning.

What was the Palace of the Inquisition is in ruins, but the eighteenth-century mahogany ceiling panels are in good condition, as a lecturing schoolteacher explains to a group of kids. Beautiful ceiling: the Inquisitors were men of taste. Almost all the Sevilian tiles the Dominicans imported to dress up the place have disappeared. Even the brick floors were brought from Spain; now you can't see them for the soot. I pause for a minute at the stone shield that proudly overlooked the archway of this palace, the shield with its cross, sword, and laurel. Now it sits on a broken-down sawhorse.

The Inquisitors set up here in 1584, after having spent their first fifteen years facing the Church of La Merced. They bought the property from don Sancho de Ribera, son of one of the founders of Lima, for a small sum, and from this spot they watched out for the spiritual purity of what is today Peru, Ecuador, Colombia, Venezuela, Panama, Bolivia, Argentina, Chile, and Paraguay. From this audience chamber, behind this massive table whose top is made of a single slab of wood, and which has sea monsters instead of feet, the Inquisitors in their white habits and with their army of lawyers, notaries, secretaries, jailers, and executioners struggled valiantly against witchcraft, Satanism, Judaism, blasphemy, polygamy, Protestantism, and perversions. All heterodoxies, all schisms, he thought. It was an arduous task, rigorous, legalistic, maniacal, that of the gentlemen Inquisitors, among whom there figured (their collaborators) the most illustrious intellectuals of the era: lawyers, professors, theological orators, versifiers, writers of prose. He thought: How many homosexuals could they have burned? A detailed investigation that filled innumerable pages of a file carefully stored away would precede each condemnation and auto-da-fé. He thought: How many mad people could they have tortured? How many simple people could they have hanged? Years would pass before the High Tribunal of the Holy Office would pass judgment from this table decorated with a skull, with silver inkstands with etched figures of swords, crosses, fish, and the inscription: "I, the light of the truth, guide your conscience and your hand. If you do not mete out justice, in your failure you work your own ruination." He thought: How many real saints, how many daring people, how many poor devils could they have burned?

Because it wasn't the light of the truth that guided the hand of the Inquisition: it was informers. They were the ones who filled these cells, dungeons, moist and deep caves in which no sunlight enters, and from which the prisoner would emerge crippled. He thought: You would have ended up here in any case, Mayta. For your way of life, of sex. The informer was protected to the utmost and his anonymity guaranteed, so he could collaborate without fear of reprisals. Here, still intact, is the Door of the Secret. Mayta, with a feeling of anguish, peered through the crack, linking himself with that accuser who, without being seen by the accused, would identify him by a simple nod of his head. The accused could be sent to prison for many years, his property confiscated, himself condemned to a degrading life or burned alive. He got goose bumps: how easy it was to get rid of a rival. All you had to do was enter this little room and, with your hand on the Bible, testify. Anatolio could come, spy though the crack, nod, pointing at him, and condemn him to the flames.

A doubtfully spelled notice informs us that they didn't in fact burn very many: thirty-five in three centuries. It isn't an overwhelming statistic. And of the thirty-five—a meager consolation—thirty were garroted before the fire devoured their cadavers. The first to have the lead in the grand spectacle of the Lima auto-da-fé was not garroted first: Mateo Salade, a French-

107

man, was burned alive because he had carried out some chemical experiments that someone denounced as "dealings with Satan." Salado? he thought. This poor frog must have contributed the Peruvian expression *salado*, a person with bad luck. He thought: From now on, you won't be a *salado* revolutionary.

But even though the Holy Tribunal didn't burn many people, it did torture an enormous number. After the informers, physical torture was the most frequently used device for sending victims, of both sexes, of all conditions and states, to the auto-da-fés. Here we see in all its glory a real circus of horrors, the instruments the Holy Office used—the verb is mathematically precise—to "extract the truth" from the suspect. Some cardboard dummies instruct the visitor about the pulleys and strappados—the rope from which the suspect was hung, hands tied behind his back and a hundred-pound weight strapped to his feet. Or how the victim was stretched out on the "pony," an operating table that used four tourniquets to wrench out the limbs, one by one, or all four at once. The most banal of the devices was the stock, which immobilized the criminal's head in a yoke as he was beaten. The most imaginative was the rack, of surrealistic refinement and fantasy—a kind of chair in which, using a system of hand and ankle cuffs, the executioner could torture the legs, arms, forearms, neck, and chest of the criminal. The most contemporary of the tortures is the hood—a cloth placed over the nose or in the mouth, through which water was poured, so that the victim could not breathe. The most spectacular was the brazier, placed next to the condemned person's feet, which had previously been basted with oil so that they would roast evenly. Nowadays, Mayta thought, they use electric shocks on the testicles, sodium-pentothal injections, immersion in tubs of shit, cigarette burns. Not much progress in this field.

Ten times over, he thought: What are you doing here, Mayta? Is this a time for wasting a single minute? Don't you have more important things to do? But he was moved even more deeply by the small wardrobe that for months, years, or in perpetuity, the people accused of Judaism, witchcraft, or of trafficking with the devil or of having blasphemed, and who had "vehemently repented," abjured their sins, and promised to redeem them-selves, had to wear. A room full of costumes: amid these horrors, this seems more human. Here is the "crown," the conical hat, the hair shirt, white, embroidered with crosses, serpents, devils, and flames, in which the condemned marched to the Plaza Mayor —after a stop at the Callejón de la Cruz, where they were to kneel before a Dominican cross—where they would be whipped or sentenced. Garments they might also have to wear day and night, for as long as their sentence required. That's the final image, the one that remains fixed in my memory, when, my visit over, I head for the exit, the idea of those condemned people who would go back to their normal business, wearing that uniform, which would inspire horror, panic, repulsion, nausea, scorn, and hatred wherever they went. He imagined what those days, months, and years must have been for the people who had to deck themselves out that way and be pointed out in the street, avoided like mad dogs. He thought: This museum is really worth a visit. Instructive, fascinating. Con-densed in a few striking images and objects, there is an essential ingredient, always present in the history of this country, from the most remote times: violence. Violence of all kinds: moral, physical, fanatical, intransigent, ideological, corrupt, stupid—all of which have gone hand in hand with power here. And that other violence—dirty, petty, low, vengeful, vested, and selfish—which lives off the other kinds. It's good to come here to this museum, to see how we have come to be what we are, why we are in the condition in which we find ourselves.

At the entrance to the Museum of the Inquisition, I see that at least another dozen old people, men, women, and children have joined the family in rags I saw before. They constitute a sort of grotesque royal court of tatters, grime, and scabs. As soon as they see me, they stretch out their black-nailed hands and beg. Violence behind me and hunger in front of me. Here, on these stairs, my country summarized. Here, touching each other, the two sides of Peruvian history. And I understand why Mayta accompanied me obsessively on my tour of the museum.

I virtually run to the Plaza San Martín to catch the bus. It's late, and a half hour before the curfew, all traffic stops. I'm afraid the curfew is going to catch me in between my house and Avenida Grau. It's only a few blocks, but when it gets dark there, it's dangerous. There have been muggings, and just last week a rape. Luis Saldías's wife—they just got married, he's a hydraulic engineer, and they live right across the street from me. Her car broke down and she was outside after curfew, walking home from San Isidro. Right in those last few blocks, a patrol caught her. Three cops: they threw her into their car, stripped her—after beating her up for fighting back—and raped her. Then they let her out in front of her house, saying, "Just be thankful we didn't shoot you." That's the standing order they have when they catch someone violating curfew. Luis Saldías told me everything, with his eyes filled with rage, and he added that, ever since, he's happy whenever someone shoots a cop. He says he doesn't care if the terrorists win, because "nothing could be worse than what we're already living." I know he's wrong, that it can still get worse, that there are no limits to our deterioration, but I respect his grief and keep my mouth shut.

Five

You get to Jauja by train. You buy your ticket the night before and get down to the Desamparados Station at six in the morning. I was told that the train is always packed, and sure enough, I have to fight my way onto a car. But I'm lucky and get a seat, while most of the passengers have to stand. There are no lavatories, so the more venturesome piss from the steps as the train rolls along. Even though I ate something just before leaving Lima, I start feeling hungry after a few hours. You can't buy anything at any of the stops: Chosica, San Bartolomé, Matucana, San Mateo, Casapalca, and La Oroya. Twenty-five years ago, the food vendors would pile onto the train at every stop, carrying fruit, sodas, sandwiches, and candy. Now all they sell are trinkets and herb tea.

The trip is uncomfortable and slow, but full of surprises. First, there is the train itself, inching its way from sea level to an altitude of three miles. It crosses the Andes at Anticona Pass and stops when it reaches the foot of Meiggs Mountain. Looking at the sublime spectacle, I forget the armed soldiers posted in every car and the machine gun on the roof of the locomotive, in case of attack. How can this train stay in service? The terrorists are constantly cutting the highway to the central mountain range by blasting landslides out of the slopes. Road travel is practically impossible. Why haven't they blown up the train, why haven't they blocked the tunnels, or destroyed the bridges? Perhaps the terrorists have some strategic need to keep communications open between Lima and Junín. I'm glad; I couldn't reconstruct Mayta's adventure without making the trip to Jauja.

Peak follows peak, some separated by abysses at the bottom of which roar rushing rivers. The little train goes over bridges and through tunnels. It's impossible not to think of the engineer Meiggs and what he accomplished here. Over eighty years ago, he directed the laying of these tracks in this geography of gorges, snow-capped mountains, peaks buffeted by wind, and under constant threat of flash floods. Did Mayta the revolutionary think about that engineer's odyssey as he took this train for the first time one morning in February or March, twenty-five years ago? He would have thought about the suffering of the workers as they laid these rails, erected these bridges, and bored out these tunnels—the thousands of *cholos* and Indians who worked for a symbolic salary, at times nothing more than a fistful of bad food and some coca, who sweated twelve hours a day, splitting rocks, blasting stone, carrying ties, leveling the bed so that the highest railroad in the world would become a reality. How many of them lost fingers, hands, and eyes dynamiting the mountains? How many fell into these precipices or were buried by the landslides that rolled over the camps where they were sleeping, one on top of another, trembling with cold, groggy with fatigue, stupefied with coca, kept warm only by their ponchos and the breath of their buddies? He began to feel the altitude: a certain difficulty in breathing, the pounding blood in his temples, his accelerated heart rate. At the same time, he could barely hide his excitement. He felt like smiling, whistling, and shaking hands with everyone in the car. He was dying with impatience to see Vallejos again.

"I am Professor Ubilluz," he tells me, stretching out his hand when I emerge from Jauja Station, where, after an interminable wait, two policemen in street clothes frisk me and pick through the bag in which I'm carrying my pajamas. "Shorty to my friends. And, if it's all right with you, we are already friends."

I wrote, telling him I was going to visit, and he'd come to meet me. Right around the station, there is a considerable military presence: soldiers with rifles, roadblocks, and barbed wire. And patrolling the street at a snail's pace, an armored car. We start walking. "Are things bad here?"

"It's been a bit quieter these past few weeks," Ubilluz says. "They've actually lifted the curfew. We can go out to gaze at the stars. We'd forgotten what they look like."

He tells me that a month ago there was a massive attack by the insurgents. The firing went on all night, and the next day there were bodies all over the place. They smelled so bad and there were so many of them that they had to be doused with kerosene and burned. Ever since, the rebels haven't attempted another important action in the city. Of course, every morning you wake up and see the mountains covered with little red hammer-and-sickle flags. Every afternoon, the army patrols yank them out.

"I've reserved a room for you over at the Paca Inn," he adds. "A beautiful place, you'll see."

He's a little old man, neat, stuffed into a striped suit he keeps buttoned up, which makes him look like a kind of moving package. His tie has a tiny knot, and his shoes look as if they've been dipped in mud.

He's got that ceremonious manner typical of mountain people, and his Spanish is carefully enunciated, although from time to time he uses a Quechua expression. We find an old taxi near the plaza. The city hasn't changed much since the last time I was here. Outwardly, at any rate, there are few traces of war. There

113

are no garbage dumps or crowds of beggars. The tiny houses seem clean and immortal, with their decrepit portals and complicated ironwork. Professor Ubilluz spent thirty years teaching science in the Colegio Nacional San José. When he retired—about the same time that the movement we took for a simple act of terrorism by a group of extremists began to take on the proportions of a civil war—there was a ceremony in his honor attended by all the graduates who had been his students. When he gave his farewell address, he wept.

"Whuddya say, brother," said Vallejos.

"How are ya', kid," said Mayta.

"So you finally made it here," said Vallejos.

"You said it." Mayta smiled. "Finally."

They hugged each other. How can the Paca Inn stay open? Do tourists still come to Jauja? Of course not. What would they come to see? All festivals, even the famous Carnival, have been canceled. But the inn stays open because the functionaries who come from Lima stay there, and, at times, so do military missions. None must be here now, because there are no guards anywhere. The inn hasn't been painted for ages and looks miserably run-down. There is no staff, no one behind the desk: just a watchman, who does everything. After I leave my bag in the small, cobwebbed room, I walk down and sit on the terrace that faces the lake, where Professor Ubilluz is waiting for me.

Did I know the famous story about Paca? He points to the glittering water, the blue sky, the fine line of peaks that surround the lake. This, hundreds of years ago, was a city of greedy folk. The beggar appeared one radiantly sunny morning when the air was clear. He went begging from house to house, and at every one, he was chased away with insults and dogs. But at one of the last houses he found a charitable widow who lived with a small child. She gave the beggar something to eat and some words of encouragement. Then the beggar began to glow and showed the charitable woman his true face—he was Jesus—

114

and gave her this order: "Take your son and leave Paca immediately, carrying all you can. Don't look back, no matter what you hear." The widow obeyed and left Paca. But as she was going up the mountain she heard a loud noise, like a huge drum, and out of curiosity turned around. She managed to see the horrifying landslide of rocks and mud that buried Paca and its inhabitants and the waters that turned the town into a tranquil lake filled with ducks, trout, mallards. Neither she nor her son saw or heard anything more, because statues can't see or hear. But the citizens of Jauja can and do see both of them, in the distance: two rocky formations staring out at the lake from a spot to which processions of pilgrims go to devote a moment to the people God punished for being greedy and insensible and who lie under those waters on which frogs croak, ducks quack, and where, formerly, tourists rowed.

"What do you think, comrade?"

Mayta could see that Vallejos was as happy and excited as he was himself. They walked to the boardinghouse where the lieutenant lived, on Tarapacá Street. How was the trip? Very good, and most of all, very moving, he'd never forget the Infiernillo Pass. Without stopping his chatter, he took note of the colonial houses, the clear air, the rosy cheeks of the Jauja girls. You were in Jauja, Mayta, but you didn't feel very well.

"I think I've got mountain sickness. A really weird feeling. As if I were going to faint."

"A bad beginning for the revolution." Vallejos laughed, snatching Mayta's suitcase out of his hands. Vallejos was wearing khaki trousers and shirt, boots with enormous soles, and he had a crew cut. "Some coca tea, a little snooze, and you'll be a new man. At eight we'll meet over at Professor Ubilluz's place. A great guy, you'll see."

Vallejos had ordered a cot set up in his own room at the boardinghouse, the top floor of a house with rooms lining either side of a railed gallery. He left Mayta there, advising him to sleep awhile to get over the mountain sickness. He left, and

Mayta saw a shower in the bathroom. I'm going to shower when I get up and again at bedtime every day I'm in Jauja, he thought. He would stock up on showers for when he'd have to go back to Lima. He went to bed fully clothed, only taking off his shoes before he closed his eyes. But he couldn't sleep.

You didn't know much about Jauja, Mayta. What, for example? More legend than reality, like that biblical explanation of the birth of Paca. The Indians who lived here had been part of the Huanaca civilization, one of the most vigorous conquered by the Incan Empire. Because of that, the Xauxas allied themselves with Pizarro and the Conquistadores, and took vengeance on their old masters. This region must have been immensely wealthy—who could ever guess, seeing how modest a place it is today—during colonial times, when the name Jauja was a synonym for abundance.

He knew that this little town was the first capital of Peru, designated as such by Pizarro during his Homeric trek from Cajamarca to Cuzco along one of those four Inca highways that went up and down the Andes in the same way the revolutionary columns snake their way nowadays. Those months when it could boast being the capital were its most glorious. Then, when Lima snatched the scepter from it, Jauja, like all the cities and cultures of the Andes, went into an irreversible decline and servitude, subordinate to that new center of national life set in the most unhealthy corner of the coast, from which it would go on ceaselessly expropriating all the energies of the country for its own use.

His heart was pounding, he felt dizzy, and Professor Ubilluz, with the lake as background, just goes on talking. I stop paying attention, pursued by the nightmare images I associated with the name Jauja when I was a child. The city for people with tuberculosis! Because they had been coming here since the last century, all those Peruvians suffering from that terrifying illness, mythified by romantic literature and sadomasochism, that tuberculosis for which the dry climate of Jauja was considered extraordinarily curative. They came here from the four cardinal points of the nation, first on mules over trails, then on the steep railroad built by the engineer Meiggs. All Peruvians who began to spit blood and who could pay for the trip and who had the money to convalesce or die in the pavilions of the Olavegoya Sanatorium, which, because of that continuous invasion, grew and grew, until, at one moment, it engulfed the city.

The name that centuries ago had aroused greed, admiration, dreams of gold doubloons and golden mountains came to mean perforated lungs, fits of coughing, bloody sputum, hemorrhage, death from consumption. Jauja, a fickle name, he thought. And pressing his hand to his chest to count the beats, he remembered that his godmother, in her house in Surquillo, in those days when he had gone on his hunger strike, had admonished him with her index finger in the air and her generous fat face: "Do you want us to send you to Jauja, you silly boy?" Alicia and Zoilita would drive him crazy every time they heard him cough: "Uh-oh, cousin, that's how it begins, a little cough; soon we'll see you on the road to Jauja." What would Aunt Josefa, Zoilita, and Alicia say when they found out what he had come to Jauja to do? Later, while Vallejos was introducing him to Shorty Ubilluz, a ceremonious gentleman who made a little bow as they shook hands, and to half a dozen boys who looked more like lower-school kids from the Colegio San José and not secondary-school seniors, Mayta, his body still covered with goose bumps from the icy shower, told himself that soon, to those other images, another would have to be added: Jauja, cradle of the Peruvian revolution. Would that, too, be part of the place? Jauja of the revolution, like Jauja of gold, or Jauja for tuberculars? This was Professor Ubilluz's house, and Mayta could see, through a dirty window, adobe buildings, tile or zinc roofs, a fragment of cobblestoned street, and the raised sidewalks because of the torrents that—as Vallejos had explained as they walked over—formed in the storms of January and February. He thought: Jauja, cradle of the socialist revolution in Peru. It was difficult to believe, it sounded so unreal, like the city of gold or the city of the consumptives. I tell him that at least outwardly there would seem to be less hunger and want in Jauja than in Lima. Am I right? Instead of answering, Professor Ubilluz, putting on a serious face, suddenly revives, on this solitary shore of the lake, the subject that has brought me to his land: "You have probably heard many stories about Vallejos, of course. And you will hear even more in the days to come."

"It's always the same, when you're trying to delve into a historical event," I reply. "One thing you learn, when you try to reconstruct an event from eyewitness accounts, is that each version is just someone's story, and that all stories mix truth and lies."

He suggests we go on to his house. A cart pulled by two burros catches up to us, and the driver agrees to take us to the city. He drops us off, half an hour later, in front of Ubilluz's little house, nine blocks up on Jirón Alfonso Ugarte. It just about faces the jail. "Yes," he tells me, even before I ask. "This was the lieutenant's territory, that's where it all started." The jail takes up the whole block on the other side of the street and closes off Jirón Alfonso Ugarte. At that gray wall and those tile-covered eaves, the city ends. Beyond is the country: the fields, the eucalyptus trees, and the peaks. I see, just beyond, trenches, barbed wire, and soldier boys scattered here and there, doing guard duty. One of the persistent rumors last year was that the guerrillas were preparing to attack Jauja in order to declare it the capital of liberated Peru. But hasn't the same rumor gone around about Arequipa, Puno, Cuzco, Trujillo, Cajamarca, and even Iquitos?

The jail and Professor Ubilluz's house are in a neighborhood with a religious name, one that carries connotations of martyrdom and expiation: Cross of Thorns. It's a modest place, low and dark, with a large framed photograph from which beams a gentleman of another era—string tie, straw hat, waxed mustachios, high starched collar, vest, Mephistophelian goatee— who must be the professor's father or grandfather, to judge by the resemblance. There is a long chaise, covered with a multi-colored poncho, and chairs painted in several different colors, all of them so worn they seem about to collapse. In a glass-doored bookcase, there are disorderly stacks of newspapers. Some buzzing flies circle our heads, and one of the joeboys helped pass around a plateful of sliced fresh cheese and some crusty little rolls that made Mayta's mouth water. I'm dying of hunger and I ask Professor Ubilluz if there is someplace where I can buy some food. "At this time of day, no," he says. "At nightfall, perhaps we'll get some baked potatoes at a place I know. In any case, I can offer you some very good *pisco*.

"They say the most absurd things about my friendship with Vallejos," he adds. "That we met in Lima when I was in the army. That we began to conspire then and that we went on plotting here, when he came to be chief of the jail. The only truth in all that is that I did retire from the army. But when I was in, Vallejos was still at his mother's breast . . ." He laughs, with a forced little giggle, and exclaims, "Pure fantasy! We met here, a few days after Vallejos came to take up his post. I also have the honor to be able to tell you that I taught him all he knew about Marxism. Because you have to understand"—he lowers his voice and looks around with apprehension, pointing out, as he does so, some empty shelves—"that I had the most complete Marxist library in Jauja."

A long digression distracts him from Vallejos. Despite the fact that he's an old, sick man—he's had a kidney removed, he's got high blood pressure, and varicose veins that put him through the tortures of the damned—that he's retired from all political action, the authorities, a couple of years ago, when terrorist activities were at a fever pitch in the province, burned all his books and had him incarcerated for a week. They attached electrodes to his testicles to make him confess his complicity in the guerrilla campaign. What complicity could there be when it was common knowledge that the insurgents had him on their hit list—all because of some infamous calumnies. He gets up, opens a drawer, and takes out a piece of paper, which he then

shows me: "The people sentence you to death, traitor scum."
He shrugs. He was old, and life no longer mattered to him. Let
them kill him, what a crock of shit. He didn't take any precautions: he lived alone and didn't even have a stick for self-
defense.

"So it was you who taught Vallejos Marxism." I take advantage of his pause to interrupt him. "I thought all this time
it had been Mayta."

"The Trotskyite?" He twists around in his chair, gesturing
scornfully. "Poor Mayta! He went around in Jauja like a sleep-
walker, because of the mountain sickness . . ."

It was true. He had never felt anything like that pressure
in his temples and that giddiness in his heart, which was suddenly
punctuated by some disconcerting pauses in which it seemed to
stop pumping. Mayta had the sensation of being empty, as if
his bones, muscles, and veins had suddenly disappeared and a
polar chill was freezing the huge void under his skin. Was he
going to faint? Was he going to die? It was a sinuous, treach-
erous malaise: it came and went. He was at the edge of a preci-
pice, but the threat of falling into the abyss never materialized.
It seemed as though everyone in Shorty Ubilluz's crowded little
room realized what was happening to him. Some were smoking,
and a grayish cloud, with flies in it, distorted the faces of the
boys sitting on the floor, who from time to time interrupted
Ubilluz's monologue with questions. Mayta had lost the thread
of the conversation. He was next to Vallejos on a bench, with
his back resting against the bookcase, and even though he wanted
to listen, he could only pay attention to his veins, his temples,
and his heart.

In addition to his mountain sickness, he felt ridiculous. Are
you the revolutionary who's come to test these comrades? He
thought: The three-mile altitude has turned you into a faded
flower with a pounding heart. He could only vaguely hear
Ubilluz explaining to the boys—was he trying to impress him
with his confused knowledge of Marxism?—that the way to
move the revolution forward was by understanding both the

social contradictions and the traits the class struggle took on in each of its phases. He thought: Cleopatra's nose. Yes, there it was: the unforeseeable element that upsets the laws of history and turns science into poetry. How stupid he had been not to foresee the most obvious thing, that a man who goes up into the Andes can suffer mountain sickness; why hadn't he bought some pills to counteract the effect of the difference in atmospheric pressure on his body.

Vallejos asked him, "Do you feel okay?" "Sure, fine." He thought: I've come to Jauja so this hick professor who doesn't know shit can give me a class on Marxism. Now Shorty Ubilluz was pointing to him, welcoming him: the comrade from Lima that Vallejos had spoken to them about, someone with enormous revolutionary and union experience. He invited Mayta to speak and told the boys to ask him questions. Mayta smiled at the half-dozen beardless faces that had turned to gaze at him with curiosity and a certain admiration. He opened his mouth.

"He was the real guilty party, if we're looking for guilty parties," Professor Ubilluz repeats, with his vinegary expression. "He made fools of us. We thought he was the link with the Lima revolutionaries, with the unions, with the party, which consisted of hundreds of comrades. In reality, he represented no one and was no one. A Trotskyite, to top things off. His very presence sealed off any possibility that the Communist Party might support us. We were very naïve, it's true. I knew about Marxism, but I had no idea of the strength of the party, and much less about the divisions among the left-wing groups. And Vallejos, of course, knew even less than I. So you thought that Mayta the Trotskyite indoctrinated the lieutenant? Not a chance. They barely had time to see each other, only when Vallejos could get to Lima. It was in this room right here that the lieutenant learned about dialectics and materialism."

Professor Ubilluz comes from an old Jauja family in which there have been sub-prefects, mayors, and lots of lawyers. (Law is the great profession in the mountains, and Jauja beats most places even there in numbers of lawyers per citizen.) They

121

must have been well-off because, he tells me, many of his relatives have managed to go abroad: Mexico, Buenos Aires, Miami. Not him. He's going to stay here until the end, threats or no threats, and he'll sink with whatever's left when it's over. Not only because he doesn't have the means to leave, but because of his contrary nature, that rebelliousness that caused him, unlike his cousins, uncles, and brothers, who were busy with farms, small businesses, or legal practices, to devote himself to teaching and to become the first Marxist in the city. He's paid for it, he adds: jailed countless times, beaten up, insulted. And even worse, the ingratitude of the left, which has now grown and is about to take power, but which forgets the people who opened the way and laid down the foundation.

"The real lessons in philosophy and history, the ones I couldn't give in the Colegio San José, I gave in this little room," he exclaims proudly. "My house was a people's university."

He falls silent because we hear a metallic sound and military voices. I get up to peek through the curtains. The armored car is passing by, the same one I saw at the station. Next to it, under the command of an officer, that's a platoon of soldiers. They disappear around the corner of the jail.

"Wasn't it Mayta who planned everything, then?" I abruptly ask him. "Wasn't it he who orchestrated all the details of the uprising?"

The surprise reflected in his half-reddened face, which is full of white spots from his whiskers, seems genuine. As if he had heard incorrectly and knew nothing about what I was saying.

"Trotskyite Mayta the intellectual author of the uprising?" He carefully pronounces the words, with that overly precise mountain diction, which barely allows the syllables out of his mouth. "What an idea! When he got here, everything had already been arranged by Vallejos and me. He had nothing to do with it until the very end. I'm going to say something else. He was only informed of the details at the last minute."

"Because you didn't trust him?" I interrupt.

"Just as a precaution," says Professor Ubilluz. "Well, if you prefer the word 'trust,' then yes, because we didn't trust him. Not that we thought he was a squealer, but that he might be afraid. Vallejos and I decided to keep him in ignorance, as soon as we figured out that he had no one behind him, that he was on his own. Would it have been surprising that at the critical moment the poor guy would turn tail and run? He wasn't one of us, and he couldn't really take the altitude. He had no knowledge of weapons. Vallejos taught him how to shoot on a beach near Lima. A hell of a revolutionary to dig up! They say he was even a fag."

He laughs, with his usual forced giggle. I'm just about to say that, unlike him, who wasn't where he was supposed to be—and I hope he explains why—Mayta, despite his mountain sickness and his representing no one else, was alongside Vallejos when—to use Ubilluz's own expression—"the potatoes fell in the fire." I'm just about to tell him that lots of other people have said about him exactly what he's saying about Mayta: that he was really the one to blame, that he was the deserter. But of course I say nothing at all. I'm not here to contradict anyone. My job is to listen, observe, compare stories, mix it all together and weave a fantasy. Again, we hear the metallic sound of the armored car and the trotting soldiers.

When one of the boys said, "It's time to go," Mayta felt relieved. He was feeling better, after having gone through some moments of agony. He answered the questions posed by Ubilluz, Vallejos, the joeboys, and at the same time he was keenly aware of the malaise that was crushing his head and chest and seemed to be churning his blood. Had he answered well? At least he seemed sure of himself, even if nothing was further from the truth, and in allaying the fears of the boys, he had tried not to lie even as he avoided telling truths that might dampen their enthusiasm.

It wasn't easy. Would the Lima working class support them once the revolutionary action began? Yes, but not right away. At the beginning, the workers would be indecisive, confused because of the misinformation the newspapers and radio would spread and because of the lies those in power and the bourgeois parties would tell. They would be paralyzed by brutality and repression. But that very repression would quickly open their eyes, revealing just which group was defending their interests, and which was, in addition to exploiting them, deceiving them. The revolutionary action would push the class struggle to heights of violence.

Mayta was moved by the boys' wide-open eyes and their attentive immobility. They believe everything you tell them. Now, while the joeboys were saying goodbye to him, ceremoniously shaking his hand, he asked himself just what in fact the attitude of the Lima proletariat would be when the action began. Hostility? Scorn for that vanguard fighting for them out in the mountains? The fact was that APRA controlled the unions, that they were allied with the Prado government, and opposed to anything that smacked of socialism. It might be different with a few unions, like Civil Construction, in which the Communist Party had some influence. No, probably not. Those guys would accuse us of being provocateurs, of playing along with the government, of serving them on a silver platter the pretext for outlawing the party and deporting and jailing the progressives. He could imagine the headlines in *Unity*, the comments in the handbills they would distribute, and the articles that would appear in the *Workers Voice* published by the rival RWP. Yes, that would all hold true for the first phase. But, he was sure, if the uprising were to last, develop, undermine bourgeois power here and there, oblige it to discard its liberal mask and show its bloodied face, the working class would shake off its lethargy, all the reformist deceptions, all its corrupt leaders, all those illusions of being able to coexist with the sellouts, and would join the struggle.

"Well, the chicks have gone to roost." Shorty Ubilluz went to the pile of books, pamphlets, newspapers, cobwebs in his studio and dug out a jug and some glasses. "Now let's have a drink."

"How did the boys seem to you?" Vallejos asked him.

"Very enthusiastic, but still wet behind the ears," Mayta said. "Some of them can't be more than fifteen, right? Are you sure you can depend on them?"

"You have no faith in our young people." Vallejos laughed. "Sure we can depend on them."

"Remember González Prada." Shorty Ubilluz began to quote, sliding around the bookcases like a gnome and getting back into his chair. "The old fogies to the grave, and the young to work."

"And every man to his assigned job." Vallejos smacked his fist into his palm, and Mayta thought: I hear him and I have no doubts. It seems that everything will bend to his will, he's a born leader, a central committee all by himself. "Nobody's going to make these boys shoot anyone. They're going to be messengers."

"The messenger boys of the revolution," Shorty Ubilluz baptized them. "I've known them since they learned how to crawl. They're the best of the joeboys."

"They'll be in charge of communications," Vallejos explained, waving his arms back and forth. "They'll maintain contact between the guerrillas and the city; they'll carry dispatches, supplies, medicine, matériel. And because they're kids, they won't be noticed. They know these mountains like the back of their hands. We've taken long hikes, and I've trained them in forced marches. They're terrific."

They jumped off ridges and landed on their feet without breaking their heads, as if they were made of rubber. They swam rushing creeks like fish, without being swept downstream or smashed against the rocks. They went through snow without suffering from the cold, and they ran and jumped at the highest altitudes without any problems. His heart rate had speeded up and the pressure of his blood on his temples was once again intolerable. Should he say something about it? Should he ask for some coca tea, anything, to relieve that anguish?

"Tomorrow, in Ricrán, you'll meet the ones who will do the

fighting," Vallejos said. "Get ready to climb some mountains and to see llamas and mountain grass."

Despite his malaise, Mayta became aware of the silence. It came from outside, it was tangible, it would be there whenever Shorty Ubilluz or Vallejos fell silent. Between a question and an answer, any time a speaker paused—that absence of motors, horns, screeching brakes, acceleration, and voices seemed to have its own sound. That silence must have covered Jauja like a night laid over the night; it was a thick presence in the room, and it rattled him. That exterior void, that lack of animal, mechanical, or human life out there on the street seemed so strange to him. He never remembered having experienced such an outrageous silence in Lima, not even in the prisons (the Sexto, the Panóptico, the Frontón) where he'd spent a few seasons. When Vallejos and Ubilluz broke it, they seemed to profane something.

His malaise had diminished, but his anxiety remained, because he knew the loss of breath, the racing pulse, the pressure, the icy chill could come back at any moment. Shorty toasted him, and he, making an effort to smile, raised the glass to his lips. The fiery *pisco* shook him. How absurd, he thought. It's only 180 miles to Lima, and it's as if you were a foreigner in an unknown world. What kind of a country is this where, by just going from one place to another, you turn into a gringo or a Martian? He felt ashamed of knowing nothing at all about the mountains, of knowing nothing at all about the world of the peasants. He paid attention again to what Vallejos and Ubilluz were saying. They were talking about a community on the eastern slope of the mountains, the one that ran right into the jungle: Uchubamba.

"Where is it?"

"Not far in miles," says Professor Ubilluz. "Close, if you look on the map. But it might as well be on the moon if you want to get there from Jauja." Years later, during Belaúnde's government, they put in a highway that went one fourth of the way.

Before, one could only get there on foot, over the peaks, down the gorges and slopes that meet the jungle.

Is there any way I can get there? Of course not, it's been a battleground for a year now, at least. And, rumor has it, a huge cemetery. They say that more people have died there than in all the rest of Peru. I will not, therefore, be able to visit some key places in Mayta's story; my investigation will be cut short. Besides, even if I could slip through the army and guerrilla lines, I wouldn't learn much. In Jauja, everybody is sure that both Chunán and Ricrán have disappeared. Yes, yes, Professor Ubilluz has it from a good source. Chunán six months ago, more or less. It was an insurgent stronghold, and it seems they even had an antiaircraft gun. That's why the air force wiped out Chunán with napalm—even the ants were killed.

There was another massacre at Ricrán, maybe two months ago. We never did find out what really happened. The people from Ricrán had captured a guerrilla detachment and, some said, they had lynched them for having eaten their crops and their animals. Other people said that they turned the rebels over to the army, which shot them in the plaza, up against the church wall. Then a revenge squad came to Ricrán and did a number five on them. Did I know what a number five was? No. Count off: one, two, three, four, you—outside! Every fifth person was hacked, stoned, or stabbed right there in the same plaza. Now there is no more Ricrán. The survivors are here in Jauja in that immigrant zone that sprang up on the north side, either here or wandering in the jungle. I shouldn't have any illusions about what was going on. The professor takes a sip and picks up the thread of our conversation.

"Getting to Uchubamba was for tough guys, unafraid of snow or avalanches," he says. For people without the varicose veins this old man has now. "I was strong and could take it then, and I got there once. A sight you can't imagine, when you see the Andes turn into jungle, covered with vegetation, animals, mist. Ruins everywhere. Uchubamba, that's the place. Don't

127

you remember it? Damn! Well, the members of the Uchubamba commune set all of Peru talking."

No, the name means nothing to me. But I do remember very well the phenomenon Professor Ubilluz has evoked, as I warm the glass of *pisco* he's just served me (a *pisco* called Devil of the Andes, a remnant of better days, when, he says, you could buy anything in the local shops, before this rationing that's starving us to death and killing us with thirst). Although a complete surprise to official, urban, coastal Peru, about halfway through the fifties, expropriations of land began to take place in different parts of the southern and central mountains. I was in Paris, and I, along with a group of café revolutionaries, avidly followed those remote events, which were succinctly reported in *Le Monde*, from which we in our imagination reconstructed the exciting spectacle: armed with sticks, slings, rocks, with their elderly, their women and children, and their animals in front, they would move, at dawn or at midnight, en masse to the neighboring lands. They felt, no doubt rightly so, that they had been dispossessed from those lands by the feudal lord, or his father, grandfather, great-grandfather, or the great-grandson of the feudal lord, so they dug up the property markers and returned the land to the commune. They branded the animals with their mark, they set up their houses, and next day they began to work the land as their own.

"Is this the beginning?" we asked ourselves, openmouthed and euphoric. "Is the volcano finally reawakening?" Perhaps that really was the beginning. In the Paris bistros, under the whispering chestnut trees, we deduced, on the basis of four lines in *Le Monde*, that those seizures were the work of revolutionaries, new narodniks, who had gone out to the country to persuade the Indians to carry out the agrarian reform that for years every government had promised and none had implemented. Later we found out that the takeovers were not the work of agitators sent by the Communist Party or the Trotskyist groups, that their origin was not even political. They sprang up

128

spontaneously from the peasant masses, who, spurred on by the immemorial abuse under which they lived, by their hunger for land, and, to some degree, by the heated-up atmosphere of slogans and proclamations in favor of social justice that prevailed in Peru then—after the collapse of the Odría dictatorship —decided one day to take action. Uchubamba? Names of other communities—those that took over lands and were kicked out again, bearing their dead and wounded, or still others, which managed to keep the land—whirl around in my memory: Algolán, in Cerro de Pasco; the Valle de la Convención communities, in Cuzco. But Uchubamba, in Junín?

"Yes, sir," said Vallejos, exultant that he could surprise him that much. "Indians with light skin and blue eyes, more gringo than either of us."

"First, the Incas conquered them and made them work under the aegis of the Quipumayocs of Cuzco," lectured Shorty Ubilluz. "Later the Spaniards took away their best lands and made them go up to work in the mines. That is, to die in the mines after a little while, with their lungs turned to sieves. The ones that were left in Uchubamba they gave over for 'Christianizing' to the Peláez Rioja family, who bled them dry for three centuries."

"But, you see, they couldn't finish them off," concluded Vallejos.

They had left Ubilluz's house to take a walk, and they were sitting on a bench in the Plaza de Armas. Over their heads, they had a marvelous silence and thousands of stars. Mayta forgot the cold and the mountain sickness. He was in a state of exaltation. He was trying to remember the great peasant uprisings: Túpac Amaru, Juan Bustamante, and Atusparia. And so, though the centuries passed, and they went on being exploited and humiliated, the communities of Uchubamba had gone on dreaming about the lands they had lost and had gone on asking to have them returned. First, they asked the snakes and the birds. Later, the Blessed Virgin and the saints. After that, they asked all the courts in the region, in lawsuits they always lost. But now, just a few months or weeks ago, if what he had heard was true, they had taken the decisive step. One fine day, they had simply moved onto the lands with their hogs, their dogs, their burros, and their horses, saying, "We want what is rightfully ours." All that had happened, and you, Mayta, didn't you know about it?

"Not a single word," Mayta said softly, rubbing his arms, goose-bumpy from the cold. "Not even a rumor. In Lima, we knew nothing about it."

He spoke while gazing at the sky, amazed at the brightness of the stars in that jet-black, sparkling dome, and by the images that what he was learning called forth in his mind. Ubilluz offered him a cigarette, and the lieutenant lit it for him.

"It happened just as I'm telling you," affirmed Vallejos. "They took over the Aína ranch, and the government had to send the Guardia Civil to get them out. The company that left Huancayo took a week to get to Uchubamba. They got them out, but only by resorting to shooting. Several dead and wounded, of course. But the community is still stirred up and unsettled. Now they know what they have to do."

"It's not that the Uchubamba community means to fight," Shorty Ubilluz said. "They're fighting already; they've already started the revolution. What we are going to do is simply channel it."

The cold came and went, like vertigo. Mayta took a deep drag. "Does your information come from a good source?"

"As good a source as myself." Vallejos laughed. "I've been there. I've seen with my own eyes."

"*We've* been there," Shorty Ubilluz corrected him in his pompously proper enunciation. "We have seen and we have conversed with them. And we have left all things in readiness."

Mayta didn't know what to say. Now he was sure that Vallejos was not the green, impulsive boy he thought he was at the beginning, but someone much more serious, solid, and complex, with more foresight, with his feet solidly on the ground.

130

He had gone much further than he had said in Lima, he had more people, and his plan had more ramifications than Mayta had imagined. It was a pity Anatolio hadn't come. So the two of them could exchange ideas, reflect—to straighten out between them that confusion of fantasy and enthusiasm which was eating him up. What a shame that all the comrades from the RWP(T) weren't here so they could see that it was no pipe dream but a burning reality. Although it still wasn't 10 p.m., the three seemed to be the only people in Jauja.

"I hope you realize that I wasn't exaggerating when I told you the Andes are ripe." Vallejos laughed again. "Just as I told you again and again, brother—a volcano. And we're gonna make it erupt, goddamn it!"

"Of course, we didn't go out to Uchubamba empty-handed." Professor Ubilluz again lowers his voice and looks around as if that episode could still get him into trouble. "We brought three sub-machine guns and a few Mausers the lieutenant got God knows where. Also first-aid equipment. We left it all well hidden in waterproof wrappings."

He falls silent, to take a sip of his drink, and whispers that for what he's telling me we could both be shot in the twinkling of an eye.

"As you can see, it wasn't as harebrained as everyone thought," he adds once the echo of the metallic passage of the armored car fades in the night: we've heard it going by the house all afternoon at regular intervals. "It was something planned objectively, scientifically, and it would have worked if Vallejos hadn't made the stupid mistake of moving the date forward. We worked with the patience of ants, a real spiderweb. Wasn't the area well chosen? Aren't the guerrillas today lords and masters of the region? The army doesn't even dare go there. Vietnam and El Salvador are nothing, compared to this. Your health!"

Out there, a man, a group of men, an entire detachment was a needle in a haystack. And under the mantle of glittering stars, Mayta saw it: thick, leafy, closed, hieroglyphic; and he saw himself, next to Vallejos and Ubilluz and an army of shadows, traversing it over sinuous paths. It wasn't the Amazonian flat-lands but an undulating forest, the brow of a mountainous forest, with slopes, gulches, gorges, narrow passes, defiles, ideal pitfalls where ambushes could be set up, where the enemy's communications could be cut, where he could be dizzied, con-fused, driven mad, where he could be attacked when he least expected it, where he would be forced to disperse, to dilute his strength, to atomize himself in the indescribable labyrinth. His beard had grown, he was thin, in his eyes there was an un-conquerable resolve, and his fingers had grown callused from squeezing the trigger, lighting fuses, and throwing dynamite. Any sign of depression he might feel would disappear as soon as he saw how new militants joined every day, how the front widened, and how there, in the cities, the workers, servants, students, and poor employees began understanding that the revolution was for them, belonged to them. He felt an anguished need to have Anatolio near, to be able to talk with him all night. He thought: With him here, I wouldn't feel this cold.

"Would you mind if we spoke a bit more about Mayta, Professor? Going back to that trip you all made in March of '58. He'd met you and the joeboys; he knew that you had contact with the Uchubamba communities and that it was there that Vallejos thought he would launch the guerrilla war. Did he do anything more, did he learn anything more on that first trip?"

He looks at me with his beady, disenchanted eyes as he raises his glass of *pisco*. He smacks his lips, satisfied. How can he make that little drink last so long? He must sip a drop at a time. "When this bottle's empty, I know I'll never have another drop until I die," he says softly. "Because things will get worse and worse." Since I stopped drinking a long time ago, the *pisco* goes to my head. My thinking's out of kilter; I'm dizzy, just as Mayta must have been with his mountain sickness.

"The poor guy got the surprise of his life," he says, in the contemptuous tone he uses when he talks about Mayta. Is it just resentment of Mayta, or is it something more general and abstract, a provincial's resentment of everything and everyone from Lima, the capital, the coast? "He came here with all the experience of a revolutionary who's already been to jail, sure he was going to take over, and he found that everything had already been taken care of, and well taken care of."

He sighs, with an expression of grief over the *pisco* that's running out, over his lost youth, over that guy from the coast he and Vallejos had taught a lesson to, over the hunger everyone's experiencing, and the uncertainty everyone's living through. In the short time we've been talking, I've come to realize that he's a man full of contradictions, difficult to understand. Sometimes he gets excited and justifies his revolutionary past. Other times, he blurts out remarks such as, "At any moment, the guerrillas will come in here, pass sentence on me, and hang a 'Stinking Traitor' sign around my neck. Or a death squad will charge in, cut the balls off my corpse, and stick them in my mouth. That's what they do around here—in Lima, too?" Sometimes he gets angry at me: "How can you go on writing novels in this nightmare?" Will he ever go back to what matters most to me? Yes: there he goes.

"Of course I can tell you what he did, said, saw, and heard on that first trip. He stuck to me like a leech. We organized a couple of meetings for him, first with the joeboys and later with comrades who had seen fighting. Miners from La Oroya, from Casapalca, from Morococha. Men from Jauja who had gone to work in the mines of the great imperialist octopus of the time, the Cerro de Pasco Copper Corporation. They would come back for holidays and occasionally for weekends."

"Were they also committed to the project?"

Vallejos and Ubilluz said they were, but Mayta wouldn't have sworn to it. There were five of them. They had talked the following morning, also in Shorty's house, almost two hours straight. He thought the meeting was terrific and that communication with all of them was easy—above all, with the

Parrot, the best-read and most politicized of the bunch—but at no time did any of them say they would give up their jobs and leave their homes to fight. At the same time, Mayta wasn't so sure they wouldn't do so. They're sensible, he thought. They were workers and knew what they were risking. They were seeing him for the first time. Wasn't it logical they would be cautious? They seemed to be old friends of Ubilluz. At least one of them, the one with a mouth full of gold teeth, the Parrot, had been a militant in APRA. Now he said he was a socialist. When they talked about the gringos in Cerro de Pasco, they were decidedly anti-imperialist. When they talked about salaries, accidents, the diseases they contracted in the tunnels, they were absolutely revolutionary. But every time Mayta tried to get them to say exactly how they would participate in the uprising, their answers were vague. When they went from the general to the specific, their resolve seemed to weaken.

"We also went to Ricrán," adds Professor Ubilluz, dropping out his pearls one by one. "I brought him myself, in a truck that belonged to one of my nephews, because Vallejos had to stay at the jail that day. Ricrán, which has now disappeared. Do you know how many villages like Ricrán have been destroyed in this war? A judge was telling me the other day that, according to a colonel on the General Staff, the secret statistics of the armed forces list half a million dead, since all this started. Yes, I brought him to Ricrán. Four hours of bouncing around, climbing up to a valley about twenty-five hundred feet above sea level. Poor Trotskyite! His nose began to bleed, and his handkerchief was soaked. He just wasn't cut out for high altitudes. The gorges scared the hell out of him. He got dizzy just looking, I swear."

He thought he would die, fall off a cliff, that his nose would never stop bleeding. Nevertheless, that twenty-four-hour trip to the Ricrán district, way out there in a corner of the mountains, was the most stimulating thing that he did in Jauja. A land of condors, snow, clear sky, jagged, ocher peaks. He had thought: "Incredible how they can live at these altitudes, domi-

134

nate these mountains, sow and cultivate on these slopes, build a civilization in this wasteland. The men to whom Shorty Ubilluz introduced him—a dozen subsistence farmers and artisans—were highly motivated. He was able to communicate with them because they all spoke Spanish. They asked him lots of questions, and infused with enthusiasm, he gave them even more assurances than he gave the joeboys about the support of the progressive sectors in Lima. How encouraging it was to see the naturalness with which these humble men, some wearing sandals, talked about the revolution. As if it were imminent, concrete, decided, irreversible. There were no euphemisms at all in their conversation: they talked about arms, hideouts, and their participation in the action from day one on. But Mayta did have one difficult moment. What help would the U.S.S.R. give them? He didn't have the heart to talk to them about the betrayed revolution, the Stalinist bureaucratization, about Trotsky. He felt it wouldn't be prudent to confuse them with all that stuff just yet. The U.S.S.R. and the other socialist countries would help, but later, when the Peruvian revolution was a fact. Before, they would lend only their moral support—words, not deeds. The same as some Peruvian progressives. They would extend a hand only when all the others pressed them to do it. But they would be pressed, because the revolution, once in motion, would be unstoppable.

"In sum, Ricrán left you with your mouth hanging open," Vallejos said. "I knew it would, brother."

They were in front of the train station, in a small restaurant with oilcloth on the tables and calico curtains on the windows: the Duckpull. From their table, Mayta could see the mountains, on the other side of the railing and the tracks. They were turning black and gray after having been ocher and golden. They had been there for several hours, ever since lunch. The owner knew Ubilluz and Vallejo and would come over to chat with them. Whenever he did, they would change the subject, and Mayta would ask about Jauja. Where did that name "Duckpull" come from? Because of a local game played on the festival of January 20 in the Yauyos neighborhood: they would dance the *pandilla* and they would hang up a live duck that horsemen and dancers would try to decapitate by grabbing at it and pulling.

"Lucky times those, when there were ducks to decapitate in the Duckpull festival," growls Professor Ubilluz. "We thought we had touched bottom. And yet there were ducks within reach of anyone's budget, and people in Jauja ate twice a day, something that children today can't even believe." He sighs again. "It was a beautiful festival, more fun and more to drink even than during Carnival."

"All we ask is that when we get moving, the party comes through for us," Vallejos said. "They're revolutionaries, right? I've read every single *Workers Voice* you gave me, backwards and forwards. Every single article is about the revolution. Well, I hope they'll come across with actions to back up their words."

Mayta became nervous. It was the first time Vallejos had let him know he had doubts about the support of the RWP(T). Mayta hadn't mentioned a word about the internal debates concerning the project and concerning Vallejos himself.

"The party will come through. But it has to be sure this is a serious, well-planned action that is likely to succeed."

"Well, it was during those days that our Trotskyite saw that our project was neither hastily organized nor mad." Professor Ubilluz returns to the subject. "He just couldn't believe that we had prepared things that well."

"It's true, it's more serious than I'd thought." Mayta turned to Vallejos. "You know you completely faked me out? You had a network of insurgents, made up of peasants, workers, and students. I tip my hat to you, comrade."

They put on the lights in the Duckpull. Mayta saw that buzzing insects were beginning to smash into the bulb that swayed over them, hanging from a long wire.

"I, too, had to take precautions, as you did with me," said

136

the lieutenant, speaking suddenly with that aplomb which, when it emerged, made him into another man. "I had to be sure I could confide in you."

"You learned the lesson well." Mayta smiled at him. He paused to take a deep breath. Today the mountain sickness bothered him less. He was able to sleep for a few hours, after having had insomnia for two days. Were the mountains accepting him? "Two more comrades, Anatolio and Jacinto, will be coming next week. Their report will be decisive as far as the party's going all the way is concerned. I'm optimistic. When they see what I've seen, they'll understand that there's no reason to hold back."

It was here, no doubt about it, during his first visit to Jauja, that the idea that brought him so many problems lodged in his head. Did he share it with them in the Duckpull? Did he unfold it in a low voice, choosing his words carefully so he wouldn't upset them with revelations about the divisions in what they thought was a united left? Professor Ubilluz assures me he didn't say anything about it. "Even though this body of mine is the worse for wear, my memory is still good." Mayta never told him about his intention to involve other groups or parties. Could he have told only Vallejos about it? In any case, it's certain that he had already decided on the plan in Jauja, because Mayta was not impulsive. If he went to see Blacquer and, probably, the people from the other RWP when he went back to Lima, it's because he had seriously thought things over in the mountains.

It was on one of those insomniac, heart-pounding nights in the boardinghouse on Tarapacá Street, as he listened to his friend's tranquil breathing and his own roaring pulse. Wasn't what was at risk too important for just the tiny RWP(T) to take charge of the uprising? It was cold, and he curled up under the blanket. With his hand on his chest, he felt his heart beat. The logic was crystal-clear. The divisions on the left derived to a large extent from the absence of real action, from their sterile gesturing: that's what made them splinter and eat each other alive—that, even more than ideological controversies. Guerrilla fighting could change the situation and bring together the genuine revolutionaries by showing them just how byzantine their differences were. Yes, action would be the remedy for the party politics that resulted from political impotence. Action would break the vicious circle, would open the eyes of the opposing comrades. Someone would have to be daring and rise to the occasion. "What do Pabloism and Anti-Pabloism matter, when the revolution is at stake, comrades?" He imagined in the cold of the Jauja night the sky spattered with stars, and he thought: This clear air is inspiring you, Mayta. He dropped his hand from his chest to his penis and, thinking about Anatolio, began to rub it.

"He didn't tell you that the plan was too important for it to be the exclusive monopoly of a Trotskyist splinter group?" I insist. "Why would he have bothered trying to get help from the other RWP, and even from the Communist Party?"

"He never said a word," Professor Ubilluz answers quickly. "He told us nothing about it and tried to conceal from us the fact that the left was divided and that the RWP(T) was insignificant. He deceived us, deliberately and treacherously. He talked about the party. The party this and the party that. I thought he was talking about the Communist Party, which would have meant thousands of workers and students."

In the distance, we hear a flurry of rifle shots. Or is it a clap of thunder? We hear it again in a few seconds, and remain silent, listening. We hear another salvo, even farther off, and the professor says softly, "It's dynamite caps the guerrilla fighters set off out in the hills. To break the nerve of the garrison soldiers. Psychological warfare." No: it was ducks. A flock flew over the reed patches, quacking. They had gone out for a walk, and Mayta had his bag in his hand. Within a short hour, he would be on the return train to Lima.

"There's room for everyone, of course," Vallejos said. "The

138

more, the merrier. Of course. There will be enough weapons for all who want to fight. All I ask is that you carry out your negotiations fast."

They were walking on the outskirts of the city, and in the distance some roofs with red tiles glowed. The wind sang through the eucalyptus trees and the willows.

"We have all the time we need," said Mayta. "No need to rush things."

"Yes, there is," said Vallejos dryly. He turned to look at him, and there was a blind resolve in his eyes. Mayta thought: There's something else, I'm going to find out something else. "The two leaders of the Uchubamba land seizure, the ones who led the takeover of the Aína hacienda, are here."

"In Jauja?" asked Mayta. "Why haven't you introduced them to me? I would have wanted to meet them."

"They're in jail and are not receiving guests." Vallejos smiled. "That's right—prisoners."

They had been brought in by the Civil Guard patrol that had gone out to undo the land takeover. But it wasn't certain the two would remain in Jauja for long. At any moment, an order could come, transferring them to Huancayo or Lima. And the whole plan depended to a great extent on them. They would lead them from Jauja to Uchubamba quickly and surely, and they would guarantee the collaboration of the communities. Did he see why there was so little time?

"Alejandro Condori and Zenón Gonzales," I tell him, naming names before he has a chance to do it. Ubilluz gapes. The light from the bulb has faded and we are almost in darkness.

"Right, those are their names. You are very well informed."

Am I? I think I've read everything that came out in newspapers and magazines about this story, and I've talked with an infinite number of participants and witnesses. But the more I investigate, the less I feel I know what really happened. Because, with each new fact, more contradictions, conjectures, mysteries, and incongruities crop up. How did it happen that those two peasant leaders, from a remote community in the jungle region of Junín, ended up in the Jauja jail?

"A fantastic accident," Vallejos explained. "I had nothing to do with it. This was the jail they were sent to because this is where they would come before the prosecution. My sister would say that God is helping us, see?"

"Were they in with you before they were captured?"

"In a general way," says Ubilluz. "We spoke with them during the trip we made to Uchubamba, and they helped us hide the weapons. But they only came in with us all the way in the month they were imprisoned. They really got close to their jailer. That is, the lieutenant. I think he didn't tell them the whole plan until the thing blew open."

That part of the story, the end, makes Professor Ubilluz uncomfortable, even though so much time has passed. About that part he knows only what he's heard, and his role is both disputed and doubtful. We hear another volley, far off. "They may be shooting the accomplices of the terrorists," he says, grunting. This is the time they usually choose to take them from their homes, in a jeep or an armored car, and bring them to the outskirts. The corpses turn up the next day on the roads. And suddenly, with no transition, he asks me, "Does it make any sense to be writing a novel with Peru in this condition and Peruvians all living on borrowed time?" Does it make any sense? I tell him it certainly does, since I'm doing it.

There's something depressing about Professor Ubilluz. Everything he says has a sad cast to it. Maybe I'm prejudiced, but I can't get rid of the notion that he's always on the defensive and that everything he tells me is aimed at some kind of self-justification. But doesn't everyone do the same thing? Why is it I have no confidence in him? The fact that he's still alive? That I've heard so much gossip and so many rumors about him? But am I not also aware of the fact that in political controversies this country was always a garbage heap, until it became the cemetery it is today? Don't I know the infinite horrors which have no basis in fact that enemies ascribe to each other? No, that isn't what seems so pitiful to me in him, but, simply, his decadence, his bitterness, the quarantine in which he lives.

"So then, in short, Mayta's part in the plan of action was nil," I say.

"To be fair, let's say minimal," he corrects me, shrugging his shoulders. He yawns, and his face fills with wrinkles. "With him or without him, it would have turned out the same. We let him in because we thought he was a political and union leader of some importance. We needed the support of workers and revolutionaries in the rest of the country. That was to be Mayta's function. But it turned out he didn't even represent his own group, the RWP(T). Politically speaking, he was a total orphan."

"A total orphan." The expression rings in my ear as I bid Professor Ubilluz goodbye and go out onto the deserted streets of Jauja, heading toward the Paca Inn, under a sky glistening with stars. The professor tells me that, if I'm afraid of such a long walk, I can sleep in his tiny living room. But I prefer to leave: I need air and solitude. I have to quell the static inside my head and put some distance between me and a person whose mere presence depresses my work. The volleys have ceased, and it's as if there were a curfew, because there's not a soul around. I walk down the middle of the street, banging my heels, making every effort to be noticed, so that if a patrol comes along, they won't think I'm trying to sneak by. The sky glows—an unusual sight for someone from Lima, where you almost never see the stars through the mist. The cold chaps my lips. I don't feel as hungry as I did in the afternoon.

A total orphan. That's what he became, by being a militant in smaller and smaller, ever more radical sects, looking for an ideological purity he never found. He was the supreme orphan when he threw himself into this extraordinary conspiracy to start a war in the heights of Junín, with a twenty-two-year-old second-lieutenant jailer and a secondary-school teacher, both of them totally disconnected from the Peruvian left. It certainly was fascinating. It kept on fascinating me for a year after I made the investigation, just as much as it fascinated me that day when I found out in Paris what had happened in Jauja . . . The wretched light of the widely spaced streetlights wraps around the old façades of the houses, some with enormous gateways and ironclad doors, wrought-iron bars on their windows, and shuttered balconies. Behind all that, I can imagine entranceways, patios with plants and trees, and a life once upon a time ordered and monotonous and now, doubtless, beside itself with fear.

In that first visit to Jauja, nevertheless, the total orphan must have felt exultation and happiness such as he never felt before. He was going to act, the revolt was becoming tangible: faces, places, dialogues, concrete action. As if suddenly his whole life as a militant, a conspirator, a persecuted individual, a political prisoner was justified and at the same time catapulted into a higher reality. Besides, it all coincided with the attainment of something which until a week ago had seemed a wild dream. Hadn't he dreamed? No, it was as true and concrete as the imminent revolt: he had had in his arms the boy he had desired for so many years. He had made him experience pleasure and he had experienced pleasure himself. He had heard him whimper under his caresses. He felt a burning in his testicles, the prelude to an erection, and he thought: Have you gone crazy? Here? Right in the station? Here, in front of Vallejos? He thought: It's happiness. You have never felt like this before, comrade.

Nothing's open, and I remember from a previous visit, years ago, before all this, the eternal shops of Jauja at dusk, illuminated with kerosene lamps: the tailor shops, the candlemaker's shop, the barbershops, the jewelers, the bakeries, the hat stores. And also that hanging from the balconies you could sometimes see rows of rabbits drying in the sun. Suddenly I'm hungry again, and my mouth waters. I think about Mayta. Excited, happy, he got ready to return to Lima, certain that his comrades in the RWP(T) would approve the plan of action without reservations. He thought: I'll see Anatolio, we'll spend the night talking, I'll tell him everything, we'll laugh, he'll help me to get the others excited. And later . . . There is a placid silence, the kind you find in books by the Spanish writer Azorín, broken from time to time by the cry of a night bird, invisible under the eaves of a house.

Now I'm leaving the town. This is where it took place, this is where they did it, in these little streets, so tranquil, so timeless then, in that plaza of such beautiful proportions, which twenty-five years ago had a weeping willow and a border of cypresses. Here in this land where it would be difficult to imagine that things could be worse, that hunger, murder, and the danger of disintegration would reach the extremes of today. Here, before returning to Lima, when they said goodbye in the station, the total orphan indicated to the impulsive second lieutenant that in order to give a greater impetus to the start of the rebellion he should consider a few armed acts of propaganda.

"And just what is that?" Vallejos asked.

The train was in the station and people were shoving their way on. They talked near the stairs, taking advantage of the last minutes.

"Translated into Catholic language, it means to preach by example," said Mayta. "Actions that educate the masses, that take hold in their imagination, that give them ideas, show them their own power. One armed act of propaganda is worth hundreds of issues of the *Workers Voice*."

They were speaking in low tones, but there was no danger of their being heard, because of the pandemonium all around them.

"And you want more armed acts of propaganda than taking over the Jauja jail and seizing the weapons? More than seizing the police station and the Civil Guard post?"

"Yes, I want more than that," said Mayta.

Capturing those places was a belligerent, military act, which would seem like a traditional military coup because a lieutenant was doing it. It wasn't sufficiently explicit from the ideological point of view. He would have to take maximum advantage of those first hours. Newspapers and radios would be reporting nonstop. Everything they did in those first hours would reverberate and remain engraved in the memory of the people. So he would have to take full advantage and carry out acts that would have a symbolic charge to them, whose message would be both about revolution and about the class struggle, which would reach the militants, students, intellectuals, workers, and peasants.

"You know something?" said Vallejos. "I think you're right."

"The important thing is how much time we have."

"A few hours. With the telephone and telegraph lines cut and the radio out of commission, the only way to sound the alarm is for someone to go to Huancayo. While they go and come back and mobilize the police—let's say, five hours."

"More than enough for some didactic action," said Mayta. "Action that will show the masses that our movement is against bourgeois power, imperialism, and capitalism."

"Now you're making a speech." Vallejos laughed, hugging him. "Get on, get on. And now that you're going back, don't forget the surprise I gave you. You're going to need it."

"The plan was perfect," Professor Ubilluz said several times during our chat. What went wrong then, Professor? "That it was changed, rushed, turned upside down." Who did all that? "I couldn't tell you, exactly. Vallejos, naturally. But perhaps influenced by the Trotskyite. I'll wonder about that until I die." A doubt, he says, that has eaten away at his life, that is still eating away at it, even more than the infamous calumnies against him, even more than being on the insurgents' blacklist. I have gone halfway back to the inn without running into a patrol, armored car, man, or beast: only invisible chirps. The stars and the moon render visible the quiet, bluish countryside, the fields, the eucalyptus trees, the mountains, the small houses along the road sealed up with mud and rocks, just like those in the city. The waters of the lake, in a night like this, should be worth seeing. When I get to the inn, I'll go out to look at them. The walk has restored my enthusiasm for my book. I'll go out on the terrace and the dock, no stray or intended shots will interrupt me. And I shall think, remember, and imagine until, just before dawn, I give form to this episode in the real life of Alejandro Mayta. A whistle blew and the train began to move.

Six

"It was the most terrifying encounter I ever had in my life," says Blacquer. "I stood there blinking, not really believing he was actually standing there. Was it really Mayta? 'Yes, it's me,' said Mayta quickly. 'Can I come in? It's urgent.'"

"Can you imagine me letting a Trot in?" Blacquer smiles, remembering the shiver that ran down his spine that morning when he found himself face to face with that apparition. "I don't think you and I have anything to say to each other, Mayta."

"It's important, it's urgent, it goes way beyond our differences." He spoke vehemently, and seemed not to have slept or washed. You could see he was really excited. "If you're afraid you'll be compromised if you let me in, we can go anywhere you like."

"We saw each other three times," Blacquer adds. "The first two were before that meeting of the RWP(T) when they threw him out for being a traitor. I mean, for coming to see me. Me, a Stalinist."

He smiles again, exposing his tobacco-stained teeth, and

behind his thick glasses his myopic eyes look me up and down disagreeably. We are in the convalescent Café Haiti in Miraflores, which still hasn't been put back together after the bombing: its windows still have no glass in them, the counter and the floor are both still smashed and scorched. But out here in the street you don't see all that. All around us, people are talking about the same thing, as if everyone sitting at the twenty or so tables is having the same conversation. Could it be true that Cuban troops had crossed the Bolivian border? That for the last three days the rebels, along with the Cuban and Bolivian "volunteers" who support them, have pushed the army back? That the Junta has warned the United States that if it doesn't intervene, the insurgents will take Arequipa in a matter of days and from there will be able to proclaim the Socialist Republic of Peru? But Blacquer and I skirt these momentous issues and chat about that insignificant, forgotten episode of a quarter century ago, the key to my novel.

"I really was one," he adds after a while. "Like everybody else at that time. Weren't you, after all? Weren't you moved by the hagiography Barbusse wrote about Stalin? Didn't you know by heart the poem Neruda wrote in his honor? Didn't you have a poster with the drawing Picasso did of him? Didn't you weep when he died?"

Blacquer was my first teacher of Marxism—thirty-five years ago—in a secret study group organized by the Young Communists in a house over in Pueblo Libre. At that time he was a Stalinist; I mean, a machine programmed to repeat official statements, an automaton who spoke in stereotypes. Now he is a man who has grown old, who survives by working in a print shop. Is he still a militant? Perhaps, but he's nothing more than an outsider as far as the party is concerned: he'll never rise in the hierarchy. The proof is the fact that he's here with me right out in broad daylight—well, it's a gray day with lowering, ashen clouds that themselves look like bad omens, in keeping with the rumors about the internationalization of the war in the south. No one's hunting him down, while even the lowest-level leaders

147

of the Communist Party—or of any party on the extreme left—are in hiding, in jail, or dead. I have only heard about his confused history, and I don't intend to find out about it now. (If the rumors turn out to be true and the war really is growing more general, I'll barely have time to finish my novel. If the war reaches the streets of Lima, my own front door, I doubt I'll be able to do it.)

What I want to hear is his account of those three meetings they had twenty-five years ago on the eve of the Jauja uprising. They were opposites: the Stalinist and the Trotskyist. But I've always been intrigued by the fact that Blacquer, who seemed destined by fate to reach the Central Committee and perhaps to be head of the Communist Party, is today a nobody. It was something that happened to him in some Central European country—Hungary or Czechoslovakia—where he was sent to study and where he got involved in some mess or other. From the sotto voce accusations that circulated at the time—the usual: factional activity, ultra-individualism, petit-bourgeois pride, lack of discipline, sabotaging the party line—it was impossible to know what he had said or done to deserve excommunication. Had he committed the ultimate crime—criticizing the U.S.S.R.? If he did, why did he do it? All we know is that he was expelled for a few years, and lived in the infinitely sad limbo of purged communists—no one can be more an orphan than a militant expelled from the party, not even a priest who puts aside his vows—where he deteriorated in all possible ways, until, it seems, he could return, having gone through, I suppose, the obligatory rite of self-criticism. Coming back to the flock didn't help him very much, judging by what's become of him since. As far as I know, the party had him correcting the proofs of *Unity* as well as some pamphlets and leaflets. At least, that is, until the insurrection took on the dimensions it has now and the communists were declared outlaws and began to be persecuted or assassinated by the death squads. But it's hardly likely that anyone, except through some monumental error or stupidity, is going to jail or murder the ruined and useless man Blacquer has

148

become. His acid memories have probably ended his illusions. Every time I've seen him over the past few years—always in a group; this is the first time in ten or fifteen years that we've spoken alone—he's impressed me as being a bitter man interested in nothing.

"They didn't expel Mayta from the RWP(T)," I correct him. "He resigned. At that last session, to be precise. His letter of resignation appeared in *Workers Voice (T)*. I clipped it out."

"They threw him out," he firmly corrects me in turn. "I know all about that Trot meeting, just as if I'd been there myself. Mayta told me all about it the last time we met. The third time. I'd like more coffee, if you don't mind."

Coffee and soda is all anyone can have, now that even saltines are rationed. Actually, they're not supposed to serve more than one cup of coffee to a customer. But no one pays much attention to that law. The people around us are very excited, all talking loudly. Even though I try not to be distracted, I find myself listening to a young man with glasses: at the Ministry of the Exterior, they estimate that "several thousand" Cubans and Bolivians have crossed the border. The girl with him opens her eyes wide: "Could Fidel Castro be with them?" "No, he's too old for that rough stuff," the boy says, smashing her illusions. The barefoot, ragged boys in the Diagonal attack every car like a pack of dogs, offering to wash it, guard it, scrub the white-walls. Others wander from table to table, offering to make the customers' shoes shine like mirrors. (They say the bomb that exploded here was placed by boys like these.) There are also clusters of women who assault the passersby and the drivers (when the lights turn red) to sell them blackmarket cigarettes. With the scarcities we're forced to put up with, the one thing we don't lack is cigarettes. Why doesn't the blackmarket sell preserves and crackers, something we can use to stave off the hunger we feel when we wake up and when we go to sleep?

"I'll tell you all about it," said Mayta, panting. He spoke calmly and methodically, and Blacquer listened politely. He told him what he wanted to tell him. Had he acted properly or not?

He didn't know and didn't care. It was as if all the fatigue of a sleepless night had suddenly welled up in him. "See? I had a good reason for knocking at your door."

Blacquer remained silent, looking at him, his cigarette burning down between his thin, yellowed fingers. The little room led several lives—office, dining room, foyer—and was stuffed with furniture, chairs, a few books. The greenish wallpaper was water-stained. As he was speaking, Mayta had heard the voice of a woman and the crying of a child coming from upstairs. Blacquer remained so still that Mayta would have thought he was asleep, if it weren't that he had his myopic eyes fixed on him. This sector of Jesús María was quiet, devoid of cars.

"As a provocation directed against the party, it couldn't be any cruder," he said finally, his voice devoid of inflection. The ash from his cigarette fell to the floor, and Blacquer stepped on it. "I thought you Trots were a little subtler with your tricks. You needn't have bothered to visit me, Mayta."

He wasn't surprised: Blacquer had said, more or less, what he was supposed to say. Mayta admitted to himself that he was right: a militant should be suspicious, and Blacquer was a good militant. This he knew from the time they were in jail together. Before he answered, Mayta lit a cigarette and yawned. Upstairs, the child began to cry again. The woman quieted him down, in low tones.

"Just remember, I'm not here to ask your party for anything. I just wanted to inform you. This goes beyond our differences and concerns all revolutionaries."

"Even the Stalinists who betrayed the October Revolution?" asked Blacquer quietly.

"Even the Stalinists who betrayed the October Revolution." Mayta nodded. His tone changed. "I thought about taking this step all night before actually doing it. I'm as suspicious of you as you are of me. Don't you realize that? Do you think I don't know what I'm risking? I'm putting a powerful weapon in your hands and in the hands of your party. Nevertheless, here I am.

Don't talk about provocations even you don't believe in. Just think a little."

This is one of the things I understand least in this story, the strangest episode. Wasn't it absurd to reveal details about an uprising to a political enemy, to whom—this was the icing on the cake—he was not even going to propose a pact, a joint action, from whom he was not going to ask a thing? What sense was there in all that? "Early this morning, over that radio over there, they said that red flags have been flying since last night over Puno, and that before tomorrow they will be flying over Arequipa and Cuzco," someone says. "Fabrications," someone else counters.

"When he came to see me, I also thought it didn't make any sense," agrees Blacquer. "First, I thought it was a trap. Or that Mayta had gotten involved in something, was sorry he ever did it, and was now trying to weasel out by creating complications and difficulties . . . Later on, after what happened, it was all clear."

"The only clear thing in all this is a knife in our backs," roared Comrade Pallardi. "To ask for help from the Stalinists for this adventure isn't merely indiscipline. It's purely and simply betrayal."

"I'll explain it to you all over again, if I have to," Mayta interrupted him, without getting upset. He was sitting on a pile of back numbers of *Workers Voice* and was leaning on the poster with Trotsky's face on it. Within a few seconds, an electric tension had galvanized the garage on Jirón Zorritos. "But before I do, comrade, clear something up for me. When you say adventure, are you referring to the revolution?"

Blacquer slowly savors his watery coffee and runs the tip of his tongue over his cracked lips. He narrows his eyes and remains silent, seeming to reflect on the dialogue taking place at a nearby table: "If this news is right, tomorrow or the day after, the war will be right here in Lima." "Do you really think so, Pacho? A war would really be somethin', doncha think?"

The afternoon passes and the automobile traffic intensifies. The Diagonal is bumper-to-bumper. The beggar kids and the women selling cigarettes have also become more numerous. "I'm happy the Cubans and Bolivians have crossed the border," exclaims an irritable guy. "Now the Marines in Ecuador have no reason to stay out. It may well be that they're already in Piura or Chiclayo. I hope they kill the people they have to kill and that they put an end to all this once and for all, goddamn it." I barely hear him, because, in fact, at this very moment his bloody speculation has less life to it than those two meetings in that Lima of fewer cars, fewer beggars, and fewer blackmarket dealers, where the things that are happening now would seem impossible: Mayta going to share his plot with his Stalinist enemy, Mayta fighting it out with his comrades in the final session of the Central Committee of the RWP(T).

"Coming to see me was the only sensible thing he did in that entire crazy business he got involved in," adds Blacquer. He's taken off his glasses to clean them, and he looks blind. "If the guerrilla war really took off, they would have needed urban support. Networks that would send them medicine and information, that could hide and nurse the wounded and recruit new fighters. Networks that would broadcast the actions of the advance guard. Who was going to create those networks? The twenty-odd Peruvian Trots?"

"Actually, there are only seven of us," I correct him.

Had Blacquer understood him? He was still as a statue again. Leaning his head forward, realizing that he was sweating, trying to find the words that fatigue and worry were stealing from him, hearing from time to time, in that invisible upper floor, the child and the woman, I explained it to him again. No one was asking the militants of the Communist Party to go out to the mountains—he had taken the precaution not to mention to him Vallejos, Jauja, or any date whatsoever—or that they give up any of their theories, ideas, prejudices, dogmas, anything. Only that they be informed and alert. Soon they would be in a situation where they'd have only two alternatives: put their convictions into practice or renounce them. Soon they would have to show the masses they really wanted to topple the exploitive system and replace it with a revolutionary worker-peasant regime. Or they would show that all they had been saying was just rhetoric: they could vegetate in the shadow of the powerful ally that had adopted them and wait for the revolution to fall on Peru someday like a gift from heaven.

"When you attack us, then you seem like your old self," said Blacquer. "What are you asking for? Make your point."

"All I'm asking is that you be ready, nothing more." I thought: Will I lose my voice? I had never been so exhausted. I had to make a huge effort to articulate every syllable. Overhead, the child began to wail again. "Because, when we act, there is going to be a massive counterstrike. And of course you all won't be exempt from the repression."

"Of course," muttered Blacquer. "If what you're telling me isn't a lie, the government, the press, and everybody else will say that it was planned and executed by us, that it was paid for with Moscow gold and carried out under orders from Moscow. Right?"

"That's probably the way it'll be." I nod. The child was crying even more loudly, and its wailing began to rattle me. "But now that you've been warned, you can take precautions. Besides . . ."

I stood there with my mouth hanging open, without the spirit to finish, and for the first time since my talk with Blacquer began, I hesitated. Sweat was pouring down my face, my pupils were dilated, and my hands shook. Adventure and betrayal?

"They're the words that sum up what you've done, and I stand by them," said Comrade Carlos in a flat voice. "Comrade Pallardi has simply spoken the truth."

"Stick to the Vallejos business for now," the general secretary chided him. "We said we would discuss the Jauja matter first. The meeting between Comrade Mayta and Blacquer comes second."

"Right," replied Comrade Carlos, and Mayta thought:

153

They're all turning against me. A lieutenant who plans a revolution as if it were a Putsch, without union support, without the participation of the masses. What else can this thing be called but an adventure?

"We could call it a provocation or a big joke," Comrade Medardo interrupted. He looked at Mayta and added, with a lapidary gesture: "The party can't sacrifice itself for something that hasn't got a chance in the world."

Mayta felt that the pile of *Workers Voice* he was sitting on had begun to tip over and he thought how ridiculous it would be if he slipped and took a fall. He stole a look at his comrades, and understood why, when he came in, they had greeted him so distantly, and why no one was absent from this meeting. Were they all against him? Even the members of the Action Group? Would Anatolio be against him, too? Instead of depression, he felt a wave of rage roll over him.

"And, 'besides,' what?" Blacquer encouraged me to go on.

"Rifles," I said in a small voice. "We have more than we need. If the Communist Party wants to defend itself when the bullets start flying, we'll give you weapons. Free of charge, of course."

Blacquer was lighting his ten millionth cigarette of the morning. But his matches went out twice in a row, and when he took his first drag, he choked. "You're sure that this time it's for real." I saw him stand up, smoke pouring out of his nose and mouth, poke his head into the next room, and shout, "Take him for a walk. We can't talk with all that crying." There was no answer, but the child instantly quieted down. Blacquer sat down again, to stare at me and calm down.

"I still don't know if this is a trap, Mayta," he said, muttering. "But I do know one thing. You've gone crazy. Do you really think the party would ever, under any circumstances, join forces with the Trots?"

"Not with the Trots. With the revolution," I answered. "Yes, I do think so. That's why I'm here."

"A petit-bourgeois adventure, if we want to put it precisely," said Anatolio, and when I realized how much he was stuttering,

I knew exactly what he was going to say next, that he had memorized what he was saying. "The masses have not been invited to participate and don't figure in the plan in any way. By the same token, what guarantee is there that the people from Uchubamba will rise up if we go out there? None at all. Have any of us seen those imprisoned leaders? No. Who's going to run this show? Us? No. A lieutenant with a Putschist, ultra-adventurist mentality. What role are we being offered? To be the caboose, the cannon fodder." Now he did turn and he did have enough guts to look me in the eye. "My obligation is to say what I think, comrade."

That's not what you thought last night, I mentally answered him. Or maybe it was that his attitude last night had been a fake, just to keep me off guard. Carefully, so I would have something to keep me busy, I straightened up the newspapers I had been sitting on and leaned them back against the wall. By then, the whole thing had become clear: there had been an earlier meeting in which the Central Committee of the RWP(T) had decided on what was now happening. Anatolio must have been there. I felt a bitter taste, a pain in my bones. It was too much of a farce. Hadn't we talked over so many things last night in the room over on Jirón Zepita? Didn't we review the action plan? Will you say goodbye to anyone before you go out to the mountains? Only my mother. What'll you tell her? That I've won a scholarship to go to Mexico: I'll write you once a week, Mama. Had there been in him any hesitation, doubt, contradiction—was he uncomfortable? Not a thing. He seemed enthusiastic and very sincere. We were in bed in the dark, the cot creaked, and every time the sound of the racing little feet above our heads came back, his body, pressed against mine, tensed up. That sudden vibration showed me, just for an instant, patches of Anatolio's skin, and I anxiously waited for it to happen again. With my mouth against his, I said, suddenly, "I don't want you to die, ever." And a moment later: "Have you thought that you might die?" With a voice made soft and languid by desire, he answered me instantly: "Of course I've thought about it. And it doesn't matter to me at all." In pain and trembling, on the pile of *Workers Voice*, which once again threatened to tip over, I thought: Actually, it does matter quite a bit to you.

"I thought it was just a pose, that he was having emotional problems, I thought that . . ." Blacquer stops talking because the girl at the next table has burst out laughing. "It would happen from time to time among the comrades, the same way that one fine day a soldier wakes up and thinks he's Napoleon. I thought: This morning, he woke up and thought he was Lenin arriving at the Finland Station."

He's quiet again, because of the girl's laughter. At another table, a man shouts instructions: Fill tubs, pots, pans, barrels, and put them in every room, in every corner, even if you have to use salt water. If the Reds come in, the United States will bomb us and the fires will be even worse than the bombs. That should be our top priority, believe me—enough water available to put out the fire as soon as it starts.

"But, despite the fact that it sounded fantastic, it was the truth," Blacquer goes on. "It was all the truth. They had more than enough weapons. The second lieutenant had pilfered lots from an army armory, right here in Lima. He had them hidden somewhere. You knew that he gave Mayta a sub-machine gun, right? It seems it was from that lot he stole. The idea of rebelling must have been an obsession Vallejos had even when he was a cadet. He wasn't crazy, his plan was sincere. Stupid but sincere."

The false smile bares his stained teeth. With a brusque gesture, he pushes aside a small boy who tries to shine his shoes. "They had no one to give them to, they had no one to shoulder those rifles," he mocks.

"How did the party react?"

"Nobody thought it of any importance, nobody believed a single word. Not about the rifles, not about the uprising. In the summer of 1958, months before the *barbudos* marched into Havana, who was going to believe those things? The party

156

reacted in a logical way. I had to sever all relations with the Trot, because he had to have some trick up his sleeve. Naturally, I did exactly that."

A lady tells the man who'd been talking about filling the pots of water that he's an ignoramus. When the bombs start falling, all you can do is pray! Pots of water against bombs! What did he think, that war was like a carnival, stupid asshole? "I'm sorry you're not a man, lady, or I'd knock your teeth down your throat," roars the gentleman. To which the lady's male friend gallantly adds, "I'm a man, come on and knock mine down my throat." It looks as though they're going to fight for real.

"Trap, madness, whatever—we don't want to have anything more to do with it," quoted Blacquer. "And I don't want you here ever again."

"Just what I expected. You all are what you are, and you'll go on being just that for quite a while."

The two men are pulled apart, and as quickly as they got wrangled up, they calm down. The girl says, "Don't fight among yourselves. In times like these, we have to be united." A hunchback is looking at her legs.

"It was a real blow for him." Blacquer shoos away another kneeling boy trying to shine his shoes. "To come to see me, he had to overcome lots of inhibitions. No doubt about it, he actually thought the insurrection could flatten the mountains that separated us. Spineless naïveté."

He throws his cigarette butt away, and instantly a ragged, filthy figure jumps on it, picks it up, and anxiously takes a drag, to extract one final mouthful of smoke. Was he like that when he decided to visit Blacquer? Was I that anguished when I realized that zero hour was coming and there were only a handful of us to carry out an uprising, and we lacked even a minimal support organization in the city?

"The coup de grâce was yet to come," Blacquer adds. "His own party was going to expel him as a traitor."

That's what Jacinto Zevallos had said, exactly that. For the

157

veteran, the worker, the Trotskyist relic of Peru to say it, was the most upsetting thing to occur at a meeting where he had already heard so many hostile words. Even more painful was Anatolio's turnaround. Because he both respected and cared for old Zevallos. The secretary general was speaking indignantly, and no one moved a muscle.

"Yes, comrade, to ask help from those Creole Stalinists for this project behind our backs, and in the party's name, is more than mere fractionization. It is betrayal. Your explanations make matters even worse. Instead of recognizing your mistake, you have simply explained your reasons. I have to request your separation from the party, Mayta."

What explanations did I give them? Even though none of those who were there at that session would even admit it took place, I feel the unquenchable need to believe it did, and just as Blacquer described it. What could I say to them that would justify my visit to the arch-enemy? With the aid of hindsight, it doesn't seem so inconceivable. The Reds who may enter Lima tomorrow, or the day after, belong to a vast Marxist spectrum, which includes Communist Party members, Trotskyists, and Maoists, all apparently fighting under one flag. The revolution was too important, serious, and difficult to be monopolized by anyone, to be the private property of a single organization, even if that organization had interpreted Peruvian reality more correctly than the others. The revolution would be possible only if all revolutionaries, setting aside their quarrels, but without giving up their individual concepts, united in a concrete action against class enemies. Badly dressed, in his forties, sweaty, over-excited, blinking, he tried to sell them that marvelous toy which had changed his life and which—he was sure—could change theirs and that of the entire left: action, purifying, redemptive, absolute action. Action would file away the rough spots, the rivalries, the byzantine differences; it would abolish the enmities born out of egoism and the cult of personality; it would sweep away the groups and factions in an unquenchable current that would carry along all revolutionaries, comrades.

That's why I went to talk to Blacquer. Not to reveal any key information to him: I mentioned no names, no dates, and not a single location. And I in no way compromised the RWP(T). The first thing I told Blacquer was that I was speaking only for myself and that any future agreements would have to be made party to party. I went to see him without requesting authorization, so I could save time, comrades. Wasn't I on my way to Jauja? I went simply to notify them that the revolution was going to begin, so they could come to the proper conclusions, if, that is, they really were the revolutionaries and Marxists they said they were. So they would be ready to take part in the struggle. Because the reactionaries would defend themselves, would fight like cornered rats, and so as not to be bitten, we all had to form a common front . . . Did they listen to me until I finished? Did they make me shut up? Did they throw me out of the garage on Jirón Zorritos, kicking and insulting me?

"They let him speak several times," Blacquer assures me. "There was a lot of tension, and a lot of personal things came to the surface. Mayta and Joaquín almost started swinging at each other. And then, instead of killing him off once and for all, they picked him up off the floor where they'd left him like a dirty rag, and they gave him an out. A Trotskyite melodrama. I suppose that last meeting of the RWP(T) is going to be quite useful to you."

"Yes, I suppose so. But I still don't get it. Why do Moisés, Anatolio, Pallardi, and Joaquín absolutely deny that it ever took place? Their version of what happened shows discrepancies in many areas, but they all agree on this one point: Mayta's resignation reached them by mail, he resigned on his own when he went to Jauja, once the RWP(T) decided not to participate in the uprising. Bad collective memory?"

"Bad collective conscience," Blacquer says in a low voice. "Mayta couldn't have made up that meeting. He came to tell me all about it a few hours after it happened. It was the coup de grâce, and it must still trouble them. Because, as they started piling charge after charge on him, everything started coming

159

out, even his Achilles' heel. Can you imagine them being that cruel?"

"What you really mean to say is that the end of the world is coming, buddy," a confused patron exclaims. The girl is still laughing her dumb and happy laugh, and the beggar kids leave us in peace for a moment as they start kicking a can around among the pedestrians.

"He actually told you about that?" I'm surprised. "It was a subject he never mentioned, not even to his best friends. Why did he come to you at that particular moment? I just don't understand."

"At the beginning, I didn't get it either, but now I think I do," says Blacquer. "He was a revolutionary, one hundred percent, don't forget. The RWP(T) had just thrown him out. Perhaps he thought that would make us reconsider our refusal. Maybe now we would take his plan seriously."

"As a matter of fact, we should have expelled him a long time ago," affirms Comrade Joaquín. He turned to look at Mayta in such a way that I thought: Why does he hate me? "I'm going to tell you what I think without pulling any punches, as a Marxist and as a revolutionary. I'm not surprised at what you have done, not about the plot, not about having secretly talked with that Stalinist policeman Blacquer. You can't do anything straight, because you aren't straight, you're just not a man, Mayta."

"Let's keep personal differences out of this," the secretary general interrupted him.

What Joaquín said took him so by surprise that Mayta couldn't say a word. All I could do was shrink back. Why did it surprise me so much? Wasn't it something that was always in the back of my mind, something I always feared would come up in debates, a quick low blow that would lay me out and keep me on my back for the rest of the discussion? With a cramp in every part of his body, he leaned back on the pile of newspapers. I felt a hot wave roll over me and in despair I thought: Anatolio is going to stand up and confess that we slept together

160

last night. What was Anatolio going to say? What was he going to do?

"It isn't a personal difference, because it's directly related to what's happened," replied Comrade Joaquín. Even with all my fear and perturbation, Mayta knew that Joaquín really did hate him. What did I ever do to him that was so serious, so wounding to him that he would take this kind of revenge? "That way of doing things of his, complicated, capricious, that idea of going to see our worst enemy, is feminine, comrades. It's a subject that's never been brought up here out of consideration for Mayta, the very kind of consideration he didn't have for us. Is it possible to be a loyal revolutionary and a homosexual at the same time? That's the real question we've got to decide, comrades."

Why does he say homosexual and not fag? I thought absurdly. Isn't fag the right word? Recovering, he raised his hand, signaling to Comrade Jacinto that he wanted to speak.

"Are you sure that it was Mayta himself who told them he'd gone to see you?"

"Yes, I'm sure." Blacquer nods. "He thought he had done the right thing. He wanted to have a motion approved. That once the three who had to go went up to Jauja, the ones who stayed in Lima would again try to set up an agreement with us. It was his biggest mistake. For the Trots, who couldn't figure out how they were going to get out of the Jauja operation—which they never believed in, and which they thought Mayta had dragged them into—this was the perfect pretext. They could get rid of Jauja and Mayta all in one shot. Which meant splitting up even more. That's always been the Trots' favorite sport: purges, divisions, fractions, and expulsions."

He laughs, showing his nicotine-stained teeth.

"Personal differences have nothing to do with it, and neither do sexual or family differences," I answered, without taking my eyes off the back of Anatolio's head, as he sat on one of the little milking stools, his eyes fixed on the floor. "And that's why I'm

161

not going to pay attention to that provocation. Because there's only one way to respond to what you said, Joaquín."

"It's against the rules to get personal. Threats are also against the rules." The secretary general raised his voice.

"Well, are you homosexual or not, Mayta?" he heard Comrade Joaquín say right to his face. I saw that his fists were clenched, that he was ready to defend himself or to attack. "At least be frank about your vice."

"Private conversations are not allowed," insisted the secretary general. "And if you want to fight, go outside."

"You're right, comrade," said Mayta, looking at Jacinto Zevallos. "No conversations and no fights, nothing to distract us from our business. This argument isn't about sex. We'll take it up another time, if Comrade Joaquín thinks it's so important. Let's go back to our agenda. And I hope I won't be interrupted, at least."

I'd recovered my self-control, and they actually did let me speak. But even as he spoke, he knew inside that it wasn't going to be much use. They'd already decided, that's right, behind my back, to wash their hands of the insurrection, and no amount of talk was going to change their minds. As he spoke, he never revealed his pessimism. I forcefully repeated all the reasons I'd already given them, which circumstance gave them, reasons that even now, despite reverses and objections, still seem irrefutable to me as I heard them spoken aloud.

Didn't the objective conditions exist? Weren't the victims of latifundism, bossism, and capitalist and imperialist exploitation a revolutionary potential? If that is the case, then the revolutionary vanguard would create the subjective conditions by means of armed acts of propaganda, striking at the enemy in pedagogic operations that would mobilize the masses and gradually incorporate them into the action. Weren't there lots of examples? Indochina, Algeria, Cuba—there they were, the proof that a determined vanguard could start the revolution. It was false to say that Jauja was a petit-bourgeois adventure. It was a well-planned action and it had its own small but sufficient infrastructure. It would be successful if all of us would do our jobs. It was also false to say that the RWP(T) was being dragged along in the operation: it would have ideological control over the revolution, Vallejos would only have military control. We would have to take a more liberal, more generous, more Marxist, and more Trotskyist point of view, comrades. We cannot afford sectarian squabbles. Here in Lima, you're right, support is weak. That's why we have to be open to support from other left groups, because the fight is going to be long, difficult, and . . .

"There is a motion on the floor asking for Mayta's expulsion, and that's what we have to discuss," remembered Comrade Pallardi.

"Didn't I make myself clear when I said we shouldn't see each other ever again?" said Blacquer, closing the door of his house.

"It's a long story," replied Mayta. "I can't compromise you anymore. Because I came to speak to you, I've been expelled from the RWP(T)."

"And because I spoke to him, my party expelled me," Blacquer says in his bleak voice. "Ten years later."

"Your problems with the party came about because of those conversations?"

We've left the Haiti and we're walking along Miraflores Park, toward the corner of Larco, where Blacquer will take a bus. A thick mass of people stroll among and trip over the vendors who have their trinkets spread out all over the ground. The excitement the news of the invasion has caused is general. Our chat is spattered with the words Cubans, Bolivians, bombings, Marines, war, Reds.

"No, that's not true," Blacquer clarifies. "My problems began when I started questioning the party line. But I was castigated for reasons that outwardly had nothing to do with my questions. Among the many charges brought against me was that I had supposedly flirted with Trotskyism. They said that I'd proposed to the party a plan of action that involved the Trots. The

163

same old story: discredit the critic, so that anything he says is garbage. In that kind of game, nobody's better than we are."

"So you were also a kind of victim of the Jauja thing," I say to him.

"In a way." He looks at me again, with his old, parchment-colored face humanized by a half smile. "Other proofs of my collusion with the Trots existed, but they didn't know about them. I inherited Mayta's books when he went out to the mountains."

"I don't have anyone else to give them to," I said jokingly. "I am bereft of comrades. Better you than the informers. If you look at it that way, you needn't have any scruples. Take my books and learn something."

"There was a huge amount of Trotskyite shit, which I read in secret, the way we read Vargas Vila in secondary school." Blacquer laughs. "In secret, right. I even ripped out the pages where Mayta had written down his initials, so there'd be no criminal evidence."

He laughs again. There is a small crowd of people all craning their necks, trying to hear a news bulletin from a portable radio some passerby holds over his head. We just catch the end of a communiqué: the Junta for National Restoration announces to the community of nations the invasion of the fatherland by Cuban–Bolivian–Soviet forces. The invasion began at dawn, and the enemy has violated our sacred Peruvian soil at three places on the border, in the province of Puno. At 8 p.m., the committee will address the nation on the radio and television to report on this outrageous affront, which has electrified all Peruvians and made them into a single fist in defense of . . . So it was true, they had invaded. It must also be true, then, that the Marines will be moving in from their Ecuadorian bases, if they haven't already. We start walking again, among people either stunned or frightened by the news.

"It doesn't matter who wins, because I lose anyway," Blacquer suddenly says, more bored than alarmed. "If the Marines win,

I lose because I must be on their list as an old agent of international communism. If the rebels win, I lose because I'm a revisionist, a socialist-imperialist, and an ex-traitor to the cause. I'm not going to follow the advice that guy in the Haití was giving. I'm not going to fill pots and pans with water. For me, the fires may be the solution."

At the bus stop, in front of the Tiendecita Blanca, there is such a crowd that he'll have to wait a long time before he can get on a bus. In the years he spent in the limbo of the expelled, he tells me, he understood the Mayta of that day. I hear him, but I'm distanced from him, thinking. That the events in Jauja contributed years later, even indirectly, to Blacquer's fall to the status of nonperson in which he's lived is yet another proof of how mysterious and unforeseeable the ramifications of events are, that unbelievably complex web of causes and effects, reverberations and accidents that make up human history. It seems, in any case, that he doesn't resent Mayta's impulsive visits. It even seems that at a distance he respects Mayta.

"Nobody's abstaining, you can count the hands," said Jacinto Zevallos. "Unanimity, Mayta. You are no longer a member of the RWP(T). You have expelled yourself."

There was a sepulchral silence, and no one moved. Should he just leave? Should he say anything? Should he walk out, leaving the doors open or just tell them to go fuck themselves?

"Ten minutes ago, we both knew we were enemies to the death," shouted Blacquer furiously as he paced in front of Mayta's chair. "And now you act as if we'd been comrades all our lives. It's grotesque!"

"Don't anybody leave," said Comrade Medardo softly. "I have a request for a reconsideration, comrades."

"We are in different trenches, but we are both revolutionaries," said Mayta. "And we resemble each other in something else: for you and for me, personal matters always take a back seat to politics. So stop bitching and let's talk."

A reconsideration? All eyes were fixed on Comrade Medardo.

There was so much smoke that from the corner where he was sitting, next to the pile of *Workers Voice*, Mayta saw their faces as if in a cloud.

"Was he desperate, crushed, did he feel his world was collapsing?"

"He was confident, calm, even optimistic, or at least that's how he appeared." Blacquer moves his head in negation. "He wanted to show me that being expelled didn't affect him in the slightest. It might well have been true. Did you ever meet one of these guys who discovers sex or religion in old age? They get anxious, fiery, indefatigable. That's how he was. He had discovered action and he seemed like a kid with a new toy. He looked ridiculous, like an old man trying to do the latest dance steps. At the same time, it was hard not to envy him a little."

"We've been enemies for ideological reasons, and for the very same reasons we can be friends now." Mayta smiled at him. "Being friends or enemies, as far as we're concerned, is purely a matter of tactics."

"Are you going to go through the rite of self-criticism and request membership in the party?" Blacquer ended up, laughing.

The veteran revolutionary in decline who one fine day discovers action and throws himself into it without thinking, impatient, hopeful that the fighting and the marching are going to recompense him for years of impotence—that's the Mayta of those days, the one I perceive best among all the other Maytas. Were friendship and love things he understood only in political terms? No: he talked that way only to win Blacquer over. If he had been able to control his sentiments and instincts, he wouldn't have led the double life he led, he wouldn't have had to deal with the intrinsic split between being, by day, a clandestine militant totally given over to the task of changing the world, and, by night, a pervert on the prowl for faggots. There's no doubt that he could pull out all the stops when he had to—we see the proof of it in that last attempt to attain the impossible, the support of his arch-enemies for an uncertain revolt. Two,

166

three buses pass and Blacquer still can't get on. We decide to walk down Larco; maybe on Benavides it'll be easier.

"If news of this gets out, the only people who will gain by it will be the reactionaries. It's also a black eye for the party," Comrade Medardo explained delicately. "Our enemies will be rubbing their hands with glee, even the ones from the other RWP. There they go, they'll say, tearing themselves to bits in one more internal struggle. Don't interrupt me, Joaquín, I'm not asking for an act of Christian forgiveness or anything like that. Yes, I'll explain what kind of reconsideration I'm talking about."

The atmosphere of the garage on Jirón Zorritos had thickened. The smoke was so dense that Mayta's eyes were burning. He saw that they were listening to Moisés with relief burgeoning on their faces, as if, surprised at having defeated him so easily, they were thankful that someone was giving them an out whereby they could leave with a clear conscience.

"Comrade Mayta has been castigated. He knows it, and so do we," added Comrade Medardo. "He will not come back to the RWP(T), at least not for now, not as long as current conditions last. But, comrades, he's said it. Vallejos's plans are still in effect. The uprising will take place, with or without us. Whether we like it or not, it's going to affect us."

What was Moisés's point? Mayta was surprised to hear Moisés refer to him still as "comrade." He suspected what the point was, and in an instant all the depression and anger he had felt when he saw all those raised arms in favor of the motion disappeared: this was a chance he'd have to take.

"Trotskyism will not participate in the guerrilla war," he said. "The RWP(T) has unanimously decided to turn its back on us. The other RWP isn't even aware of the plan. But the plan is serious and solid. Don't you see? The Communist Party has a great opportunity here to fill a vacuum."

"To stick its neck in the guillotine. A great privilege!" growled Blacquer. "Drink your coffee and, if you like, tell me

167

about your tragic love affair with the Trots. But don't say a word about that uprising, Mayta."

"Don't make up your minds now, not even in a week—take all the time you need," Mayta went on, paying no attention to him. "The main obstacle for you all was the RWP(T). That obstacle has vanished. The insurrection is now the sole property of a worker-peasant group of independent revolutionaries."

"You, an independent revolutionary?" Blacquer said, enunciating carefully.

"Buy the next issue of *Workers Voice (T)* and you'll see for yourself," said Mayta. "That's what I've become: a revolutionary without a party. See? You've got a golden opportunity here. To run things, stand at the head of it all."

"That was the resignation you read," Blacquer says. He takes off his glasses to breathe on them and clean them with his handkerchief. "A decoy. No one believed in that resignation—neither the guy who signed it nor the ones who printed it. So why did they bother? To trick the readers? What readers? Did *Workers Voice (T)* have any readers beyond the—how many, seven—the seven Trots in the party? That's the way history is written, comrade."

All the stores on Avenida Larco are closed, even though it's still early. Because of the news about the invasion down south? Around here, there are fewer people than on the Diagonal or in the park. And even the gangs of beggars that overrun the streets and the cars are thinner than usual. The side of the Municipal Building is covered with an enormous graffito in red paint: "The People's Victory Is Coming Soon." It's decorated with the hammer and sickle. It wasn't there when I passed by three hours ago. A commando came with paint and brushes and painted it right in front of the cops? But now I realize that there are no police guarding the building.

"Let's at least give him a chance, then, to do a little less damage to the party," Comrade Medardo went on cautiously. "He should resign. We'll publish his resignation in *Workers Voice (T)*. Besides, it would be proof that the party bears no responsibility

168

for whatever he does in Jauja. A reconsideration in that sense of the word, comrades."

Mayta saw that various members of the Central Committee of the RWP(T) were nodding in approval. Moisés/Medardo's proposal might be accepted. He thought it over quickly, balancing the advantages and disadvantages. Yes, it was the lesser of two evils. He raised his hand: Could he speak?

At Benevides, there are as many people waiting for buses as there were at the Tiendecita Blanca. Blacquer shrugs: patience. I tell him I'll wait with him until he gets on. Several people near us are talking about the invasion.

"Over the years, I've come to realize that he wasn't so crazy," Blacquer says. "If the first action had lasted longer, things might have turned out the way Mayta planned. If the insurrection had caught on, the party would have been forced to enter and try to take over. As it has with this revolt. Who remembers that, for the first two years, we opposed it? And now we're fighting the Maoists for control, right? But Comrade Father Time shows no pity. Mayta was twenty-five years too early with his plans."

Intrigued by the way he talks about the party, I ask him if he was readmitted or not. He gives me a cryptic answer: "Only halfway." A lady with a child in her arms who seemed to be listening to him suddenly interrupts us. "Is it true the Russians are in it, too? What did we ever do to them? What's going to happen to my daughter?" "Calm down, nothing's going to happen. It's a lot of baloney," Blacquer consoles her as he waves at an overloaded bus that just keeps on going.

In an atmosphere totally unlike that of the meeting a few minutes earlier, the secretary general whispered that Comrade Medardo's proposal was reasonable. It would keep the divisionists of the other RWP from taking advantage. He looked at him: there was no problem about having the central figure comment. "You have the floor, Mayta."

"We talked for quite a while. In spite of what had just happened to him, he became euphoric, talking about the uprising," says Blacquer, lighting a cigarette. "I found out that it would take place in a matter of days, but I didn't know where. I would never have imagined Jauja. I thought maybe Cuzco, because some groups were seizing land there. But a revolution in the Jauja jail—who'd ever think of a thing like that?"

I listen to his flat laugh again. Without thinking, we start walking again, toward the bus stop on 28 de Julio. Time passes, and there he is, sweating, his clothes wrinkled and filthy, shadows under his eyes, his stiff hair all messed up. He's sitting on the edge of his chair in Blacquer's poor, tiny, crowded living room. He talks, waves his arms, and punctuates his words with decisive gestures. In his eyes, there is an irrefutable conviction. "Is the party going to refuse to enter into history, refuse to make history?" he berates Blacquer.

"Everything about this incident turned out to be contradictory," I hear Blacquer say half a block later. "Because the very RWP(T) that expelled Mayta for wanting to involve them in Jauja threw itself into something even more sterile: the 'expropriation' of banks."

Was it Fidel Castro's entrance into Havana, which had taken place in the meantime, that transformed the prudent RWP(T), which had slid out of Mayta's conspiracy, into a bellicose organization that set about emptying the banks of the bourgeoisie? They attacked the branch of the Banco Internacional that we've just passed—Joaquín was captured in the operation—and then, a few days later, the Banco Wiese in La Victoria, where Pallardi fell. These two actions disintegrated the RWP(T). Or was there, as well, a modicum of guilty conscience, a desire to prove that, even though they'd turned their backs on Mayta and Vallejos, they were capable of risking all on a single toss of the dice?

"Not remorse, not anything even like it," says Blacquer. "It was Cuba. The Cuban Revolution broke through the taboos. It killed that superego that ordered us to accept the dictum that 'conditions aren't right,' that the revolution was an interminable conspiracy. With Fidel's entrance into Havana, the revolution seemed to put itself within reach of anyone who would dare fight."

"If you don't take them, the guy who owns my house will sell them all off in La Parada," Mayta insisted. "You can pick them up after Monday. And there aren't that many, anyway."

"Okay, I'll take the books." Blacquer gave in. "Let's say I'll store them for you for the time being."

At the 28 de Julio stop, we find the same mob we found at the earlier stops. A man wearing a hat has a portable radio, and—nervously watched by all those around him—he's trying to find some station broadcasting news. He can't find one. All he gets is music. For almost half an hour, I wait with Blacquer. Two buses pass by, packed to the roof, without stopping. Finally I say goodbye, because I want to get home in time to hear the message of the committee about the invasion. At the corner of Manco Cápac, I turn around: Blacquer is still there; I can make out his ruinous face and his air of being lost as he stands at the edge of the sidewalk, as if he didn't know what to do or where to go. That's the way Mayta must have been that day after the meeting. And yet Blacquer assures me that after leaving him his books and showing him where to hide the key to his room, Mayta left exuding optimism. "He grew under punishment" is what he said. No doubt about it: his resistance and his daring became stronger in adversity.

Although all the stores are closed, the sidewalks in this part of Larco are still crowded with people selling handicrafts, trinkets, and pictures: views of the Andes, portraits, and caricatures. I thread my way around blankets covered with bracelets and necklaces, watched over by boys with ponytails and girls wearing saris. The air is filled with incense. In this enclave of aesthetes and street mystics, there is no perceptible alarm, not even any curiosity about what's going on down south. You'd say that they don't even know that in the last few hours the war has taken a much more serious turn and that at any minute it could be right here on top of them. At the corner of Ocharán, I hear a dog

171

bark: it's a strange sound that seems to come from the past, because ever since the food shortage began, domestic animals have disappeared from the streets. How did Mayta feel that morning? The long night had begun in the garage on Jirón Zorritos with his expulsion from the RWP(T), then moved on to his agreement to disguise it as a resignation, and ended with that conversation with Blacquer, which transformed him from an enemy into a confidant, a shoulder to cry on.

Sleepy, hungry, and exhausted, but in the same frame of mind he was in when he returned from Jauja, and still convinced that he had acted properly. They hadn't thrown him out because he'd gone to see Blacquer: they'd agreed on the pullout before. Their feigned anger, the accusations of betrayal were just a trick to preclude any possibility of reviewing the decision. Was it out of fear of fighting? No, it was their pessimism, their lack of willpower, their psychological inability to break with routine and go on to real action. He had taken a bus and had to stand, hanging on to the rail, crushed between two black women carrying baskets. Didn't he know that way of thinking all too well? "Wasn't it your own for so many years?" They had no faith in the masses because they had no contact with them; they doubted the revolution and their own ideas because the intriguing that went on among sects had rendered them incapable of action.

Looking at him, one of the black women began to laugh, and Mayta realized he was talking to himself. He laughed, too. But if that's the way they thought, then it was better that they didn't take part, because they'd just be dead weight. Yes, they would be missed, because now there would be no urban support in Lima. But as new adherants emerged, a support organization would spring up here and elsewhere. The comrades of the RWP(T), when they saw that the vanguard was respected and that the masses were joining them, would regret their indecision. The Stalinists, too. The meeting with Blacquer was a time bomb. When they saw that the trickle was turning into a raging torrent, they would remember that the door was open and that

they would be welcome. They would come; they would participate. He was so distracted that he forgot to get off at his corner
and only realized he'd passed it two stops later.

He reached the alley completely worn out. In the patio,
there was a long line of women with pots, all shouting because
the first one was taking too long at the tap. He went into his
room and stretched out on the bed, without even taking off his
shoes. He just didn't have the energy to go down and get in
line. But how good it would have been now to sink his tired
feet in a pan of cool water. He closed his eyes and, fighting
sleep, chose the words for the letter he was to bring that afternoon to Jacinto so it could come out in the issue of *Workers
Voice (T)* that was at the press.

That issue barely covers four pages, a single sheet folded in
four, now so yellow that as I pick it up—sitting in front of the
television, where the generals of the Junta have yet to appear,
even though it's eight o'clock—I get the feeling it's going to
crumble in my hands. The resignation is not on the first page,
which consists of two long articles and a smaller one, boxed, at
the bottom. The editorial, set in small caps, takes up the left
column: "Halt, Fascists!" It concerns some incidents that took
place in the central mountains regarding a strike over two
mining contracts with the Cerro de Pasco Copper Corporation.
When the police removed the strikers, they shot a few of them,
one of whom later died. This is not random violence but is,
instead, part of a plan to intimidate and immobilize the working
classes, a plan hatched by the police, the army, and reactionary
groups, in accord with Pentagon and CIA Latin American
policy. What's it all about?

They've started playing military music, and pictures of the
national emblem and the flag are followed by busts and portraits
of national heroes. Are they going to start or what? To halt
the advance, every day more powerful and unstoppable, of the
workers toward socialism. Those methods cannot surprise anyone who has learned the lessons of history: they were used by

Mussolini in Italy, Hitler in Germany, and now Washington is applying them to Latin America. But they will not succeed, they will be counterproductive, a nutrient fertilizer, as Leon Trotsky wrote: For the working classes, the blows of repression are like pruning for plants. There they are: the Navy, the Air Force, the Army, and behind them, the advisers, the ministers, the heads of garrisons and military units in the Lima region. Their somber faces seem to confirm the worst rumors. The editorial in *Workers Voice (T)* ends with an exhortation to workers, peasants, students, and progressives to close ranks against the Nazi-Facist conspiracy. They're singing the National Anthem.

The other article is about Ceylon. It's true, at that time Trotskyism had taken hold there. The text asserts that Trotskyism is the second most powerful force in the Parliament and the most powerful among the unions. From the way the tenses go, it would seem the article was translated from the French—by Mayta himself, perhaps? The names, beginning with that of Madame Bandaranaike, the Prime Minister, are difficult to remember.

Okay, the National Anthem is over, and the representative of the army, the usual spokesman for the Junta, steps forward. In an unusual move, he skips the pompous patriotic rhetoric he normally uses, and instead gets right to the heart of the matter. His voice has less of a military ring and is more tremulous. Three military columns, made up of Cubans and Bolivians, have penetrated deep into our territory, supported by planes which, beginning last night, have been bombing civilian targets in Puno, Cuzco, and Arequipa. An open violation of all international laws and agreements. There are many casualties, and considerable property damage. In the very heart of the city of Puno, bombs have destroyed part of the Social Security Hospital, causing an as yet undetermined number of deaths. The description of the disasters takes him several minutes. Will he tell us if the Marines have crossed the Ecuadorian border?

The small box at the bottom of the page announces that

174

shortly the RWP(T) will present at the union hall of the Civil Construction Union its previously postponed program on "The Betrayed Revolution: A Trotskyist Interpretation of the Soviet Union." To find Mayta's resignation, you have to turn the page. It's in a corner, below an extensive article entitled "Let's Set Up Soviets in the Barracks!" With no heading or frame: "Resigns from the RWP(T)." The spokesman now assures us that the Peruvian troops, despite the fact that they are fighting against superior numbers and greater logistical support, are heroically resisting the criminal invasion of international communist terrorism, and have the decided support of the civilian populace. The committee, invoking martial law, has this afternoon activated three new divisions of reservists. Will he tell us if U.S. planes are bombing the invaders?

Comrade Secretary General of the RWP(T)
Lima

Comrade:

I take this opportunity to communicate to you my irrevocable decision to resign from the ranks of the Revolutionary Workers' Party (Trotskyist), in which I have been a militant for more than ten years. I have taken this decision for personal reasons. I wish to be independent again and to act under my own responsibility, so that anything I might say or do will not compromise the party in any way. I need my freedom of action in these moments in which our country is foundering once again in the struggle between revolution and reaction.

My voluntary withdrawal from the RWP(T) does not mean that I am breaking with the ideals that have marked the path of revolutionary socialism for the workers of the world. I would like, comrade, to reaffirm once again my faith in the Peruvian proletariat, my conviction that the revolution will become a reality that will once and for all break the chains of exploitation and obscurantism which have weighed so heavily on our people for centuries. The process of liberation will be carried out in the light of that theory—more solid and stronger than ever before—

conceived by Marx and Engels and implemented by Lenin and Trotsky.

I request that my resignation be published in *Workers Voice (T)* so that the public will be informed.

Long live the Revolution!
A. Mayta Avendaño

He's only said it at the end, very quickly, with less firmness, as if he wasn't very sure. In the name of the Peruvian people, who are gloriously fighting in defense of Western civilization and Christianity in the free world, against the onslaught of collectivist and totalitarian atheism, the Junta has requested and obtained from the government of the United States of America support troops and logistical supplies to repel the communist Russo–Cuban–Bolivian invasion that seeks to enslave our homeland. So this is true as well. Here we go. The war is no longer a Peruvian affair. Peru is just one more theater for the war the Great Powers are waging, directly and through satellites or allies. Whoever wins, the fact is that hundreds of thousands, maybe millions, will die. If Peru survives, it will be prostrate. I was so sleepy I didn't feel I had enough energy even to turn off the TV.

His anxiety was justified when he turned around: Anatolio was pointing a pistol at him. He wasn't afraid, just sorry: the delay it would cause! And what about Vallejos? The plan had to be carried out step by step with absolute precision, and it was clear that Anatolio wasn't there to kill him but to keep him from getting to Jauja. He strode firmly toward the boy to try to convince him to be reasonable, but Anatolio stretched out his arm energetically and Mayta saw that he was going to squeeze the trigger. He raised his hands over his head, thinking: To die without even having fought. He felt a lacerating sadness; he'd never be with them, there on Calvary when the Epiphany began. "Why are you doing this, Anatolio?" His own voice disgusted him: a real revolutionary is logical and cold, not sentimental. "Because you're a faggot," said Anatolio in a calm, leaden, forceful, irreversible tone, one Mayta wished he could use just now. "Because you're a queer and you've got to pay the price," confirmed the secretary general, his jaundiced face and pointy ears jutting forward. "Because you're a faggot and disgusting," added Comrade Moisés/Medardo, sticking his profile over Comrade Jacinto's shoulder. The whole Central Committee of the RWP(T) was there, one behind the other, all armed with pistols. He had been judged, sentenced, and they were now going to execute him. Not for indiscipline, errors, or betrayal, but—how petty, how asinine—for having slid his tongue, like a stiletto, between Anatolio's teeth. He lost all composure and began to cry out for Vallejos, Ubilluz, Lorito, the peasants from Ricrán, the joeboys: "Get me out of this trap, comrades." With his back soaking wet, he woke up. From the edge of the bed, Anatolio was looking at him.

"I couldn't make out what you were saying," he heard him whisper.

"What are you doing here?" Mayta stuttered, still partly in his nightmare.

"I just came by," said Anatolio. He was looking at him without blinking, with an intriguing little light in his eyes. "Are you mad at me?"

"The truth is that you're hard to figure," Mayta said softly, without moving. He had a bitter taste in his mouth, his eyes were bleary, and he still had goose bumps from the scare he'd had. "The truth is, you're a cynic, Anatolio."

"You taught me everything," said the boy gently, always looking him in the eye with an undefinable expression that irritated Mayta and made him remorseful. A horsefly began to buzz around the light bulb.

"I taught you to screw like a man, not to be a hypocrite," said Mayta, making an effort to control his rage: Calm down, don't insult him, don't hit him, don't argue. Just get him out of here.

"The Jauja idea is crazy. We talked it over, and we all agreed that you had to be stopped," said Anatolio without moving,

177

with a certain vehemence. "No one was going to kick you out. Why did you go to Blacquer? No one would have expelled you."

"I'm not going to argue with you," said Mayta. "This is all ancient history. Why don't you just leave."

But the boy didn't move a muscle and didn't stop looking at him with that look that had both provocation and scorn.

"We aren't comrades or friends anymore," said Mayta. "What the fuck do you want?"

"I want you to give me a blowjob," said the boy slowly, looking him in the eye and touching his knee with his five fingers.

Seven

"What are you doing here, Mayta?" exclaimed Adelaida. "What do you want?"

Rospigliosi Castle marks the border between Lince and Santa Beatriz, neighborhoods that have become indistinguishable. But when Mayta and Adelaida were married, there was a class struggle going on between them. Lince was always modest, lower-middle-class tending toward proletarian, with narrow, colorless little houses, tenements and their alleys, cracked sidewalks and rocky little gardens. Santa Beatriz, on the other hand, was a pretentious neighborhood where a few well-off families built mansions in "colonial," "Sevilian," or "neo-Gothic" style—like this monument to extravagance, the Rospigliosi Castle, a castle with battlements and pointed arches made of reinforced concrete. The inhabitants of Lince viewed their neighbors in Santa Beatriz with resentment and envy, while the good citizens of Santa Beatriz looked down their noses at the Linceans and scorned them.

"I'd just like a word with you," said Mayta. "And, if you don't mind, I'd like to see my son."

Nowadays Santa Beatriz and Lince are the same: one decayed and the other improved, until they finally met at a median point. It's a shapeless region, inhabited by white-collar workers, business and professional people neither rich nor impoverished, but hard pressed to get to the end of the month without money problems. This mediocrity is personified perfectly by Adelaida's husband, don Juan Zárate, an employee of the Mail and Telegraph Service with many years' service. His photo is next to the curtainless window. Looking through that window, I can see the Rospigliosi Castle. Since the building is used by the Air Ministry, it is surrounded by coils of barbed wire and sandbag walls, behind which I can see the guards' helmets and rifle barrels. One of those patrols stopped me as I was on my way over here and frisked me from head to toe before letting me pass. The air-force men are on edge, their fingers wrapped around their triggers. Justifiably so, given the situation we're in. In the photo, don Juan Zárate wears a suit and a tie and looks serious. Adelaida, clinging to his arm, also looks stern.

"That's when we got married, over in Cañete. We spent three days there, in a house that belonged to one of Juan's brothers. I was seven months' pregnant. Barely shows, right?"

She is right. No one could ever guess she was so far advanced in her pregnancy. The photograph must be almost thirty years old. It's unbelievable how well preserved this woman, who for a short time was the wife of my schoolmate from the Salesian School, is.

"It was Mayta's child," Adelaida adds.

I pay close attention to what she says and observe her carefully. I still can't get over the impression her looks made on me when I walked into that lugubrious little house. I'd only spoken with her over the telephone and I never thought that harsh voice could be connected to a woman who was still attractive despite her age. Her hair is gray and falls in waves to her shoulders. Her face has soft features, with prominent, fleshy lips, and deep eyes.

180

She crosses her legs: smooth, well-rounded, long, solid. When she was married to Mayta, she must have been a knockout.

"A fine time to be remembering your son," Adelaida exclaimed.

"I always remember him," Mayta replied. "It's one thing not to see him and another not to think of him. We made a deal, and I've stuck by it."

But there's something desolate about her, a depression, an air of defeat. And an absolute indifference: it doesn't seem to matter to her that the rebels have taken Cuzco and established a government there, that there were undecipherable shots last night in the streets of Lima, not even whether or not it's true that hundreds of Marines have just reached the La Joya base in Arequipa to reinforce the army, which seems to have collapsed all along the southern front. She doesn't even mention the events that have all of Lima in suspense and that—despite the genuine triumph it is for me to be speaking with her—distract me with recurring images of red flags, rifle shots, and shouts of victory on the streets of Cuzco.

"This is how you stick by it—coming to my house?" said Adelaida, pushing back a curl that had fallen over her forehead. "Do you have any idea the mess you'd be making if my husband finds out?"

As I listen to her tell how her wedding to Juan Zárate was moved forward so that Mayta's child could be born with another name and another father, in a real home, I remind myself that I am wrong to be distracted: I haven't got much more time. Being here is my reward for being persistent. Adelaida refused to see me several times, and the third or fourth time I called, she just hung up on me. I had to insist, beg, swear that neither her name nor Juan Zárate's nor her son's would ever appear in what I wrote. Finally, I had to suggest to her that since this was business —I wanted her to tell me about her life with Mayta and that final meeting just hours before he went to Jauja—I would pay for her time. She's granted me an hour of conversation for a stiff price. She will not discuss anything she considers "too private."

"It's something special," insisted Mayta. "I'll be gone in a minute, you'll see, I swear."

"I thought he was on the run and had no place to go," Adelaida says. "The usual thing. Because, from when I first met him until we separated, he always felt he was being watched. Rightly and wrongly. And full of secrets, even from me."

Did she ever love him? She couldn't have any other reason for living with him. How did she meet him? At a fair, by the wheel of fortune at Plaza Sucre. She bet on number 17 and someone next to her bet on 15. The wheel stopped right on 15. "What luck! The little bear," exclaimed Adelaida. Her neighbor: "It's yours. Will you accept it as a gift? How do you do? My name's Mayta."

"Okay, okay, I'd rather the gossip who lives across the hall not see us together here." Adelaida finally opened the door to him. "Five minutes and that's it, please. If Juan finds you here, he'll be really mad. You've already given me enough headaches for one lifetime."

Didn't she suspect from his nervousness and his fidgeting that this unusual visit had been prompted by the fact that he was on the verge of doing something extraordinary? Not in the slightest. Because, in fact, she didn't see any sign of nerves or excitement in him. He was his normal self: calm, badly dressed, a little thinner. When they'd got to know each other better, Mayta confessed that the meeting at the wheel of fortune in Plaza Sucre was not accidental: he had seen her, followed her, and hung around, looking for a way to strike up a conversation.

"He convinced me that he'd fallen in love with me at first sight," Adelaida adds in a sarcastic tone. Every time she mentions his name, she becomes bitter. Despite the fact that it all happened a long time ago, there's an open wound somewhere inside her. "A total fraud, and I fell for it like the sucker I am. He was never in love with me. And he was so self-centered he never even realized how much he hurt me."

Mayta took a look around: a sea of red flags, a sea of fists held high, a sea of rifles, and ten thousand throats hoarse from shouting. Being here in Adelaida's house seemed incomprehensible to him, in the same way that it seemed incomprehensible that any son of his, even if he had someone else's name, could live with these armchairs covered with clear plastic, surrounded by these walls and their cracked paint. Was I right to come? Wasn't this visit merely a meaningless, gratuitous, sentimental gesture? Wouldn't Adelaida figure something strange was going on? Was that song they were singing "The International" in Quechua?

"I'm going away and I don't know when I'll be back to Peru," Mayta explained to her, sitting on the arm of the nearest chair. "I didn't want to leave without meeting him. Would it bother you if I saw him for a minute?"

"It sure would bother me," Adelaida cut him off brusquely. "He doesn't have your name, and Juan is the only father he knows. Don't you know what it cost me to get him a normal home and a real father? You're not going to ruin it on me now."

"I don't want to ruin anything," Mayta said. "I've always respected our deal. I just wanted to meet him. I won't tell him who I am, and if that's the way you want it, I won't even talk to him."

He said nothing about his real activities when they first began seeing each other, only that he worked as a journalist. You couldn't say he was good-looking, with that gait of his, as if he were walking on eggs, and with those spaces between his teeth. He didn't even have a good job, judging by his clothes. But in spite of all that, you liked something about him. What was there about this revolutionary that appealed to the cute employee of the Banco de Crédito over in Lince? The airmen guarding Rospigliosi Castle are uptight. They stop every passerby and ask to see his papers. Then they frisk him in hysterical detail. Has something else happened? Do they know something that hasn't been announced yet over the radio? A young girl carrying baskets who stubbornly refused to be frisked has just been hit with a rifle butt.

"When I was with him, I felt I was learning things," Adelaida says. "Not that he was so well-educated. It was that he talked about things the other guys I went out with never mentioned. Since I didn't understand anything, I was like a mouse hypnotized by a cat."

She was also impressed by the fact that he respected her, that he was so relaxed, so sure of himself. He said beautiful things to her. Why didn't he kiss her? One day, he brought her to meet an aunt of his over in Surquillo, the only relative of Mayta's she would ever meet. Aunt Josefa prepared them a lunch, complete with little cakes, and was affectionate toward Adelaida. They were chatting away when suddenly doña Josefa had to step out. They stayed in the living room listening to the radio, and Adelaida thought: Now is the moment. Mayta was right next to her on the sofa, and she waited. But he didn't even try to hold her hand, and she said to herself: He must really be in love with me. The girl with the baskets has finally resigned herself to being frisked. Then they let her go. As she passes opposite the window, I see her lips moving as she insults them.

"I'm begging you, don't ask to talk to him," Adelaida said. "Besides, he's in school. Why would you want to meet him, what for? If he put two and two together, it would be awful."

"Just by seeing my face he's miraculously going to discover I'm his father?" Mayta mocks.

"It frightens me, like tempting fate," Adelaida stuttered.

In fact, her voice and face were consumed with worry. It was useless to make any more demands. Wasn't this flash of sentimentality, this desire to see the son he rarely remembered, a bad symptom? He was wasting precious moments; it was foolish to have come. If Juan Zárate found him, there would be a scene, and any scandal, no matter how small, would have negative repercussions for the plan. Get up, say goodbye. But he was glued to the armchair.

"Juan was postmaster here in Lince," Adelaida says. "He would come to see me when I went to work at the bank and again when I got off. He followed me, he asked me out, he asked me to marry him once a week. He put up with my rejections and never gave up."

"Did he offer to give his name to the child?"

"That was the condition I set for our getting married." I glance at the photo taken in Cañete, and now I understand why the beautiful employee would marry this ugly, older bureaucrat. Mayta's son must be thirty years old. Did he have the normal life his mother wanted for him? What can he think about the current situation? Is he supporting the rebels and internationalists, or is he backing the army and the Marines? Or, like his mother, does he believe that either alternative is pure garbage? "Even though he hadn't kissed me by our fifth or sixth date, he gave me a big surprise."

"What would you say if I were to propose to you?"

"Let's wait until that day and you'll find out," she said, playing the coquette.

"I'm proposing, then," said Mayta. "Would you marry me, Adelaida?"

"He hadn't even kissed me," she repeats, nodding. "And he proposed just like that. I cooked my own goose in all of this, so I can't blame anyone else."

"Proof that you were in love."

"It isn't that I was dying to get married," she asserts. Once again, she makes the gesture I've seen several times: she throws her hair back off her face. "I was young, quite good-looking, and lots of guys were interested in me. Juan Zárate wasn't the only one. And I said yes to the one who was as poor as a church mouse, the revolutionary, the one who had other problems, too. Wasn't I a jerk?"

"Okay, I won't see him," Mayta says softly. But he still didn't get off the arm of the chair. "Tell me something about him, at least. And about yourself. Has married life been good for you?"

"Better than my life with you," said Adelaida, in a resigned, even melancholic tone. "I live quietly, without worrying whether the cops might barge in day or night, break the place

185

up, and arrest my husband. With Juan, I know that we'll be eating every day and that we won't be evicted for not paying the rent."

"To judge by the way you say it, you don't seem so happy," said Mayta. Wasn't this conversation, at this precise moment, absurd? Shouldn't he be buying medicines, picking up his money down at France-Presse, packing his bag?

"No, I'm not," said Adelaida, who displayed more hospitality since Mayta had agreed not to see the boy. "Juan made me quit working at the bank. If I were still working, we'd be living better, and I'd see people, know what's going on. Here in the house, I spend my time sweeping, washing, and cooking. Not exactly the kind of life to make you happy."

"No, it isn't," said Mayta, looking around the living room. "And yet, compared to millions of people, Adelaida, you're living very well."

"Are you starting in with politics now?" She gets riled up. "In that case, get out. It's your fault that I've come to hate politics above everything."

They were married three weeks later in a civil ceremony in the Lince town hall. Then she began to know the real Mayta. Under that clear blue sky, and over the roofs of red tiles in Cuzco, wave hundreds, thousands of red flags, and the old façades of its churches and palaces and the ancient stones of its streets are red with the blood of the recent fighting. At the beginning, she didn't understand all that stuff about the RWP. She knew that in Peru there was one party, the APRA, which General Ordía had outlawed and which Prado had made legal again when he took office. But a party called the RWP? Screaming demonstrations, shots fired in the air, and frenetic speeches proclaim the beginning of another era, the advent of the new man. Have the executions of traitors, informers, torturers, and collaborators with the old regime begun in the beautiful Plaza de Armas, where the viceregal authorities had Túpac Amaru drawn and quartered? Mayta gave her a partial explanation: the Revolutionary Workers' Party was still small.

"I didn't think it was important, because it seemed like a game to me," she says, pushing back a falling lock of hair. "But before a month was out, one night when I was alone I heard knocking at the door. It was two investigators. Under the pretext of carrying on a search, they cleaned the place out—they even took away a bag of rice I had in the kitchen. That's how the nightmare began."

She barely ever saw her husband, never knowing if he was at meetings, at the print shop, or in hiding. Mayta's life was not France-Presse, because he only got an hourly and extremely low wage from them. They couldn't have survived if she hadn't gone on working at the bank. She quickly realized that the only thing important to Mayta was politics. There were times when he'd come home with those guys and argue until all hours of the morning. "So the RWP is communist?" she asked him. "We're the real communists," he answered. Who is this man you've married? she began to ask herself.

"I thought Juan Zárate loved you and turned himself inside out to make you happy."

"He loved me before you turned up," she said. "And he must have loved me when he agreed to give his name to your son. But once he went through with it, he began to resent me."

Did he mistreat her? No, he treated her well enough, but always made her feel that it was he who had been the generous one. With the kid, on the other hand, he was good, he took charge of his education. What are you doing here, Mayta? Wasting your last hours in Lima talking about all this? But some kind of inertia kept him from leaving. That they were talking about conjugal problems in that final conversation, when Mayta was already halfway to Jauja, disappoints me. I was hoping to find something spectacular, something dramatic in that last conversation, something that would throw a conflicting light on what Mayta was feeling and dreaming on the eve of the uprising. But, to judge by what I'm hearing, I see that you two spoke more about you than about him. Sorry for interrupting, let's go on. So his political activities brought you suffering?

"I suffered more because he was queer," she replies. She blushes and goes on, "More because I found out he'd married me to cover up what he was."

Finally, a dramatic revelation. And yet my attention is still split between Adelaida and the flags, the blood, the shootings, and the euphoria of the insurgents and internationalists in Cuzco. Is that how Lima will be in a few weeks? On the bus I took to Lince, the driver assured me that the army, starting last night, had begun publicly shooting presumed terrorists in Villa el Salvador, Comas, Ciudad del Niño, and other new towns. Will we see the same lynchings and murders in Lima that were perpetrated in Lima when the Chileans occupied the city during the War of the Pacific in 1881?

I can hear, quite clearly, the lecture a historian gave in London, based on the account of the British consul in Lima. While the Peruvian volunteers sacrificed themselves to hold the line against the Chilean attack in Chorrillos and Miraflores, the Lima mob murdered the Chinese in their shops, hanging them, stabbing them, and burning them in the street after accusing them of being accomplices of the Chileans. Then they went on to loot the houses of the rich, terrified ladies and gentlemen who were praying the invaders would get there quickly. They discovered that they were less afraid of the Chileans than of those frenzied masses of Indians, *cholos*, mulattoes, and blacks who had taken over the city. Would something like that happen now? Would the hungry masses loot the houses of San Isidro, Las Casuarinas, Miraflores, Chacarilla, as the last vestiges of the army melted away before the final rebel offensive? Would there be a stampede toward embassies and consulates, while generals, admirals, functionaries, and ministers boarded planes and ships with all the jewels, dollars, and deeds they could dig out of their hiding places at the last minute? Would Lima burn, the way the city of Cuatro Suyos is burning now?

"It would seem you haven't forgiven him for that," I say to her.

"Whenever I remember, my blood freezes in my veins," Adelaida admits.

That time? That night—rather, that dawn. She heard the car's brakes, a skid out in front of the house. And since she lived in fear of the police, she jumped out of bed to take a look. Through the window, she saw the car. In the bluish light of dawn, she could see Mayta's faceless silhouette get out of the car on one side. On the other side, she could make out the driver. She was going back to bed, when something—something strange, unusual, difficult to explain, to define—upset her. She pressed her face to the window. Because the other man had made a gesture as if to say goodbye to Mayta, a movement it didn't seem right to make to her husband. The kind of obscene gesture you'd see jokers, drunks, and playboys make. But Mayta was never playful or familiar. So? The guy, as if he were saying goodbye, had grabbed his fly. His fly. He still held on to it, and Mayta, instead of slapping his hand away—Let go, you stinking drunk!—nuzzled up to him. He was hugging him. They were kissing. On the face, on the mouth. "It's a woman," she wished, hoped, begged heaven it would be, all the time feeling her hands and knees shaking. A woman wearing trousers and a jacket? The foggy glow kept her from seeing clearly who was kissing and rubbing her husband down there on that deserted street, but there could be no doubt—because of his size, his build, his head, his hair—it was a man. She felt the desire to run out, half dressed as she was, and shout at them: "Queers, queers!" But a few seconds later, when the two separated and Mayta walked toward the house, she pretended to be asleep. In the darkness, mortified with shame, she glimpsed him coming in. She hoped that he would be so drunk that anyone who saw them would say, "He didn't know what he was doing or with whom." But of course he hadn't even had a single drink. Did he ever drink? She saw him undress in the darkness, except for the underpants he slept in, and slip into bed with her, carefully, so as not to wake her up. Then Adelaida began to throw up.

"I don't know how long," Mayta replied, as if the question had taken him by surprise. "It'll all depend on how I do. I want to change my life-style. I don't even know if I'll come back to Peru."

"Are you going to give up politics?" a surprised Adelaida asked him.

"In a way," he said. "I'm going because of something you always used to get on me about. I've finally proven you right."

"A little late, don't you think?" she said.

"Better late than never." Mayta smiled. He was thirsty, as if he had eaten fish. Why not just leave?

Adelaida had that expression of disgust on her face that he remembered so well, and the crowd didn't even manage to understand until—noisy and cataclysmic—the first bombs exploded. Roofs, walls, the bell towers of Cuzco all began to collapse. Debris of all sorts—stones, roof tiles, bricks—flew all over. Then they started to machine-gun the people who were running. In their panic, the crowd created as many casualties as the bursts of fire from the strafing planes. In the confusion of moans, bullets, and screams, those with rifles fired at the sky dirty with smoke.

"You were the only person Mayta said goodbye to," I assure her. "He didn't even visit his Aunt Josefa. Doesn't his visit, when you think about it after so many years, seem strange to you?"

"He told me he was leaving the country and that he wanted to find out how his son was doing," Adelaida says. "Naturally, I understood everything later, when it was in the papers."

Outside, there is a sudden flare-up of activity at the entrance to the Rospigliosi Castle, as if, behind the barbed wire and the sandbags, they were redoubling their guard. Out there, not even the horror of the bombing has brought the looting under control. Frenzied bands of escaped convicts are breaking into the downtown stores. The rebel commanders are ordering anyone found looting to be shot where he stands. The buzzards are tracing circles over the bodies of those shot, who are soon indis-

190

tinguishable from the victims of the bombing. It all smells of gunpowder, rotten flesh, burning.

"Take advantage of things, so you can be cured," whispers Adelaida, so low that I barely heard her. But her words have the same effect on me as a slap in the face.

"I'm not sick," Mayta stuttered. "Tell me about the kid before I go."

"You *are* sick," Adelaida insisted, trying to look him in the eye. "Are you cured, maybe?"

"It isn't a sickness, Adelaida," I stammered. I could feel that my palms were sweaty, and I was even thirstier.

"In your case, it is," she said, and Matya thought something had reawakened all her resentment of before. It was his fault: What were you doing there, why didn't you leave? "In others, it's degenerate, but that kind of vice has nothing to do with you. I know all about it, I talked to that doctor about it. He said it could be cured, and you didn't want to try shock treatments. I offered to get a loan from the bank for the therapy, but you said no, no, no. Now that it's all over, tell me the truth. Why didn't you want to go through with it? Were you scared?"

"Shock treatment is useless for these things," I said, muttering. "Let's not talk about it. Could I please have a glass of water?"

Wasn't it possible that marrying you was his "therapy," ma'am? Couldn't he have married her, thinking that living with a young, attractive woman would "cure" him?

"That's what he wanted me to believe, when we finally got around to talking," Adelaida says softly, pushing back her hair. "A lie, of course. If he had wanted to be cured, he would have tried. He married me to cover up. Above all, in front of his revolutionary buddies. I was the screen for his filthy activities."

"If you don't want to, you don't have to answer this question. Did you two have a normal sex life?"

She doesn't seem to be uncomfortable. Because there are so many dead and it's impossible to bury them, the rebel commanders order them doused with anything flammable and burned. The rotting bodies scattered through the city must not be the cause of infection. The air is so thick and polluted that you can scarcely breathe. Adelaida uncrosses her legs, makes herself comfortable, and scrutinizes me. Otherwise, there is a clamor. An armored car has taken up a position in front of the barbed wire. There are more guards. Things must have gotten worse. It looks as if they're getting ready for something.

As if she had read my mind, Adelaida says softly, "If they are attacked, we'll be the first to be fired on." The crackling of the bonfires of corpses doesn't silence the irrepressible, maddened voices of the relatives and friends who try to stop the burning, who demand Christian burial for the victims. Swathed in smoke, stench, fear, and despair, some try to wrench the bodies away from the revolutionaries. From a monastery, church, or convent there comes a funeral procession. It advances, ghostlike, the people chanting prayers and imprecations amid the dying and the ruin that is Cuzco.

"I had no idea what normal or abnormal relations were," she says, pushing back her hair in her ritual gesture. "I couldn't make any comparisons. In those days, you didn't discuss those things with your girlfriends. So I thought they were normal."

But they weren't. They lived together and from time to time they made love. Which meant that on certain nights they hugged and kissed, finished rapidly, and went to sleep. Something superficial, routine, hygienic, something that—as she realized later—was incomplete, far short of her needs and desires. It isn't that she didn't like Mayta's politeness—he always turned out the light beforehand. But she had the feeling that he was in a hurry, on edge, thinking about something else even as he caressed her. Was his mind somewhere else? Yes, as he asked himself at what moment this desire that had aroused his body by means of fantasies and memories would begin to fade, to sink, to plunge him into that well of anguish from which he would try to extricate himself by stammering stupid explanations that Adelaida, luckily, seemed to believe. His thoughts were on other nights or dawns, when his desire did not fade and even seemed to get sharper if his hands and mouth were kept busy, not with

192

Adelaida, but with one of those little fags that, after great hesitation, he dared to seek out in Porvenir or Callao. In fact, they made love only a few times, and at first Adelaida didn't know how to ask him not to finish so quickly. Later, when she was surer of herself, she did ask him. She begged him, implored him not to withdraw from her, exhausted, exactly when she had begun to feel a stirring, a vertigo. Most often, she didn't even feel that, because Mayta would suddenly seem to be sorry for what he was doing. And she was such a sucker that, until that night, she had tortured herself wondering: Is it my fault? Am I frigid? Can't I get him excited?

"May I have another glass of water?" Mayta said. "Then I'm on my way, Adelaida."

She got up, and when she returned to the small living room, she brought, with the water, a handful of photographs. She handed them over without saying a word. The newborn child, the child a few months old in diapers, in Juan Zárate's arms; at a birthday party, next to a cake with two candles; in short pants and in shoes, at attention, staring at the photographer. I examined them again and again, examining himself at the same time that he studied the features, the positions, the gestures, the clothes of his child, whom he had never seen and whom he would never see in the future. Would he remember these pictures tomorrow in Jauja? Would I remember them, would they go with me, would they give me courage on the march in the cold uplands, in the jungle, during attacks, while I wait in ambush? What did he feel as he looked at them? Would he feel, when he remembered them, that the struggle, the sacrifices, the murders were things he'd do for his sake? Right now, did he feel tenderness, remorse, anguish, love? No, just curiosity, and gratitude toward Adelaida for having shown him the photographs. Was this the reason that brought him to this house before he left for Jauja? Or, more than meeting his son, could it have been to find out if Adelaida was still resentful for that thing which doubtless was the agony of her existence?

"I don't know," says Adelaida. "If that's why he came, he

went away knowing that, despite the many years that had gone by, I hadn't forgiven him for ruining my life."

"But even though you knew, you stayed with him for quite a while. You even became pregnant."

"Inertia," she whispers. "Being pregnant gave me the strength to end the whole farce."

She had suspected it for weeks, because her period had never been so late. The day she received the positive test results, she began to cry with excitement. Almost immediately, however, she was overcome with the thought that someday her son or daughter would know what she knew. Over the previous weeks, they had had several arguments about shock treatments.

"It wasn't because I was afraid," he said in a low voice as he looked at her. "It was because I didn't want to be cured, Adelaida."

So, in that last conversation, you two spoke about the unmentionable. Yes, and even Mayta had been much more frank than he'd been when they were living together. The procession kept picking up people from the streets it passed along, horrifying, somnambulistic men and women, children and old people stunned because they saw sons, brothers, grandchildren with their bones splintered, crushed by falling rubble, and burned in the hygienic fires. This chanting and tearful serpent squeezing through the ruinous, narrow streets of Cuzco seemed to console and reconcile the survivors. Suddenly, in the area that had been the Plaza del Rey, fighters and their supporters waving rifles and red flags tried to raise the spirit of the people and to keep them from becoming demoralized by starting a demonstration. There was an avalanche of shouts, stones, shots, and a terrified howling.

"If I didn't know it was against your principles, I'd ask you to have an abortion," said Mayta, as if he had prepared the statement. "There are plenty of good reasons. The life I lead, that we lead. Is it possible to bring up a child in the midst of that kind of life? What I do requires total dedication. I just can't hang that around my neck. Anyway, if it isn't against your principles. If it is, we'll just have to do our best."

She didn't cry and they didn't even argue. "I don't know, let me see, I'll think about it." And at that moment she knew what she had to do, clearly and absolutely.

"So you lied to me." Adelaida smiled, with a little air of triumph. "When you told me that you were ashamed of yourself, that it made you feel like garbage, that it was the disgrace of your life. I'm happy to see that you finally admit it."

"It made and still makes me ashamed sometimes," said Mayta. My cheeks were burning, and my tongue felt coated, but I wasn't sorry to be talking about these things. "It's still the disgrace of my life."

"So then, why didn't you want to get better," Adelaida repeated.

"I want to be what I am," I muttered, "I'm a revolutionary and I have flat feet. I'm also a queer. I don't want to stop being one. It's difficult to explain it to you. In this society, there are rules and prejudices; whatever seems abnormal seems a crime or a sickness. All because society is rotten, full of stupid ideas. That's why we need a revolution, see?"

"And at the same time he told me himself that in the U.S.S.R. he would have been thrown into an insane asylum, and in China he would have been shot, because that's how they deal with queers," Adelaida tells me. "Is that why you want to start a revolution?"

Amid the dust of the collapsing buildings, the smoke from the fires, the prayers of the believers, the howls of the wounded, the despair of the unharmed, the sound of rifle shots echoed only a few seconds. Suddenly there came again the sound of screaming engines. Even before the people who had been throwing stones at each other, punching each other, and cursing each other could understand what was happening, bombs and machine-gun fire rained down on Cuzco.

"That's why I want to start *another* revolution," Mayta said, as he passed his tongue over his dry lips. He was dying of thirst but didn't dare ask for a third glass of water. "No half measures, but the true, the integral revolution. A revolution that will wipe out all injustice, a revolution that will guarantee that no one will have any reason to be afraid of being what he is."

"And you're going to bring about that revolution with your pals from the RWP?" Adelaida laughed.

"I'm going to have to bring it about all by myself." Mayta smiled at her. "I'm not in the RWP anymore. I resigned last night."

She woke up the next day, and the idea was in her head, perfected by a night's sleep. She caressed it, she turned it over, she spun it around as she got dressed, waited for the bus, and rattled toward the Banco de Crédito in Lince, and while she checked the balance in an account in her Lilliputian office. At eleven, she asked permission to go to the post office. Juan Zárate was still there, behind the four-paned windows. She managed to let him see her, and when he greeted her, she answered with a Technicolor smile. Juan Zárate, of course, took off his glasses, straightened his tie, and dashed out to shake her hand. The breakdown is total. The broken-up streets are strewn with more dead, more houses collapse, and those still standing are looted. Few of those who moan, weep, steal, die, or search for their dead seem to hear the orders given on every corner by the rebel patrols: "The order is to abandon the city, comrades. Abandon the city, abandon the city."

"I'm still shocked that I had the nerve," says Adelaida, looking at her honeymoon photo.

So that, during that last conversation, in this little living room, Mayta spoke to the woman who had been his wife about intimate, ideal things: the true, the integral revolution, the one that would abolish all injustices without inflicting new ones. So that, despite the last-minute reverses and setbacks, he felt, as Blacquer assured me, euphoric and even lyrical.

"If only our revolution would light the way for the others.

196

Yes, Adelaida. I hope our Peru sets the example for the rest of the world."

"It's better to be frank, and that's just how I'm going to talk to you—frankly." Adelaida couldn't believe her own self-confidence and daring. Even as she was saying these things, she was able to smile, strike a pose, and shake her hair in such a way that the head of the Lince post office looked at her in ecstasy. "You were wild about marrying me, isn't that right, Juan?"

"You said it, Adelaidita." Juan Zárate bent forward over the little table in the Petit Thouars coffee shop where they were having a soda. "Crazy about you, and even more than crazy."

"Look me in the eye, Juan, and answer me truthfully. Do you still like me as much as you did years ago?"

"More than ever." The head of the Lince post office swallowed hard. "You're even prettier now than then, Adelaidita."

"Well then, if you like, you may marry me." Her voice hadn't failed her, and it doesn't fail her now. "I don't want to cheat you, Juan. I'm not in love with you. But I'll try to love you, to comply with your wishes, I'll respect you, and I'll do whatever I can to be a good wife."

Juan Zárate stared at her, blinking. The soda in his hand began to tremble.

"Are you speaking seriously, Adelaidita?" he managed finally to blurt out.

"I certainly am." And even now she didn't hesitate. "I ask only one thing from you. That you give your name to the child I'm expecting."

"Give me another glass of water," said Mayta. "I just can't stop drinking, I don't know what's wrong with me."

"You've been making speeches," she said, getting up. She went on, from the kitchen: "You haven't changed a bit. You're even worse. Now you want to start a revolution not just for the poor but also for the queers. I swear you make me laugh, Mayta."

A revolution for the queers, too, I thought. Yes, for the poor queers, too. He wasn't the slightest bit angry about Adelaida's burst of laughter. Amid the smoke and pestilence, you could make out the columns of people fleeing from the destroyed city, tripping over the broken pavement, covering their mouths and noses. The dead, the badly wounded, the very old, and the very young remained among the ruins. And looters, who, defying asphyxiation, fire, and sporadic bombing, broke into the houses still standing, looking for money and food.

"And he accepted," I conclude. "Don Juan Zárate must have really loved you, ma'am."

"We had a church wedding while we waited for my divorce from Mayta to go through." Adelaida sighs, looking at the Cañete photograph. "It was two years before the divorce was official. Then we had a civil ceremony."

How did Mayta take this story? Without any surprise, certainly with relief. He had gone through the charade of telling her how very concerned he was that she should marry that way, with no feelings at all.

"Wasn't that what you did with me? But with one difference. You tricked me, and I told Juan everything."

"But your calculations were wrong," said Mayta. He had just finished the glass of water and was feeling bloated. "Don't you remember that I warned you? Right from the beginning, I warned you that . . ."

"No more speeches, please," Adelaida interrupted him.

She is silent, tapping her fingers on the arm of the chair, and I can see by the look on her face that she has estimated that the hour is up. But I look at my watch and there are fifteen minutes left. Just then, we hear shots: one isolated report, then two more, than a burst of fire. Adelaida and I jump to the window and look out. The guards have disappeared, no doubt crouching behind the barbed wire and sandbags. But on the left, seemingly unconcerned, a patrol of airmen advances toward Rospigliosi Castle. It's true that the shots sounded quite far away. Executions in the slums? Has the fighting on the outskirts of Lima begun?

"And did it really work out as you wished?" I take up the conversation again. She looks away from the window, at me. The expression of alarm on her face when she heard the shots has been replaced by the sour expression which seems to be habitual in her. "The business about the boy."

"It worked out until he discovered that Juan wasn't his father," she says. She remains there, with her lips parted, trembling, and her eyes, which stare fixedly at me, begin to shine.

"Well, that doesn't really have anything to do with the story, we don't have to talk about your son." I excuse myself. "Let's get back to Mayta."

"I'm not going to make another speech," he said, to calm her. He drank the last drop of water. What if being so thirsty is a sign of fever, Mayta? "I'm going to be frank with you, Adelaida. I wanted to find out about my son before I leave the country, but I wanted to find out how you were doing, too. I'm no better off for having found out. I hoped I'd find you happy, at peace. But all I see is resentment, toward me and everybody else."

"If it makes you feel any better, I resent you less than I resent myself. Because I made all my own trouble."

Far off, there are more shots. From the surrounding valleys, ridges, peaks, and plateaus, Cuzco is a cloud of smoke filled with groans.

"Juan didn't tell him. I did," she whispers, in a hesitant voice. "Juan will never forgive me. He always loved Johnny as if he were his own son."

And she tells me the old story that must gnaw at her day and night, a story that combines religion, jealousy, and grudge. From the beginning, Johnny favored his false father over his mother, was more attached to him than to her, perhaps because in some obscure way he sensed that it was Adelaida's fault that there was a huge lie in his life.

"Do you mean that your husband takes him to Mass every Sunday?" Mayta said, thinking aloud. My memory brought back to me a whirlwind of prayers, chants, communions, and childhood confessions, the collection of colorful holy pictures I stored in my notebook as if they were precious objects. "Well, at least in that, he has something in common with me. When I was his age, I went to Mass every day."

"Juan is a very devout Catholic," said Adelaida. "Catholic, Apostolic, Roman, a pious old lady, he says jokingly. But it's the absolute truth. And he wants Johnny to be that way, of course."

"Of course." Mayta nodded. But he was free-associating, thinking about the boys from the San José school in Jauja who had listened so attentively, almost hypnotized, to what he told them about Marxism and revolution. He saw them: they were printing the communiqués their leaders sent them, on mimeograph machines hidden under tarpaulins and boxes; they were distributing handbills outside factories, schools, markets, movie houses. He saw them multiplying like the loaves of bread in the Bible, every day recruiting scores of boys as poor and self-denying as themselves, coming and going along dangerous paths, along snowdrifts in the mountains, slipping through obstacles and army patrols, sliding at night over the roofs of public buildings and the tops of peaks to leave red flags with the hammer and sickle. And I saw them arrive, sweaty, joyful, and formidable at remote encampments with the medicine, information, clothing, and food the guerrillas would need. His son was one of them. They were very young, fourteen, fifteen, sixteen years old. Thanks to them, the guerrillas would surely be victorious.

The assault on heaven, I thought. We shall bring heaven down from heaven, establish it on earth; heaven and earth were becoming one in this twilight hour. The ashen clouds in the sky met the ashen clouds from the fires. And those little black spots that flew, innumerable, from all four points on the compass toward Cuzco—they weren't ashes but vultures. Spurred on by hunger, braving smoke and flames, they dove on toward their desirable prey. From the heights, the survivors, parents, wounded, the fighters, the internationalists, all of them, with a minimum of fantasy, could hear the anxious tearing, the febrile

200

pecking, the abject beating of wings, and smell the horrifying stench.

"And so . . . ?" I urge her to continue. Now we hear shots all the time, always far off, but neither of us looks out on the street again.

"And so the subject was never brought up in front of Johnny," she goes on. I listen to her and I try to get interested in her story, but I still see and smell the carnage.

It was a taboo subject, down at the very roots of their relationship, undermining it like slow acid. Juan Zárate loved the boy, but he had never forgiven her that agreement, the price she made him pay to marry her. The story took an unexpected turn the day Johnny—he'd finished secondary school and entered pharmacy school—discovered his father had a lover. Don Juan Zárate had a lover? Yes, and she had her own little house. The very idea would have made Adelaida roar with laughter—jealousy was out of the question: that old coot, dragging his feet, practically blind, with a lover. She was dying of laughter. A woman is jealous when she is in love, and she had never loved Juan Zárate. She had stoically put up with him. She was just annoyed that, with the pittance he earned, he supported two households . . .

"But my son, on the other hand, was devastated. It drove him crazy," she adds, in a hypnotic state. "He became embittered, shriveled up. That his father could have a sweetheart seemed like the end of the world to him. Was it because he's been raised so piously? In a child, I would have understood a reaction like that. But how can you figure it in a young man twenty years old?"

"He suffered for your sake," I tell her.

"It was religion," Adelaida insists. "Juan brought him up that way, four-square religious. He went crazy. He wouldn't accept that his father, who had taught him to be one hundred percent Catholic, could be a hypocrite. That's what he said, and he was already twenty."

She falls silent because the shots sound closer this time. I look

201

out the window. It can't be anything serious; the guards seem calm across the barbed wire. They are looking south, as if the shots come from San Isidro or Miraflores.

"Maybe he inherited it from Mayta," I say to her. "When he was a kid, that's how he was: an unwavering believer, convinced that you had to toe the line at every instant. He would make no compromises. Nothing bothered him more than someone who believed one thing and did something else. Didn't he tell you about the hunger strike he went on so he could be like the poor? People like that aren't usually happy in life, ma'am."

"When I saw him suffering so much, I thought I could help him by telling him the truth," Adelaida says softly, her face twisted. "I went crazy too, right?"

"Yes, I'm leaving, but one last favor," Mayta said, and as soon as he was on his feet, he was sorry he hadn't left earlier. "Don't tell anyone you've seen me. Keep it to yourself."

She had never taken seriously those secrets, precautions, fears, that distrust, despite the fact that, while they were together, she had seen the police in the house several times. The effect it had on her was like that of seeing grown men playing children's games, a persecution complex that poisoned life. How can you enjoy life if you're constantly afraid of a universal conspiracy of informers, the army, the APRA, the capitalists, the Stalinists, the imperialists, etc., etc., against you? Mayta's words brought back the nightmare it had been to hear, several times a day: "Careful, don't repeat this, don't tell anyone, no one's supposed to know, no one can . . ." But she didn't argue. Sure, sure, not a word to anyone. Mayta nodded and with a half smile, waving goodbye, he went off hurriedly, walking that funny little walk of his, the walk of a man with blisters on the soles of his feet.

"He didn't cry, there was no melodrama," Adelaida adds, staring into space. "He asked me a few questions, as if out of mere curiosity. What was Mayta like? Why did we get divorced? Nothing else. He seemed to calm down, to the point that I thought: Judging by what little effect it's had on him, telling him seems to have been a waste of time."

But the next day, the boy disappeared. Adelaida hasn't seen him for ten years. Her voice breaks, and I see her wring her hands as if she wants to tear the skin off.

"Is that how Catholics behave?" she whispers. "To break off with a mother because of something that at worst was only a mistake. Everything I did, didn't I do it for his sake?"

She even went to the Missing Persons Bureau, though the boy was nearly of legal age. I'm sorry to see how tormented she is and I understand that she's added this episode to the list of Mayta's crimes, but, at the same time, I feel distant from her grief, nearer to Mayta, following him through the streets of Lince toward Avenida Arequipa, to get the bus. Did he walk slumped over because of the bitterness of that visit to his ex-wife and the frustration of not having seen that son he would certainly never see? Was he demoralized, pained? He was euphoric, charged with energy, impatient, mentally allocating the time he had left in Lima. He knew how to overcome reverses by an emotive leap, knew how to draw strength from them for the task he had in front of him. Before, the simple, precise, daily manual labor that wiped out his depression and self-pity was painting walls, working in the Cocharcas print shop, distributing handbills on Avenida Argentina and Plaza Dos de Mayo, correcting proofs, translating an article from French for *Workers Voice*. Now it was a flesh-and-blood revolution, the real thing, which would begin any moment now. He thought: The revolution *you* are going to start. Was he going to waste time torturing himself because of domestic complications? He went through his pockets, took out the list, reread what he had to buy. Would they have his severance pay ready for him at France-Presse?

"At first, I thought he'd killed himself," Adelaida says, furiously wringing her hands. "That I'd have to kill myself to make up for his death."

They learned nothing about him for weeks and months, until one day Juan Zárate received a letter. Serene, measured, well-thought-out. He thanked Juan for what he had done for him, said he wished he could repay him for his generosity. He said he was sorry that he had left in such a brusque fashion, but he thought it best to avoid explanations that would be painful to both of them. He shouldn't worry about him. Is he high up in the mountains which are beginning to fade into the night? Is he one of the men who jumps and runs back and forth among the survivors—his sub-machine gun on his shoulder, his pistol in his belt—trying to impose order on chaos.

"The letter came from Pucallpa," says Adelaida. "He didn't even mention my name."

Yes, his severance pay was ready—and in cash, not a check: 43,000 *soles*. He could buy everything on the list and still have some left over. Naturally, he did not bid the editors at France-Presse a fond farewell. When the chief asked him if he could stand in for someone on Sunday, Mayta said he was going to Chiclayo. He walked out in high spirits, hurrying toward Avenida Abancay. He never had the patience to go shopping, but this time he went to several stores, looking for the best-quality khaki trousers, a pair that could stand up to a harsh climate, rough terrain, and heavy action. He bought two pairs, each in a different store, and then, from a vendor out on the sidewalk, he purchased a pair of sandals. The vendor lent him his bench, leaning on the walls of the National Library, so he could try them on. He went into a pharmacy on Jirón Lampa. He was about to take out his list and hand it to the pharmacist, when he stopped himself, repeating, as he had thousands of times in his life, "You can't take enough precautions." He decided to buy the bandages, the antiseptics, the coagulants, the sulfa, and the other first-aid materials Vallejos had told him to get, in several different pharmacies.

"And you haven't seen him since then?"

"I haven't," Adelaida says.

But Juan Zárate has. Every so often, he would come to Lima from Pucallpa or Yurimaguas, where he was working in lumber camps, and they would have lunch. But ever since this stuff began—the attacks, the kidnappings, the bombings, the war—he hasn't written or come: he's either dead or he is one of them.

Night has fallen and the survivors have huddled together to protect themselves from the cold and the darkness of Cuzco. The crowd babbles in its sleep, hearing spectral planes and bombs that multiply those of the previous day. But Mayta's son is not asleep. In the small headquarters dugout, he argues, trying to impose his point of view. The people should return to Cuzco as soon as the noxious fumes from the fires dissipate, and begin to rebuild. There are commanders with other opinions: there they will be all too easy a target for renewed bombings, and a slaughter like today's hamstrings the masses. It would be better for the people to stay in the country, scattered in the outlying districts, settlements, and camps, less vulnerable to air attacks. Mayta's son replies, argues, raises his voice in the glare of the small fire. His face seems tanned, scarred, serious. He hasn't taken his sub-machine gun off his shoulder or removed his pistol from his belt. The cigarette between his fingers has gone out and he doesn't realize it. His voice is that of a man who has overcome all tests—cold, hunger, fatigue, retreat, terror, crime—and is sure of an inevitable, imminent victory. So far, he has never been wrong, and it doesn't look as though he'll make any mistakes in the future.

"The few times he came, he would pick up Juan and they'd go out together," Adelaida repeats. "He never came to see me, never called me, and never let Juan even mention the possibility of his visiting me. Can you understand that kind of resentment, that kind of hate? At the beginning, I wrote him lots of letters. Later I just gave up."

He picked up the package, handed over the receipt, and went out. With the sulfa and Mercurochrome from the last pharmacy, he'd finished up the list. The packages were big and heavy. When he got to his room on Jirón Zepita, his arms hurt. He had his bag ready: the sweaters, the shirts, and right in the middle, the sub-machine gun Vallejos had given him. He packed the medicine and looked over the piles of books. Would Blacquer come to take them? He went out and hid the key between the two loose boards on the landing. If Blacquer didn't come, the landlord would sell them to make up for the unpaid rent. What did that matter now, anyway? He took a taxi to Parque Universitario. What did his room, his books, Adelaida, his son, or his former comrades matter now? He felt his heart pounding as the driver put the valise on the luggage rack. The bus would leave for Jauja in a few minutes. He thought: From this trip, there is no return, Mayta.

I get up, I give her the money, I thank her, and she sees me to the door, which she closes as soon as I cross the threshold. It seems strange to see the phony façade of the Rospigliosi Castle in the fading light. Once again, I have to allow the airmen to frisk me. They let me pass. As I walk along, past houses sealed up with stone and mud, all around me I hear noises that are no longer exclusively shots. There are hand grenades exploding, and cannon being fired.

Eight

He looks like one of Arcimboldo's figures: his nose a twisted carrot, his cheeks two quinces, his chin a protruding potato covered with eyes, and his neck a cluster of half-skinned grapes. His ugliness is so outrageous that it's charming. If you didn't know better, you'd say all that greasy hair hanging in tufts over don Ezequiel's shoulders is a wig. His body seems even spongier than it really is, because it's stuffed into those baggy pants and that tattered sweater. Only one of his shoes has laces; the other threatens to fall off with each step he takes. Nevertheless, don Ezequiel is not a beggar but the owner of the furniture and housewares store located in the Plaza de Armas of Jauja, next to the Colegio del Carmen and the Iglesia de las Madres Franciscanas. The gossips of Jauja say that this man before us is the richest merchant in the city. Why hasn't he fled, like the other rich people? The insurgents kidnapped him a few months ago, and the vox populi has it he paid a high ransom. Ever since then, they've left him alone, because, as they say, he's paid his "revolutionary taxes."

"I know who sent you here. I know it was that son of a bitch Shorty Ubilluz." He stops me dead as soon as he sees me walk into his store. "You're wasting your time, I don't know anything, I never saw anything, and I was never involved in that dumb bullshit. I have nothing to say. I know you're writing about Vallejos. Don't put me in it, or I'll sue you. I'm telling you without getting mad, just so you'll get the idea through your thick skull."

As he speaks to me, his eyes are burning with indignation. His shouts are so loud that some troops on patrol in the plaza come over to see if there's anything wrong. No, nothing. When they leave, I go into my usual routine: No reason to get upset, don Ezequiel, I'm not going to use your name, not once. Not a single person who participated in the action, not even Second Lieutenant Vallejos or Mayta, appears by name. No one could tell from what I'm writing what really happened.

"So why the fuck did you bother coming to Jauja?" he retorts, gesturing with fingers that look like hooks. "Why the fuck are you asking questions up and down every street in town? What the fuck is all this gossip-collecting for?"

"So I will know what I'm doing when I lie," I say for the hundredth time this year. "At least let me try to explain it to you, don Ezequiel. Just two minutes of your time. Okay? May I come in?"

The light that bathes Jauja is like the dawn, like first light, hesitant, blackish, and in it the outline of the cathedral, the balconies, and the fenced-in garden constantly dissolve and reappear. The sharp breeze gives him goose bumps. Was it nerves? Was it fear? He wasn't nervous or frightened, just slightly anxious, and not about what was going to happen but because of the damn altitude, which made him aware of his heart every second. He'd slept a few hours, despite the cold that came in through the broken windows, despite the fact that the barbershop chair was not an ideal bed. At five, a crowing rooster had awakened him, and the first thing he thought was:

208

Today's the day. He got up, stretched and yawned in the darkness, and, banging into one thing after another, went over to the washbowl filled with water. He sat down on one of the chairs where Ezequiel shaved his customers, and, closing his eyes, went over his orders. He was confident, serene, and if it weren't for that shortness of breath, he would have felt happy. Minutes later, he heard the door open. In the glow of a lantern, he saw Ezequiel, carrying hot coffee in a canteen cup.

"Was it very uncomfortable sleeping in here?"

"I slept very well," said Mayta. "Is it five-thirty already?"

"Just about," whispered Ezequiel. "Go out the back way, and don't make any noise."

"Thanks for your hospitality," Mayta said, bidding him goodbye. "Good luck."

"Bad luck is what it was. My big mistake was being a nice guy, an asshole." His nose swells up, and myriad wine-colored veins pop out. His frenetic eyes dance in his head. "My big mistake was to feel sorry for an outsider I didn't know and to let him sleep for one single night in my barbershop. And who was it who came to me with the sad tale of how this poor fellow had no place to stay and wouldn't I put him up? Who else but that son of a bitch Shorty Ubilluz!"

"But that was twenty-five years ago, don Ezequiel," I say, trying to calm him down. "It's an old story no one remembers. Don't get so worked up."

"I get worked up because that bastard isn't happy with what he did to me then. Now he's going around saying I've sold out to the terrorists. Let's see if the army shoots me—the world will finally be rid of me." Don Ezequiel snorts. "I get worked up because nothing ever happened to that smart-aleck shithead—but me, who knew nothing, who understood nothing, who saw nothing, they locked me up in jail, they broke my ribs, and they had me pissing blood, they kicked me so many times in the kidneys and the balls."

"But they let you out of jail, you started over, and now

you're the envy of everyone in Jauja. Don Ezequiel, you shouldn't let yourself get like this, don't lose your temper. Forget it."

"How can I forget it if you come around here bothering me to tell you things I don't know anything about," he says, growling, and stretches out his fingers as if to scratch me. "It's the dumbest thing I ever heard. The one who knew the least about what was going on was the only one to get fucked up."

He went down the hall, made sure there was no one in the street, opened the half door of the barbershop, went out, and closed the door behind him. There wasn't a soul in the plaza, and the timid light was barely strong enough for him to see where he was walking. He went to the bench. The Ricrán men hadn't arrived yet. He sat down, put his suitcase between his feet, pulled up the collar of his sweater so he could breathe through it, and stuck his hands in his pockets. He would have to be a machine. It was something he remembered from his military instruction course: a lucid robot, who is neither early nor late, and, above all, who never doubts; a fighter who executes his orders with the precision of an electric mixer or a lathe. If everyone did just that, the toughest test, the one they'd face today, would be no problem. The second test would be even easier, and from then on, there would be a clear road to victory.

He heard roosters he couldn't see; behind him, in the grass of the little garden, a toad croaked. Would they be late? The truck from Ricrán would park in the Plaza de Santa Isabel, where all the vehicles carrying merchandise for the market came. From there, divided into small groups, they would take up their positions. He didn't even know the names of the two comrades who would go with him to seize the jail and then the telephone company. "Who's today's saint?" "St. Edmund Dantés." Behind the collar that covered half his face, he smiled. He'd thought of the password while remembering *The Count of Monte Cristo*. Just then, the punctual joeboy appeared. His name was Feliciano Tapia and he was in uniform—khaki shirt and trousers, cap of the same color, and a gray sweater—carrying books under his arm. They are going to help us start the revolution and then go to school, he thought. We have to hurry, so they won't be late for class. Each group had a joeboy attached to it as messenger, in case they had to communicate something unforeseen. Once each group began its withdrawal, the joeboy was supposed to return to his normal life.

"The guys from Ricrán are late," said Mayta. "Could the mountain road be blocked?"

The kid looked at the clouds. "No, it hasn't rained."

It was improbable that a rainstorm or a landslide would close the road at this time of year. If it did happen, their backup plan had the Ricrán people heading across the mountains to Quero. The joeboy looked enviously at Mayta. He was just a little kid, with rabbit teeth and fuzz on his cheeks.

"Are your buddies on time like you?"

"Roberto is already on the corner by the orphanage, and I saw Melquíades on his way to Santa Isabel."

It was quickly growing light, and Mayta was sorry he hadn't checked over the sub-machine gun once more. He had oiled it the night before in the barbershop, and before going to sleep, he'd clicked the safety on and off, to check if the gun was loaded. What need was there for another check? Now there was some movement in the plaza. Women with cloaked heads were walking by, heading for the cathedral, and from time to time a van or a truck passed, loaded with bundles or barrels. It was five minutes to six. He stood up and grabbed his suitcase.

"Run to Santa Isabel, and if the truck's there, tell my group to park in front of the jail. At six-thirty I'll let them in. Got it?"

"I don't have anything to hide, so I'll tell you the way it was. The guy in charge of everything wasn't Vallejos or the outsider but Ubilluz." Don Ezequiel scratches the bumpy wattles on his throat with his black fingernails, and snorts. "He was responsible for what happened and what didn't happen that morning. You're wasting your time shooting the shit with anyone else. He's the

211

guy you want. That fuckup is the only one who knows just exactly what the fuck happened."

A radio turned up full blast and broadcasting in English drowns out his voice. It's a station set up for the American Marines and pilots, who are using the Colegio San José as a headquarters.

"There goes the radio station of the motherfucking gringos!" barks don Ezequiel, covering his ears.

I tell him how surprised I am not to have seen Marines on the streets, that all the patrols around are Peruvian soldiers and national guardsmen.

"The gringos must be sleeping it off or resting after screwing so much," he bellows, enraged. "They've corrupted Jauja totally, even the nuns are prostitutes now. How could it be otherwise when they've got dollars and we're dying of hunger? They say they even bring their water in by plane. It isn't true that their money helps local commerce. Not a single one has ever come in here to buy anything. They only spend money on cocaine, you bet; they pay anything for cocaine. It's a lie that they've come here to fight the communists. They've come to snort cocaine and screw Jauja girls. They even brought blacks with them, how the hell do you like that?"

Even though I'm paying attention to don Ezequiel's tantrum, I don't forget about what Mayta was doing that early morning twenty-five years ago, in that Jauja free of revolutionaries and Marines, as he walked down the morning street Alfonso Ugarte, carrying his weapon in his suitcase. Was he worried that the truck was late? He must have been. Even though they knew that someone was bound to be late, this first problem—even before the plan went into effect—must have troubled him. As to the plan itself, I think I've figured it out fairly well, despite all the lies and fantasies surrounding it, up until the moment when, about eleven in the morning, the revolutionaries were to leave Jauja and head for the bridge at Molinos.

From that point on, I get lost, because of the contradictions in the various accounts I've heard. I'm increasingly sure that only a small nucleus—perhaps only Vallejos and Ubilluz, maybe just those two and Mayta, perhaps only the lieutenant—knew *everything* they'd planned. The decision to keep the others ignorant of the entire plan hampered them terribly. What could Mayta have been thinking about on the last block of Alfonso Ugarte, when he saw on his left the adobe walls and the tile-covered eaves of the jail? That, to the right, behind the curtains in Ubilluz's house, Shorty and the comrades from La Oroya, Casapalca, and Morocha, ensconced there since the night before or at least for some hours now, were perhaps watching him pass. Should he warn them that the truck hadn't come? No, he should just follow orders. Besides, just from seeing him there alone, they would understand that the truck was held up. If it arrived in the next half hour, the Ricrán men would get into the fray. And if it didn't, they would meet with them in Quero, where the latecomers were supposed to go.

He reached the stone façade of the jail, and as the lieutenant had said, there was no guard. The rusty door opened and Vallejos appeared. Signaling him to be quiet, he took Mayta by the arm and brought him in, after checking to see if anyone was following him. With a gesture, he told him to go into the warden's office. Then he disappeared. Mayta observed the entranceway with its columns, the door of the room in front, which had the word *Guardroom* on it, and the little patio with cherry trees, which had long, thin leaves and clusters of fruit. In the room where he stood, there was the national emblem, a blackboard, a desk, a chair, and a small window. Through the dirty glass, he could just make out the street. He stood there with the suitcase in his hands, not knowing what to do.

Then Vallejos came back. "Just wanted to see if anyone noticed you come in," he said in a low voice. "Didn't the truck come?"

"Seems not. I sent Feliciano to wait for it and to tell my group to be here at six-thirty. Will we need the Ricrán people?"

213

"No problem," said Vallejos. "Hide in here and wait. Don't make a sound."

Mayta was reassured by the calm and sureness of the lieutenant. He was wearing fatigues, boots, and a black turtleneck sweater instead of his commando shirt. He went into the warden's inner office, which seemed to him a kind of large closet with white walls. That cabinet must have been a weapons locker, they must put rifles in those niches over there. When he closed the door, he found himself in semi-darkness. He had to struggle to open the suitcase, because the lock jammed. He took out the sub-machine gun and put the ammunition clips in his pockets. As suddenly as it came alive, the radio fell silent. What had happened to the truck from Ricrán?

"It had arrived very early at Santa Isabel, where it was supposed to go." Don Ezequiel bursts into laughter, and it's as if poison were pouring out of his eyes, mouth, and ears. "And when the thing at the jail began, it had already left. But not heading for Quero, where it was supposed to go, but for Lima. And not carrying communists or stolen weapons. No, sir. What was it carrying? Beans! As fucking crazy as it sounds. The revolution's truck, just when the revolution was starting, went off to Lima with a shipment of beans. Why don't you ask me whose beans they were?"

"I'm not going to ask you, because you're going to tell me they were Shorty Ubilluz's beans," I say.

Don Ezequiel gives another one of his monstrous cackles. "Why don't you ask me who was driving it?" He raises his dirty hands, and as if punching someone, he points to the plaza. "I saw him go by, I recognized that traitor. I saw him hanging on to the steering wheel, wearing a faggoty blue cap. I saw the sacks of beans. What the fuck is going on here? What do you think was going to happen—that damned son of a bitch was screwing Vallejos, the outsider, and me."

"Tell me just one thing more, and then I'll leave you in peace, don Ezequiel. Why didn't you go, too, that morning?

214

Why did you stay so peacefully in your barbershop? Why didn't you at least hide?"

His fruit-like face contemplates me horribly for several seconds, in slow fury. I watch him pick his nose and tear at the skin on his neck. When he answers, he still feels the need to lie. "Why the hell should I hide when I had nothing to do with anything? What the hell for?"

"Don Ezequiel, don Ezequiel," I chide him. "Twenty-five years have gone by, Peru's going down the drain, people are thinking only of saving themselves from a war that isn't even being fought by Peruvians, you and I might be dead in the next raid or skirmish. Who cares anymore what happened that day? Tell me the truth, help me to end my story before this homicidal chaos our country has become eats both of us up. You were supposed to cut the telephone lines and hire some taxis, using a phony barbeque over in Molinos as a pretext. Don't you remember what time you were supposed to be at the telephone company? Five minutes after they opened up. The taxis were going to wait at the corner of Alfonso Ugarte and La Mar, where Mayta's group was going to commandeer them. But you didn't hire the cabs, you didn't go to the telephone company, and when the joeboy came to ask you what was going on, you told him: 'Nothing's going on, it's all gone to hell, run to school and forget you even know who I am.' That joeboy is Telésforo Salinas, director of physical education for this province, don Ezequiel."

"A pack of lies! More of Ubilluz's slander!" he growls, purple with rage. "I knew nothing and I had no reason to hide or flee. Get out, go away, disappear. Stinking slanderer! Shiteating gossip!"

Hidden in the semi-darkness, with the sub-machine gun in his hands, Mayta could hear nothing. Nor could he see anything, except two streaks of light where the planks of the door met. But he had no difficulty guessing that at that very instant Vallejos was going into the barracks of the fourteen guards and was waking them up with his thundering voice: Ateeenshun! Rifle inspection! The officer in charge of the Huancayo armory had just told him he would be coming to hold an inspection early in the morning. Be careful, you've got to be fanatics about oiling both the outside and the bolts of the rifles. I don't want anybody written up for a rusty piece. Second Lieutenant Vallejos didn't want any more bad reports from the armory officer. The working weapons and the ammunition for each republican guard—ninety cartridges—would be taken to the guardroom. Fall in out in the patio! Now it would be his turn. The wheels were beginning to turn, the cogs were moving, this is action, this was it. Have the Ricrán guys gotten here yet? He looked through the cracks, waiting for the silhouettes of the guards carrying their Mausers and their bullets to the little room in front, one behind the other, and among them, Antolín Torres.

He is a retired republican guard who lives on Manco Cápac Street, halfway between the jail and don Ezequiel's store. To keep the ex-barber from taking a swing at me or from having a fit of apoplexy, I have to retreat. Sitting on a bench in Jauja's majestic plaza—disfigured now by police barriers and barbed wire on the corners where the municipal building and the sub-prefecture are—I think about Antolín Torres. I talked to him this morning. He's been a happy man ever since the Marines hired him as a guide and translator.

He used to have a little farm, but the war ruined it. He was dying of hunger until the gringos came. His job is to accompany the patrols as they reconnoiter the area around Jauja. (His Spanish is as good as his Quechua.) He knows that his work may cost him his life. Many of the people in Jauja turn their backs on him, and the façade of his house is covered with graffiti: "Traitor" and "Condemned to Death by the Revolutionary Tribunal."

From what Antolín has told me and from don Ezequiel's curses, I conclude that relations between the Marines and the locals are bad, awful. Even the people who oppose the insurgents

216

resent these foreigners they can't understand, who, above all, eat well, smoke, and suffer no privations—in a town where even the formerly rich experience dearth. A sixty-year-old with a bull neck and a huge stomach, an Ayacucho man from Cangallo who has lived most of his life in Jauja, Antolín Torres speaks a wonderful Spanish spiced with Quechuanisms. "People say the communists are going to kill me. Okay, but when they come to kill me they're going to find a guy who eats well, drinks well, and smokes American cigarettes." He's a storyteller who knows how to achieve dramatic effects with pauses and exclamations. That day, twenty-five years ago, he went on duty at eight, when he was supposed to replace Huáscar Toledo on guard duty at the front door. Huáscar wasn't in the sentry box but inside with the others, oiling his Mauser in preparation for the visit of the armory officer. Second Lieutenant Vallejos was hurrying them, and Antolín Torres suspected something.

"But why, Mr. Torres? What was so strange about an arms inspection?"

What was strange was that the lieutenant was walking around with his sub-machine gun on his shoulder. What reason could he have for being armed? And why did we have to leave our weapons in the guardroom? This is really strange, sergeant. Where does this stuff come from about separating a trooper from his rifle for an inspection? Don't think so much, Antolín, it gets in the way of promotion, is what the sergeant said. I obeyed, I cleaned my Mauser, and I left it in the guardroom along with my ninety cartridges. Then I went to fall in in the patio. But I could smell something fishy. But not what happened later. I thought it was something to do with the prisoners. There were maybe fifty in the cells. An escape attempt, I don't know what, but something.

"Now." Mayta pushed the door open. From being so long in one position, his legs were completely cramped. His heart pounded like a drum, and he was overwhelmed by a sensation of something final, irreversible, as he walked out into the patio with his oiled sub-machine gun. He took up a position in front of the judge's office, facing the troops, and said, "Don't force me to shoot. I don't want to hurt anyone."

Vallejos had his sub-machine gun trained on his subordinates. The bleary eyes of the fourteen guards swung back and forth from him to the lieutenant, from the lieutenant back to him, without understanding: Are we awake or dreaming? Is this really happening, or is it a nightmare?

"And then the lieutenant spoke, isn't that a fact, Mr. Torres? Remember what he said?"

"I don't want to drag you in, but I've become a rebel, a revolutionary socialist." Antolín Torres imitates him and acts out the scene, his Adam's apple rising and falling. "If anyone wants to follow me of his own free will, let him come. I'm doing this for the sake of the poor, the suffering, and because our leaders have let us down. And you, pay sergeant, buy beer on Sunday for everyone, and take it out of my back pay." "While the lieutenant was speaking, the other enemy, the one from Lima, had us covered with his sub-machine gun, blocking the way to the Mausers. They made fools of us. The commander punished us with two weeks' confinement to barracks."

Mayta had heard Vallejos but hadn't paid any attention to what he was saying because of his own excitement. "Like a machine, like a soldier." The lieutenant herded the guards to their barracks, and they obeyed docilely, still not understanding. He saw that the lieutenant, after closing the door, bolted it. Then, with rapid, precise movements, his weapon in his left hand, he ran, with a large key in his other hand, to open a cell door. Were the Uchubamba men there? They had to have seen and heard what had just happened. On the other hand, the other prisoners, the ones in cells on the other side of the patio with its cherry trees, were too far away. From his position next to the guardroom, he saw two men come out behind Vallejos. There they were, yes, the comrades he until now only knew by name. Which one was Condori and which Zenón Gonzales? Before he could find out, an argument broke out with the younger of the two, a fair-skinned little guy with long hair. Even though Mayta had been told that the peasants from the eastern region usually had light skin and hair, he was shocked: the Indian agitators who had led the seizure of the Aína hacienda looked like two little gringos. One was wearing sandals.

"Gonna chicken out now, motherfucker?" he heard Vallejos say, his face close to one of the men. "Now that things have begun, now that the fat's in the fire, you want to mouse out?"

"I'm not chickening out," Zenón Gonzales said truculently, stepping back. "It's that . . . it's that . . ."

"It's that you're yellow, Zenón," Vallejos shouted. "Too bad for you. Get back to your cell. I hope they send you away for a long time. Rot in the Frontón, then. I don't know why I don't just shoot you like a dog, you son of a bitch."

"Wait up, hold it, let's talk calmly without fighting," said Condori, stepping between them. He was the one wearing sandals, and Mayta was happy to see someone who might be his own age. "Don't go off the deep end, Vallejos. Let me talk to Zenón for a minute."

In three strides, the lieutenant was at Mayta's side.

"What a faggot," he said, no longer furious as he was a moment before, but disillusioned. "Last night, he agreed. Now come the doubts—maybe it would be better to stay here, and later on we'll see. That's what you call fear, not doubt."

What doubts moved the young leader from Uchubamba to provoke this incident? Did he think, when the rebellion was about to begin, that perhaps there were too few of them? Did he doubt that he and Condori could drag the rest of the community into the uprising? Did he have an inkling of the defeat? Or, simply, did he hesitate when he thought that he would have to kill people and that someone might kill him?

Condori and Gonzales whispered together. Mayta heard the odd word and sometimes saw them gesture. Once, Condori grabbed his comrade by the arm. He must have had some power over him, because Gonzales, even though complaining, remained respectful. A moment later, they came over.

219

"Okay, Vallejos," said Condori. "Everything's okay now. No problem."

"Okay, Zenón." Vallejos squeezed his hand. "I'm sorry I got mad. No hard feelings?"

The young man nodded. As he squeezed his hand, Vallejos said again, "No hard feelings. We're doing this for Peru, Zenón." Judging by his face, Gonzales seemed more resigned than convinced.

Vallejos turned to Mayta. "Have the weapons loaded into the taxis. I'm going to talk to the prisoners."

He went off toward the cherry trees, and Mayta ran to the main entrance. Through the small window in the door, he looked out on the street. Instead of taxis, Ubilluz, and the miners from La Droya, he saw a small group of joeboys headed by the cadet commander, Cordero Espinoza.

"What are you doing here?" he asked them. "Why aren't you at your posts?"

"We aren't at our posts because everyone's gone," says Cordero Espinoza, with a yawn that warms his smile. "We got tired of waiting. We couldn't be messengers for people who weren't there. I was assigned the police station. I got there good and early, and no one else showed up. After a while, Hernando Huasasquiche came to tell me that Professor Ubilluz wasn't at home or anywhere around here. And that he'd seen him driving his truck on the main road. A little later, we found out that the Ricrán people had just disappeared, the La Oroya men had either never come or had gone back. We got really scared! We got together in the plaza. We were all worried, just standing around waiting to go to school. We'd been fooled, the whole thing was some kind of phony story. Right then, Felicio Tapia turned up. He told us that the guy from Lima had gone to the jail after being stood up by the Ricrán men. So we went to the jail to see what was happening. Vallejos and Mayta had locked up the guards, captured the rifles, and freed Condori and Gonzales. Can you imagine anything as ridiculous as that?"

Dr. Cordero Espinoza is certainly right. What else could you say but that it was ridiculous? They take over the jail, they've got fourteen rifles and twelve hundred cartridges. But there aren't any revolutionaries, because not one of the thirty or forty conspirators turned up. Was that what Mayta thought when he peered through the window and found only seven boys in uniform?

"Nobody came? None? Not a single one?"

"Well, we're here," said the kid with the half-shaved head, and despite his confusion, Mayta remembered what Ubilluz had said about him when they were introduced: Cordero Espinoza, commander of his class, number one, a brain. "But it looks like the others have taken off."

Shock, rage, an intimation of the catastrophe closing in on them? Or, rather, the tacit confirmation of something as yet undefined, which he'd feared since earlier, when the Ricrán men weren't in the plaza, or maybe earlier still, when his Lima comrades from the RWP(T) decided to withdraw their support, or when he'd understood that his attempt at Blacquer's to get the Communist Party involved in the uprising was useless? Was it since one of those moments that he'd been waiting, without even admitting it to himself, for this coup de grâce? The revolution wouldn't even begin? But it has begun, Mayta, don't you realize it, it has begun.

"That's why we're here, that's why we've come," exclaimed Cordero Espinoza. "Don't you think we can replace those guys?"

Mayta saw that the joeboys were clustered around their commander and were nodding in agreement and support. But all he could think of at that instant was that some passerby, someone from the neighborhood, might take notice of that little group of schoolboys at the jail door.

"It struck me that we should volunteer right then and there. I didn't even talk it over with my buddies," remembers Dr. Cordero Espinoza. "It just hit me when I saw the look on poor Mayta's face when he found out that nobody showed up."

We're in his office on Junín Street, where law offices abound. Law is still *the* profession in Jauja, even though, over the past few years, war and catastrophes have seriously dampened local legal business. Until fairly recently, in every Jauja family at least one or two sons came into the world with a briefcase of legal documents under their arms. Lawsuits are a sport practiced by all classes in this province, at least as popular as soccer and Carnival. In the throng of lawyers in Jauja, the old cadet commandant and top student at Colegio San José—where he used to teach a course on political economy a couple of times a week, until the war caused classes to be suspended—is still the star.

He's an easygoing, friendly man. His office glitters with diplomas from the congresses he's attended, the honors he's won as city councilman, president of the Jauja Lions Club, president of the Committee for a Highway to the East, and various other civic functions. Of all the people I've talked with, he's the one who evokes those events with the greatest precision, ease, and —at least it seems to me—objectivity. The handsomeness of his office contrasts with the entrance hall, which has a hole in the floor and half of one wall shattered. As he leads me through, he points to it, saying, "It was a guerrilla bomb. I've left it this way to remind me of the precautions I have to take every day if I want to keep my head on my shoulders."

With the same wit, he told me, soon after, that when the guerrillas attacked his house, they were more efficient: the two dynamite charges burned it to the ground. "They killed my cook, a little old lady sixty years old. My wife and children, fortunately, were already out of Jauja." They live in Lima and are about to leave the country. Which is what he will do as soon as he can wrap up his business. Because, as he says, with the way things are going, what sense does it make to go on risking one's neck? Hasn't Jauja's security improved since the Marines came? Things are even worse. Because the people resent the foreign troops so much, they help the guerrillas—by hiding

222

them, supplying them with alibis, or just by keeping quiet. They say something similar is happening among the Peruvian guerrillas and the Cuban and Bolivian internationalists. That there are confrontations between them. Nationalism, as we all know, is stronger than any other ideology. I can't help liking the ex-cadet commander: he says all these things naturally, without melodrama or arrogance, and even with a sense of humor.

"As soon as they heard me offer them as volunteers, they got all excited," he continues. "In fact, the seven of us were like brothers. A kids' game, compared to what we have today, right?"

"Yes, yes, we'll be their replacements."

"Open the door, let us in, we can do it."

"We are revolutionaries and we'll be their replacements."

Mayta was looking at them, listening to them, and his head was filled with static, disorder.

"How old are you?"

"Huasasquiche and I are seventeen," says Cordero Espinoza. "The others are fifteen or sixteen." Lucky for us, because they couldn't bring us up on charges, since we were still minors. They sent us to juvenile court, where they didn't take the matter too seriously. Don't you think it's paradoxical that I was a pioneer in the armed struggle in Peru and that now I'm a target of the guerrillas?" He shrugs.

"I suppose that by that time there was no way for Mayta and Vallejos to turn back," I say.

"Yes, there was. Vallejos could have let the guards out of the barracks where he'd locked them up and cursed them up and down: 'You have demonstrated that you're really nothing, pansies, if there really was an attack on the jail by subversives. Not a single one of you has passed the test I just put you to, shitasses.'" Dr. Cordero Espinoza offers me a cigarette, and before lighting his own, he places it in a holder. "They would have swallowed the story, I'm sure of it. He could have sent us off to school, put Gonzales and Condori back in the lockup, and gotten off scot-free. All of them could have, even then. But of course they didn't. Mayta and Vallejos weren't men who would just give in. In that sense, even though one was in his forties and the other in his twenties, they were more kids than we were."

So it was Mayta who first accepted that romantic and preposterous offer. His hesitation and perplexity lasted a few seconds. He decided suddenly. He opened the main door, said, "Quickly, quickly," to the joeboys, and as they invaded the patio, he looked down the street. It was empty of people and cars, the houses were all shuttered. His strength came back to him, his blood rushed through his veins, there was no reason to despair. He closed the door after the last boy. There they were: seven anxious and impassioned little faces. Both Condori and Gonzales were now carrying rifles, and they looked with fascination at the kids. Vallejos appeared behind the cherry trees, having finished his inspection of the prisoners.

Mayta went to meet him. "Ubilluz and the others haven't come. But we have volunteers to take their places."

Did Vallejos pull up short? Did Mayta see that his face twisted into a hideous grin? Did he see that the young second lieutenant labored to appear calm? Did he hear Vallejos say under his breath, "Ubilluz hasn't come? Ezequiel either? The Parrot either?"

"We can't go back now, comrade." Mayta shook him by the arm. "I told you, I warned you that it would happen. Action selects. Now there's no going back. We can't. Accept the boys. They got all fired up coming over here. They are revolutionaries, what other proof could you want. Are we turning yellow, brother?"

The more he spoke, the more he convinced himself, and for a second time, he repeated his exorcism against good sense: "Like a machine, like a soldier." Vallejos, mute, scrutinized him— doubting? trying to determine if what he was saying was also what he was thinking? But when Mayta stopped talking, the lieutenant once again became a tissue of controlled nerves and instant decisions. He then approached the joeboys, who had listened to the dialogue.

"I'm happy this has happened," he said, standing among them. "I'm happy because, thanks to this, I know there are some brave men in this world like you. Welcome to the struggle, boys. I want to shake hands with every one of you."

Actually, he began to hug them, to press them to his breast. Mayta took off his hat, hugging and being hugged, and behind clouds, he saw Zenón Gonzales and Condori joining in. A profound emotion overwhelmed him. He had a knot in his throat. Several boys wept, and the tears poured down their jubilant faces as they embraced the lieutenant, Mayta, Gonzales, Condori, and one another. Long live the revolution! shouted one, and another shouted: Long live socialism! Vallejos ordered them to be quiet.

"I don't think I ever felt as happy as I did at that moment," says Dr. Cordero Espinoza. "It was beautiful, so much naïveté, so much idealism. We felt as if our mustaches and beards had suddenly sprouted, as if we had grown taller and stronger. Probably not a single one of us had even set foot in a whorehouse. I, at least, was a virgin. And it seemed to me I was losing my virginity."

"Did any of you know how to use a rifle?"

"In the military training course, they gave us some rifle classes. Maybe a few of us had fired shotguns. But we made up for inexperience right then and there. It was the first thing Vallejos did after hugging us: he taught us what a Mauser was all about."

While the lieutenant gave the joeboys a lesson on how to fire a rifle, Mayta explained what had happened to Condori and Zenón Gonzales. They didn't raise the roof when they found out they had no one else to count on. They weren't outraged to learn that the whole revolutionary body might consist of them and the little group of soldier boys. They were serious as they listened, and asked no questions. Vallejos ordered two boys to get some taxis. Felicio Tapia and Huasasquiche took off on the run. Then Vallejos got Mayta and the peasants together. He had restructured the plan. Divided into two groups, they would seize the police station and the Civil Guard post. Mayta was listening, but out of the corner of his eye he took note of how the peasants reacted. Would Gonzales be saying, "See? I told you I was right to have my doubts about all this." No, he said nothing. He was inscrutable as he listened to the lieutenant.

"Here come the taxis," shouted Perico Temoche, from the main door.

"I was never a real taxi driver," Mr. Onaka assures me, pointing melancholically to the empty shelves in his store, shelves that used to be filled with food and domestic articles. "I was always the owner of this store, which I ran. You may not believe it, but it was the best-stocked shop in Junín province."

Bitterness twists his yellow face. Mr. Onaka has been a favorite victim of the rebels, who have robbed his store an incredible number of times. "Eight," he informs me. "The last was three weeks ago, with the Marines already here. So you see, gringos or no gringos, it's the same shit. They came at six, wearing masks. They locked the door and said, 'Where's the food hidden, pig?' Hidden? Go look for it and take whatever you can find. It's because of you that I haven't got a thing. They found nothing, of course. Why don't you take my wife instead? She's all you've left me. Why don't you kill me? Have a good time, kill the guy whose life you've ruined. We don't waste bullets on vultures, one of them said. And all that happened at six in the afternoon, with the police, soldiers, and Marines walking the streets of Jauja. Doesn't that prove that they're all the same bunch of crooks?" He snorts, takes a deep breath, and looks at his wife, who, bent over the counter, tries to read the paper by bringing the page right up to her eyes. Both of them are decrepit.

"Since she could take care of the customers by herself, I did a little taxi driving with the Ford," Mr. Onaka continues. "It

226

was my bad luck that I got tangled up in the Vallejos business. I cracked up the car because of it, and I had to spend a fortune fixing it. Because of that, I was hit on the head—they split my brow right here—and thrown in jail, while they investigated and found out that I wasn't an accomplice but a victim."

We are in a corner of his run-down store, each standing on his own side of the counter. At the other end, Mrs. Onaka looks away from her newspaper every time a customer comes in to buy candles or cigarettes, the only things the store seems well stocked with. The Onakas are of Japanese descent—the grand-children of immigrants—but in Jauja they're called "the Chinks," a misnomer that doesn't bother Mr. Onaka.

Unlike Dr. Cordero Espinoza, Mr. Onaka doesn't accept his disasters with philosophical good humor. Anyone can see he's demoralized, resentful about everything. He and Cordero Espinoza are the only people, among all those I've talked to in Jauja, who speak openly against the guerrillas. The others, even those who have been victims of their attacks, keep absolutely silent about the revolutionaries.

"I had just opened up when the Tapia kid—the family lives over on Villarreal—shows up. An emergency, Mr. Onaka. You have to take a sick lady to the hospital. I started up the car, the Tapia boy sat down next to me, and then the little actor said, 'Hurry up, the lady's dying.' In front of the jail, there was an-other taxi being loaded with rifles. I parked behind it. I asked the lieutenant, 'Where's the sick lady?' He didn't even answer me. Right then, the other guy, the one from Lima, Mayta—right?—steps up and sticks his gun in my chest: 'Do what you're told and you'll be all right.' I thought I'd shit in my pants—if you don't mind my saying so. I was really afraid. After all, those were the first revolutionaries I'd ever seen. What a jerk I was. At the time, I had a little money. I could have gone away with my wife. We could be living out our old age in peace."

Condori, Mayta, Felicio Tapia, Cordero Espinoza, and Teófilo Puertas got into the car after loading it with half the rifles and ammunition. Mayta ordered Onaka to drive off: "If you make any funny moves, you're dead." He was in the back seat, and his mouth was dry as cotton. But his hands were sweating. Squeezed in next to him, the cadet commander and Puertas were sitting on the rifles. In front, with Felicio Tapia, was Condori.

"I don't know why I didn't crash or run someone over." Mr. Onaka speaks out of a toothless mouth. "I thought they were thieves, murderers, escaped convicts. But how could the lieutenant be with them? What could the Tapia kid and the child of that gentleman Dr. Cordero be doing mixed up with murderers? They talked about the revolution and I don't know what else. What is this? What's going on? They made me take them over to the Civil Guard station, on Jirón Manco Cápac. The guy from Lima, Condori, and the Tapia boy got out there. They left the other two guarding me, and Mayta said to them, 'If he tries to get away, kill him.'

"Afterward, the kids swore it was only playacting, that they would never have shot me. But now we know that even kids kill, with hatchets, stones, and knives, right? Anyway, now we know lots of things that nobody knew then. Easy now, boys, don't get excited. You know me, I wouldn't hurt a fly, and I've given you credit lots of times. Why are you doing this to me? And besides, what's going on over there? What are they going to do at the station? The socialist revolution, Mr. Onaka, said Corderito—the guy whose house they burned down and whose office they almost blew up. The socialist revolution! What? What is that? I think it was the first time I ever heard the words. That's when I found out that four grown men and seven joeboys had chosen my poor Ford to carry out a socialist revolution. Holy shit!"

At the door of the station there were no guards, and Mayta signaled to Condori and Felicio Tapia: he would go in first, they should cover him. Condori looked calm, but Tapia was very pale and Mayta saw that his hands were red from holding on so tight to the rifle. He walked into the room bent over, with the

228

safety off the sub-machine gun, shouting: "Hands up or I'll shoot!"

In the half-darkened room, Mayta surprised a man wearing underpants and an undershirt in mid-yawn, a yawn that froze, turning his face into a stupid mask. He sat there staring, and only when he saw Condori and Felicio Tapia appear behind Mayta, they too pointing rifles at him, did he raise his hands.

"Watch him," said Mayta, and he ran to the back of the building. He passed through a narrow hall that led to an unpaved patio. Two guards, wearing trousers and boots but without shirts on, were washing their faces and hands in a basin of soapy water. One smiled at Mayta, mistaking him for a buddy.

"Get your hands up, or I'll fire!" Mayta said, not shouting this time. "Hands up, goddamn it!"

The two obeyed, and one of them moved so quickly that he knocked the basin over. The water darkened the dirt of the patio. "What's all the racket, for Christ's sake?" called out a sleepy voice. How many could there be in there? Condori was next to him, and Mayta whispered, "Take these two out," without taking his eyes off the room where he'd heard the voice. He crossed the little patio on the run, bent forward. He passed under a climbing vine, and on the threshold of the room, he stopped short, holding back the "Hands up!" he was about to shout. It was the sleeping room. There were two rows of bunks against the walls, and on three bunks there were men, two sleeping and the third smoking, flat on his back. A transistor radio was next to him, and he was listening to country music. When he saw Mayta, he choked and jumped to his feet, staring fixedly at the sub-machine gun.

"I thought it was all a joke," he stuttered, dropping the cigarette and placing his hands on his head.

"Wake those two up," said Mayta, pointing to the sleeping men. "Don't make me shoot: I don't want to kill you."

Without turning his back on Mayta or taking his eyes off the weapon, the guard edged along sideways, like a crab, until he reached the others. He shook them. "Wake up, wake up, I don't know what's going on."

"I was expecting shots, a huge racket. I thought I'd see Mayta, Condori, and the Tapia kid bleeding, and that in the confusion the guards would shoot me, thinking I was an attacker," says Mr. Onaka. "But there wasn't a single shot. Before I knew what was going on inside, the other taxi came with Vallejos. He'd already captured the police station over on Jirón Bolívar and locked Lieutenant Dongo and three guards in a cell. He asked the kids: Everything okay? We don't know. I begged him: Let me go, lieutenant, my wife is really sick. Don't be afraid, Mr. Onaka, we need you because none of us drives. Can you imagine anything as dumb as that? They were going to make a revolution and they didn't even know how to drive a car."

"No problem," said Mayta, relieved to see them again. "What about the police station?"

"A breeze," answered Vallejos. "Well done, I congratulate all of you. And we have ten more rifles."

"We aren't going to have enough men for so many rifles," said Mayta.

"We'll have enough," replied the lieutenant, as he looked over the new Mausers. "In Uchubamba there are more than enough, right, Condori?"

It seemed incredible that everything was going so well, Mayta.

"They loaded another pile of rifles in my Ford," Mr. Onaka says, sighing. "They ordered me to drive to the telephone company, and what else could I do?"

"When I got to work, I saw two cars there, and I recognized the Chink from the store, that Onaka character, the crook," says Mrs. Adriana Tello, a tiny, wrinkled-up old lady with a firm voice and gnarled hands. "He had such a face on that I thought he's either gotten up on the wrong side of the bed or he's a neurotic Chinaman. As soon as they saw me, some guys got out and went into the office with me. Why should I have been suspicious? In those days there weren't even robberies in Jauja, much less revolutions, so why be suspicious? Wait, we're not open yet. But it was as if they hadn't heard a word. They jumped over the counter, and one turned Asuntita Asís's—may she rest in peace—desk over. What's all this? What are you doing? What do you want? To knock out the telephone and telegraph. Good gracious! I'll be out of a job. Ha, ha, I swear that's just what I was thinking. I don't know how I can still laugh with all the things that are going on. Have you seen the impudence of these gringos who say they have come to help us? They can't even speak Spanish, and they walk around with their rifles and just go into any house they please, what nerve. As if we were their colony. There must not be any more patriots left in our Peru when we have to put up with that kind of humiliation."

When she saw Mayta and Vallejos kicking the switchboard apart, smashing the machinery with their rifle butts, and pulling out all the wires, Mrs. Adriana Tello tried to run out. But Condori and Zenón Gonzales held her while the lieutenant and Mayta finished breaking things up.

"Now we can take it easy," said Vallejos. "With the guards locked up and the telephone line cut, we're out of immediate danger. We don't have to split up."

"Will the people with the horses be in Quero?" Mayta was thinking aloud.

Vallejos shrugged. Could anyone be counted on?

"The peasants," murmured Mayta, pointing at Condori and Zenón Gonzales, who, after the lieutenant signaled to them, had released the woman, who ran, terrified, out of the building. "If we get to Uchubamba, I'm sure they won't let us down."

"We'll get there." Vallejos smiled. "They won't let us down."

They'd go on foot to the plaza, comrade. Vallejos ordered Gualberto Bravo and Perico Temoche to take the taxis to the corner of the Plaza de Armas and Bolognesi. That would be where they'd meet. He went to the head of those who remained and gave an order that left Mayta with goose bumps: "Forward, march!" They must have been a strange, unimaginable, disconcerting group—those four adults and five schoolboys, all

231

armed, marching along the cobblestone streets toward the Plaza de Armas. They would attract attention, they would stop anyone on the sidewalks, they would cause people to come to windows and doors. What did the good citizens of Jauja think as they saw them pass?

"I was shaving, because in those days I'd get up sort of late," says don Joaquín Zamudio, ex-hatmaker, ex-businessman, and now vendor of lottery tickets on the streets of Jauja. "I saw them from my room and thought they were rehearsing for the national holidays. But why so early in the year? I poked my head out the window and asked: What parade is this? The lieutenant didn't answer me and instead shouted: Long live the revolution! The others shouted: Hurrah, hurrah! What revolution is it? I asked them, thinking they were fooling around. And Corderito answered: The one we're starting, the socialist revolution. Later I found out that they went along just the way I'd seen them, marching and cheering, and robbed two banks."

They marched into the Plaza de Armas, and Mayta saw few passersby. When people did turn to look at them, it was with indifference. A group of Indians with ponchos and packs, sitting on a bench, just followed them with their eyes. There weren't enough people for a demonstration yet. It was ridiculous to be marching, because instead of looking like revolutionaries, they looked like boy scouts. But Vallejos set the example, and the joeboys, Condori, and Gonzales followed suit, so Mayta had no choice but to get in step. He had an ambiguous feeling, exaltation and anxiety, because even though the police were locked up, and their weapons captured, and the telephone and telegraph knocked out, wasn't their little group extremely vulnerable? Could you begin a revolution just like that? He gritted his teeth. You could. You had to be able to.

"They walked through the main door, practically singing," says don Ernesto Durán Huarcaya, ex-president of the International Bank and today an invalid dying of cancer on a cot in the Olavegoya Sanatorium. "I saw them from the window and thought that they couldn't even get in step, that they couldn't march worth a damn. Later, since they headed straight for the International Bank, I said here comes another request for money, for some carnival or parade. There was no more mystery after they got inside, because they turned their guns on us and Vallejos shouted: We've come to take the money that belongs to the people and not to the imperialists. I'm not going to put up with this, hell no, I'm going to face them down."

"He got down on all fours under his desk," says Adelita Campos, retired from the bank and now a seller of herb concoctions. "A real macho when it came to docking us for coming in late or pinching us when we passed too close to him. But when he saw the rifles—zoom—down he went under the desk, not even ashamed. If the president did that, what were we employees supposed to do? We were scared, of course. More of the kids than of the old guys. Because the boys were bawling like calves: Long live Peru! Long live the revolution! They were so wild they could easily start shooting. The person who had the great idea was the teller, old man Rojas. What could have become of him? I guess he's dead, probably someone killed him, because the way things have been going in Jauja, no one dies of old age anymore. Somebody kills you. And you never know who."

"When I saw them come up to my window, I opened the box on the left side," says old man Rojas, ex-teller at the International Bank, in the squalid quarters where he's waiting to die in the Jauja old-folks home. "That's where I had the morning deposits and the small bills we used to make change, nothing much. I raised my hands and prayed: 'Holy Mother, let them believe this one.' They did. They went right to the open box and took what they saw: fifty thousand *soles*, or thereabouts. Now that's nothing, but then it was quite a tidy sum, but nothing compared to what there was in the box on the right—almost a million *soles* that hadn't yet been put in the vault. They were amateurs, not like the ones that came later. Shh, now, sir, don't repeat what I've told you."

"Is that all?"

"Yes, that's all." The teller trembled. "It's early, only a few people have come in."

"This money isn't for us but for the revolution," Mayta interrupted him. He spoke into the incredulous faces of the employees. "For the people, for those who have sweated. This isn't stealing, it's expropriation. You have no reason to be frightened. The enemies of the people are the bankers, the oligarchs, and the imperialists. All of you are being exploited by them."

"Yes, of course," the teller said, quaking. "What you say is true, sir."

When they got out into the plaza, the boys went on cheering. Mayta, carrying the moneybag, went up to Vallejos: Let's go to the Regional, there aren't enough people here for a meeting. He saw very few people, and although they looked at the insurgents with curiosity, they wouldn't come too close.

"But we've got to move quickly," agreed Vallejos, "before they bolt the door on us."

He started running, and the others followed him, lining up in the same order in which they'd been marching. A few seconds of running eliminated Mayta's ability to think. Shortness of breath, pressure in his temples: the malaise came back, even though they weren't running that quickly, but almost, as it were, warming up before a game. When, two blocks later, they stopped at the doors of the Regional Bank, Mayta was seeing stars and his mouth was hanging open. You can't faint now, Mayta. He entered with the group, but in a dream. Leaning on the counter, seeing the shock on the face of the woman in front of him, he heard Vallejos explain: "This is a revolutionary action, we've come to recover the money stolen from the people." Someone protested. The lieutenant shoved a man and punched him.

He had to help, move, but he didn't do a thing, because he knew that if he stepped away from the counter, he'd fall down. Propped on his elbows, he pointed his weapon at the group of employees—some shouting, some seemingly about to defend the man who had protested—and saw Condori and Zenón Gonzales grab the man from the big desk, the one Vallejos had hit. The lieutenant pointed his sub-machine gun at him with a menacing gesture. The man finally gave in and opened the safe next to his desk. When Condori had finished putting the money into the bag, Mayta began to feel better. You should have come a week earlier to acclimatize yourself to the altitude, you just don't know how to do things.

"Are you okay?" Vallejos asked him on the way out.

"A touch of mountain sickness from running. Let's hold the meeting with whatever people are here. We've got to do it."

One of the boys euphorically shouted: "Long live the revolution!"

"Hurrah!" bellowed the other joeboys. One of them pointed his Mauser at the sky and fired. The first shot of the day. The other four followed. They invaded the plaza, cheering the revolution, firing shots in the air, and telling people to gather around.

"Everyone's told you there was no meeting, because nobody wanted to hear what they had to say. They called to the people walking on the square, standing in doorways, anyone—but no one would come," says Anthero Huillmo, ex-street photographer, now blind and selling novenas, religious pictures, and rosaries from eight in the morning until eight at night at the cathedral door. "They even tried to stop the truck drivers: 'Stop!' 'Get out!' 'Come on!' But the drivers had their doubts and just stepped on the gas. But there was a meeting. I was there, I saw it and heard it. That was before God saw fit to send that tear-gas grenade that burned my face. Now I can't see, but then I could and did. Actually, it was a meeting held exclusively for me."

Was that the first sign that their calculations were wrong not just about the people involved in the uprising but about the people of Jauja? The purpose of the meeting was crystal-clear in his mind: inform the man on the street about what had gone on that morning, explain the class struggle in its historic and social sense, and show their conviction—maybe even give some of the poorest money. But in the center of the plaza, to which Mayta had made his way, there was no one but a street photographer, the little bunch of Indians petrified on their bench, trying their best not to look at the revolutionaries, and the five joeboys. They vainly waved and called to the groups of curious people on the corners near the cathedral and the Colegio del Carmen. If the joeboys tried to approach them, they ran off. Did the shots scare them? Could the news have spread already, so that these people would be afraid to be taken for revolutionaries if the police were suddenly to appear? Did it make any sense to go on waiting?

Cupping his hands over his mouth, Mayta shouted: "We are rebelling against the bourgeois order, so the people can throw off their chains! To end the exploitation of the masses! To give land to the people who work it! To stop the imperialist rape of our nation!"

"Don't shout yourself hoarse. They're far away and can't hear you," said Vallejos, jumping off the little wall around the garden in the plaza. "We're wasting our time."

Mayta obeyed and began walking alongside him toward the corner of Bolognesi, where the taxis, guarded by Gualberto Bravo and Perico Temoche, were waiting. Well, there was no meeting, but at least his mountain sickness was better. Would they get to Quero? Would the people who were supposed to be there really be there with horses and mules?

As if there were telepathic communication between them, Mayta heard Vallejos say, "Even if the Ricrán guys don't show up in Quero, there won't be any problem, because there are lots of horses and mules there. It's a cattle town."

"We'll buy them, in that case," said Mayta, patting the bag he carried in his right hand. He turned to Condori, who marched behind him: "How is the road to Uchubamba?"

"When it's dry, easy," replied Condori. "I've done it a thousand times. It's only rough at night because of the cold. But as soon as you get to the jungle, easy as pie."

Gualberto Bravo and Perico Temoche, who were sitting next to the taxi drivers, got out to meet them. Envious of not having gone with them to the banks, they kept saying, "Tell us about it, tell us." But Vallejos ordered an immediate departure.

"We mustn't separate under any circumstance," said the lieutenant, coming up to Mayta, who, with Condori and the three joeboys, was already in Mr. Onaka's taxi. "No need to speed. First stop, Molinos."

He went to the other taxi, and Mayta thought: We'll get to Quero, we'll load the Mausers on mules, we'll cross the mountains, go down to the jungle, and in Uchubamba the community will receive us with open arms. We'll give them weapons, and Uchubamba will be our first base camp. He had to be optimistic. Although there had been desertions, and even if the Ricrán men didn't show up in Quero, he couldn't allow himself to doubt. Hadn't everything gone so well this morning?

"That's what we thought," says Colonel Felicio Tapia, a doctor drafted into the army, a married man with four sons, one an invalid and another an army man, wounded in action in the Azángaro sector. He's passing through Jauja because he has to make constant inspections of the clinics in the Junín zone. "We thought the guards and the lieutenant we'd left locked up would take a long time to get out, and since communications were cut, they'd have to go to Huancayo to get reinforcements. Five or six hours, at least. By then, we'd be well on our way to the jungle. Who'd find us then? Vallejitos had chosen the place very well.

"It's the area where we've had the most trouble carrying out operations. Ideal for ambushes. The Reds are out there in their dens, and the only way to root them out is by saturation bombing, by destroying everything, and attacking with bayonets—which means heavy casualties. If people knew how many men we've lost, they'd be shocked. Well, I don't suppose Peruvians are shocked by anything nowadays. Where were we? Oh yeah, that's what we thought. But Lieutenant Dongo got right out of the cell. He went to the telegraph office and saw everything smashed, so he went down to the station and found the telegraph there working perfectly. He telegraphed, and a busload of police left Huancayo about the time we were leaving Jauja. Instead of five hours, we barely had a two-hour lead on them. How stupid! To knock out the telegraph at the train station would have taken two minutes."

"So why didn't you do it?"

He shrugs and blows smoke out his mouth and nose. He's old before his time, his mustache stained by nicotine. He gasps. We are talking in the infirmary at the Jauja barracks. From time to time, Colonel Tapia glances into the waiting room crowded with sick and wounded being looked after by nurses.

"You know, I don't know why we didn't do it. Underdevelopment, I suppose. In the original plan, in which there were going to be some forty people, I think, not counting the joeboys, one group was supposed to seize the station. At least that's how I remember it. Then, in the confusion of changing plans, Vallejitos must have forgotten about that. Probably no one remembered that there was a telegraph at the station. The fact is, we left happy, thinking we had all the time in the world."

In fact, they weren't very happy. When Mr. Onaka (whining that he couldn't go to Molinos with his wife sick, that he didn't have enough gas to get there) started up, the incident with the watchmaker took place. Mayta saw him appear suddenly, snorting like a wild bull, right in front of the glass door with gothic letters on it: "Jewels and Watches: Pedro Bautista Lozada." He was an older man, thin, wearing glasses, his face red with indignation. He was carrying a shotgun. Mayta took the safety off his sub-machine gun, but he was calm enough not to fire—after all, the man was howling like a banshee, but he wasn't even aiming his gun at them. He was waving it around like a cane, shouting: "Fucking communists, you don't scare

238

me," while stumbling around by the curb, his glasses bouncing on his nose. "Fucking communists! Alight if you've got any balls!"

"Get going and don't stop," Mayta ordered the driver, sticking his finger in his back. At least, no one shot that old grouch. "He's a Spaniard," Felicio Tapia said, laughing. "What does alight mean?"

"Everyone in Jauja says you are the most pacific man in the world, don Pedro, a person who makes no trouble for anyone. What got into you that morning that you went out and insulted the revolutionaries?"

"I don't know what got into me." He talks through his nose, his toothless mouth dripping saliva. He lies under the vicuña blanket in his chair in the shop where he's passed the more than forty years since he came to Jauja: don Pedro Bautista Lozada. "I just got mad. I saw them go into the International and carry out the money in a bag. That didn't bother me. Then I heard them give communist cheers and shoot off their rifles. They didn't care that their stray shots could hurt someone. What was all that foolishness? So I took my shotgun, this one I have between my legs in case of unannounced guests. Then I noticed I hadn't even loaded it."

The dust, the junk, the disorder, and the character's incredible age remind me of a movie I saw when I was a kid: *The Prodigious Magician*. Don Pedro's face is a prune and his eyebrows are bushy and huge. He's told me he lives alone and prepares his own food—his principles forbid him to have servants.

"Tell me something else, don Pedro. When the police from Huancayo arrived and Lieutenant Dongo began to look for guides to track down the rebels, you refused to go. Could it be you weren't really so mad at them? Or was it that you were unfamiliar with the Jauja mountains?"

"I knew them better than anyone, good deer hunter that I was," he drones and dribbles, wiping away the gook that pours out of his eyes. "But even though I don't like communists, I

239

don't like cops either. I'm talking about then, because nowadays I don't even know what I like anymore. I only have a few watches left and this spit that keeps slipping out because I have no teeth. I'm an anarchist and will be one until I die. If anyone walks in here with bad intentions, guerrilla or police agent, this shotgun goes off. Down with communism, goddamn it. Death to the cops."

The taxis, one behind the other, passed through Plaza Santa Isabel, where they were to have loaded the Ricrán truck with the weapons captured at the jail, the police station, and the Civil Guard post. But no one around Mayta in the jam-packed car in which they could barely move was complaining about the change. The joeboys couldn't stop hugging each other and cheering. Condori, reserved, looked at them without partaking of their enthusiasm. Mayta was silent. But this happiness and excitement moved him. In the other taxi, the same scene was undoubtedly taking place.

At the same time, Mayta was taking note of the driver's edginess, watching him carefully, worried about the sloppy way he was driving. The car bounced and pitched. Mr. Onaka went into every pothole, hit every rock, and seemed intent on running over every dog, burro, horse, or person who crossed his path. Was it fear, or deliberate? Just then, only a few hunderd yards outside Jauja, the car went off the road and smashed against a pile of rocks alongside the ditch, flattening a fender and throwing the passengers into each other and against doors and windows. The five of them thought Mr. Onaka had done it on purpose. They roughed him up, insulted him, and Condori gave him a punch that split his eyebrow. Onaka whined that he hadn't crashed on purpose. When they got out of the car, Mayta smelled eucalyptus: a cool breeze from the nearby mountains was wafting it in. Vallejos's taxi doubled back, raising a cloud of red dust.

"That little joke cost us fifteen minutes, maybe more," says Juan Rosas, sub-contractor, truck driver, and owner of a bean and potato farm. He happens to be in Jauja, recovering from a hernia operation at his son-in-law's house. "We were waiting for another car to replace the Chink's. Not even a burro came by. The worst bad luck, because there were always trucks on that road coming and going to and from Molinos, Quero, or Buena Vista. That day, nothing. Mayta told Vallejos, 'You go on with your group—the one I was in—and see about the horses.' Because no one thought the Ricrán people would be waiting for us. Vallejos didn't want to go. So we stayed. Finally, a pickup came by. Fairly new, a full tank, good retreads. Not bad. We stopped it, there was an argument, the driver didn't want to cooperate, we had to scare him. In the end, we just commandeered it. The lieutenant, Condori, and Gonzales were up front. Mayta got in the back with the plain folk—us—and all the Mausers. We were concerned about the loss of time, but as soon as we got started again, we began to sing."

The pickup jumped along the roadbed filled with potholes, and the joeboys, their hair flying all over, their fists in the air, cheered Peru and the socialist revolution. Mayta, sitting with his back against the cab, looked at them. Then, suddenly, it occurred to him: "Why don't we sing 'The International,' comrades?"

The little faces, white with dust, nodded agreement, and several said, "Yes, yes, let's sing it." But then he realized that none of them knew the words or had ever heard "The International." There they were, under the diaphanous mountain sky, in their wrinkled uniforms, looking at him and looking at each other, each one waiting for the others to begin singing. He felt a wave of tenderness for the seven boys. They were years away from being men, but had already graduated into the revolution. They were risking everything in the marvelous spontaneity of their fifteen, sixteen, or seventeen years, even though they lacked political experience and any ideological formation. Weren't they worth more than the experienced revolutionaries of the RWP(T), who had stayed back in Lima, or the lettered Dr. Ubilluz and his worker-peasant legions, who had evaporated that same morning? Yes, they were. They'd chosen action. He wanted to hug them.

"I'll teach you the words," he said, standing up in the bouncing truck. "Let's sing, sing along with me. 'Arise, ye prisoners of starvation . . .' "

Screeching, out of key, exalted, laughing themselves sick because of their mistakes and cracked voices, raising a left fist in the air, cheering the revolution, socialism, and Peru: that's how the mule drivers and farmers on the outskirts of Jauja saw them, and also the rare travelers trekking down toward the city through waterfalls and bushy ferns, along that rocky, humid gorge that runs from Quero to the provincial capital. They tried to sing "The International" for quite a while, but because Mayta couldn't carry a tune, they never got it right. They ended up singing the National Anthem and the anthem of the Colegio Nacional de San José de Jauja. Then they reached the Molinos bridge. The truck didn't stop until Mayta forced it to by banging on the roof.

"What's the problem?" asked Vallejos, sticking his head out the half-open door.

"Weren't we going to blow up this bridge?"

The lieutenant made a face. "How? With our hands? The dynamite's at Ubilluz's place."

Mayta remembered that in every one of their discussions Vallejos had insisted on blowing up the bridge. With it destroyed, the police would have to go up to Quero on foot or on horseback, which would be one more advantage.

"Don't worry." Vallejos quieted him down. "We've done enough. Keep on singing, it makes the trip go faster."

The pickup started to move again, and the seven joeboys began singing and joking once more. But Mayta didn't sing along. He stood with his back against the cab, and as he watched the landscape with its huge trees go by, he listened to the sound of the waterfalls, the trill of the finches, and felt the clear air filling his lungs with oxygen. Lulled by the happiness of the adolescents, he let his imagination run wild. How would Peru be in a few years? A busy hive, whose atmosphere would reflect,

242

on a national scale, the atmosphere of this truck, stirred by the idealism of these boys.

The peasants, owners of their own lands by then; the workers, owners of their own factories by then; government officials, conscious that now they were serving the community and not imperialists, millionaires, political bosses, or local parties, would feel the same. With discrimination and exploitation abolished, the foundations of equality established through the abolition of inherited wealth, the replacement of the elitist army with a popular militia, the nationalization of private schools, and the expropriation of all companies, banks, businesses, and urban property, millions of Peruvians would feel that now indeed they were progressing, the poorest first. The hardest-working, most talented, and most revolutionary would get the important jobs, instead of the richest or the best connected.

And every day the chasms that separated the proletariat from the bourgeoisie, the whites from the Indians, blacks, and Asiatics, the coastal people from the mountain and jungle people, the Spanish speakers from the Quechua speakers, would be bridged just a bit more. Everyone, except the tiny group that would flee to the United States or die defending their privileges, would take part in the great production effort to develop the country, end illiteracy, and do away with the stranglehold of central authority. The fog of religion would fade with the systematic rise of science. The worker and peasant councils, in their factories, on their collective farms, and in government ministries, would prevent the outsized growth and consequent ossification of a bureaucracy that would freeze the revolution and use it for its own benefit.

What would he do in that new society, if he was still alive? He wouldn't accept any important place in government, in the armed forces, or in the diplomatic service. Maybe a political post, a minor one, perhaps in the country, on a collective farm in the Andes, or on some colonization project in the Amazon region. Social, moral, and sexual prejudices would give way little

243

by little, and it wouldn't matter to anyone, in that crucible of work and faith that Peru would be in the future, that he would be living with Anatolio. By then, they would have gotten back together, and it would be more or less obvious that, alone, free of stares, with all due discretion, they could love each other and enjoy each other. He secretly touched his fly with the hand grip of his weapon. Beautiful, isn't it, Mayta? Very. But how far off it seemed . . .

Nine

The community of Quero is one of the most ancient in Junín province. Today, the people of Quero—just as they did twenty-five years ago and probably just as they did centuries ago—grow potatoes, beans, and coca. They pasture their cattle on mountains which can be reached from Jauja by following a steep trail. If the rains don't turn the road into a swamp, the trip takes a couple of hours. The potholes make the pickup seem like a bucking bronco, but the countryside more than makes up for the rough ride: a deep pass, bound at each end by twin mountains, paralleled by a foamy, rushing river whose name changes—first it's called Molinos, and then, nearer to the town, Quero. Luxuriant cinchonas, their leaves made even greener by the morning dew, line the route toward the little town that stretches out along the pass. We go in at about eleven.

In Jauja, I heard contradictory versions of what took place in Quero. The town itself is in a war zone and in recent years has been the scene of innumerable attacks, executions, and large-scale operations by both the rebels and counterinsurgency forces. According to some, Quero was under rebel control and its plaza was fortified. Others said the army had an artillery company stationed there, as well as a training camp complete with U.S. advisers. One person was sure I'd never be allowed to enter Quero, because the army uses it as a concentration camp and torture center. "That's where they bring prisoners from all over the Mantaro Valley to make them talk. They use the most up-to-date methods. When they've finished with the prisoners, they take them up in helicopters and drop them out over the jungle to terrorize the Reds, who are supposedly watching from below."

Tales. In Quero, there's not a sign of either insurgents or soldiers. I'm not surprised that reality contradicts these rumors. Information in this country has ceased to be objective and has become pure fantasy—in newspapers, radio, television, and ordinary conversation. "To report" among us now means either to interpret reality according to our desires or fears, or to say simply what is convenient. It's an attempt to make up for our ignorance of what's going on—which in our heart of hearts we understand is irremediable and definitive. Since it is impossible to know what's really happening, we Peruvians lie, invent, dream, and take refuge in illusion. Because of these strange circumstances, Peruvian life, a life in which so few actually do read, has become literary.

The real Quero, where I'm walking around now, bears no resemblance to its image in the fictions I've heard. You see not a trace of war or combatants (of either side) anywhere. Why is the town deserted? I supposed that all eligible men would have been conscripted either by the army or by the guerrillas, but, as a matter of fact, you don't see old men or boys either. They must be working in the fields or inside their houses. Probably they get scared whenever an outsider walks into town. As I stroll through the little church, built in 1946, with its stone tower and tile roof, and wander around the gazebo in the center of the plaza, surrounded by cypress and eucalyptus trees, I get the feeling it's a ghost town. Could it have had the same image that morning when the revolutionaries rolled in?

"The sun was shining brightly, and the plaza was full of people, because it was the time for communal labor," don Eugenio Fernández Cristóbal assures me, as he points his cane at the sky filled with ashen clouds. "I was here in the square. They came right around that corner over there. About this time of day, more or less."

Don Eugenio was justice of the peace in Quero at that time. Now he's retired. What's extraordinary is that after all those events in which he was absolutely and totally involved—at least since Vallejos, Mayta, Condori, Zenón Gonzales, and their following of seven children arrived here—he went back to his judicial functions and lived several years more in Quero, finally retiring. Now he lives on the outskirts of Jauja. Despite all the apocalyptic tales about the region, I didn't have to ask him twice to go with me to Quero. "I always liked adventure," he tells me. And I didn't have to ask him twice to tell what he remembered about that day, the most important in his long life. He answers my questions quickly and with absolute certitude, even with regard to insignificant details. He never doubts, never contradicts himself, and leaves no loose threads that might call his memory into question. Not an easy game for an octogenarian who, besides, I have no doubt, hides some things from me and lies about many others. What exactly was his part in the adventure? No one knows for sure. Does he know himself, or does the version he's cooked up convince him as well?

"I took no notice, because it wasn't odd for pickups carrying people from Jauja to come to Quero. They parked right over there, next to Tadeo Canchis's house. They asked where they could eat. They were very hungry."

"And you didn't notice that they were all armed, don Eugenio? That, besides the weapon each one had, there were rifles in the truck?"

"I asked them if they were going hunting," don Eugenio

says. "Because this is not a good season for deer hunting, lieutenant."

"We're just going to do a little target practice, doctor," he says Vallejos told him. Up on the pampa.

"Wasn't it perfectly normal for some boys from the Colegio San José to come here for training?" don Eugenio asks himself. "Weren't they taking military training courses? Wasn't the lieutenant a soldier? The explanation seemed more than satisfactory to me."

"I'll tell you something. Until we got here, I hadn't given up hope."

"That the Ricrán guys would be waiting for us with horses?" Vallejos smiled.

"And Shorty Ubilluz, too, with the miners," confessed Mayta. "I still had my hopes."

He looked over Quero's small, green plaza a couple of times, as if trying to make the missing men appear by an act of will. His brow was furrowed and his mouth trembled. A bit farther on, Condori and Zenón Gonzales were talking with some people from the community. The joeboys stayed by the truck, keeping an eye on the Mausers.

"A real knife in the back," he added, in a barely audible voice.

"Unless some accident held them up on the highway," said the justice of the peace, standing next to him.

"There was no accident. They aren't here because they didn't want to be here," said Mayta. "What else could you expect? Why waste time feeling sorry about what they've done. They didn't come and that's that, what's the big deal?"

"That's the spirit." Vallejos clapped him on the back. "Better on our own than in bad company, damn it."

Mayta made an effort. He'd have to shake off this depression. Let's get to work, get the horses and mules, buy supplies, get going. Only one idea should be in your head, Mayta: Cross the mountains and get to Uchubamba. There, out of danger, they would be able to recruit men and calmly go over their strategy.

248

On the road, while he was standing in the pickup, his mountain sickness had disappeared. But now, in Quero, as he began to move around, he felt the pressure in his temples again, the same accelerated heart rate, the same dizziness, the same vertigo. He tried to cover it up as he walked through Quero, Vallejos on one side, the justice of the peace on the other, trying to find people who would rent them pack animals. Condori and Zenón Gonzales, who knew people in the village, went to get something to eat and to buy supplies. Cash, of course.

They should have held a meeting here to explain the insurrection to the peasants. But, without even talking it over with Vallejos, he rejected the idea. After this morning's failure he didn't want to remind the lieutenant of it. Why was he so depressed? He just couldn't shake it off. The euphoria he'd felt on the road had kept him from thinking over the day's events. But now he reviewed their situation again and again: four adults and seven adolescents hell-bent on putting plans into action that fell apart with each step they took. This is defeatism, Mayta, the road to failure. Like a machine, remember. He smiled and tried to show he understood what the justice of the peace and the lady who owned the house where they had stopped were saying in Quechua. You should have learned Quechua instead of French.

"They screwed themselves by staying here so long." Don Eugenio takes one last drag from the minuscule butt of his cigarette. How long did they stay? At least two hours. They got here around ten and left after twelve.

He really should say, "We left." Didn't he go with them? But don Eugenio, eighty years of age and all, commits not the slightest lapse that might even suggest that he was an accomplice of the rebels. We are in the gazebo in the center of the plaza, besieged by an impertinent rain the gray, hunchback clouds pour over the town. An intense, rapid cloudburst, followed by the most beautiful rainbow. When the sky clears, there always remains a light, imperceptible drizzle, the kind we get all the time in Lima, which makes the grass in the Quero plaza glisten.

Little by little, the people who still live there emerge. They appear from out of the houses like unreal figures—Indian women lost under multiple skirts, babies wearing hats, ancient peasants wearing sandals. They come over to say hello to don Eugenio, to embrace him. Some leave after exchanging a few words with him; others remain with us. They listen to him recall that episode of times past, at times nodding slightly; at other times, they interpolate brief comments. But when I try to find out how things are now, they all lapse into an unbreachable silence. Or they lie: they haven't seen soldiers or guerrillas, and know nothing about the war. As I supposed, there is not a single man or woman of fighting age among them. With his vest buttoned up tight, his wool cap pulled down to his eyes, and with the shoulders of his shiny old jacket too wide for his body, the old justice of the peace of Quero looks like a character out of a book, a gnome who's lost his way among these Andean peaks. His voice has a metallic quality, as if he were speaking from inside a tunnel.

"Why did they stay so long in Quero?" he asks himself, his thumbs stuck in the buttonholes of his vest. He observes the sky as if the answer were in the clouds. Because they had a hard time getting the pack animals. These people here can't rent out the animals they need for work just like that. No one wanted to rent, even though they were willing to pay top dollar. Finally they convinced the widow, doña Teofrasia Soto de Almaraz. By the way, what became of doña Teofrasia? There's a murmur, some remarks in Quechua, and one of the women crosses herself. Ah, she died. In the bombing? So the guerrillas had been here after all. Damn. Had they gone already? Did many die? Why did they put doña Teofrasia's son on trial?

Thanks to don Eugenio's marginal comments in Spanish during his conversation in Quechua with the townspeople, I begin sorting out the episode that obliquely reintroduces the present into Mayta's story. The guerrillas were in Quero and had "meted out justice" to several people, doña Teofrasia's son among them. But they had already gone their way, when a plane flew over the town, strafing the place. Among the victims was doña Teofrasia, who, when she heard the plane, had gone out to see what it looked like. She died in the doorway of the church.

"What a sad way to go," comments don Eugenio. She lived right down this street. Hunchbacked and a bit of a witch, according to local gossip. Well, it was she who accepted their offer after letting them plead with her. But her animals were out in the pasture, and it took her more than an hour to round them up. At the same time, they were held up by the food. I told you already, they were hungry, and they ordered lunch over at Gertrudis Sapollacu's place—she had a little inn and rented rooms.

"So they were sure of themselves."

"The police almost caught them with bowls of chicken soup in front of them," don Eugenio agrees.

The chronology is clear enough. Everyone agrees. An hour after things had calmed down, the busload of Civil Guards from Huancayo, commanded by a lieutenant named Silva and a corporal named Lituma, arrived at Jauja. They stopped briefly in the city to get a guide and to pick up Lieutenant Dongo and the guards under his command. The chase began immediately.

"And how is it you went with them, sir," I ask him point-blank, just to see if I can rattle him.

The lieutenant tried to get him to stay in Quero. Mayta listed the reasons why he should come with them. They needed someone to act as bridge between the city and the country, especially now, after all that had happened. They had to set up auxiliary networks, recruit people, get information. He was the right man for the job. All the arguing was useless. Vallejos's orders and Mayta's entreaties were obliterated by the resolve of the diminutive lawyer. No, gentlemen, I'm no fool, I'm not going to wait around here for the police so I can pay the piper. He was going with them whether they liked it or not. The polite exchange of ideas turned into an altercation. The voices of Vallejos and the justice of the peace grew louder, and in the

251

somber room reeking of grease and garlic, Mayta noticed that
Condori, Zenón Gonzales, and the joeboys had stopped eating to
listen. It was unwise to let the argument turn bitter. They had
enough problems already, and there were too few of them for
internal squabbles.

"It's not worthwhile arguing like this, comrades. If the doctor
insists on coming, let him come."

He was afraid the lieutenant would contradict him, but
Vallejos chose instead to eat his lunch. The justice did the same,
and in a few minutes the air was clear. Vallejos had posted cadet
commander Cordero Espinoza out on a hill to keep an eye on the
road as they ate. The stop in Quero was growing longer, and as he
nibbled smoked pieces of chicken, Mayta told himself it was
foolish to be taking so long.

"We really should be getting out of here."

Vallejos agreed, glancing at his watch, but he continued
eating unhurriedly. Mayta knew inwardly that he was right.
Yes, what a bother it was to stand up, to stretch your legs, limber
up your muscles, run out to the hills, and walk—for how many
hours? What if he fainted from mountain sickness? They'd put
him on a mule, like a sack. It was ridiculous to be bothered by
this illness. He felt as if mountain sickness were a luxury unac-
ceptable in a revolutionary. But the physical discomfort was
very real: shivers, headaches, a generalized lassitude. And, worst
of all, that pounding in his chest.

He was relieved to see that Vallejos and the justice of the
peace were chatting animatedly. How to explain why the Ricrán
people were scared off? Did they have a meeting yesterday to
decide not to come? Did Shorty Ubilluz order them not to
come? It would be an incredible coincidence for Ubilluz, the
miners, and the Ricrán men all to have decided to back out
independently, without talking to each other. Was this of any
importance now, Mayta? Not the slightest. Later it would be,
when history demanded a reckoning and established the truth.
(But I, in this case, am history, and I know that things aren't

252

that simple, that time doesn't always let the truth come out. About this specific matter, the last-minute absences, there is no way of knowing with absolute certainty whether the missing men deserted or if the protagonists went into action ahead of time, or if it all turned out to be the result of a misunderstanding about dates, days, and hours. And there is no way of setting the record straight, because even the actors don't know the facts.)

He swallowed the last mouthful and wiped his mouth with his handkerchief. The semi-darkness in the room had at first hidden the flies, but now he could see them. They formed a constellation on the walls and ceiling, and they strolled arrogantly over the plates of food and the fingers of those eating. All the houses in Quero had to be like that: no light, no running water, no drainage, and no bath. Flies, lice, and a thousand other bugs must be part of the poor furniture, lords and masters of pots and pelts, of the rustic beds pushed up against the daub-and-wattle walls, of the faded images of the Virgin and of saints nailed to the doors. If they had to pee at night, they probably wouldn't feel like getting up and going outside. They pee right here, next to the bed where they sleep and the stove where they cook. After all, the floor is just dirt, and dirt soaks up urine, leaving no trace. And the smell doesn't matter much because it disappears, mixed in with the other smells, thickening the multiple smells of garbage and filth that make up the household atmosphere. And if at midnight they had to shit? Would they have enough energy to go out into the darkness and the cold, the wind and the rain? They'd shit right here, between the stove and the bed.

As they walked in, the lady of the house, an old Indian woman all wrinkly and rheumy, with two long pigtails that bounced off her shoulders as she walked, put some cavies that had been walking loose in the room in a corner behind a trunk. Did the animals sleep with her, cuddled up against her old body in search of warmth? How many months, how many years had that lady been wearing those skirts she had on, which no doubt had grown old with her? How long had it been since she had washed herself

253

from head to toe with soap? Months? Years? Had she ever done it in her entire life? The dizziness of the mountain sickness disappeared, replaced by sadness.

Yes, Mayta, millions of Peruvians lived in this same grime, in this same abandonment, amid their own urine and excrement, without light or water, living the same vegetable life, the same animal routine, the same elemental existence that this woman was living. This woman with whom, despite his efforts, he hadn't been able to exchange more than a few words, because she barely knew any Spanish. Just looking around here justified what they had done and what they were going to do, didn't it? When Peruvians like this woman came to understand that they did have power, that all they had to do was become aware of it and use it, the whole pyramid of exploitation, servitude, and horror that was Peru would collapse like a rotten roof. When they understood that by rebelling they would finally begin to humanize their inhuman lives, the revolution would be unstoppable.

"Get ready, we're moving out," said Vallejos, standing up. "Let's load the rifles."

They all hustled out to the street. Mayta felt uplifted again as he passed from the darkness to the light. He went to help the joeboys remove the rifles from the pickup and tie them on to the mules. In the plaza, the Indians went on buying and selling, uninterested in them.

"They convinced me in the simplest way," says don Eugenio, with a mournful expression, pitying his own credulity. "Lieutenant Vallejos explained to me that, besides training the boys, he was going to hand the Aína hacienda over to the Uchubamba commune. Remember, Condori was president of the commune, and Zenón Gonzales vice president. Why shouldn't I believe him? There had been problems in Aína for months. The commune there had occupied the hacienda lands and claimed them, using colonial titles as their proof of ownership. Wasn't the lieutenant a military authority in the province? I had to do my duty, I wasn't a justice for nothing, you know. So, and mind you the hike was no laughing matter—I was around sixty at the

254

time—I went with them willingly. Wasn't it the natural thing to do?"

You'd certainly say it was, to hear the naturalness with which he says it. The sun has come out. Don Eugenio's face glows.

"You must have been really surprised when the shooting began."

"You'd better believe it," he says without hesitation. "It began just after we left, when we went into Huayjaco gulch."

He frowns—his eyelids wrinkle, his eyebrows bristle—and his eyes turn watery. It must be the effect of the glare. I can't imagine the former justice of the peace weeping tears of nostalgia over what happened that afternoon. Although it may be that at his age, all his past life, even the most painful parts, arouses his nostalgia.

"They were in such a hurry that I didn't even have time to pack a bag," he says softly. "I left dressed just the way you see me now, wearing a tie, a vest, and a cap. We started walking, and an hour, an hour and a half later, the fun began."

He laughs a little, and the people around us laugh as well. There six, four men and two women, all of them old. Sitting on the rusty railing that runs around the gazebo are several boys. I ask the adults if they were there when the police came. After looking at the justice out of the corner of their eye, as if asking his permission to speak, they say they were. I push on, turning to the oldest of the peasants: Tell me what happened, what took place after the revolutionaries left. He points to the corner of the plaza, where the road ends: That's where the bus carrying the police came into town. It was smoking and backfiring. How many? A lot. How many would you say? About fifty, maybe. Spurred on by his example, the others also begin to speak and all at once start telling me what they remember. It's hard for me to follow the thread in this labyrinth where Quechua mixes with Spanish, where the events of twenty-five years ago suddenly get confused with the air strike of a few days or weeks ago—when it took place, in fact, is also unclear—and with the guerrilla trials. In the minds of the peasants there is, naturally, an association that it's cost me a lot of work to make and that very few of my compatriots see. What I finally establish is that the fifty or sixty policemen thought the rebels were hiding in Quero, so they spent about half an hour searching the town, going in and out of the tiny houses, asking everyone where the rebels were. Did they ask where the "revolutionaries" were? Did they call them communists? No, they didn't use those names. They said thieves, rustlers, bandits. Are you sure?

"Of course they're sure," says don Eugenio, speaking for all of them. "You have to remember that those were other times—who would ever have thought that was a revolution? Remember, too, that they robbed two banks before leaving Jauja . . ."

He laughs, and the others laugh as well. In that half hour they were here, were there any incidents involving police and members of the community? No, none. The guards were convinced right then and there that the "rustlers" had gone and that the people of Quero had nothing to do with them and knew nothing about what had happened in Jauja. Other times, no doubt about it: then the police didn't think that any man wearing a poncho and sandals was—until he proved otherwise—an accomplice of the subversives. The Andean world hadn't yet been polarized to the degree it has today, when its inhabitants can only be either accomplices of the rebels or accomplices of the repressors of the rebels.

"In the meantime," says the justice of the peace, his eyes once again watery, "we were getting soaked to the skin."

The rain poured down fifteen minutes after they'd left Quero. A rain so heavy it sometimes seemed like hail. They considered looking for a place to stay dry until it let up, but there was no place. How the landscape has changed, Mayta said to himself. He was probably the only one not bothered by the cloudburst. The water poured off his skin, saturated his hair, ran between his lips, and felt like balm. At the point where the Quero farms ended, the land immediately began to curve upward. It was as if they had once again crossed into a different region or country,

256

because this land had nothing whatever in common with the land between Jauja and Quero. The dense cinchonas, the pastures, the birds, the roar of the waterfalls, the wildflowers, and the reeds waving along the side of the road had all disappeared. On this bald slope, there wasn't even a trace of a road, and the only vegetation was some giant, thick-armed, spiny cacti that looked like candelabra.

The very earth had become black and hunchbacked, with huge, sinister-looking rocks and stones. They walked in three groups: the mules and arms in front, with Condori and three joeboys; then the rest of the boys, led by Zenón Gonzales, about a hundred yards behind; and finally the last group, the lieutenant, Mayta, and the justice of the peace. He also knew the way to Aína, in case they lost the others. But up to now Mayta was able to keep the other two groups in sight, up ahead, above, at the foot of the mountains, two spots that appeared and disappeared as the land rose or fell and the rain got lighter or heavier. It must have been the middle of the afternoon, although the grayness of the sky suggested nightfall. "What time is it?" he asked Vallejos. "Two-thirty." When he heard that, Mayta remembered a joke the students at the Salesian School would make whenever someone asked the time. "I don't know, my cock has stopped," and they'd point to their fly. He smiled, and in that moment of distraction, he almost fell.

"Carry your weapon with the barrel pointing down, so the rain doesn't get in," Vallejos said to him. The rain made the ground muddy, and Mayta tried to step from stone to stone, but the stones had loosened because of the rain, so he was constantly slipping. On the other hand, on his right side, the Quero lawyer —tiny, huddled over, his hat oozing water, his nose and mouth covered with a multicolored handkerchief, his ancient boots caked with mud—walked this mountain trail as if he were on a smooth sidewalk. Vallejos, too, walked easily, hunched forward a bit, his sub-machine gun on his shoulder, and his head down, so he could watch where he stepped. He led the way the whole time, and Mayta and don Eugenio would have to sprint from time to time to catch up to him. Since leaving Quero, they had barely spoken a word. The idea was to reach the pass called Viena, on the eastern slope, where it was milder. Condori and Zenón Gonzales thought it would be possible to get there before nightfall, if they hurried. It wasn't advisable to camp out on the uplands because of the danger of snow or a storm.

Although he was tired and still occasionally bothered by the altitude, Mayta felt fine. Were the Andes finally accepting him after tormenting him for so long? Had he received his baptism? Yet, a short time later, when Vallejos said they could take a rest, he dropped to the muddy ground, exhausted. The rain had stopped, the sky was clearing, and he could no longer see the other two groups. The three men were in a deep hollow, flanked by rock walls from which sprouted moist clumps of ichu grass. Vallejos came over, sat next to him, and asked to see his weapon. He looked it over carefully, moving the safety on and off. He returned it without saying a word, and lit a cigarette. The young man's face was covered with drops of water, and, through the cigarette smoke, Mayta could see he was tense with worry.

"You're the one who's always optimistic," he said to him.

"I'm still optimistic," replied Vallejos, taking a drag and expelling smoke out his nose and mouth. "But . . ."

"But you still can't figure out what happened this morning," said Mayta. "You've lost your political virginity, my friend. The revolution is more complicated than any fairy tale, brother."

"I don't want to discuss what happened this morning," Vallejos cut him off. "There are more important things to do now."

They heard a snore. The justice of the peace had settled down on his back on the ground, with his hat over his face, and appeared to have fallen asleep.

Vallejos looked at his watch. "If I'm right, the guards should be getting to Jauja now. We've got about four hours on them. And out here in these badlands we're like a needle in a haystack.

258

We're out of danger, I think. Okay, let's wake up the justice and be on our way."

No sooner had he heard Vallejos's last words than don Eugenio jumped to his feet. Instantly he clapped his soaking hat on his head. "Always ready, lieutenant," he said, giving a military salute. "I'm an owl, I close only one eye when I sleep."

"I'm amazed you're with us, doctor," said Mayta. "At your age, and with all the work you have, you have good reasons to look out for yourself."

"Well, frankly, if someone had given me the word, I probably would have taken off," the justice confessed, without the slightest embarrassment. "But they never said a word to me, they treated me like trash. So what else could I do? Wait for the police, so I could be the sacrificial lamb? What jerk would do that?"

Mayta began to laugh. They had started walking again and were scrambling up out of the hollow, slipping all the time, when he saw Vallejos freeze, crouched over. He looked from side to side, listening.

"Shots," he heard him say in a low voice.

"Thunder, man," said Mayta. "Sure it's shots?"

"I'm going to see where they're coming from," said Vallejos, moving off. "You two stay here, don't make a sound."

"And the police believed all that when you told them, don Eugenio?"

"Of course they believed me. Wasn't it the truth? But beforehand they put me through the wringer."

With his thumbs in his vest and his wrinkled face turned toward the sky, he goes on telling his story. Standing in a circle in the gazebo, there are now about twenty old people and children. They had him for three days in the Jauja jail, then a couple of weeks in the Civil Guard headquarters over in Huancayo, demanding he confess to being an accomplice of the revolutionaries. But he, of course, remained stubborn, indefatigable, and repeated his tale about being tricked into going with them, that he believed Vallejos and the others when they said they needed a justice of the peace to hand over the Aína hacienda to the Uchubamba community, and that the arms were for the joeboys' military training exercises. They had to accept his story; yes, sir, they did. After three weeks, he was back in Quero, back to his job as justice of the peace, clean as a whistle, and with a good story for his friends. He laughs, and in his laugh I detect a touch of mockery. Now the air is dry, and on the village buildings, on the farmland, and on the nearby mountains, there is a play of ocher, slate, gold, and various shades of green. "It's sad to see these fields lying fallow," don Eugenio laments. "All this was excellent farmland. Damn the war! It's killing Quero, it's not fair. And to think that twenty-five years ago the town seemed so poor. But things can always get worse, there is no limit when it comes to misery." I don't let him get distracted by current events and make him return to the past and to fiction. What did he do during the exchange of fire? How long did it last? Did they ever get out of the Huayjaco gulch? From the beginning to the end, and don't leave a thing out, don Eugenio.

Shots, no doubt about it. Mayta was down on one knee, submachine gun at the ready, looking all around him. But, down in the hollow, his field of vision was limited: a horizon broken by toothlike crags. A shadow passed, flapping its wings. A condor? He never remembered seeing one, except in photographs. He noticed that the justice of the peace was crossing himself and that, with his eyes closed and his hands pressed together, he had begun to pray. He heard another volley in the same area as the first one. When would Vallejos come back? As if in answer to his wish, the lieutenant appeared at the edge of the hollow. And, behind him, the face of one of the joeboys from the middle group: Perico Temoche. They slid into the hollow and came toward them. Temoche's face was red and his hands and the butt of his Mauser stained with mud, as if he had fallen.

"They're firing at the first group," said Vallejos. "But they're far away, the second group hasn't seen them yet."

"What do we do?" asked Mayta.

"We advance," replied Vallejos forcefully. "The first group is the important one, we've got to save those weapons. We'll try to distract them until the first group gets away. Let's get going. Spread out."

As they climbed out of the hollow, Mayta wondered why it hadn't occurred to anyone to give don Eugenio a rifle and why he hadn't asked for one. If they had to fight, the justice was in for a rough time. He wasn't anxious or afraid. He was totally serene. He wasn't surprised about the shots. He had been waiting for them ever since they left Jauja and had never believed they had as big a lead as the lieutenant claimed. How stupid it was to have stayed so long in Quero.

At the top of the hollow, they crouched down to take a look. They couldn't see anyone: only the gray-brown, rolling terrain, always rising, with occasional ridges and cliffs, where he thought they could take cover if their pursuers appeared from around a hill.

"Take cover among the rocks," said Vallejos. He was carrying his sub-machine gun in his left hand, while with his right he was gesturing for them to fan out more. He was virtually running, bent over, looking all around. Behind him came the justice, with Mayta and Perico Temoche bringing up the rear. He hadn't heard any more shots. The sky was clearing: there were fewer clouds, and they were not leaden, heavy storm-clouds, but white, spongy, fair-weather clouds. Bad luck, now it would be better if it were raining, he thought. He moved forward, concerned about his heart, afraid he'd be overcome again by shortness of breath, irregular heart rate, fatigue. But he wasn't; he felt well, although a bit cold. Straining his eyes, he tried to pick out the forward groups. It was impossible, because of the irregularity of the terrain and the abundance of blind spots. Then, between two high points, he seemed to make out the moving spots.

He beckoned Perico Temoche over. "Is that your group?"

The boy nodded several times, without speaking. He seemed

even more of a child this way, with his face twisted. He was hugging his rifle as if someone were going to try to take it away from him, and he seemed to have lost his voice.

"There haven't been any more shots." He tried to raise the boy's spirits. "Maybe it was just a false alarm."

"No, it was no false alarm," stammered Perico Temoche. "The shots were real."

And in a very low voice, trying his best to keep his self-control, he told Mayta that, when the first shots rang out, his whole group could see that, out in front, the vanguard was scattering, while someone, most likely Condori, raised his rifle to reply to the attack. Zenón Gonzales shouted: "Hit the dirt, hit the dirt." They remained flat on their faces until Vallejos appeared and ordered them to go on. Vallejos had brought him back so he could be their runner.

"And I know why." Mayta smiled at him. "Because you're the fastest. And the cleverest, too?"

The joeboy smiled slightly, without opening his mouth. They went on walking together, looking to each side. Vallejos and the justice of the peace were about twenty yards in front of them. Minutes later, they heard another volley.

"The funny part is that right in the middle of all that shooting I caught a cold," says don Eugenio. "The rain had been heavy and I was soaked, see?"

Yes, the small man in his vest and hat, surrounded by guerrillas, ducking bullets being fired by guards from up in the mountains, begins to sneeze. Trying to put the squeeze on him, I ask when did he realize that those he was with were insurgents and that the business about maneuvers and the handing over of Aína was pure make-believe. He isn't fazed.

"When the bullets began to fly," he says, with absolute conviction, "the situation became self-evident. Damn it, man, put yourself in my place. Without knowing how, there I was, with bullets whizzing all around me."

He pauses, his eyes watery again, and I remember that afternoon in Paris two or three days after the afternoon we're recalling. At that hour of the day, I religiously stopped writing, went out to buy *Le Monde*, to read it while drinking an espresso at the Le Tournon bistro near my house. His name was misspelled, they'd changed the *y* to an *i*, but I hadn't the slightest doubt that it was my schoolmate from the Salesian. His name appeared in a news item about Peru, so small it was almost invisible, barely six or seven lines, no more than a hundred words. "Insurrection Attempt Fails," or something like that, and although it wasn't clear whether the movement had any further ramifications, the article did say that the leaders were either dead or captured. Was Mayta captured or dead? That was my first thought as the Gauloise I was smoking fell out of my mouth and I read and reread the notice, unable to accept that in my far-off land such a thing had taken place and that my fellow reader of *The Count of Monte Cristo* was the main character. But that the Mayta spelled with an *i* in *Le Monde* was my Mayta, I was sure of from the start.

"What time did the prisoners begin to get here?" don Eugenio repeats my question, as if I had asked it of him. Actually, I asked the old people from Quero, but it's good that it's the justice of the peace, a man well known to the locals, who shows interest in finding out. "It must have been at night, don't you think?"

There is a chorus of no's, heads shaking, voices that try to speak over one another. Night hadn't fallen, it was still afternoon. The guards came back in two groups. The first brought the president of the community of Uchubamba tied onto one of doña Teofrasia's mules. Was Condori already dead? Dying. He'd been shot twice, once in the back and once in the neck, and he was covered with blood. They also brought several of the joeboys, with their hands tied behind them. In those days, the winners took prisoners. Nowadays, it's better to die fighting, because when they catch you, they get what they want out of you and kill you anyway, isn't that right, sir? Anyway, they'd taken the boys' shoelaces, so they couldn't try to escape. It was as if they were walking on eggs, and though they dragged their feet, some lost their shoes. They brought Condori to the lieutenant governor's house and gave him first aid, but it was a joke, because he died right away. About a half hour later, the others arrived. Vallejos waved to them to hurry.

"Faster, faster," he heard him shout.

Mayta tried, but he couldn't. Now Perico Temoche was several yards in front of him. There were scattered shots, but he couldn't tell where they were coming from or if they were farther away or closer than before. He was trembling, not from mountain sickness, but from the cold. Just then, he saw Vallejos raise his sub-machine gun: the blast exploded in his ears. He looked at the ridge the lieutenant had fired at, and all he saw were rocks, earth, clumps of ichu grass, jagged peaks, blue sky, and little white clouds. He aimed in the same direction, his finger on the trigger.

"Why the fuck are you stopping"—Vallejos urged them on again. "Go on, go on."

Mayta obeyed and walked very quickly for a good stretch, his body hunched over, jumping over stony patches, breaking into a run sometimes, tripping, feeling the cold right down to his bones, and his heart going crazy. He heard more shots, and at one time was sure that a bullet had smashed into some stones a short distance away. But, no matter how hard he looked at the ridges, he couldn't see a single enemy soldier. He had finally become an unthinking machine, a machine with no doubts, no memory, a body concentrated on the task of running, so he wouldn't be left behind. Suddenly his knees buckled and he stopped, out of breath. Staggering, he went a few steps farther and took cover behind some mossy rocks. The justice of the peace, Vallejos, and Perico Temoche continued to advance very rapidly. You'll never catch up to them, Mayta.

The lieutenant turned around, and Mayta signaled him to keep going. Just as he was gesturing, he noticed, this time without any doubt, that a bullet struck a few steps away from him: it gouged a small smoky hole in the ground. He crouched as low as he could, looked, searched, and finally saw, peering over the wall of rocks on his right side, the head of a guard, and a rifle pointed straight at him. He had taken cover on the wrong side. He crawled around the rocks, flattened out on the ground, and felt shots going right over his head. When he could finally aim and fire, trying to apply Vallejos's instructions—the target should be right in the sights—the guard was no longer on the wall. The burst of fire knocked him back and dazed him. He saw that his shots had splintered the stones a yard below, where he'd seen the guard.

"Run, run, I'll cover you," he heard Vallejos shout. The lieutenant was aiming at the wall.

Mayta got up and ran. He was stiff from the cold; his bones seemed to creak under his skin. It was a cold both freezing and boiling, which made him sweat, as if he had a fever. When he was next to Vallejos, he went down on his knees and aimed at the rocks.

"There are maybe three or four there," said the lieutenant, pointing. "We're moving forward in jumps, by stages. We can't stay in one place, or they'll surround us. They mustn't cut us off from the others. Cover me."

And, without waiting for a reply, he got up and began to run. Mayta kept watching the cliffs on the right, his finger on the trigger, but there was no sign of life. Finally, he looked for Vallejos and saw him far off, waving him on. He would cover him. He began to run, and after a few steps, he heard shots again. But he didn't stop, he kept running. Soon he found out it was the lieutenant who was shooting. When he reached him, they were together with Perico Temoche and the justice of the peace. The boy was loading a clip which he'd taken out of a bag hanging on his cartridge belt. So he'd been firing, too.

"And the other groups?" Mayta asked. There was a stony rise in front of them, so they could see nothing.

"We've lost them, but they know they can't stand still," said Vallejos urgently, without ceasing to look around him. And,

265

after a pause: "If they surround us, we're fucked. We've got to keep going until nightfall. When it's dark, we'll be out of danger. There's no way to hunt us down at night."

Till it gets dark, thought Mayta. How much longer would that be? Three, five, six hours? He didn't ask Vallejos what time it was. Instead, he stuck his hand into his pack—he'd done it dozens of times that day—and made sure he had lots of clips.

"We'll move two by two," ordered Vallejos. "First the doctor and me, then you and Perico. One pair covers the other. Pay attention, be careful, run in a crouch. Let's go, doc."

He took off, and Mayta saw that now the justice of the peace had a revolver in his hand. Where did he get it? It had to be the lieutenant's, that's why his holster was open. Right then, he saw two silhouettes above his head, between two rifle barrels. One shouted: "Give up, motherfucker." He and Perico fired at the same time.

"They didn't catch all of them that same day," don Eugenio says. Two joeboys got away: Teófilo Puertas and Felicio Tapia.

I got this story directly from the people involved, but I don't interrupt him, just to see how his version squares with theirs. A few details either way: the old justice of the peace's version is very similar to what I've already heard. Puertas and Felicio were in the first group, under Condori's command. They were the first to be spotted by one of the patrols the guards had divided into to search the area. On Vallejos's orders, Condori tried to move forward, while Vallejos held off the attack, but he was soon wounded. This caused a panic. The boys started running, abandoning the mules and rifles. Puertas and Tapia hid in a cave. They stayed there all night, half frozen. The next day, hungry, confused, and with colds, they retraced their steps and reached Jauja without being caught. Accompanied by their parents, they turned themselves in at the jail.

"Felicio was all swollen up," the justice of the peace tells me. Because of the beating he'd been given for trying to be a revolutionary.

Out of all those people from Quero who'd been with us, there

266

was left in the gazebo only one old couple now. Both remember Zenón Gonzales's entrance—tied to a horse, barefoot, and with his shirt ripped, as if he'd struggled with the guards. Behind him came the rest of the joeboys, also tied up and without shoelaces. One of them—no one knows which one—was crying. A dark-skinned kid, they say, one of the little ones. Was he crying because they'd beaten him? Because he was wounded or frightened? Who knows. Maybe because of the lieutenant's bad luck.

And so, climbing up, always up, two by two, they went on for a period that to Mayta seemed like hours, but which couldn't have been because it hadn't grown a bit darker. They constantly changed partners: Vallejos and the lawyer, Mayta and Perico Temoche, or Vallejos and the joeboy, and Mayta and the lawyer. Two ran and two covered. They were together enough of the time to buck each other up, catch their breath, and move on. They would see the guards' faces at every turn, and they fired shots that never seemed to hit their target. There weren't three or four, as Vallejos had imagined, but many more; otherwise, they would have had to be ubiquitous to appear in so many different spots. They would peer out from the high ground, sometimes on both sides, although the more dangerous side was the right, where the wall of stones was very close to the path they were running along.

They were following them along the line of the ridge, and even though Mayta from time to time thought they had left them behind, they always reappeared. He'd already changed clips a couple of times. He didn't feel ill; cold, yes, but his body was holding up well under the tremendous strain of running at this altitude. Why hasn't anyone been wounded? he thought. After all, the guards had taken lots of shots at them. It's that the guards are being cautious, they barely stick out their heads and take potshots, just to do their duty, without pausing to aim, afraid of being easy targets for the rebels. It seemed like a game, a noisy but inoffensive ritual. Would it last until dark? Could they slip away from the guards? It seemed impossible that night would ever come, that this clear sky would ever darken. He didn't feel discouraged. Without arrogance, without even feeling sorry for himself, he thought: Rightly or wrongly, Mayta, you're doing just what you always wanted to do.

"Get ready, don Eugenio. Let's run. They're covering us."

"You go on without me, my legs have given out," said the justice of the peace very slowly. "I'll stay behind. Take this, too."

Instead of handing it to him, don Eugenio threw him the revolver, which Mayta had to bend over to pick up. The justice of the peace was sitting down, with his legs spread apart. He was perspiring copiously and his mouth was twisted into an anxious grimace, as if he'd been left without air to breathe. His posture and his expression were those of a man who's reached the limits of his resistance, who's been rendered indifferent by exhaustion. Mayta understood there was no point in arguing with him.

"Good luck, don Eugenio," he said, starting to run. He quickly crossed the thirty or forty yards that separated him from Vallejos and Perico Temoche and didn't hear a single shot. When he reached them, they were on their knees, firing. He tried to explain what had happened to the justice of the peace, but he was gasping so furiously that he couldn't get the words out. He tried to fire from the ground, but couldn't. His weapon was jammed. He fired the revolver, the three final rounds, with the feeling that he was doing it for fun. The wall was very close and there was a line of rifles aimed at them: the enemy caps appeared and disappeared. He heard them shout threats that the wind brought to them quite clearly: "Give up, damn you." "Give up, motherfuckers." "Your accomplices have already surrendered." "Start praying, assholes." It occurred to him: They've got orders to take us alive. That's why no one's wounded. They were only firing to scare us. Could it be true that the first group had given up? He was calmer and tried to tell Vallejos about don Eugenio, but the lieutenant cut him off with an energetic gesture. "Run, I'll cover you."

268

Mayta realized, from his voice and face, that this time he was really alarmed. "Quickly, this is a bad spot, they're cutting us off. Run, run." And he gave him a pat on the back.

Perico Temoche began to run. Mayta got up and ran, too, hearing the shots whistle by him. But he didn't stop. Gasping, feeling ice piercing his muscles, his bones, his very blood vessels, he kept on running, and even though he tripped and fell twice and once lost the revolver he held in his left hand, he got right up both times and went on, making a superhuman effort. Until his legs gave out and he fell to his knees. He huddled on the ground.

"We've gotten ahead of them," he heard Perico Temoche say. And an instant later: "Where's Vallejos? Do you see him?" There was a long pause, with gasps. "Mayta, Mayta, I think those motherfuckers have got him."

Through the sweat that clouded his vision, he saw that down there where the lieutenant had remained to cover them—they'd run about two hundred yards—there were some greenish silhouettes moving about.

"Let's run, come on," he said, panting, trying to stand up. But neither his arms nor his legs would move. Then he bellowed, "Run, Perico. I'll cover you. Run, run."

"They brought Vallejos in at night, I saw him myself, didn't all of you?" says the justice of the peace. The two old folks with us in the gazebo confirm what he says by nodding. Don Eugenio points again to the little house with the shield on it, the government office. "I saw it from there. They put us prisoners in that room with the balcony. They brought him in on a horse, wrapped in a blanket they could barely pull off him because it stuck to the blood pouring out of all his wounds. He was very dead when they brought him into Quero."

I listen to him ramble on about who killed Vallejos and how. It's a story I've heard many times from so many people, both in Jauja and in Lima, that I know no one can tell me what I don't already know. The former justice of the peace for Quero will not help me determine which among all the hypotheses is the correct

269

one. That Vallejos died in the exchange of fire between the insurgents and the Civil Guards. That he was only wounded and Lieutenant Dongo finished him off, to avenge the humiliation Vallejos inflicted when he captured his police station and locked him up in his own jail. That he wasn't wounded when they captured him, and was executed on orders from above, out there in the Huayjaco flatlands, to set an example to officers with revolutionary fancies. The justice of the peace recites all these hypotheses and—with his usual prudence—intimates that he accepts the thesis that Vallejos was executed by Lieutenant Dongo.

Personal vengeance, the confrontation between the idealist and the conformist, the rebel and authority: these are images that correspond to the romantic appetites of our people. Which doesn't mean, of course, that they can't be true. The fact is that this part of the story—under what circumstances Vallejos died —will never be cleared up. We won't even know how many times he was shot: there was no autopsy, and the death certificate doesn't say a thing. The witnesses give the most disparate accounts: from a single shot in the back of the neck to a body turned into a sieve. All we know is that he was dead when they brought him into Quero tied to a horse, that from here they brought him to Jauja, and that his family took him back to Lima the next day. He was buried in the old cemetery in Surco. It's not used anymore; the old headstones are in ruins, and the paths are covered with weeds. Around the lieutenant's tomb, which gives only his name and the date of his death, there is a thick crop of wild grass.

"And did you see Mayta when they brought him in, don Eugenio?"

Mayta, who never took his eyes off the guards gathered around down below, where Vallejos was, began to catch his breath, to come back to life. He was still on the ground, pointing at nothing in particular with his jammed sub-machine gun. He tried not to think about Vallejos, about what could have happened to him, but about recovering his strength, getting to his feet, and catching up to Perico Temoche. Taking deep breaths, he sat upright, and then, almost bent double, he ran, without knowing if he was being shot at, without knowing where he was going, until he finally had to stop. He threw himself on the ground with his eyes closed, waiting for the bullets to pierce his body. You are going to die, Mayta. This is what it is to be dead.

"What should we do, what should we do?" stammered the joeboy at his side.

"I'll cover you," he said, panting, trying to pick up the sub-machine gun and aim.

"We're surrounded," whimpered the boy. "They're going to kill us."

Through the sweat pouring down his forehead, he saw guards all around him, some prone, others hunched down. Their rifles were all pointed at them. Their lips were moving, and there were some unintelligible sounds. But he didn't have to understand to know that they were shouting: "Give up! Drop your weapons!" Surrender? They would kill him, in any case. Or they would torture him. He pulled the trigger with all his strength, but it was still jammed. He worked the action for a few seconds, listening all the time to Perico Temoche's whimpering.

"Put down your guns! Put your hands on your heads!" bellowed a voice that was very near. Or you're dead.

"Don't cry, don't give them the satisfaction," said Mayta to the joeboy. "Go ahead, Perico, throw away your rifle."

He threw the sub-machine far away, and, imitated by Perico Temoche, he stood up with his hands on his head.

"Corporal Lituma!" The voice seemed to come from a bull-horn. "Frisk them. One false move, shoot them."

"Yes, lieutenant."

Uniformed figures with rifles came running from all sides. He waited, motionless, for them to come at him, convinced they would beat him, his fatigue and the coldness increasing with every second. But he only felt shoves as they searched him from head to foot. They ripped the pouch off his belt, and calling him "rustler" and "thief," they ordered him to take the shoelaces off his sneakers. They tied his hands behind his back with a rope, and did the same to Perico Temoche. Mayta heard Corporal Lituma sermonizing the boy, asking if he wasn't ashamed to be a "rustler" when he was just a snotnose. Rustlers? Did they think they stole cattle? He felt like laughing at the stupidity of his captors. Then he was struck in the back with a rifle butt and ordered to move. He walked, dragging his feet, which were swimming inside his loose sneakers. He was ceasing to be the machine he'd been. He began to think, doubt, remember, and ask himself questions again. He felt he was trembling. Wouldn't it be better to be dead than to have to drink the bitter brew he had ahead of him? No, Mayta, no.

"The delay in returning to Jauja wasn't caused by the two casualties," says the justice of the peace. "It was the money. Where was it? They went crazy looking for it, and it just didn't turn up. Mayta, Zenón Gonzales, and the joeboys swore that it was on the mules, except for the *soles* they'd given to the widow, Teofrasia Soto de Almaraz, for her animals, and to Gertrudis Sapollacu for lunch. The guards who captured Condori's group swore they didn't find a penny on the mules, only Mausers, bullets, and some pots of food. They spent a lot of time interrogating us about the whereabouts of the money. That's why we got to Jauja at dawn."

We, too, are going to arrive later than we had planned. The hours flew by in the Quero gazebo, and it's getting dark fast. The pickup's lights are on. All I can see are dark, fleeting tree trunks and the stones and shiny pebbles we bounce over. I vaguely think about the risk of being ambushed at one of the switchbacks, about being blown up by a mine, about getting to Jauja after curfew and being locked up.

"What could have happened to the money from the robbery?" don Eugenio wonders, unstoppable now in his evocation of those events. "Could the guards have split it up?"

Just one more enigma to add to the others. In this case, at

least, I have some solid clues. An abundance of lies clouds the whole story. How much could the insurgents have taken away with them from Jauja? My guess is that the bank employees inflated the amount and that the revolutionaries never knew how much they had stolen, because they never had time to count it. They carried the money in bags, which they tied to the mules. Did anybody know how much was in each bag? No one, probably. Probably, too, their captors emptied some of the money into their own pockets, so the total sum returned to the banks was barely fifteen thousand *soles*, much less than the amount the rebels "expropriated," and much, much less than the amount the banks said they had stolen.

"Perhaps that's the saddest part of the story," I think aloud. "That what had begun as a revolution—as crazy as it was, it was a revolution, nevertheless—should end in a dispute as to how much they had stolen and who ended up with the loot."

"That's life," philosophizes don Eugenio.

He imagined what the Lima newspapers would say, tomorrow, the day after, or the day after that; what the comrades from the RWP and the RWP(T) would say, and what their enemies in the PC would say, when they read the exaggerated, fantastic, sensationalist, yellow-journal versions of what happened which would appear in the papers. He imagined the meeting the RWP(T) would devote to distilling revolutionary doctrine from the episode, and he could almost hear the inflections and tones of each of his old comrades, asserting that reality had confirmed the scientific, Marxist, Trotskyist analysis the party had made, and completely justified its distrust and its refusal to participate in a petit-bourgeois adventure destined to fail.

Would anyone suggest that their distrust and refusal had contributed to the failure? The idea would never even occur to them. Would the rebellion have turned out differently if all the cadres of the RWP(T) had participated in it, and resolutely? He thought so. That would have brought the miners in, as well as Professor Ubilluz, and the Ricrán people. Things would have been planned and executed better, and right now they'd be on their way to Aína safe and sound. Were you being honest, Mayta? Did you try to think lucidly? No. It happened too fast, everything was too compressed. In tranquillity, when all of it was over, it would be necessary to analyze what had taken place from the beginning, to determine objectively if the rebellion would have had better luck if it had been conceived differently, with the participation of those who did take part as well as the RWP(T), or if a different plan would merely have delayed the defeat and made it more bloody.

He felt sadness, but also a desire to feel Anatolio's head against his breast, to hear that slow, rhythmic, almost musical breathing of his when he was worn out and sleeping on his body. He let out a sigh and realized his teeth were chattering. He felt a rifle butt slam into his back: "Hurry it up." Every time Vallejos's image came into his mind, the cold became overwhelming, so he tried to blot it all out. He didn't want to think about him, to wonder if he was a prisoner, if he was wounded, dead, if they were beating him, torturing him, because he knew depression would leave him defenseless against what was coming. He was going to need courage, more than was necessary just to resist the rushing wind that beat at his face.

Where had they taken Perico Temoche? Where were the others? Could any of them have managed to escape? He was walking alone between two columns of Civil Guards. They sometimes looked at him out of the corner of their eye, as if he were a rare bird, and forgetting what had just happened, they amused themselves by talking, smoking, and walking with their hands in their pockets, as if coming back from a stroll. Well, I don't think I'll ever be bothered by mountain sickness again, he thought. He tried to figure out where he was, because they were doubling back along the route he'd taken earlier, but now that it wasn't raining, the landscape looked different. The colors were more sharply contrasting, and the edges of things were not as sharp. The ground was muddy and his sneakers constantly slipped off. He had to stop each time to put them back on, and every time he stopped, the guard behind him gave him a shove.

Are you sorry, Mayta? Did you act too quickly? Did you act irresponsibly? No, no, no. On the contrary. Despite the failure, the mistakes, the foolishness, he was proud. For the first time, he had the feeling he'd done something worthwhile, he'd brought the revolution forward, even if only in a minuscule way. He wasn't depressed about being arrested, as he had been other times; then he'd had a sense of waste. They had failed, but they had done the experiment: four intrepid men and a handful of schoolboys had occupied a city, disarmed the police, expropriated the banks, and fled to the mountains. It was possible to do, and they had proven it. In the future, the left would have to take this precedent into account: someone in this country wasn't content with merely predicting revolution, and had tried to do it. You know what it is, he thought, as his sneaker came off. He put it back on and was struck again with a rifle butt.

I wake don Eugenio, who fell asleep halfway back, and I let him off at his place on the outskirts of Jauja, thanking him for his company and his memories. I go straight to the Paca Inn. The kitchen is still open and I could get something to eat, but all I want is a beer. I drink it on the small terrace above the lake. The water sparkles, and the reeds on the shore are lit by the moon, which shines round and white in a sky spattered with stars. In Paca at night, all kinds of noises can be heard: the whistling wind, toads croaking, nightbirds singing. But not tonight. Tonight, even the animals are silent. The only other guests at the inn are two traveling salesmen, in the beer business, whom I hear talking on the other side of the windows, in the dining room.

This is the end of the main part of the story, its core of drama. It didn't last twelve hours, beginning at dawn with the seizure of the jail and ending before nightfall with the deaths of Vallejos and Condori and the capture of the others. They brought them to the Jauja jail, where they held them for a week, and then they sent them to the Huancayo jail, where they remained for a month. There they discretely began to free the joeboys, following the decision of the juvenile court, which placed them in the custody of their families, under a kind of

275

house arrest. The justice of the peace for Quero went back to work, "free of dust and dirt," after three weeks. Mayta and Zenón Gonzales were taken to Lima, locked up in the Sexto, then in the Frontón, and later returned to the Sexto. Both were amnestied—there never was a trial—years later, when a new president took office. Zenón Gonzales still runs the Uchubamba commune, which has owned the Aína hacienda since the agrarian reform of 1971, and belongs to the Popular Action Party, of which he is the local boss.

During the first days, the newspapers were filled with these events and devoted front pages, headlines, editorials, and articles to what, because of Mayta's past record, they deemed an attempted communist insurrection. An unrecognizable photo of him behind bars in some jail or other appeared in *La Prensa*. But, after a week, people stopped talking about it. Later, when there were outbreaks of guerrilla fighting in the mountains and the jungle in 1963, 1964, 1965, and 1966—all inspired by the Cuban Revolution—no newspaper remembered that the forerunner of those attempts to raise up the people in armed struggle to establish socialism in Peru had been that minor episode, rendered ghostlike by the years, which had taken place in Jauja province. Today no one remembers who took part in it.

As I fall asleep, I hear a rhythmic noise. No, it isn't the night birds. It's the wind, which slaps the waters of Lake Paca against the terrace of the inn. That soft music and the beautiful, starry night sky of Jauja suggest a peaceful land and happy, tranquil people. They lie, because all fictions are lies.

Ten

I visited Lurigancho for the first time five years ago. The prisoners housed in building number 2 invited me to the opening of a library, which someone decided ought to be named after me. So I accepted their invitation, in part because I was curious to find out if what people said was really true about the Lima prison.

To get there by car, you have to drive by the Plaza de Toros, cross the Zárate neighborhood, then go through some slums. The slums eventually turn into garbage dumps, where you can see the hogs from the so-called clandestine pig farms feeding. Then the asphalt runs out, replaced by potholes. Soon the cement buildings emerge in the humid morning light, partially blurred by the mist. They are as colorless as the sand flats around them. Even from a distance, you can see that the innumerable windows have no glass in them—if, in fact, they ever had glass—and that the movement in the tiny symmetrical squares are faces and eyes peering out.

What I remember vividly from that first visit is the overcrowding, those six thousand prisoners suffocating in an area meant for fifteen hundred, the indescribable filth, the atmosphere of pent-up violence on the point of exploding. Mayta was in that anonymous mass, more a horde or a pack than a human collectivity—I'm absolutely certain of it. It may be that I saw him and that we waved to each other. Could he have been in building number 2? Would he have bothered to attend the opening of the library?

The buildings stand in two rows, the odd-numbered ones in front, the even-numbered ones in back. The symmetry is broken up by the cell block for fags, which is up against the wire fence along the western wall. The even-numbered buildings are for recidivists or felons, and the odd-numbered ones house first offenders who haven't been sentenced yet or are serving light terms. Which means that Mayta has been an inmate of an even-numbered building for years. The prisoners are housed according to their Lima neighborhoods: Agustino, Villa El Salvador, La Victoria, El Porvenir. Where would they have put Mayta?

My car moves forward slowly, and I realize that unconsciously I've taken my foot off the accelerator, I'm trying to postpone my second visit to Lurigancho as long as possible. Am I frightened by the thought of finally facing the character I've been investigating, about whom I've been questioning people, whom I've been imagining and writing about for a year? Or is my repugnance for this place stronger than my curiosity about Mayta? At the end of my first visit, I thought: It isn't true that the convicts live like animals: animals have more room to move around. Kennels, chickenhouses, and stables are more hygienic than Lurigancho.

Between the buildings runs what is sarcastically called Jirón de la Unión, a narrow, crowded alley, dark by day and totally black at night. It's there that the bloodiest fights between gangs and between individual killers take place, and where the pimps peddle their living goods. I remember clearly walking through this nightmare, rubbing elbows with that pitiful, almost sleepwalking fauna: half-naked blacks, half-breeds covered with tattoos, mulattoes with intricate hairdos—veritable jungles

278

cascading down to their waists—and stupefied, bearded whites, foreigners with blue eyes and with scars, squalid Chinese, Indians huddled against the wall, and madmen talking to themselves. I know that for years Mayta has been running a kiosk where he sells things to eat and drink in Jirón de la Unión. But no matter how hard I try to remember, I just can't seem to evoke the image of a food stand in the sultry alleyway. Was I so upset that I didn't realize what it was? Or was the "kiosk" nothing more than a blanket on the ground where Mayta, hunkered down, offered juice, fruit, cigarettes, sodas?

To reach building 2, I had to circle the uneven cell blocks and cross two wire fences. The warden, leaving me at the first fence, told me I was on my own now; not even the National Guard enters that sector, or anyone else carrying firearms. As soon as I passed through the fence, I was surrounded by a multitude waving their arms, all speaking at the same time. The delegation that had invited me formed a circle around me then, and that's how we made our way: me in the center of a ring of men, and outside the ring, a mass of criminals. The convicts must have mistaken me for some official or other, because they began to spout out their case histories, rave, protest abuses, shout, and demand services. Some were coherent, but the majority were chaotic. They all seemed on edge, violent, not quite in focus mentally. As we walked, I discovered the source of the solid stench and the clouds of flies: a wall about a yard high, where all the garbage from the jail must have been accumulating for months, even years. A naked inmate was sleeping soundly, stretched out on the trash. He was one of the insane, normally assigned to the less dangerous buildings, the odd-numbered ones. I remember having said to myself after that first visit that the really strange thing was not that there were madmen in Lurigancho but that there were so few. It was incredible that all six thousand inmates hadn't gone crazy in that abject ignominy. And what if, after all these years, Mayta had gone mad?

He was sent back to prison twice after having served four years for the Jauja affair, the first time seven months after being amnestied. It's extremely difficult to reconstruct his story—his police and prison history—after that, because, unlike the Jauja business, there are almost no written documents relating to the actions he was accused of participating in and no witnesses willing to talk about them. The newspaper accounts I've been able to find in the periodical section of the National Library are so sketchy that it's practically impossible to figure out his role in the robberies in which he was supposed to have participated. It's also impossible to determine whether they were political actions or just ordinary crimes. Knowing Mayta, you'd think they were probably political, but, after all, what does it mean to say "knowing Mayta"? The Mayta I've been researching was in his forties. The Mayta of today is over sixty. Is he the same man?

In which cell block in Lurigancho could he have been spending these last ten years? Four, six, eight? They must all be more or less like the one I saw: low-ceilinged places with faint light (when there isn't a blackout), cold and humid, with large windows covered with rusty bars, and a hole in the floor for sanitary purposes. To find a place to sleep amid all that excrement, vermin, and filth is a daily war. During the ceremony for the library—a painted box and a few secondhand books—I saw several drunks staggering around. When they passed around little cans so we could drink a toast, I found out that they get drunk on a *chicha* they make from fermented *yuca*. Unbelievably strong stuff, made right in the prison. Would my supposed fellow student also get drunk on that *chicha* when he's feeling too high or too low?

The event that sent Mayta back to prison after the Jauja affair, twenty-one years ago, took place in La Victoria, near the street that was the shame of the neighborhood—Jirón Huatica, which literally crawled with prostitutes. Three gangsters, according to *La Crónica*, the only newspaper to write it up, seized a garage where Teodoro Ruiz Candia had an auto-repair shop. When he came to open up at eight in the morning, he found three armed men waiting for him. They also captured Ruiz Candia's assistant,

Eliseno Carabías López. The objective of these criminals was the Banco Popular. At the rear of the garage, there was a window that opened onto a lot; the rear door of the Banco Popular opened onto the same lot. Every day at noon, a van went into the lot, to take away the day's deposits, to bring them to the Central Bank, or to deliver money to the branch for the day's transactions. Until noon, the thieves remained in the shop with their two prisoners. They looked out through the window and smoked. Though they wore masks, the owner and his assistant swore one of them was Mayta. They also said it was he who gave the orders.

When they heard a car motor, they jumped out the window into the lot. Actually, no shots were fired. The thieves surprised the driver and the guard and disarmed them both, just after the bank employees had placed a sealed sack containing three million *soles* in the van. After forcing the driver and the guard to lie face down on the ground, one of the gangsters opened the gates of the lot that led to Avenida 28 de Julio. Then he ran back to the bank van, where his other two accomplices were waiting with the loot. They sped out. Because of nerves or careless driving, the van ran over a man sharpening knives, and then smashed against a taxi. According to *La Crónica*, the van turned over twice and came to rest upside down. But the thieves managed to get out and run away. Mayta was captured some hours later. The article does not say whether the money was recovered, and I haven't been able to find out if the other two were ever caught.

And I haven't been able to find out if Mayta was ever sentenced for the robbery. A police report I was able to pull from the archives of the La Victoria precinct house more or less repeats the same information as the article in *La Crónica* (although the humidity has ruined the paper to such an extent that it's difficult to make it out). There is no sign of a prosecutor's report. In the files at the Ministry of Justice, where statistics on crime and data on criminals are stored, the event shows up most ambiguously in Mayta's file. There is a date—April 16, 1963—when he must have been sent from the police station to prison, followed by the note "Attempted robbery of branch bank, people wounded and beaten, also forced detention, traffic accident, and attack on pedestrian," and, finally, a reference to the court handling the matter. Nothing else. It's possible that the prosecution was slow, that the judge died or lost his job, and that the whole case remained stuck where it was, or simply that the file was lost.

How many years did Mayta spend in Lurigancho for that? I couldn't find that out, either. I found a registry note for his entering prison, but none for his having left. That's another thing I'd like to ask him about. In any case, I lost track of him ten years ago when he went back to jail a second time after Jauja. On that occasion, he had a proper trial and was sentenced to fifteen years for "extortion, kidnapping, and robbery leading to the loss of life." If the dates on the file are correct, he's been in Lurigancho for just under eleven years.

I've finally arrived. I go through the usual ritual. The National Guards frisk me from head to toe, and I turn in all my identification papers, which will remain at the guardhouse until my visit ends. The warden has left orders that I am to be sent to his office. An aide in civilian clothes brings me here, after crossing a patio outside the wire fences. From here, you can see the entire prison. This is the best-maintained area, the least sordid in the place.

The warden's office is on the second floor of a cold and crumbling building made of reinforced concrete. The office itself is tiny and contains a metal desk and a couple of chairs. The walls are completely bare, and there isn't even a pencil or piece of paper on the desk. This warden is not the one who was here five years ago, but a younger man. He knows why I'm here and orders the guards to bring the criminal I want to speak to. He will lend me his office for the interview, since it is the only place where no one will bother us. "You've probably seen that here in Lurigancho there isn't an inch of space, because of over-crowding."

While we wait, he adds that things never work right, no matter how hard they try. Now, for example, the convicts are all riled up and are threatening a hunger strike because they think their visiting rights are being cut. It's just not true, he assures me. It's simply that, in order to keep tabs on the visits, the usual way drugs, alcohol, and weapons are smuggled in, he's set visits for the women on one day and for the men the next. That way, there will be fewer people each day, and each visitor can be searched more thoroughly. If they at least could cut down on the cocaine, they would keep a lot of people from getting killed. Because of cocaine, they fight it out with knives. More than because of alcohol, money, or queers, it's the drugs. But until now it's been impossible to keep it out. Don't the guards sell drugs, too? He looks at me as if to say, "Why ask what you already know?"

"You can't stop it. No matter what control systems we de-vise, they always beat them. Look, by just sneaking in a few grams of coke, just once, a guard doubles his monthly salary. Do you know how much they make? So there's nothing sur-prising about it. People talk a lot about 'the Lurigancho prob-lem.' This place isn't the problem. The whole country's the problem."

He says it without bitterness, as if it were a fact I should be aware of. He seems earnest and well-intentioned. I certainly don't envy him his job. A knock at the door interrupts us.

"I'll leave you with the prisoner," he says, going to the door. "Take all the time you need."

The person who enters the office is a skinny little guy with curly white hair and a scraggly beard, who is trembling all over. He's wearing an overcoat that's much too big for him. He's got on worn-out sneakers, and his frightened eyes jump around in his head. Why is he shaking like that? Is he sick, or frightened? I can't say a word. How can this be Mayta? He doesn't look even slightly like the Mayta in the photos. That Mayta would be twenty years younger than this guy.

"I wanted to talk with Alejandro Mayta," I stammer.

"That's me," he answers in a tremulous voice. His hands, his skin, even his hair seem vexed with disquiet.

"You're the Mayta of the Jauja business with Lieutenant Vallejos?" I hesitatingly ask.

"No, I'm not that one," he blurts out, realizing what's going on. "He's not here anymore."

He seems relieved, as if being brought to the warden's office entailed some danger which has just vanished. He turns halfway around and bangs on the door until it opens and the warden appears with two men. Still shaking, the curly-headed old man explains that there's been a mistake, that I'm looking for the other Mayta. He walks out in a hurry on his silent sneakers, shaking constantly.

"Know which one he's talking about, Carrillo?" the warden asks one of his assistants.

"Sure, sure," says a fat man, his gray hair in a crew cut and his belly slopping over his belt. "The other Mayta. Wasn't that one mixed up in politics?"

"Yes," I say. "That's the one I'm looking for."

"You just missed him, as you might say," he quickly explains. "He got out last month."

I think I've lost him and that I'll never find him and that maybe it's better that way. It could be that, instead of helping me, a meeting with the flesh-and-blood Mayta would undo everything I've accomplished so far. Don't you know where he's gone? No one has an address where he might be found? They don't, and have no idea where he might be. I tell the warden not to bother coming with me, and as we go downstairs, I ask him if he remembers Mayta. Of course he does; he's been here as long as the oldest convict. He came in as a simple office boy, and now he's vice warden of the whole penitentiary. He's seen God only knows what things!

284

"A very correct, easygoing prisoner, never got into any trouble," he says. "Ran a food kiosk in building 4. Hardworking guy. He managed to support his family while serving his sentence. He was here at least ten years the last time."

"His family?"

"Wife and four kids," he adds. "She came to see him once a week. I remember Mayta very well. Walked as if he were walking on eggs, right?"

We're crossing the patio, between the wire fences, heading toward the guardhouse, when the vice warden stops. "Hold it. Arispe may have his address. He inherited the food kiosk. I think they're still partners, even now. I'll have him brought down, maybe you'll be lucky."

Carrillo and I remain in the patio, standing in front of the wire fences. To kill time, I ask him about Lurigancho and he, like the warden, says that there are always problems here. "Because here we've got, and I really mean it, the bad ones, people who seem to have been born for the express purpose of doing indescribable things to their fellow man." Off in the distance, breaking the symmetry of the buildings, stands the one reserved for fags. Do they still lock them up there? Yes. Not that it's of any real use; despite the walls and the bars, the other prisoners get in and the fags get out. Business as usual. Anyway, since they've got their own building, there are fewer problems. Before, when they were mixed in with the others, the fights and murders they'd cause were much worse.

I remember, from my first visit, a short talk I had with one of the prison doctors about the rapes of incoming prisoners. "The most common problem is infections of the rectum, complicated by gangrene or cancer." I ask Carrillo if there are still as many rapes. He laughs. "It's inevitable, with people who have nothing else, don't you think? They have to let go somehow." Finally, the prisoner the warden had called down appears. I explain that I'm looking for Mayta, does he know where I might find him?

He's a respectable-looking guy, dressed relatively well. He

listens without asking any questions. But I see that he has doubts, and I'm sure he's not going to tell me anything. I ask him to give Mayta my telephone number the next time he sees him.

Suddenly he decides. "He works in an ice-cream parlor," he says. "In Miraflores."

It's a small ice-cream parlor which has been there for many years. It's on Bolognesi Street, a street I know very well because when I was a kid I knew a beautiful girl who lived there. She had the improbable name of Flora Flores. I'm sure the ice-cream parlor was there then and that I went in with the beautiful Flora Flores to have a sundae. It's an unusual place for a street where there are no stores, only the typical Miraflores houses: two stories, front lawn, the inevitable geraniums, bougainvillea, and poincianas with big red flowers. I have an attack of nerves as I turn off the Malecón onto Bolognesi. Yes, it's exactly where I remember it, a few steps away from that gray house with balconies, where Flora's sweet face and incandescent eyes would appear. I park a short distance from the ice-cream parlor, but I can barely get the key out of the ignition, because I've suddenly become jittery.

"Alejandro Mayta," I say, stretching out my hand. "Right?"

He looks at me for a few seconds and smiles, opening a mouth not overpopulated with teeth. He blinks, trying to remember me. Finally, he gives up.

"I'm sorry, but I can't place you," he says. "I thought you might be Santos, but you aren't Santos, right?"

"I've been looking for you for a long time," I say, leaning on the counter. "You're going to be surprised," I warn him. "Just now, I've come from Lurigancho. The guy who told me how to find you was your partner in building 4—Arispe."

I study him carefully, to see how he reacts. He seems neither surprised nor upset. He looks at me with curiosity, the hint of a smile still on his dark face. He's wearing a cotton T-shirt, and I see hands that are rough, the rough hands of a porter or a day laborer. What I notice most is his absurd haircut. Someone has really chopped him up: his head looks like a mop, laughable.

He makes me remember my first year in Paris, when I was really poor, and a friend of mine and I would get our hair cut at a school for barbers, near the Bastille. The students, just kids, would cut our hair for free, but they would leave us looking like my invented classmate. He looks at me, squinting up his dark, tired eyes—crow's-feet at each end—with distrust growing in them.

"I've been investigating you for a year now, talking with the people who knew you," I say. "Imagining you, even dreaming about you. Because I've written a novel that in a remote way deals with the Jauja business."

He looks at me without saying a word, quite surprised now, not understanding, not sure he's heard correctly, but very jumpy.

"But . . ." he stammers. "Why would you even bother, how can it be . . ."

"I don't really know why, but that's what I've been doing all this year," I say to him quickly, afraid of his fear, afraid he'll refuse to talk to me now or ever again. I try to explain: In a novel there are always more lies than truths, a novel is never a faithful account of events. This investigation, these interviews, I didn't do it all so I could relate what really happened in Jauja, but so I could lie and know what I'm lying about.

I realize that, instead of calming him down, I'm confusing and alarming him. He blinks and stands there with his mouth open, mute.

"Now I know who you are. You're the writer." Now he's out of the difficulty. "Sure, I recognized you. I even read one of your novels, at least I think so, years back."

Just then, three sweaty boys come in from some game, judging by the equipment they're carrying. They order ice cream and sodas. While Mayta takes care of them, I observe how he handles himself in the ice-cream parlor. He opens the freezer, fills the ice-cream dishes, opens the bottles, reaches for the glasses with an ease and familiarity that reflect a lot of practice. I try to imagine him in building 4 in Lurigancho, serving fruit juice, packages of cookies, cups of coffee, selling cigarettes to the other convicts, every morning, every afternoon, over the course of ten years. Physically, he doesn't seem worn down; he's a tough-looking guy, and carries his sixty-plus years with dignity. After settling the bill of the three athletes, he comes back to me, with a forced smile on his face.

"Damn," he says. "That's the last thing I'd ever imagine. A novel?"

And he moves his head incredulously from right to left and left to right.

"Naturally, your real name never appears even once," I assure him. "Of course I've changed dates, places, characters, I've created complications, added and taken away thousands of things. Besides, I've invented an apocalyptic Peru, devastated by war, terrorism, and foreign intervention. Of course, no one will recognize anything, and everyone will think it's pure fantasy. I've pretended as well that we were schoolmates, that we were the same age, and lifelong friends.

"Of course," he says, as if he were spelling it out, scrutinizing me with doubt, deciphering me bit by bit.

"I'd like to talk with you," I add. "Ask you a few questions, clear up a couple of points. Only what you want to tell me or feel you can tell me, naturally. I've got a lot of puzzles bouncing around in my head. Besides, this conversation is my final chapter. You can't refuse me now, it would be like taking a cake out of the oven too soon—the novel would fall apart."

I laugh, and so does he, and we hear the three boys laughing. But they're laughing at a joke one of them has just told. And then a woman comes in and asks for a quart, half pistachio and half chocolate. After handing her the ice cream, Mayta comes back to me.

"Two or three years ago, some of the guys from *Revolutionary Vanguard* came to see me in Lurigancho," he says. "They wanted to know all about Jauja, a written account. But I wouldn't do it."

288

"I don't want anything like that," I say. "My interest isn't political but literary, that is . . ."

"Yes, I see," he interrupts me, raising a hand. "Okay, I'll give you one evening. No more, because I don't have much time, and, to tell you the truth, I don't like talking about that stuff. How about next Tuesday? It's better for me, because on Wednesday I don't start here until eleven, so I can stay up late the night before. All the other days, I have to leave home at six, because I have to take three buses to get here."

We agree that I'll pick him up when he finishes work, after eight. Just as I'm leaving, he calls me back. "Have an ice-cream cone, on the house. So you see how good our ice cream is. Maybe you'll become a regular customer."

Before I go back to Barranco, I take a little walk around the neighborhood, mentally trying to put things in their proper order. I stop for a while under the balconies of the house where that superlative beauty Flora Flores lived. She had long, chestnut-colored hair, slender legs, and violet eyes. Whenever she came to the rocky beach at Miraflores, wearing her black bathing suit, the morning would fill with light, the sun would glow hotter, the waves roll more joyously. I remember that she married a pilot and only a few months later he crashed into a peak in the Cordillera, between Lima and Tingo María. Years later, someone told me that Flora had remarried and was living in Miami. I go up to Avenida Grau. Right on this corner, there was a gang of boys with whom we—the Diego Ferré and Colón boys, from the other end of Miraflores—would have hard-fought soccer matches at the Terrazas Club. I remember how anxiously I'd wait for those matches when I was a kid, and how terribly frustrating it was when I was only on the second team. When I get back to the car, half an hour later, I've partially recovered from my meeting with Mayta.

The incident that caused him to be sent back to Lurigancho, the reason he spent the past ten years there, is well documented in newspapers and judicial archives. It occurred in Magdalena

Vieja, not far from the Anthropological Museum, at sunrise one January day in 1973. The president of the Pueblo Libre branch of the Banco de Crédito was watering his patio—he did it every morning before getting dressed—when the doorbell rang. He thought it was the milkman, coming by earlier than usual. At the door there were four men, their faces covered with ski masks and their pistols pointing straight at him. They went with him to his wife's room. They tied her up in her own bed. Then— they seemed to know the place well—they went into his only daughter's bedroom. (She was nineteen years old, studying to become a travel agent.) They waited until the girl got dressed and told the gentleman that, if he wanted to see her again, he should pack fifty million *soles* into an attaché case and bring it to Los Garifos Park, near the National Stadium. They disappeared with the girl in a taxi they'd stolen the night before.

Mr. Fuentes reported everything to the police and, following their instructions, carried an attaché case stuffed with paper to the Los Garifos Park. There were plainclothesmen stationed all around it. No one approached him, and Mr. Fuentes received no communication for three days. Just when he and his wife were getting desperate, there was a second telephone call: the kidnappers knew that he had called the police. They would, however, give him one last chance. He was to bring the money to a corner of Avenida Aviación. Mr. Fuentes explained that he couldn't get fifty million *soles*, that the bank would never give him that kind of money, but he would give them his life savings, some five million. The kidnappers insisted: fifty million or they'd kill her.

Mr. Fuentes helped himself to some money, signed notes, and succeeded in getting together nine million, which he brought that night to the place the kidnappers had indicated—this time, without telling the police. A car skidded to a halt, and the person on the passenger side grabbed the attaché case, without saying a word. The girl turned up some hours later at her parents' home. She had taken a taxi at Avenida Colonial, where her captors had left her. They'd held her for three days, blindfolded and partially chloroformed. She was so distraught that she had to be taken to the Hospital del Empleado. A few days later, she walked out of the room she was sharing with a woman just operated on for appendicitis, and, without saying a word, jumped out of a window.

The newspapers sensationalized the girl's suicide and fanned public opinion. A few days later, the police announced that they had captured the head of the group—Mayta—and that his accomplices would be captured momentarily. According to the police, Mayta admitted his guilt and gave all the details. His accomplices and the money vanished. At the trial, Mayta denied he had ever taken part in the kidnapping, denied he had even known about it, and insisted that he was tortured into making a false confession.

The trial lasted several months, and at the outset it got a lot of attention in the papers. But that quickly faded. Mayta was sentenced to fifteen years: the court found him guilty of kidnapping, criminal extortion, and complicity in a homicide. He swore he was innocent. That on the day of the kidnapping he was in Pacasmayo looking into a possible job, as he said again and again, but he could provide no witnesses, no proof. The testimony of Mr. and Mrs. Fuentes was especially damning. Both were sure that Mayta's voice and physical appearance were those of one of the men in ski masks. Mayta's lawyer, an obscure shyster whose performance during the entire trial was awkward and halting, appealed. The Supreme Court upheld the original sentence two years later. The fact that Mayta was set free after serving two-thirds of his time certainly corroborates what Mr. Carrillo told me at Lurigancho: that his behavior during those years was exemplary.

On Tuesday, at 8 p.m., when I drive over to pick him up at the ice-cream parlor, Mayta is waiting for me, carrying an airline bag, which probably contains the clothing he wears at work. He's just washed his face and combed that wild hair of his; a few drops of water run down his neck. He's wearing a blue striped shirt, a faded, much darned checked jacket, wrinkled khaki trousers, and heavy shoes, the kind used for hiking. Is he hungry? Shall we go to a restaurant? He says he never eats at night and that it would be better if we were just to look for a quiet place. A few minutes later, we're in my study, face to face, drinking soda. He doesn't want beer or anything alcoholic. He tells me he gave up smoking and drinking years ago.

The beginning of the chat is rather sad. I ask him about the Salesian School. He did study there, correct? Yes. He hasn't seen any of his schoolmates for ages, and knows only the slightest bit about a few of them, professional men, businessmen, or politicians—the ones whose names appear in the papers. And nothing about the priests, although, he tells me, just a few days ago he ran into Father Luis on the street. The one who taught the youngest students. A little old man, almost blind, bent over, dragging his feet, propelling himself along with a broomstick. He told Mayta that he was in the habit of taking his little strolls on Avenida Brazil, and that he had recognized him, but Mayta smiles; of course he had no idea to whom he was speaking. He must be a hundred years old.

When I show him the material I've gathered about him and the Jauja adventure—articles clipped out of newspapers, photocopies of reports, photographs, maps with routes traced on them, cards on the participants and on witnesses, notebooks with data and interviews—I see him sniff, look through it, and handle it, an expression of stupor and embarrassment on his face. Several times, he gets up to go to the bathroom. He has a problem with his kidneys, he explains, and constantly feels like urinating, although most of the time it's a false alarm and there are only a few drops.

"On the bus, at home, at the ice-cream parlor, it's a real pain. It's a two-hour commute, I told you already. I just can't make it all the way, no matter how much I pee before I get on. Sometimes there's nothing I can do except wet my pants like a baby."

"Were the years in Lurigancho tough?" I stupidly ask.

Disconcerted, he stares at me. There is total silence outside on the Malecón de Barranco. You can't even hear the surf.

"Well, you don't live like a prince," he answers after a bit, shamefaced. "It's hard, especially at the beginning. But you can get used to anything, don't you think?"

Finally, something that jibes with the Mayta of the witness accounts: that modesty, that reticence when it comes to speaking about his personal problems or revealing his inner feelings. What he never did get used to was the National Guard, he soon admits. He hadn't known what hate was until he discovered the feeling they inspired in the prisoners. Hatred mixed with absolute and total terror, of course. Because when they come through the wire fences to stop a riot or break up a strike, they always do it by shooting and beating, no matter who gets it, the righteous and the sinners.

"It was at the end of last year, wasn't it?" I say. "When there was that massacre."

"December 31," he says, nodding. "A hundred or so came in to celebrate New Year's Eve. They wanted to have some fun, to bring in the New Year with a bang, as they said. They were all stinking drunk."

It was around 10 p.m. They emptied their rifles from the doors and windows of the cell blocks. They stole all the money, liquor, marijuana, and coke they could find in the prison, and until dawn they went on having fun, shooting, beating the prisoners with their rifle butts, making them hop around like frogs, making them run the gauntlet, or just kicking in their teeth.

"The official figures list thirty-five dead," he says. "Actually, they killed at least twice that many, even more. The newspapers said later that they'd thwarted an escape attempt."

He makes a gesture of fatigue and his voice becomes a murmur. The convicts piled up on top of each other, like a rugby scrum, mountains of bodies, for self-protection. But that isn't his worst prison memory. The worst was probably the first months, when he was brought from Lurigancho to the Palacio de Justicia for prosecution, in one of those crowded paddy wagons with metal walls. The prisoners had to ride hunched down, with their heads touching the floor. If they raised their heads even slightly to try to sneak a look out the window, they were savagely beaten. The same thing on the return trip: to get back on the wagon from the lockup, they had to run the gauntlet, a double line of National Guards. They had to decide whether to protect their heads or their testicles, because all along the route they were hit with billy clubs, kicked, and spit on. He remains pensive—he's just returned from the bathroom—and he adds, without looking at me: "When I read that one of them's been killed, I feel really happy."

He says it with a quick and profound resentment that disappears a second later when I ask him about the other Mayta, that curly-headed, skinny guy who shook in that odd way.

"He's just a sneak thief whose brain has melted away from cocaine," he says. "He won't last long."

His voice and his expression sweeten when he talks about the food kiosk he ran with Arispe in building 4. "We created a genuine revolution," he assures me with pride. "We won the respect of the whole place. We boiled the water for making fruit juice, for coffee, for everything. We washed the knives, forks, and spoons, the glasses, and the plates before and after they were used. Hygiene, above all. A revolution, you bet. We organized a system of rebate coupons. You might not believe me, but they only tried to rob us once. I took a gash right here on my leg, but they didn't get a thing. We even set up a kind of bank, because a lot of cons gave us their money for safekeeping."

It's clear that for some reason he's really reluctant to speak of the thing that interests me the most: Jauja. Every time I try to bring it up, he starts to talk about it, and then, very quickly, inevitably, he switches to some current topic. For example, his family. He tells me he got married in the time he was free between his last two terms in Lurigancho, but that he actually met his wife in jail, the time before. She would come to visit her brother, and he introduced her to Mayta. They wrote each other, and when he was released, they got married. They have four children, three boys and a girl. It was really hard on his wife when he was imprisoned again. During the first years, she had to practically kill herself to feed the kids, until finally he could help her, thanks to the kiosk. During those first years, his wife knitted, and peddled her work from door to door. He also tried to sell her knitting—there was some demand for sweaters—in Lurigancho.

As I listen, I study him. My first impression—that he is well-conserved, healthy, and strong—is false. His health can't be good. Not only because of that problem with his kidneys that makes him go to the bathroom every other minute. He perspires a great deal; at times he chokes up, as if he were overcome by waves of vertigo. He dries his forehead with his handkerchief and some-times, in the middle of a spasm, he can't speak. Does he feel ill? Should we stop the interview? No, he's fine, let's keep going.

"It seems to me that you don't want to talk about Vallejos and Jauja," I say, point-blank. "Does it bother you because it was such a failure? Because of how it affected the rest of your life?"

He shakes his head.

"It bothers me because I realize that you know more about it than I do." He smiles. "Yes, no joke. I've forgotten lots of things, and I'm mixed up about lots of others. I'd really like to help you out and tell you about it. But the problem is that I don't know all that happened or even how it happened. It's a long time ago, don't forget."

Is he just talking, is it a pose? No. His memories are hesitant, sometimes erroneous. I have to correct him every few minutes. I'm shocked, because this whole year I've been obsessed with the subject, and I naïvely supposed the major actor in it would be too, and that his memory would still go on scratching away at what happened in those few hours a quarter century ago. Why should it be that way? All that, for Mayta, was one episode in a life in which, before and after, there were many other episodes, as important, or even more so. It's only normal that these other events would replace or blur Jauja.

"There is one thing, above all others, that I just can't understand," I say to him. "Was there a betrayal? Why did the people who were involved just disappear? Did Professor Ubilluz countermand the orders? Why did he do it? Fear? Because he didn't believe in the project? Or was it Vallejos, as Ubilluz declares, who moved the date of the uprising forward?"

Mayta reflects for a few seconds in silence. He shrugs his shoulders. "That part never was clear and never will be," he says in a low voice. "That day, it looked like betrayal to me. Later it got even more complicated. Because I hadn't known beforehand the date they'd set for the revolt. Only Vallejos and Ubilluz knew it, for security reasons. Ubilluz has always said that the date they'd agreed on was four days later, and that Vallejos moved it forward when he found out he was going to be transferred, because of an incident he'd been involved in with the APRA people two days earlier."

That there was such an incident is true; it's documented in a small Jauja newspaper. There was an APRA demonstration in the Plaza de Armas in honor of Haya de la Torre, who made a speech in the atrium of the cathedral. Vallejos, in civilian clothes, Shorty Ubilluz, and a small group of friends stationed themselves at one corner of the plaza, and when the entourage passed by, they pelted them with rotten eggs. The APRISTA toughs scattered them. Vallejos, Ubilluz, and the others tried to fight back, and then they took refuge in Ezequiel's barbershop. That's all we know for sure. Ubilluz and other people in Jauja assert that Vallejos was recognized by the APRA people and that they noisily protested the participation of the head of the prison, an officer on active duty, in action directed against an authorized political meeting. Vallejos was told that because he took part in the demonstration he was going to be transferred. They say he received an urgent message from his immediate superior in Huancayo. That's what probably pushed him into moving the rebellion up four days, without telling the others about it. Ubilluz swears he only found out what happened when the lieutenant was dead and the other rebels were in jail.

"At first, I didn't believe it. I thought they'd chickened out," says Mayta. "Later on, I just didn't know. Because, months or years later, some of the people originally involved ended up in the Sexto, the Frontón. They were jailed for other reasons— union or political stuff. They all swore that they were surprised when the uprising occurred, that Ubilluz had given them a different date, that there was no desertion, no change of heart. Frankly, I just don't know. Only Vallejos and Ubilluz knew the first date. Did Vallejos change it? He didn't tell me. But it isn't impossible. He was a really impulsive guy, really capable of doing something like that, even if he ran the risk of being all alone. What we used to call a willful individualist in those days."

Is he criticizing Vallejos? No, it's a distanced, neutral observation. He tells me that on the first night, when Vallejos's family came to claim his body, his father wouldn't speak to him. He came in when they were interrogating Mayta, and Mayta stretched his hand out to him. But the father wouldn't take it and even looked at him angrily, with tears in his eyes, as if Mayta were responsible for everything.

"I just don't know, it might have been like that," he repeats. "Or there might have been a misunderstanding. That is, Vallejos was sure of support that wasn't actually promised. At the meetings they brought me to in Ricrán between Ubilluz and the miners, they talked about revolution, and everyone seemed in agreement. But did they really offer to take a rifle and come out to the mountains on the first day? I didn't hear them say they would. Vallejos just assumed everything, he had no doubts. It may be they just made some vague promises, moral support, they would help from a distance, with their group continuing their normal lives. Or it may be that they did commit themselves and that out of fear, or because the plan didn't convince them, they just backed out. I couldn't say for sure. I just don't know."

He drums his fingers on the arm of the chair. There is a long silence.

"Were you ever sorry you got mixed up in it?" I ask him. "I imagine that in jail you must have thought quite a lot over the years about what happened."

297

"Repenting is something Catholics do. I stopped being a Catholic many years ago. Revolutionaries don't repent. They go through self-criticism, but that's different. I went through mine, and that's that." He seems angry. But a few seconds later he smiles. "You don't know how strange it is for me to talk politics, to remember political events. It's like a ghost that comes back from the pit of time to show me the dead and make me see forgotten things."

Did he stop taking an interest in politics only in these last ten years? Was it during the time before in jail? Or when he was imprisoned because of Jauja? He remains silent, deep in thought, trying to clarify his memories. Could he have forgotten that, too?

"I hadn't thought about it until now," he says softly, mopping his forehead. "It wasn't a decision I made consciously. It just happened, the force of events. Remember that when I went to Jauja for the uprising I had broken with my comrades, with my party, and with my past. I was alone, politically speaking. And my new comrades were only that for a few hours. Vallejos died, Condori died, Zenón Gonzales went back to his community, the joeboys went back to school. See what I mean? It isn't that I gave up politics. You might say that politics gave me up."

The way he says it makes me disbelieve him: he speaks in hushed tones, his eyes not meeting mine, as he wiggles around in his chair. He never saw his old friends from the RWP(T) again?

"They were good to me when I was in jail, after Jauja," he says vehemently. "They came to see me, they brought me cigarettes, they arranged it so I'd be included in the amnesty the new government put into effect. But the RWP(T) broke up a little afterward, because of what happened at La Convención, the Hugo Blanco business. When I got out of jail, the RWP(T) and the other RWP no longer existed. Other Trotskyist groups with people from Argentina sprang up. I didn't know any of them, and I was no longer interested in politics."

As he says these words, he gets up to go to the bathroom. When he comes back, I see he's washed his face as well. Sure you don't want to go out and get something to eat? He assures me he doesn't and repeats that he never eats at night. We sit there, each one immersed in his own thoughts, without speaking. The silence continues to be total tonight in the Malecón de Barranco. There are probably only silent lovers protected by the darkness, and not the drunks and marijuana smokers that raise such a ruckus on Friday and Saturday nights.

I tell him that in my novel the character is an underground revolutionary, that he's spent half his life plotting and fighting against other tiny groups as insignificant as his own, and that he flings himself into the Jauja adventure not so much because Vallejos's plans convince him—inwardly, he may be skeptical about their chances for success—but because the lieutenant opens the way to action for him. The possibility of taking concrete action, of producing verifiable and immediate changes in everyday reality electrifies him. The minute he meets that impulsive young man, he realizes how inane his revolutionary activities have been. That's why he embarks on the insurrection, even though he senses it is virtually suicide.

"Do you recognize yourself in that character?" I ask him. "Or does he have nothing at all to do with you, with the reasons why you followed Vallejos?"

He continues to look at me, thoughtful, blinking, not knowing what to say. He raises his glass and drinks the rest of the soda. His vacillation is his answer.

"Those things seem impossible when they fail," he reflects. "If they succeed, they seem perfect and well planned to everyone. For example, the Cuban Revolution. How many landed with Fidel on the *Granma*? A handful. Maybe even fewer than we had that day in Jauja. They were lucky and we weren't." He meditates for a moment. "It never seemed crazy to me, much less suicidal," he affirms. "It had been well thought out. If we had destroyed the Molinos bridge and slowed down the police, we would have crossed the Cordillera. In the jungle, they never would have found us. We would have . . ."

His voice fades. His lack of conviction is so apparent that

you'd say it was senseless to go on trying to make me believe something even he didn't believe. What does my supposed ex-fellow student believe in now? At the Salesian School, half a century ago, he ardently believed in God. Later, when God died in his heart, he believed with the same ardor in the revolution, in Marx, in Lenin, in Trotsky. Then Jauja, or perhaps before that, those long years of insipid activism, weakened and finally killed that faith as well. What came to replace it? Nothing. That's why he gives the impression of being an empty man, without the emotion to back up his words. When he began to rob banks and take part in kidnappings, could he believe in anything except getting money any way he could? Something inside me refuses to accept that. Above all now, as I look at him, dressed in those walking shoes and that shoddy clothing; above all, now that I've seen how he earns a living.

"If you don't want to, we don't have to discuss it," I point out. "But I have to say this, Mayta. It's hard for me to understand how, after you got out of prison after Jauja, you could go around robbing banks and kidnapping people. Can we talk about that?"

"No, not about that," he answers immediately, with some harshness. But he contradicts himself when he adds: "I wasn't involved. They used false evidence, they used false witnesses and made them testify against me. They condemned me because they needed a fall guy and I had a record. The real crime is that I was sent to jail."

Once again, his voice trails off, as if at that moment he'd been overcome by demoralization, fatigue, and the certitude that it is useless to try to dissuade me from believing something that over time has acquired an irreversible consistency. Is he telling the truth? Is it possible he wasn't one of the thieves in La Victoria or one of the kidnappers in Pueblo Libre? I know very well that there are innocent people in the nation's jails—perhaps as many as there are criminals outside who are supposed to be honest people—and it is not impossible that Mayta with his record became a scapegoat for judges and cops. But I glimpse in the man seated opposite me such apathy, moral abandon, and perhaps cynicism that it is perfectly possible to imagine him an accomplice in the worst crimes.

"The character in my novel is queer," I tell him after a bit.

He raises his head as if he'd been stung by a wasp. Disgust twists his face. He's sitting in a low armchair, with a wide back, and now he does seem to be sixty or more. I see him stretch his legs and rub his hands, tense.

"But why?" he finally asks.

He takes me by surprise. Do I know why? But I improvise an explanation. "To accentuate his marginality, his being a man full of contradictions. Also to show the prejudices that exist with regard to this subject among those who supposedly want to liberate society from its defects. Well, I don't really know exactly why he is."

His expression of displeasure grows. I see him reach out and pick up a glass of water he's placed on some books, clutch it, and, when he notices it's empty, put it down again in the same place.

"I was never prejudiced about anything," he says softly, after a silence. "But, about fags, I think I am prejudiced. After seeing them. In the Sexto, in the Frontón. In Lurigancho, it's even worse."

For a while, he's again deep in thought. His expression of disgust diminishes, without altogether disappearing. There is no note of compassion in what he says. "Tweezing their eyebrows, curling their eyelashes with burned matches, using lipstick, wearing skirts, creating hairdos, letting themselves be exploited the same way prostitutes are exploited by pimps. How can you not be sick to your stomach? It's unbelievable that a human being can sink so low. Faggots who'd suck someone's dick for a lousy cigarette . . ." He snorts, his forehead again bathed in perspiration. He adds, between his teeth: "They say Mao shot all the queers in China. Could that be?"

He gets up to go to the bathroom again, and while I wait for him to come back, I look out the window. In the Lima sky, which is almost always cloudy, tonight you can see the stars, some tranquil and others sparkling over the black stain that is the sea. It occurs to me that Mayta, out there in Lurigancho, must have contemplated the glittering stars, completely hypnotized on nights like this, a clean, calm, and decent spectacle. A dramatic contrast to the degradation he was living in.

When he comes back, he says he's sorry he never left the country. It was his grand illusion every time he got out of jail: to leave, to start over from zero in another country. He tried, but it was always too hard: no money, improper papers, or both. Once, he got to the border on a bus that was going to take him to Venezuela, but they made him get off at the Ecuadorian customs office because his passport wasn't properly stamped.

"In any case, I haven't given up hope of leaving," he says, with a growl. "With such a large family, it's more difficult. But that's what I'd like to do. Here, I can't get a decent job or anything. No matter where I look, I find nothing. But I still have my hopes."

But you have given up hope as far as Peru is concerned, I think. Totally and definitively, right, Mayta? You who believed in so much, who wanted so much to believe in a future for your unfortunate land. You threw in the towel, didn't you? You think, or act as if you thought, that things here will never change for the better, only for the worse. More hunger, more hatred, more oppression, more ignorance, more brutality, more barbarity. Even you, like so many others, think now only about escaping before we completely collapse.

"To Venezuela or Mexico, where they say there are lots of jobs because of oil. Even to the United States, although I don't speak English. That's what I'd like to do."

Again, his voice catches in his throat, worn out by his lack of conviction. I, too, lose something at that moment: my interest in this conversation. I know I'm not going to get from my false fellow student anything more than what I've already got: the depressing confirmation that he is a man destroyed by suffering and resentment, who has even lost his memories. Someone in essence quite different from the Mayta of my novel, that obstinate optimist, that man of faith who loves life despite the horror and misery in it. I feel uncomfortable, as if I'm abusing him by keeping him here—it's almost midnight—in a predictable conversation that has no substance. This digging away at memories must be anguishing for him, this going back and forth from my study to the bathroom, a perturbation of his daily routine, which I imagine to be monotonous, animal-like.

"I'm keeping you up too late," I say.

"Well, I do go to bed early," he says, relieved, thanking me with a smile that puts an end to our talk. "Even though I don't sleep much—I only need four or five hours. When I was a kid, on the other hand, I was a real sleeper."

We get up and go out. On the street, he asks me where he can catch a downtown bus. When I tell him I'm going to drive him home, he stammers that it would be enough just to bring him closer. He can get a bus in Rímac.

There's almost no traffic on the Vía Expresa. A light drizzle blurs the windshield. Until we get to Avenida Javier Prado, we talk only about the news—the drought down south, the floods up north, the problems on the border. When we get to the bridge, he sighs, visibly annoyed, that he's got to get out for a minute. I stop, he gets out and urinates by the car, shielding himself with the door. When he gets back in, he mutters that at night, because of the humidity, his kidney problem is worse. Has he been to a doctor? Is he being treated? First, he had to make arrangements with the insurance. Now that he has it, he'll have to go to the Hospital del Empleado to be examined, although it seems he's got a chronic condition that can't be cured.

We're quiet until we get to Plaza Grau. There, suddenly— I just passed someone selling skin cream—as if it were someone else speaking, I hear him say, "There were two robberies, it's true. Before the one in La Victoria, the one they locked me up for. What I told you is the truth: I had nothing to do with the kidnapping in Pueblo Libre, either. I wasn't even in Lima when it happened. I was in Pacasmayo, working in a sugarmill."

He is silent. I don't press him, I don't ask him anything. I drive very slowly, hoping he'll decide to go on, afraid he won't. The emotion in his voice surprises me, as does his confidential tone. The streets downtown are dark and deserted. The only noise is the car motor.

"It was when I got out of jail, after Jauja, after those four years inside," he says, looking straight ahead. "Do you remember what was going on in the Valle de La Convención, out there in Cuzco? Hugo Blanco had organized the peasants in unions and had led them in a few land seizures. Something important, very different from what all the left had been doing. They had to have support, so what happened to us in Jauja wouldn't happen to them."

I stop at a red light, on Avenida Abancay, and he stops, too. It's as if the person next to me were different from the one who was just in my study, and different from the Mayta in my story. A third, wounded, lacerated Mayta, whose memory is intact.

"So we tried to give them support, with money." He is whispering. "We planned two expropriations. At that time, it was the best way to lend a hand."

I don't ask him who his accomplices were: his old comrades from the RWP(T) or those from the RWP, revolutionaries he met in jail, or others. At that time—the early sixties—the idea of direct action was in the air, and there were countless young men who, if they weren't already taking action, spoke night and day about doing it. It couldn't have been difficult for Mayta to link up with them, charm them, lead them in an action sanctified with the all-absolving name of expropriation. What happened in Jauja must have earned him some prestige among radical groups. I don't bother to ask if he was the brain behind those robberies.

"The plan worked perfectly in both cases," he adds. "There were no arrests, no casualties. We carried them out on two consecutive days, in different parts of Lima. We expropriated"—a brief hesitation before coming up with the proper vague formula —"several million."

He falls silent once again. I see that he's concentrating, looking for the right words to say what must be the most difficult thing of all. We are at the Plaza de Acho, a mass of shadows blurred by the fog. Which way? Yes, I'm going to take you all the way home. He points the way to Zárate. It's a bitter paradox that, now that he's free, he lives in the Lurigancho area. The street here is a combination of holes, puddles, and garbage. The car shakes and bounces.

"Since the cops knew all there was to know about me, we agreed that I wouldn't bring the money out to Cuzco. That's where we were supposed to hand it over to Hugo Blanco's people. As a simple precaution, we decided that afterward I would stay away from the others. The comrades left in two groups. I helped them to leave myself. One group in a heavy truck, the other in a rented car."

He is silent again for a moment, and coughs. Then, in a dry voice, with a touch of irony, he quickly adds: "That's when the cops grabbed me. Not for the expropriations. For the robbery in La Victoria. In which I hadn't been involved, about which I knew nothing. Now there's a coincidence, I thought. Nice coincidence. Terrific. It has its positive side. It distracts them, it's going to screw them up. They won't connect me at all with the expropriations. But no, it wasn't a mere coincidence . . ."

Suddenly I know what he's going to tell me, I've guessed exactly what the climax of his story is going to be.

"I didn't understand completely until years later. Maybe because I didn't want to understand." He yawns, his face red, and chews on something. "One day in Lurigancho, I even saw a mimeographed handbill printed by some damn little group or other that accused me of being a common thief. They said I had robbed I don't know how much money from the bank in La Victoria. I paid no attention, I thought it was one of the usual low blows you get in political life. When I got out of Lurigancho, absolved for the La Victoria caper, eighteen months had gone by. I began to look for the comrades who'd taken part in the expropriations. Why, in all that time, hadn't they sent me a single message, why hadn't they contacted me? Finally, I found one of them. And we talked."

He smiles, half opening his mouth and showing his remaining teeth. The drizzle has stopped and in the headlights I can see dirt, stones, garbage, the outline of poor houses.

"Did he tell you that the money never got into Hugo Blanco's hands?" I ask.

"He swore he'd been against it, that he tried to convince the others not to pull a dirty deal like that," Mayta says. "He told me dozens of lies and blamed it all on the others. He had asked them to consult me about what they were going to do. According to him, the others didn't want to. 'Mayta's a fanatic,' he says they said. 'He wouldn't understand, he's too upright to do something like that.' Out of all the lies he told me, I managed to pick out some truths."

He sighs and asks me to stop. While I watch him, next to the door, unbutton and button his fly, I ask myself: If the Mayta who was my model could be called a fanatic, what about this one? Yes, no doubt about it, they both are. Although, perhaps, not in the same way.

"It's true. I wouldn't have understood," he says softly, when he's sitting alongside me again. "It's true. I would have said: The revolution's money will burn your hands. Don't you realize that if you keep it, you stop being revolutionaries and become thieves?"

He sighs again, deeply. I'm driving very slowly down a dark street on the sides of which we see whole families sleeping, covered with newspapers. Squalid dogs come out to bark at us, their eyes glowing in the headlights.

"I wouldn't have let them, of course," he repeats. "That's why they turned me in, that's why they implicated me in the La Victoria robbery. They knew that, before allowing such a thing, I would have shot them. They killed two birds with one stone when they squealed on me. They got rid of me, and the police found a fall guy. They knew I wouldn't turn in comrades I thought were bringing the money from our expropriations out to Hugo Blanco. When I realized during the questioning what they were accusing me of, I said, 'Perfect, they don't suspect a thing.' And for a while I was fooling them. I thought it was a good alibi."

He laughs, slowly, with his face still serious. He falls silent, and I realize that he won't say anything more. He doesn't have to. If it's true, now I know what destroyed him, now I know why he's the ghost I have beside me. It wasn't the Jauja failure, not all those years in jail, not even paying for crimes committed by others. It was finding out that the expropriations were, in fact, robberies. Finding out that, according to his own philosophy, he had acted "objectively" like a common thief. Or had he, rather, played the naïve fool with less seasoned comrades who'd been in fewer prisons than he? Was that what disillusioned him with the revolution, what made him this faded copy of what he once was?

"For a while, I thought of hunting them down one by one and settling accounts," he says.

"Like *The Count of Monte Cristo*," I interrupt. "Did you ever read it?"

But Mayta isn't listening to me.

"Later I even lost my anger and hatred," he goes on. "If you like, we can say that I forgave them. Because, as far as I could tell, they had it as bad or even worse than I did. Except one, who got to be a congressman."

He laughs, a small acid laugh.

It's not true that you've forgiven them, I think. You haven't even forgiven yourself for what happened. Should I ask him for names, dates, try to squeeze out something more? But the confession he's made is unique, a moment of weakness he may later regret. I think what it must have been like, behind the wire fences and concrete walls at Lurigancho, knowing you were the butt of the joke. But what if all this is nothing but exaggeration and lies? Couldn't it be a premeditated charade to get himself forgiven for a record that shames him? I look at him out of the corner of my eye. He's yawning and shaking as if he were cold.

Just where the turnoff to Lurigancho is, he tells me to keep going straight. The asphalt pavement runs out. This fork is a dirt road that runs into open country.

"A little farther is the new town where I live," he says. "I walk here to take the bus. Will you remember how to get back after you let me off?"

I assure him I will. I'd like to ask him how much he makes at the ice-cream parlor, how much of it he spends on the bus, and how he uses what's left. Also, if he's tried to get any other work, and if he'd like me to try to help, give him a recommendation. But all my questions wither before I can get them out.

"At one time, people said there were possibilities in the jungle," I hear him say. "I was thinking that over, too. Since it would be hard to leave the country, maybe I should go to Pucallpa, to Iquitos. They said there were lumber camps, oil wells, job possibilities. But it was a lie. Things in the jungle are the same as they are here. In this new town, there are people who've come back from Pucallpa. It's all the same. Only the cocaine dealers have work."

Now we're leaving the open country and in the darkness I can make out an agglomeration of low and tenuous shadows: the shacks. Made of adobe, corrugated sheet metal, boards, and straw matting, they give the impression of being half finished, interrupted just as they were taking shape. There is no pavement, no sidewalks, no electricity, probably no water or drains either.

"I've never been out here," I tell him. "It's huge."

"Over on the left, you can see the lights of Lurigancho," Mayta says as he guides me through the maze of the slum. "My wife was one of the founders of this new town. Eight years ago. Some two hundred families started it. They came at night in small groups, without being seen. They worked till dawn, nailing boards together, hauling rope. The next day, when the guards came, the place already existed. There was no way to get them out."

"So, when you got out of Lurigancho, you didn't know where you lived?" I ask him.

He says no with a shake of his head. And he tells me that the day he got out, after almost eleven years, he came alone, walking through the open country we've just crossed. Throwing stones at the dogs that tried to bite him. When he got to the first shacks, he began to ask, "Where does Mrs. Mayta live?" And so he reached home and gave his family the surprise of their life.

We're right in front of his house. I have it in my headlights. The façade is brick, and the side walls too, but the roof hasn't been finished yet. It's corrugated sheet metal, not even nailed to the house, but held in place by piles of stones set at regular intervals. The door is a board held to the wall with nails and rope.

"We're fighting to get water," Mayta says. "That's our biggest problem here. That and garbage, of course. You sure you can find your way back to the street?"

I assure him I can, and I say that, if he doesn't mind, I'll get back to him soon and we'll talk some more and he can tell me more about Jauja. Maybe he'll remember more details. He nods, and we say goodbye, shaking hands.

I have no trouble getting out to the road that goes to Zárate. I drive slowly, stopping to take note of the poverty, the ugliness, the abandon, and the despair of this new town. I don't even know its name. No one's on the street, not even an animal. On all sides, there are mounds of garbage. The people, I suppose, just throw it out of their houses, resigned, knowing that no city garbage truck is ever going to pick it up, lacking the spirit to join together with other neighbors to carry it farther away, to the open country, or to bury or burn it. They, too, have thrown in the towel. I imagine what daylight would reveal: neighborhood kids playing on pyramids of filth, swarming with flies, roaches, rats, vermin of all kinds. I think about the epidemics, the stench, the premature deaths.

I'm still thinking about the garbage in Mayta's slum when on the left I see Lurigancho in the distance and I remember the mad, naked inmate sleeping on the immense garbage heap in front of the odd-numbered cell blocks. And shortly afterward, when I am all the way across Zárate and the Plaza de Acho and I'm on

Avenida Abancay, on the road that takes me to Vía Expresa, San Isidro, Miraflores, and Barranco, I can already imagine the seawalls in the neighborhood where I have the good fortune to live, and the garbage you see—I'll see it myself tomorrow when I go running—if you crane your neck and peek over the edge. The garbage dump that the cliffs facing the sea have become. And I'll remember that a year ago I began to concoct this story the same way I'm ending it, by speaking about the garbage that's invading every neighborhood in the capital of Peru.

ABOUT THE AUTHOR

Mario Vargas Llosa was born in Arequipa, Peru, in 1936. His books include *Conversation in the Cathedral*, *The Green House*, *Aunt Julia and the Scriptwriter*, and *The War of the End of the World*.

THE VINTAGE LIBRARY OF
CONTEMPORARY WORLD LITERATURE

"A cornucopia of serious fiction by contemporary writers from all parts of the world...a mix of the *au courant* and authentic art."
—CHRISTIAN SCIENCE MONITOR

"These works appeal intellectually, emotionally, even physically, and transport us out of our own space and time into strange and wonderful other places."
—SAN JOSE MERCURY NEWS

"Most impressive."
—NEWSDAY

"Excellent."
—THE VILLAGE VOICE

"Ambitious...a boon for armchair explorers."
—NEWSWEEK

On sale at bookstores everywhere, but if otherwise unavailable may be ordered from us. You can use this coupon, or phone (800) 638-6460.